AN ALMOST PERFECT ROMANCE

I don't believe this is happening, said a small voice in Jackie's head. She could feel Gerald's thighs, hard and muscular, brush against hers as they danced. She'd never been promiscuous, or gone to bed with anyone on a first date, but she wanted this stranger and she wanted him more than anything else in the world.

"You're quite something, aren't you?" he said softly. "The minute I saw you tonight, I knew we would be good together."

Then the music stopped, and they were sipping champagne together, and everything was perfect and was going to be perfect . . . until Celia Atherton came up to them, and ignoring Jackie, said:

"Gerald, you must come to dinner one night. When is your wife coming over from the States to join you?"

The Palace Affair

THE
PALACE
AFFAIR

Una-Mary Parker

A SIGNET BOOK

SIGNET
Published by the Penguin Group
Penguin Books USA Inc., 375 Hudson Street,
New York, New York 10014, U.S.A.
Penguin Books Ltd, 27 Wrights Lane,
London W8 5TZ, England
Penguin Books Australia Ltd, Ringwood,
Victoria, Australia
Penguin Books Canada Ltd, 10 Alcorn Avenue,
Toronto, Ontario, Canada M4V 3B2
Penguin Books (N.Z.) Ltd, 182–190 Wairau Road,
Auckland 10, New Zealand

Penguin Books Ltd, Registered Offices:
Harmondsworth, Middlesex, England

First published by Signet, an imprint of New American Library,
a division of Penguin Books USA Inc.

First Printing, August, 1992
10 9 8 7 6 5 4 3 2 1

PUBLISHER'S NOTE
This is a work of fiction. Names, characters, places, and incidents either
are the product of the author's imagination or are used fictitiously, and any
resemblance to actual persons, living or dead, events, or locales is entirely
coincidental.

This book is dedicated to the late Archie Parker, who shared so much of the background to this story with me.

Summer 1990

———•—◄►—•———

1

The most imposing-looking invitation on the mantelpiece was the one from Buckingham Palace. It stood thick and white beside all the other cards, overshadowing them with its elegance. While many were gilt-bordered, or had ornamental deckle edges and fancy lettering, the one from the Queen was ingeniously simple, the lettering traditional copperplate engraving, printed in black, the only gilding being the embossed Crown of England centered at the top with the initials E II R. Elizabeth Regina II.

Below were the words "THE LORD CHAMBERLAIN IS COMMANDED BY HER MAJESTY TO INVITE . . ." And here "Mrs. Jacqueline Daventry" had been handwritten in blue ink. Below, it announced there was to be an afternoon party in the gardens of Buckingham Palace on Wednesday, July 4, from four to six o'clock. In the bottom-left-hand corner were instructions on what to wear. Ladies: Day Dress and Hats. Gentlemen: Morning Dress, Uniform, or Lounge Suit. In the opposite corner were the words that sent an apprehensive shiver through all those who were looking forward to attending: Weather Permitting.

Jackie Daventry, emerging sleepily from her bedroom after another late night, had been to Buckingham Palace many times, first with her parents when her father had been the American ambassador to the Court of St. James's, in the late seventies, and more recently in her capacity as social editor of *Society* magazine. Weather permitting, she would be writing an

9

account of this afternoon's garden party, describing, for the benefit of those who had never been, the velvety green lawns, the immaculate herbaceous borders, the bandstand by the lake where the band of the Grenadier Guards played evocative music, and the large white marquees where tea, iced coffee, and a variety of delicious sandwiches and cakes were served.

Hurrying across the drawing room, she pulled back the yellow silk curtains and looked out.

When Richard Daventry, to whom she'd been married for nine years, had run off eighteen months before with Stella Morton, he'd agreed to let Jackie keep their Victorian apartment as part of the settlement. It was too large for her now that she was on her own, but it was the one thing she had wanted from him, and the reason was the location.

Situated in Knightsbridge within five minutes' walk of Harrods, it backed onto Hyde Park, and from her living-room balcony she could see the Serpentine twisting its glittering way through acres of lush greenery, amid oak and beech and sycamore trees, which grew tall, their branches interlacing in some places to form leafy canopies of cool shelter.

Now, as Jackie opened the French windows, her heart sank. A thick blanket of gray cloud shrouded the tops of the buildings, and London was enveloped in a chilly mist. Below, in the park, joggers pounded along in tracksuits molded to their bodies by the rain, and a few intrepid dog owners tramped through the long wet grass, huddled under umbrellas. It did not look promising for a garden party.

Turning back into the room, which felt cold and clammy, although it was summer, she turned on the television in order to watch the weather forecast. If the party was canceled, she'd have to rearrange her column for next week's edition of *Society*. Not that she was short of material. Last night she'd covered five social functions and tonight there were five more hostesses clamoring to have their parties written up. What had started as a fun job when she'd parted from Richard had turned into a demanding career. It had even brought her fame with the media, as other journalists interviewed her about her role as a "society reporter." They were intrigued that she was invited to the sort of party no other journalist was asked to, and only last week the *Daily Mail* had quoted her as saying: "My working day starts at six in the evening and I have more ball gowns than day clothes." There were not many journalists who could say that.

Sinking onto the sofa, she waited for the forecast to come on. If the party was canceled, she wouldn't mind, but there would be others, thousands of them, who would be deeply disappointed. Outfits bought specially for the occasion would be put away unworn. Descriptions of the exciting occasion would remain unspoken, never experienced. The elegant invitations would be pasted in albums for future generations to gaze at, but there would be no memorable anecdotes to go with them.

"Hi, there! You're up early, considering!"

Jackie spun around to see her younger brother, Kip, standing in the doorway. He was already dressed in casual trousers and jacket, and he was grinning at her.

"Did you sleep well?" Jackie asked, smiling back at him. Kip Armstrong was over from Boston for a couple of weeks, on a business trip, and she enjoyed his company. Of her three brothers, he was her favorite, and although they were very different, they'd always been close.

"I slept like the proverbial log." He glanced at the television screen. "What's on?"

"I'm waiting for the forecast. There's a garden party at Buck House this afternoon, but it will be canceled unless the rain stops."

Kip sat down beside her, a large gangling man with an easy manner. "Rather you than me. Cucumber sandwiches and bowing and scraping to royalty are not my scene."

"Don't I know it! What a fuss you used to make when you were a little boy if we had to go to a party. You're the most antisocial person I know," Jackie added, her tone indulgent.

He shrugged. "It's probably a reaction to all the socializing we had to do with Mom and Dad. Do you remember how we were made to be on our best behavior at all times?—like we'd cause an international crisis if we misbehaved, or maybe even World War Three?"

Jackie burst out laughing. "I remember! All those diplomatic receptions! I must say I loved every minute of it. I was quite sad when Dad retired."

"I wasn't. I was as relieved as hell, but then, you're a social animal like the parents, and I'm not. I like to go fishing or hunting, out into the wilds where no one can disturb me." He had a faraway look as he spoke, visualizing the peace of the countryside he so loved.

"Oh, but, Kip, wasn't it wonderful when Dad was posted to this country? Remember living in Winfield House, in the middle of Regent's Park? What an ambassadorial residence that is! I went to a reception there only the other day, given by the present American ambassador, and it brought back so many wonderful memories. Remember how many staff we had? And all those magnificent rooms, with great vases of fresh flowers every day!" Jackie gave a gusty sigh. "Boy, was that the life. We'll never have it so good again."

"Oh, I don't know." Kip, content to live in a medium-size house with his wife and two small daughters, was happy with things the way they were.

A map of Great Britain filled the television screen. It was decorated with little clouds and raindrops and the occasional yellow sunburst.

"Hush," said Jackie, "I want to hear what they say."

A pretty blond girl in a summery pink dress began to announce wind speeds and isobars, low depressions and retreating cyclones, while smiling broadly into the camera.

"I wish she'd talk English," Jackie grumbled. "I only want to know if it's going to stop raining."

Kip glanced out the window. "I wouldn't like to bet on it. Do you want some coffee? I've got a meeting this morning, but I have time to fix breakfast."

"I'd adore it." Jackie spoke with only a faint trace of an American accent, and her phraseology was very Anglicized. After twelve years in London, nine of which had been spent married to an Englishman, she'd adopted Great Britain as her homeland. Sometimes she missed the family and their place just outside Boston, but to have gone back after her divorce would have felt like starting all over again, and so she'd stayed, determined to carve out a life for herself in England.

Together, brother and sister walked down the long corridor to the kitchen, Jackie tall and slender like her mother, Kip more heavily built and attractive in a burly way, like their father. They both had the same coloring, though: pale skin and black hair and vivid blue eyes the color of delphiniums, inherited from their Irish grandmother. In Kip the combination of dark hair and blue eyes made him far more handsome than he realized. In Jackie, who always protected her skin from the sun so it was alabaster white, the effect was devastating. People in the street stopped to stare at her, wondering if her hair could have been dyed such a rich color, or if it was tinted contact lenses that made her eyes such a dazzling shade of blue.

"What have you got on today?" Kip inquired, switching on the coffee percolator.

Jackie thought for a moment, visualizing the page in her appointment book. "Two drinks parties, and then a dinner, followed by a charity ball, and I think I've got to go to an exhibition of paintings at the Crane Gallery."

He shook his head. "It beats me how you can bear going out every night. Why do you work for *Society*? They don't even pay well, do they? Of course, I know there are perks that go with the job—"

"Like never having to eat in, you mean?"

"Exactly, but isn't there anything else you could write about? For Chrissakes, a party is a party is a party!"

Jackie wrinkled her small nose. "I'm not exactly over-qualified to do anything else, you know. Dad didn't believe in preparing girls to earn their own living, did he? A fine-arts degree isn't the most useful thing in the world, but luckily I do have other qualifications. Ones that are unique, actually."

"Such as?"

"I know everybody on the social scene and I have a photographic memory for faces and places. I can pick out the 'right' people at a party in seconds, and caption photographs at a glance. That's why I got this job. Bertram Marriott, the editor, couldn't find anyone else who could do it *and* string more than three words together."

"You're underestimating yourself, Jackie, although I suppose those years as an ambassador's daughter and then as Richard's wife have finally paid off."

Jackie put some cereal into a bowl and poured chilled milk, straight from the fridge, over it. "They sure have," she replied between mouthfuls. "Dick introduced me to the county set, the very backbone of English society, and of course Mom and Dad knew everyone in London who was worth knowing, so between the two I've ended up with the entrée and the know-how, much to the chagrin of a lot of other journalists." She laughed gently, almost to herself. She was more surprised than anyone that she was now a burgeoning journalist, but it had helped ease the last remaining shreds of regret she felt that her marriage to Richard was over. She had loved him so much at the beginning, and they'd had some very happy years together, but then he had betrayed her in the most awful way, for Stella had been her best friend, and by the end a slow-burning anger had replaced the love she'd originally felt. Nevertheless, there were times when she still missed him, when the pain was deep and anguished, and loneliness bit deep into her soul. Then she would wish she'd had a child by him, something that was hers that no one could take away. But then, almost immediately she was thankful she hadn't. Richard had never wanted children. Perhaps, under the circumstances, he'd been right.

"You deserve to have some fun," Kip was saying, breaking into her thoughts. "There is a bonus in this job, in that you get invited to all the best parties. Who knows . . . on this endless round of frivolity you might meet a wonderful, handsome, kind millionaire."

"That's an absolute contradiction in terms," Jackie replied dryly. Richard had wanted to be a millionaire, and he'd wanted it so much that he'd let nothing stand in his way. Stella happened to be the daughter of the chairman of the company where he worked. After all the years he and Jackie had been together, he'd decided that although her American contacts and background were impeccable, Stella's were likely to be more profitable.

"There's no such thing as a kind millionaire, Kip."

He looked at her sympathetically, knowing what she was thinking, able to interpret her feelings as he'd done since they'd been small children.

"You may be right," he said peaceably, "but I'd like to see you married again. You don't want to end up a dried old stick, do you?" He regarded her pale features and intensely blue eyes for a moment, as if searching for something.

"Even I can see you're quite pretty," he conceded at last with brotherly candor. "And you don't look—"

"I'll kill you if you say 'a day over twenty-five'!"

There was a roguish glint in his eyes. "Well . . . er . . . twenty-six and a half, maybe?"

In fact she was thirty-four and already aware that in strong daylight tiny lines showed around her eyes. No one else would have guessed her age, though.

"Why don't you write about the social scene as it really is?" he asked suddenly as he poured their coffee into large cups. "It would be a gas."

"You mean what really happens? All the bitchiness and intrigues and wheels-within-wheels that make the whole thing tick over?"

"Yup." He grinned with relish at the thought. "Real behind-the-scenes stuff! I bet the circulation of *Society* would jump right through the roof!"

Jackie cast her eyes to heaven in mock horror. "Imagine! My God, that would be like opening a can of worms!" She thought about the pettiness of those who dubbed themselves socialites, with their silly little plots and veiled threats and relentless ambition hidden beneath a surface of courtly manners and exquisite politeness. To reveal what *really* went on would be like exposing a barrel of fermenting fruit that festered and erupted and stank of rottenness. Yet those on the outside lusted to be accepted into the exclusivity of the inner circle, believing it to be a sort of paradise on earth.

Suddenly Jackie laughed. "Maybe one day I *will* write about what it is really like, but meanwhile I don't want to be compared to that famous writer Frank Harris, of whom Oscar Wilde said, 'He was invited to all the best houses . . . once!' " Then she grew serious. "Do you realize, Kip, that there are people who would kill for my job?"

It was a casual remark, once said, immediately forgotten . . . until much later.

A few miles away, on the outskirts of Chelsea, Elfreida Witley awoke in a fever of excitement. No sooner had she opened her eyes than she leapt naked out of bed, and rushing to the windows, parted the turquoise satin curtains with hands that trembled.

A voice from the bed grunted with irritation. "What the hell are you doing? What's the time?"

Ignoring her husband, Elfreida pushed aside the voile blind and peered out.

"Oh, dear God," she groaned, her Swedish accent heavy with despair.

A mound of bedding erupted and a pink balding head with ruffled spikes of gray hair emerged from the snowy depths of Irish lace and linen. "*Now* what's the matter?"

Elfreida clasped her hands as if in supplication. "It's the garden party today. You haven't forgotten? We go to Buckingham Palace this afternoon—but I think it rains!" Her voice ended in a wail.

"Oh, for God's sake, as if it mattered!" snorted Selwyn Witley, burrowing beneath the bedding again.

But to Elfreida it mattered most desperately. When the invitation had first arrived, commanding Lord and Lady Witley of Vauxhall to attend the garden party, it had seemed like a wonderful prize, a reward for all the hard work and scheming she'd done to get her where she was today. She'd been looking forward to this afternoon for *weeks*, imagining the moment when their car would slide between the gold-tipped gates of Buckingham Palace and across the courtyard to the inner quadrangle. And then they'd alight . . . and the footmen would usher them into the palace . . . and they'd join the Queen on the emerald lawns . . . Elfreida clapped her hand over her mouth to stifle an incipient sob. The rain *must* stop. If she didn't get to go now, if it went on raining and the whole thing was canceled, it would be like having a tickle in one's nose and not being able to sneeze, or to be sexually aroused and unable to reach orgasm. The denial of final fulfillment would be unbearable.

"Perhaps it will clear," she said hopefully. "It's still early."

"Humph."

"When do they decide whether to cancel or go ahead with the party, Selwyn?"

"How the hell should I know? Oh, for Christ's sake, Elfie, stop making such a bloody fuss." The pink-domed head emerged again, and tired eyes, like oysters in cold pastry, looked across the bedroom at her.

"It's a bun fight anyway," he expostulated. "Nine thousand people get invited—nine *thousand*. You won't see anything. It's a waste of time."

Elfreida's face was a study of mutinous disappointment.

"It is still honor," she said sullenly.

"*An* honor," he corrected her. "God, your English is lousy."

"I speak *good* English." Sometimes Selwyn made her very angry, she thought, still gazing down at the shining wet street below. He didn't seem to understand what a long way she'd come from being Elfreida Sjögren, youngest of eleven children who had been born and brought up in a small village overlooking the calm waters of Lake Mälaren, on the outskirts of Stockholm. Crowded into a small wooden chalet that stood surrounded by pine and spruce trees and not much else, she had longed for the luxuries of life, for beautiful clothes and a comfortable home with a bedroom just to herself; but most of all, for good food. Lots of it. Sometimes she dreamed about food, seeing it arranged on great platters on a long table, but she always woke up before she could eat any of it.

Plump and shapely, with a fresh skin, bold blue eyes, and a cheerful disposition, she had arrived in London at the age of nineteen, determined to seek her fortune. In due course she had got a job as an *au pair*, and during the next seven years she'd worked for several aristocratic families, helping to look after their children and learning all the while some of the finer points of etiquette. She had been ambitious, greedy for the good things in life, and her efforts had paid off. Now she was Lady Witley of Vauxhall, wife of the multimillionaire chairman of Witley Constructions, who had been made a life peer in 1986 in recognition of his services to the community and the Conservative party in particular. The Prime Minister, who held him in high esteem, had recommended him for the honor, and was said to have put his name forward to the Queen. Elfreida had glowed with pride when she'd heard that, but now she felt rattled by the way Selwyn was trying to hamper her advancement into real society, and she hated it when he criticized the way she spoke.

It was still raining. Her big day was about to be ruined. A small tear rolled down her healthy pink cheek and she thought if only she could go to Buckingham Palace this afternoon she would be happy. No one knew how much it meant to her.

Still grumbling, Selwyn clambered out of bed, his arthritic joints hurting, his limbs aching from last night's vast consumption of port. He glanced at his wife's pale unclothed body as she stood uninhibitedly by the window, her bottom reminding him of a large ripe pumpkin.

"Put some clothes on, for heaven's sake. Rica will be up with your breakfast tray in a minute." Then he

shambled off to the bathroom, pulling on his mono-
grammed silk robe as he did so.

Elfreida shrugged, and getting back into bed, slipped
on a gauzy see-through lace bed jacket through which
her large dark nipples protruded tautly. A moment
later their Filipino maid, Africa, slid smilingly into the
room bearing a tray almost as big as herself, with fried
eggs and hot muffins, strawberry jam and orange
juice, fresh peaches and fragrant hot chocolate. Georgian silver sparkled against the dazzling white damask
traycloth.

"Where are the newspapers?" Elfreida demanded.
She depended on the top gossip columnists of the
Daily Mail and *Daily Express*, Nigel Dempster and
Ross Benson, to keep her informed of the activities
of the People Who Mattered. After all, if she hadn't
been an avid reader of the gossip columns when she'd
worked for the Earl and Countess of Atherton, looking after their two sons, she'd never have known Who
was Who. It was only because she'd seen a photograph
of Lord Witley with his wife, at a gala concert, that
she'd realized he often dined with the Athertons. He'd
even said good evening to her on several occasions
when she'd helped the guests with their coats, and
she'd noticed how he'd eyed her legs, letting his gaze
linger on her crotch.

"They here," Africa replied, taking the newspapers
from under her arm and laying them on the bedcover.
Her command of English was no better than her mistress's. "It raining," she added unnecessarily.

Elfreida didn't answer, but snatched up the *Express*
to see if she and Selwyn had been mentioned at the
Mayfair Ball they'd attended two nights before. One
of Ross Benson's assistants had been there, and so
had their famous photographer, Richard Young, so
surely . . . Her eyes skimmed the page, saw the familiar names of Roger Moore, Joan Collins, the Duchess
of York, and Elton John, and her heart sank. Not
a mention of Lord and Lady Witley, and the only
photograph was one of the Duchess of York in a Xan-
dra Rhodes ball gown, receiving a bouquet. Fretfully

she attacked her fried eggs and spread the golden butter thickly on her muffin. When was *she* going to be pictured in the newspapers and glossy magazines? Wasn't she a member of the British aristocracy now? Listed in the new edition of *Debrett's Peerage and Baronetage* as Selwyn's second wife . . . alongside his newly and hurriedly designed coat of arms and crest bearing the motto *Semper Paratus:* Always Ready. Elfreida didn't like the motto much. She wished Selwyn had chosen a more noble-sounding one, like "With Faith and Valor" or "God Defend the Right." "Always Ready" made her think of flashlight batteries.

"Any more I get you?" inquired Africa, who had been fussing around the bedroom, picking up discarded shoes and clothing from the night before.

"No," Elfreida replied sharply. "Get on with your work downstairs." Then she leaned back against the mound of snowy pillows and wished she felt happier. If only it would stop raining. How was she going to be able to bear it if the party was canceled? Of course, she reflected fretfully, her former employer, Lady Atherton, would already be in the know about this afternoon. Royal ladies-in-waiting got told that sort of thing before anyone else, and according to the Court Circular in the *Times,* Lady Atherton was doing one of her stints of duty at the moment. Whenever the Queen carried out a public engagement, the announcement would end with the line "The Countess of Atherton was in attendance."

Of course they didn't speak these days, she and Celia Atherton. Not after what had happened. When they saw each other at a party, Celia averted her eyes and carried on talking with her friends as if Elfreida didn't exist. With supreme self-confidence, she ignored her former *au pair,* and yet she did it with such style; it was as if she really hadn't noticed Elfreida's presence at all. Hating to be snubbed and overlooked, Elfreida glowered angrily, smoldering with resentment that only served to further charge her social ambitions. Meanwhile there was one factor that consoled Elfreida greatly. Selwyn was far richer than Lord Atherton

would ever be, and although he was a bit old and
crotchety at times, he certainly wasn't stingy. She
could buy herself all the clothes she wanted, and he'd
given her some lovely jewelry when they'd got married.
He'd also bought them a house in the Boltons, one
of London's most exclusive garden squares, where the
loudest noise in the street was the purr of the waiting
Rolls-Royce engine, and the great activity was a servant
polishing a brass knocker. The building was white and
stuccoed and resembled a giant iced wedding cake.
Douglas Fairbanks had once owned the one next door.

Selwyn had even engaged Nina Campbell, who had
designed the interior of the Duke and Duchess of
York's new house, to supervise the decorations, with
the exception of their bedroom, which Elfreida had
begged to be allowed to design herself. With some
reluctance, Selwyn had agreed.

Now, as she lay in bed munching hot muffins and
fresh peaches, she looked around with deep satisfaction. Even the Countess of Atherton—even the
Queen, for that matter—would probably never have
a bedroom like this.

Turquoise satin and gilt abounded in swags and
drapes, carvings and moldings, hangings, festoons and
flounces. Searching London for the most opulently
gilded mirrors she could find to hang on the pleated
silk wall covering, she had added layer upon layer of
gilt in the form of furniture, lamps, wall brackets, and
a large golden eagle, its wings outspread, fixed over
the bed. Sarcastically, Selwyn had asked her where
she intended hanging the Stars and Stripes.

Elfreida didn't care. If the rest of the house was a
perfect example of restrained good taste, the bedroom
was where she felt happiest. Here she could lie in bed
and look up at the intricate moldings on the ceiling
and say to herself: "I've done it! I've done it!" No
more poverty. No more hard work cleaning other people's houses and looking after their children. No more
wishing for all the lovely things she so wanted and
feared she'd never have. She had it all now, thanks
to her wits and Selwyn's money. And in time those

damned English newspapers and magazines would feature her in all her glory too, even if she had to pay them to do it.

At that moment Selwyn came back into the room, his hair brushed smooth now, an aura of Paco Raban wafting about him.

"It's still raining," he announced with a hint of amused malice.

"What? Oh, no!" She'd finished her egg and was spooning raspberry jam onto her second muffin.

Selwyn sniffed. "Anything in the papers?"

"Only a picture of the Duchess of York."

He groaned with exaggerated exasperation. "I mean is there any *news*? What's happening in Lithuania? Has Gorbachev made a further statement about Estonia? Is there still fighting in the streets of Romania? A picture of Fergie is hardly of world-shattering interest."

Elfreida shrugged, not caring. "How do I get myself on more charity committees, Selwyn? What do I have to do to be made the chairman of some fund-raising gala? That's how one gets to know the right people, you know."

"Who the fuck cares!"

"But it's the way to get on." Her scathing tones indicated her husband must be a simpleton not to recognize the route to the top. How come he'd been given a life peerage when he didn't even know about charity committees?

Selwyn turned away to go to his dressing room, but not before he'd seen the wreckage of Elfreida's breakfast tray.

"You'll get fat, like your mother."

She glared balefully at him. Ever since he'd found a hidden snapshot of Mater, who was obese and had thick stumpy legs, he'd taunted her about her weight. So far she was merely curvaceous, but her large breasts and hips foretold of amplitude yet to come.

"No, I not go fat," she retorted, losing her command of the language completely.

"But you'll guzzle cream cakes at the palace this afternoon, won't you?"

"Oh, Selwyn, has it stopped raining? Please, God, let it stop raining."

Ada Pinner always arrived at the Earl and Countess of Atherton's in time to get the breakfast. They lived in a nineteenth-century terraced house in South Eaton Place, and she'd worked for them for nearly twenty years now. If her bus from Fulham was on time, she'd flick a duster around the drawing room and dining room first, before they came down; but if, like today, she was delayed by heavy traffic, there was only time to get the breakfast before they appeared.

The heavy rain had made her late this morning, snarling up the traffic so it moved sluggishly along the King's Road. When she'd reached Sloane Square, she'd hopped off the bus, and despite the rheumatism in her feet and knees, hurried down Cliveden Place into South Eaton Place, glad that she'd put on her rubber Wellington boots. The weather wasn't fit for ducks, she thought as she let herself into the house. Going straight to the kitchen, which was situated at the back overlooking the small paved garden, she put on the kettle and started to set the table with a blue linen cloth and the pretty pink-and-white china that came from France. The Athertons always had breakfast in the kitchen. "The dining room is much too formal when it's just the family," Lady Atherton had said when they'd moved into the house ten years before.

Keeping her eye on the clock, Ada Pinner proceeded to put out cartons of cereal and pots of honey and jam, and she was just about to put some bread in the toaster when the telephone, which sat on the old Welsh dresser, rang. Ignoring it, partly because she was sure either Lord or Lady Atherton would answer it and also because she hated getting involved in taking messages, she let it ring. But after a few more moments it became obvious no one was going to answer it so she lifted the receiver cautiously and put it to her ear.

"Hello?" she said guardedly.

A woman's voice, clear and young, spoke. "May I speak to Lady Atherton please?"

"Hang on. I'll get her." Mrs. Pinner nearly added that it was a bit early to go ringing people, but thought better of it. "Who is it?" she asked instead.

The voice held a hint of humor. "It's the Queen."

Mrs. Pinner's head spun, and for a moment she felt quite breathless, as if all the air had been sucked out of her. Not for a second did it cross her mind to doubt the identity of the caller.

"Oh! . . . Oh, I'll get her," she cried in a panic-stricken voice. "I'll get her, madam . . . ma'am . . . Your Majesty! I won't be half a mo!"

With legs shaking and heart pounding—wait until she told Sidney about this!—she climbed the thickly carpeted stairs to the second floor and knocked on the bedroom door.

"Your ladyship," she called out agitatedly.

The door opened and Lady Atherton, wearing a white toweling robe and with a towel wound around her wet hair, stood there.

"What is it, Mrs. Pinner?" she asked pleasantly. Younger-looking than her forty-two years, Celia Atherton was a pretty woman with fair hair and skin, and steady unwavering gray eyes which looked at people with devastating candor, as if she was searching out the truth.

"The phone!"

"Yes, I heard it just as I was getting out of the bath. Who is it?"

Ada Pinner's eyes grew wide and round. "Hurry, madam, it's . . ."

"Not the boys?" Ever since their sons, Colin and Ian, had gone away to boarding school, she'd lived in perpetual dread that one day she'd get a message to say they were ill or had suffered an accident. "Are the boys all right?"

"It's not the boys, madam, it's the Queen. She's on the phone." Mrs. Pinner took a gulp of air. "Quick!"

To her astonishment, Lady Atherton took the news quite calmly. "Thank you, Mrs. Pinner. I'll take the call up here." Then she closed the bedroom door quietly.

When Mrs. Pinner got back to the kitchen, her heart was still hammering. The Queen! Ringing up like an ordinary person! In all her years of working for the Athertons, *that* had never happened before. At least, not while she'd been in the house, but then of course she always went home at lunchtime. Lady Atherton hired caterers and butlers if she was entertaining, otherwise Mrs. Pinner was their only regular servant.

Ada Pinner had first come to work for the Athertons in 1970, when they'd been newly married. Of course, they hadn't been the Earl and Countess of Atherton then. Their name had been Gerard—the Honorable Hugo and Mrs. Gerard—and they'd lived in a flat on the Old Brompton Road. Then, in 1981, Hugo's father had died and he'd succeeded to the title. Now he was a leading light in the House of Lords and chairman of Hamilton's, a famous firm of auctioneers, while his wife had become one of the Queen's eleven ladies-in-waiting. It was a shame, though, she thought, that there had been so little money to go with the title. Atherton Hall, in Norfolk, had been sold years ago and was now a nursing home, so the house in South Eaton Place was their only residence, unlike other people in their position, who had a place in the country as well. All that Hugo's father had been able to leave him was some furniture, silver, paintings, the family jewels, which included a magnificent sapphire-and-diamond tiara, and a few thousand pounds. That was why Mrs. Pinner was their only regular domestic help, and why Celia did the cooking herself when they were on their own.

Ada looked out the window again, watching the rain fall in a heavy curtain, bouncing on the paved patio, dripping from the leaves. Surely the garden party would have to be canceled? Perhaps that was what the Queen had wanted to discuss with her ladyship. Mrs. Pinner thought about the job of Waiting, as it was always referred to, and decided she'd have hated it herself. All that standing around a few paces behind

Her Majesty, watching for signals and always being on the alert to make sure nothing went wrong. It was just as well, she reflected, that ladies-in-waiting worked for only two or three weeks at a time before handing over to someone else.

"Sort of shift work they do," Ada had explained to her husband one day. Sidney Pinner, who worked in the bottling plant of a soft-drinks factory, hadn't been very interested. He preferred football to the royals, and thought they were rather a waste of time. Mrs. Pinner, on the other hand, was besotted by them. Pictures of the Queen, Prince Charles, and Princess Diana loomed out at visitors from ornamental dishes and mugs on display in her living room, while in the kitchen their fixed expressions, gaudily printed on tea towels, wiped many a plate dry. She also went, whenever she could, to watch when they made a public appearance, especially if Lady Atherton was Waiting. Only one thing perplexed her, so much so that she felt forced to ask about it.

"What happens," she said with embarrassment one day, "if the Queen suddenly wants to go to the lavatory? You never hear of it happening, but they must want to go sometimes. It don't seem natural, somehow, so how do they manage?"

Celia Atherton had thrown back her head, laughing. "One of the first rules you're taught when you join the palace staff is to go when you have the opportunity, and not wait until you feel the need."

"But what happens if you have a weak bladder? My Sidney has to go all the time, he can't help himself, unlike Prince Philip, who never seems to have to go at all."

"I do remember being asked two questions by the Queen's private secretary just before I became a lady-in-waiting," Celia Atherton recalled. "The first one was, could I hold my tongue, because they obviously wouldn't want a gossip, but the other question was, could I hold my water."

"He never!" Mrs. Pinner blushed at such intimate

revelations. "Oh, I wouldn't have known what to say."

Celia smiled. "I told him I thought my mother must have been frightened by a camel because I hardly ever want to go, and he said the Queen would enjoy that joke and he'd have to tell it to her."

Mystified by the strange sense of humor of the upper classes, Ada Pinner had repeated the conversation to Sidney.

"Well, pissing is the same the world over, whoever you are!" he'd replied sourly. "It's no big deal."

Lady Atherton came into the kitchen just as Mrs. Pinner was placing the teapot of *Lapsang souchong* on the table. She was dressed now, in an impeccably crisp pink linen dress with a white collar, and her face was lightly and delicately made-up.

"Oh, dear, isn't it a dreadful day?" she remarked, sitting down at the table.

Mrs. Pinner knew better than to ask if the Queen had phoned to say the party had been canceled. What happened between her employer and the Queen was never discussed, nor were the workings of Buckingham Palace, except in the most general terms.

"Yes, it's raining cats and dogs," she replied. Then as a crafty afterthought she added: "Shall I press your dress for this afternoon, m'lady?" That was one way of finding out what was going on.

"Yes, please, Mrs. Pinner, and can you check that I've got clean gloves? Did I tell you that I've discovered where to get white leather gloves cleaned?" Celia added casually.

"Where, m'lady?"

"There's a company in Scotland that does them, and we'll have to send them by mail, but it's worth it. I do so hate cotton or silk gloves. The Queen's lady's maid gave me the address."

Mrs. Pinner beamed with appropriate delight. She didn't think cotton or silk gloves were the proper thing either.

Hugo appeared a few moment later, still handsome at forty-eight, almost a clichéd version of what romantics imagine an English earl to look like: tall, elegantly slim, with dark hair graying at the temples and a dark mustache. He was without doubt one of the most distinguished-looking men of his generation, with a charismatic quality that had helped him succeed in business. Celia had grown accustomed to his striking looks, seeing them through eyes blunted by fond familiarity, but then she would notice other women gazing at him and realize with a jolt that his film-star features were very attractive to them.

"Good morning, Mrs. Pinner."

"Good morning, m'lord."

"And how are you today?" His greeting was warm and courteous. He greeted everyone in this way, whether road sweeper or duchess.

"Very well, thank you, m'lord. Would you like an egg, or will you just have cereal this morning?" Mrs. Pinner admired him almost as much as she admired royalty. He was a real gentleman, in her opinion. One of the best.

Hugo looked around the kitchen. "Any danger of a grapefruit?" he asked boyishly.

Celia burst out laughing. "You sound just like the boys. 'Any danger,' indeed! That's what they always say."

Hugo grinned. "They'll be home for the holidays quite soon, won't they?" He sounded wistful. Family tradition had dictated that after preparatory school they went to Eton College, where he himself had been, but he missed them when they were away.

"Another four weeks, darling."

"As long as that?"

"I was thinking, maybe we should get a tutor to look after them next holidays? Someone who could help them keep up their studies but who would also be able to give them a game of tennis or take them swimming."

After a moment's thought Hugo nodded slowly. "That's not a bad idea. Why don't you ring up Robertson and Short? They're the best agency. I can remember my father getting a tutor for me from them when

I was about Colin's age. They'll recommend someone good."

"Yes." Celia looked meaningfully at him. "We don't want any more *au pairs,* do we?"

Hugo shot her a knowing look, remembering. "God, no! I couldn't survive another Elfreida."

"Neither could I." Elfreida Sjögren, as Celia would always think of her, had caused them so much embarrassment that Celia still flinched when she thought about it. She supposed she ought to be thankful that Elfreida hadn't tried to seduce Hugo. As it was, poor old Selwyn Witley had succumbed to her grubby charms and abandoned Helen after twenty-three years of marriage, which was doubly hard on Helen, who had stood by him during the lean years before he'd become successful.

Of course, as the debacle had mainly taken place in the Athertons' house, the newspapers had exploited the situation to the hilt.

"QUEEN'S LADY-IN-WAITING INVOLVED IN MARRIAGE BREAKUP," screamed most of the headlines, and only in much smaller print below, "*Au pair* Runs Off with Dinner Guest."

Thankfully the Queen had been more than understanding when, mortified, Celia had apologized to her.

"Believe me, Celia," she said, "I know the press better than you do. It's typical of them to mention your position here, although it's got nothing to do with you. It will soon be forgotten."

"I sincerely hope so," Celia had replied. Well, it had been forgotten as far as the general public was concerned, but Celia herself would never be allowed to forget, because Elfreida was making a determined forage into society and so it was impossible to avoid her. Elfreida was so exuberantly gloating, too, in her new role of rich peer's wife, so triumphant about her big house in the Boltons, her chauffeur-driven Rolls-Royce, her designer-label clothes and Cartier jewelry, that she was fast becoming London's latest laughing-stock. Torn between amusement at her effrontery and embarrassment at her behavior, Celia would never forget Elfreida's methods to ensnare Selwyn, and it made her feel badly about his first wife, who had been her friend.

Breakfast over, Hugo rose to leave for the auction gallery in Bond Street.

"If the party's on this afternoon, I'll come home later to change," he said as he kissed her good-bye.

"I'll get Mrs. Pinner to press your morning suit," she replied. "I'll let you know what's happening as soon as I can." She lowered her voice, out of earshot of Mrs. Pinner. "The Queen told me just now that they'll make a decision by eleven o'clock. The forecast looks better for the afternoon."

"Then I'll hope to see you later. 'Bye, sweetheart."

" 'Bye, darling." Fondly she watched him run down the front steps and into the chauffeur-driven car Hamilton's provided for his use. With a wave of his hand he was gone, and as always, she felt a tiny pang of loss when he left her side. Hugo was her rock, her life, her love. Without him she always felt she would diminish and be a mere shadow. And if she had supported him in all he'd done since they'd got married twenty years before, then he had certainly done the same for her, especially in her role as one of the royal ladies-in-waiting. When several of the Queen's friends had recommended her and suggested she would be perfect for such a role, Celia's first instinct had been one of nervousness. The fact that her father-in-law had been an equerry to the late King George V and that she herself had been invited to parties at Buckingham Palace when she married Hugo did nothing to still her initial reluctance.

"How shall I know what to do?" she'd asked Hugo.

"Don't worry, the Queen's private secretary will go through everything with you, and there are always people on the palace staff who will help you if you're in a fix," he'd assured her.

That had been six years ago. Now she could count the Queen among her closest women friends, and her spells on duty as a pleasure. Wherever the Queen went, and whatever she did, an aura of delight spread among those most closely associated with her, extending and reaching out to the crowds beyond. It was a cliché that made Celia wince when she put it into words, but the fact was, the Queen spread happiness wherever she went, and a little of that happiness and general good spirits rubbed off on those around her.

She glanced at her watch. It was half-past nine. Robertson and Short would be open. She reached for the telephone directory to get their number. Agents for Educational Tutors. Hay Hill. Mayfair. She dialed the number and immediately an educated voice answered. Explaining that she wanted someone to help look after their thirteen- and fifteen-year-old sons during the summer vacation, she was told they had several young men on their books who were highly qualified teachers. One in particular they could recommend. His name was Roland Shaw and he was thirty-one.

"Mr. Shaw has a degree in history and English from Caius College, Cambridge, and when he was at Nottingham Grammar School, from where he won a scholarship for university, he obtained seven O levels and four A levels," she was told.

"How about sports? And can he drive a car?"

"He can play tennis and cricket, and he is apparently a strong swimmer. He also has a clean driver's license."

"That all sounds very satisfactory," Celia replied. "When can I meet him?"

"Shall I arrange for an interview tomorrow morning, Lady Atherton? I can ask him to come and see you at about ten-thirty, if that is convenient? He only lives in Knightsbridge, so he's practically within walking distance of your house."

Celia consulted her diary. "That would be fine. I shall look forward to seeing him then."

She hung up and glanced out the window. It was still raining. At this rate it was doubtful the garden party would go ahead.

"I'm off now," Jackie called to Kip an hour later. He was still making business calls in the living room,

and he shouted a perfunctory "Okay. See you later."
Belting her cream raincoat, she seized an umbrella out
of the blue-and-white Chinese stand in the hall and
hurried to the elevator. Taxis were scarce on a morning like this, so as a precaution she'd put on a comfortable pair of walking shoes that wouldn't get spoiled
by the rain. Most of her mornings were spent in the
offices of *Society* magazine going through the dozens
of invitations that arrived each day, answering letters,
and making arrangements for the coming week. Sometimes she wrote her column in the office, where she
had a desk in a corner of a room shared with the
fashion editor and her assistant, but mostly she wrote
it in the peace and quiet of her own apartment, typing
it straight onto her old-fashioned IBM golfball machine
which everyone teased her about. Okay, so it was noisy,
heavy, and couldn't do all the other things a more modern machine could do, but she loved it for its solidity
and simplicity. As for word processors, she shrank from
the thought of all that technology with horror.

"I'm surprised you don't write your column with a
quill and ink," Kip teased her. "After all, Samuel
Pepys did!"

The headquarters of *Society* were situated in Berkeley Street, on the fifth floor of a Victorian house that
had long since been converted into offices, and now
contained six separate companies, including a real-
estate agent, a law firm, and a public-relations corpo-
ration. When Jackie arrived fifteen minutes later,
having been lucky enough to have caught a cab, she
found the usual hubbub of activity generating its own
energy, so that the building had an atmosphere of a humming power station. Couriers, looking like space-age figures from some galactic hell, in black leather with
gleaming helmets and smoked-glass eye goggles, charged
in and out, delivering documents for the different companies, while secretaries rushed to and fro dealing with
them.

Up on the fifth floor, in the offices of *Society*, com-
parative peace reigned. They'd put the forthcoming
issue to bed the previous evening, each department

giving an enormous sigh of relief as they did so, and now a delicious lethargy enveloped them all and would continue to do so for the next few hours before the frenzy to meet deadlines started all over again. Basking in the luxury of knowing they had seven days before the next issue went to press, they could afford to toss ideas around, spend time planning features, speculate on what would be popular with the readers and what would not.

The editor, Bertram Marriott, was in the lobby when she arrived.

"Can I talk to you for a few minutes?" he asked.

"Sure," she replied, following him into his office, which to her amazement was always bare, his desk a gleaming barren expanse of oak, the swivel captain's chair he always sat in placed precisely behind it. Two other chairs of carved mahogany and a dark green leather sofa were the only other furnishings in the large square room. On the pale green walls hung two nondescript landscapes framed in carved gilt. Bertram, who was in his late fifties, was an old-fashioned editor, yet he ran one of the most successful modern magazines to be found on any newsstand. Delegation, Jackie decided, must be his forte, coupled with the ability to choose the right people to carry out his ideas.

"There's something I want to discuss with you," he began, fastidiously flicking a speck of dust from his desktop. "I want to run a feature, over several issues, on Prince Charles and Princess Diana. The *real* Charles and Diana, not just what the inside of Kensington Palace looks like. I want you to find out their personal habits, their likes and dislikes, what they eat and drink, what they talk about when they're alone, what they wear, in bed and out of it. A complete dossier that will give readers a real insight into what goes on behind the scenes. We've got enough photographs, but I want you to write the piece. D'you think you can do it?"

Jackie had turned several shades paler while he had been talking. How on earth was she going to get that sort of insight . . . into the lives of the most famous royal couple in the world? There was no way anyone in their household would tell her anything intimate about them, and the press office at Buckingham Palace was notoriously unhelpful on such matters. They were so scared of giving anything away that their very protestations aroused curiosity and made one think there must be something to conceal, when in fact there probably wasn't. She thought quickly. Bertram was a man who didn't like to hear the problems of any situation; only the solutions. And they had better be good ones.

"All right," Jackie agreed with a flashing smile. "How long do I have?"

Bertram gazed into the middle distance, and she could see the workings of his computerlike mind. He pursed his lips. "I'd like to have four articles, each three thousand words long, by July 30. That's a Monday, and we can insert the first one in the following week's edition, which comes out on August 8. We'll run it as a major feature throughout August—perfect timing for people on holiday, who will have time on their hands and will be attracted by such a fascinating series. We'll call it 'At Home with the Waleses,' and of course you'll have a prominent byline."

"Thank you," Jackie murmured faintly. Her mind was trying to grapple with the enormity of the task. That was, unless she was going to do a rehash of all the gossipy bits that had already appeared over the years in various newspapers. What else could she do? Ask their household controller if it would be possible to interview them? The answer would almost certainly be no, especially for a popular magazine like *Society*. Now, if she'd been writing for a more serious periodical, it might have been possible to get an interview with Prince Charles on architecture or the environment, both of which he was very interested in. She might even have been able to secure a meeting with Princess Diana to ask her all about the charities of which she was patron; but to ask her what she wore in bed . . .

"Right!" Jackie said, springing to her feet. "I'd better get started. Maybe I'll get a lead at the garden party this afternoon—that is, if it isn't canceled owing to the rain."

Bertram Marriott nodded encouragingly. "See if you can have a word with Princess Diana," he suggested.

Jackie nearly burst out laughing. For all his editorial acumen, Bertram was as naive as a child about certain things, because the problem was, he never actually went anywhere. From behind the safety of his desk he thought you could go up to any member of the royal family and do a mini-interview on the spot. He was quite put out when Jackie came back from Royal Ascot one day without a quote from the Queen. "But you were in the Royal Enclosure, weren't you?" he exclaimed. "Why couldn't you have asked her about her runners when she walked down to the paddock to see the horses before the start of the race?"

Excuses about the presence of lords- and ladies-in-waiting, equerries, and plainclothes detectives surrounding the monarch did nothing to appease him. He liked to give orders and he expected his staff to carry them out.

Jackie hurried to her own cluttered office, where Rosie, the fashion editor, was draping clothes all over the furniture.

"Hi, Rosie," Jackie greeted her.

"Jackie, what do you think of this dress?" Rosie held up armfuls of white organdy, frilled and furbelowed and looped with pink satin ribbon.

Jackie looked doubtful. "It's a bit like bedroom curtains gone wrong."

Rosie raised carefully painted eyebrows. "Let me tell you, *this* is a debutante's ball gown, and it's selling for six thousand pounds."

"Six . . . ?" Jackie's expression was stunned. "I don't believe it!"

"It's true." Rosie indicated the Year Planner on the wall beside Jackie's desk. "What else are the poor little dears going to wear to all the social events you're covering?''

Jackie followed her glance, laughing ruefully. The Planner listed all the main events of the year, so that she could slot them in among all the other functions she wrote about. The first one was the Summer Exhibition of Paintings at the Royal Academy of Art, which officially signaled the start of the Season, and this was followed by the Chelsea Flower Show, which was attended by the entire royal family on the first day. From then on it was a nonstop whirl, which included Derby Day, which was a celebration of racing attended by thousands of people from the highest in the land to colorful buskers with sideshows and fun fair; the Fourth of June celebrations at Eton College, to commemorate its founding in 1440 by King Henry VI; Royal Ascot, the Wimbledon tennis tournament, Henley Regatta, followed by Cowes Regatta on the Isle of Wight, when the royal yacht *Britannia* anchored in the bay and Prince Philip whizzed around the Solent in a powerboat, and the final departure of everyone from London to go up to Scotland for the "Glorious Twelfth" of August, when the shooting season started.

Interspersed among these major events were the Glyndebourne opera season; racing at Goodwood, one of the most beautiful racecourses in England, owned by the Duke of Richmond and Gordon; the State Opening of Parliament, when all the peers and peeresses of the realm wore their ermine-and-crimson-velvet robes and coronets, and the Queen wore her crown; the Eton and Harrow cricket match at Lord's; the Cartier Polo Match at Windsor; and a large number of annual charity balls, many of which were held in stately homes around the countryside.

When Jackie had first taken on the job of social editor, she'd been overwhelmed by the amount of socializing she was expected to do. Her life was no longer her own, and at brief moments she understood how royalty must feel, locked into a constant treadmill of going to places and meeting people. At the beginning she'd loved the glamour of her position; people were nice to her because they wanted to be mentioned in her column; she was sent the best tickets for every first night, film premiere, gala concert, ballet, or opera; restaurants gave her the best table as soon as they realized who she was, and hostesses exhausted themselves in their efforts to get her to attend one of their parties. A distinct element of power also went with the job; one of the other diary columnists had been heard to remark that she could "make or break someone socially" by how often she wrote about them. Jackie did not relish this power, and it soon became obvious among the more ambitious socialites that she would write about only people she liked, even if they weren't rich or grand. She was also immune to sycophants, hustlers, and people who tried to bribe her to get a mention. If she was going to spend her life going around and around in a goldfish bowl, meeting the same people at the same functions year after year, she was determined to make it as pleasant for herself as possible, by mixing with the people she liked.

Now, as she tackled her mail, she divided it into three stacks: those that were definitely right for *Society*, those that were too down-market and therefore no good, and those that were possible and would be good fill-ins if she had any space to spare. Then there was a pile of photographs that had arrived overnight, taken at parties during the past thirty-six hours. She liked to feature a wide cross section of celebrities, from the debutante scene to the world of pop, from royalty to film stars and politicians. Jackie immediately saw several pictures that would be perfect for the next edition, and she put them to one side. One was of Princess Michael of Kent, in a shimmering ball gown; then there was a shot of Sophia Loren, looking thirty years younger than her age, attending a film premiere; a picture of Michael Jackson in a mock uniform with lots of gilt chains; and a raunchy photograph of the Duke of Carnforth's daughter, Lady

Delia Bolton, with the skirt of her ball gown hitched up around her thighs.

By the time Jackie had written a couple of dozen letters of acceptance or refusal, or thank-you-for-last-night, it was noon. She'd got no further in planning how to do the royal feature, and she'd quite forgotten about the garden party until the fashion editor made some remark about straw hats going limp in the rain.

"That not how I want it!" Elfreida shrieked, grabbing the hairbrush out of Adolfo's hand. She hurled it across the virgin white salon floor, where it skidded to a halt by the washbasins. "What sort of a hairdresser do you call yourself?"

Adolfo's face turned red, and he clenched his hands. "Lady Witley, you *asked* me to roll your hair into a chignon at the back."

"But not like *that*! Not with this bit *here*—or that bit *there*!" Elfreida tore at her blond hair, beside herself with fury. Then she picked up some of the rollers that he'd left on the mirrored shelf in front of her and threw them across the salon too. "Don't you realize I'm going to Buckingham Palace this afternoon?" she yelled, so that everyone in the salon turned, astonished, to look at her. "Don't you know who I *am*? How can I go to the palace with my hair looking like *this*! I even bring my hat for you to fix, on top, but this is such a dump, I don't suppose you even know how to do *that*!"

A sudden rustle of curtains being drawn back from a screened-off section of the salon, a charge of expectancy filling the atmosphere, the instant lowering of voices among the other clients, and a frisson of obvious excitement among the juniors made Elfreida pause uncertainly in the middle of her stream of abuse.

At that moment Her Royal Highness the Duchess of Gloucester, petite and pretty cousin of the Queen, emerged with her hair beautifully arranged, curling around the brim of a pink straw garden-party hat on which reposed a single pink silk rose.

Without a word, Adolfo seized another brush from his trolley and started brushing Elfreida's hair with short sharp strokes.

"We're going ahead with the party. The ground is not too bad, as it's been dry all week, and the Queen doesn't want to disappoint so many people," the private secretary told Celia Atherton over the phone just before noon. "Could you get here early? We've drawn up a list of people for the Queen to meet, but you might like to add to it if you think there is anyone coming she might find interesting. Otherwise it's all fairly straightforward."

"Fine. I'll arrive at the palace at about two-thirty. Will that be all right?" Celia asked.

"That will be perfect, Celia. I'll see you later."

Celia hung up, glad that a decision had been reached. It was true—thousands of people would have felt very let down if the party had been canceled.

"Can I get you some lunch before you go, m'lady?" Mrs. Pinner asked, hovering within earshot of the phone while she pretended to be doing some dusting.

"Will you put some cheese and fruit on the kitchen table, Ada, and a bottle of mineral water," Celia replied, amused.

"Very well, and your outfit is all ready, hanging on the outside of your wardrobe."

"Thank you, Mrs. Pinner."

Celia had decided to wear a simple navy-blue dress with a matching jacket, and a navy straw hat with a white brim. This was part of her "working" wardrobe, for in her role as a lady-in-waiting she must never overshadow the Queen in any way, not that Celia was conceited enough to imagine she could. But privately she loved to wear soft bright pinks and mint greens, and sometimes daffodil yellow, but as these were among the colors the Queen was also fond of wearing, it was safer to stick to dark shades.

As she was about to leave the house two hours later, the phone rang. "Is that Lady Atherton?" asked a man's voice.

"Yes. Can I help you?"

"I just wanted to confirm my appointment with you at ten-thirty tomorrow morning. This is Roland Shaw speaking. Robertson and Short have arranged for you to interview me. Is that all right?"

Celia liked the sound of him immediately: warmed to his boyish enthusiasm and delightful manners, approved of his businesslike attitude in confirming their meeting, and thought that such a person must be very reliable.

"Yes, I'm looking forward to meeting you," she replied warmly. "I'm afraid the boys are still at Eton, of course, so you won't have the chance to meet them, but I can tell you a bit about them."

"Splendid. At ten-thirty, then?"

"Yes. I'll see you tomorrow."

Celia left the house a few minutes later. The storm clouds had drifted away, out over the north channel, and a watery sun was shining fitfully down onto the newly washed pavements. It promised to be a beautiful day after all.

2

*I*t was the first time this summer that Celia had waited on the Queen at one of the garden parties. Three were held each year, during July. They were usually relaxed affairs, at which the royal family liked to meet as many people as possible, especially those drawn from organizations whose work benefited the community, and from Celia's point of view it was an easy afternoon following the Queen across the lawns to the royal tea tent.

At two-fifteen she drove her car through the right-hand gates into the palace forecourt, having been waved on by a policeman who knew her well. Guardsmen in scarlet coats and black fur busbies, reminiscent of the bearskin helmets worn by Russian hussars in by-gone days, stood to attention outside their sentry boxes, stiff as wooden toys and just as expressionless. Celia parked her car by the side entrance that led to the secretaries' offices and hurried into the palace.

In the surrounding streets the crowds had begun to gather; there were those who had been invited this afternoon, those who had come to have a look at those who had been invited, plus a collection of Japanese tourists clicking their cameras, who wondered what was going on. The Mall, Constitution Hill, and Birdcage Walk began to resemble a sort of up-market street fete in atmosphere, as guests got into line as early as one o'clock, although they wouldn't be gaining admittance to the palace for another two and a quarter hours.

There was much preening and smirking too, among some of the guests, who were not at all displeased at being ogled by tourists eating ice cream. Those who were accustomed to being invited each year would wait, of course, until three-forty-five before allowing their chauffeurs to drive them, swishing importantly in their limousines, into the inner quadrangle; but to others, to whom this was a once-in-a-lifetime experience, it was important to arrive "in good time" lest they miss a precious second of being within the four walls, even the four garden walls, of the monarch's official residence.

Celia sensed the party atmosphere inside the palace too. As in all large households, there was an excited air of expectancy about the place and a feeling of relief that the weather had cleared up in time. J. Lyons & Co., who always did the catering for garden parties, had arrived early and were setting up the buffet tea in the marquees, bringing in trays containing forty thousand tiny sandwiches, thirty thousand little cakes and strawberry tarts, fifty thousand sweet biscuits, and gallons of iced coffee and lemonade. Simple white china cups and silver urns would be used to serve Indian tea to those who preferred it, and most did, but nowadays plain caterers' teaspoons were used instead of the royal crested silver ones. Too many had gone missing—taken home as souvenirs by certain guests—for them to be used anymore. Only in the royal tea tent, where the Queen had tea with three hundred specially invited guests from government and the diplomatic corps, plus other VIPs, were the royal household's china and silver used. And it was only for this tent that the palace kitchens provided the refreshments. Nevertheless, Celia knew that each of these garden parties cost the Queen, personally, over thirty thousand pounds, and that was for nine thousand guests on each occasion. She shuddered to think what the total amount spent on entertaining must be each year as nearly fifty thousand people got invited to the palace for luncheons or dinners or banquets, and that didn't include the years when there was a royal wedding or some other special occasion.

Hurrying along the red-carpeted corridor, which was hung with paintings and engravings, Celia made her way to a large, pleasantly furnished anteroom overlooking the inner quadrangle. Here the other ladies-in-waiting and half a dozen equerries were congregating, ready to be briefed by the Queen's private secretary. On friendly terms with everyone connected with the royal household, Celia was greeted warmly when she entered, and one of the equerries, the Earl of Slaidburn, who had been at Eton at the same time as Hugo, stepped forward with outstretched arms.

"Celia, my dear. How are you?"

"Hello, Robin." She kissed him on the cheek. "I'm fine. And you?"

"Couldn't be better. I thought we'd had it for this afternoon, though, didn't you? Never seen such rain as at seven o'clock this morning." Robin Slaidburn, ruddy-complexioned and with the air of a man who is happiest on the grouse moors, stepped back to look at Celia.

"You're looking very charming, my dear," he remarked.

Celia smiled. Although he'd been happily married for nearly twenty years, Robin had always mildly fancied her, but from a safe distance. She knew that if she were to take his flirtatious manner at all seriously, he'd run for his life.

"How's Hugo?" he asked almost immediately, as if he knew what she was thinking. "Is he coming along this afternoon?"

"Yes, he'll be here in time for tea." Then she turned to the others, and pleasantries were exchanged all around. Some of the other ladies-in-waiting, to Princess Diana, Princess Anne, and the Queen Mother, were close friends of hers, although they rarely all Waited on the same occasions; but there was a bond between them, of shared experiences.

"Have you seen the guest list for today, Celia?' Robin asked, handing her a computer printout.

"There is the usual bunch of ambassadors, of course, and some bishops and rabbis, and quite a showing from the judiciary, including that mad old judge who thinks its a woman's fault if she gets raped."

Celia snorted in disgust. "Anyone else of interest?" Her eyes skimmed down the long lists of names. There were top-ranking officers from the Army, the Royal Navy, and the Royal Air Force, as was customary, some Commonwealth leaders who would be wearing their national costume, several lords lieutenant from various counties around England where they represented the Queen, mayors from local London boroughs, and people from the arts. There were also a number of aristocrats, who had been invited because of their rank or because they were personal friends of the royal family, as well as some life peers who had been invited because of their achievements in the community.

Suddenly Celia let out a little gasp.

"What is it?" Robin asked.

Then she shrugged. "I suppose it was bound to happen sooner or later," she replied. "The Witleys have been invited!"

"The Wit . . . ?" Remembering what had happened, Robin raised his dark bushy eyebrows quizzically. "Have they, indeed? Oh, well, divorce doesn't bar one from court anymore, and they could hardly be refused entry after the enormous amount of money Selwyn gave to that housing scheme Prince Charles was so interested in, but I bet *she's* as pleased as punch to be asked."

Celia nodded. "She must be delighted," she replied dryly.

Neither of them, she realized later, had mentioned Elfreida by name.

At that moment the Queen's private secretary, a retired colonel from the Army, came hurrying into the room carrying a sheaf of papers. Small and wiry, he shook hands briskly with everyone, and when he spoke, his words came rattling out like bullets from a machine gun. It was several years since he'd retired from the Grenadier Guards, but becoming a civilian had never rested happily on his persona, and when he talked, it always seemed as if he were instructing a platoon.

"Right!" he began. "Shall we sit down?"

They sat on chairs and two sofas, in a semicircle facing him. He took an upright chair in front of the fireplace, his notes on his knee.

"Right!" He glanced around the assembled company. "At sixteen hundred hours, Her Majesty the Queen, accompanied by the Duke of Edinburgh, will come out onto the terrace from the Bow Room, with Queen Elizabeth the Queen Mother, the Prince and Princess of Wales, the Duke and Duchess of York, the Princess Royal, and the Duke and Duchess of Gloucester."

Although the whole world might refer to "Princess Diana" and "Princess Anne," he would rather have died than describe them incorrectly, even in the privacy of his own office among his colleagues.

There were echoing murmurs of "right." Celia made a mental note that ten members of the royal family would be on parade today, each of whom would walk separately to the royal tea tent, on the far side of the lawn, stopping to talk with selected people and carving a swath through the crowds as they went.

As if he knew what she was thinking, the private secretary elaborated. "The Queen will take the center route; the Duke of Edinburgh, the Princess Royal, the Duke of York, and the Princess of Wales will fan out among the guests to the right. Queen Elizabeth the Queen Mother, the Duke and Duchess of Gloucester, the Duchess of York, and the Prince of Wales will fan out to the left. Everyone got that? Right!"

They all nodded again. They'd all done it many times before and knew the form. Ladies-in-waiting would follow behind, but equerries, who were usually also retired officers from the armed forces, would go ahead, dividing the crowds so that ten avenues were formed down which members of the royal family would walk.

He continued without pausing. "We estimate the Queen and her family will take twenty-five minutes to reach the royal tea tent from the terrace, so, allowing for the playing of the National Anthem, their estimated time of arrival should be sixteen-twenty-eight. Right?"

Celia's mouth twitched. Something in her longed to salute and say: "Yes, sir."

Then the private secretary turned to Robin. "Lord Slaidburn, I'm putting you in charge of organizing those who should be presented." His eyes swept over the other men in the room. "At fifteen hundred hours I'd like you to accompany Lord Slaidburn so that you can assist him." He flourished the papers he was holding. "Here are the lists. Get these guests to line the routes, at intervals, so that the presentations are spread out. There are some people who run a children's home, to meet the Princess of Wales, some workers from Save the Children Fund, whom the Princess Royal wants to talk to, and of course a representative of the World Wildlife Fund, whom the Duke of Edinburgh wants to meet. And there are various others . . . and of course if you spot someone of interest, bring them to the front. But when the time comes, keep it moving. Don't let anyone hog the limelight. We must keep on schedule." Then he sprang to his feet and left the room as abruptly as he'd entered it, with a quick good-bye.

"Well!" remarked Robin, glancing down at the list of special people to be presented. "You'll be pleased to hear one thing, Celia."

"What's that?"

"Lord and Lady Witley of Vauxhall are *not* on this list." His eyes twinkled as he spoke.

Celia lowered her voice. "Well, that won't stop her trying to get presented."

It was three-thirty. A steady stream of people were passing through the gates now, across the courtyard and under the left archway into the quadrangle, while others were being taken in their cars right up to the glass-covered entrance, where footmen were helping them to alight. For miles around, the traffic seemed to have come to a standstill, as the police tried to control the surge around Buckingham Palace and the average Londoner cursed at the inconvenience.

One who stood apart, quietly watching the fearful congestion of cars and taxis and smartly dressed people in the Mall, was Roland Shaw. Coming from the direction of Parliament Square, he had walked slowly up Birdcage Walk, mingling with the gathering crowds in all their finery as they converged on the palace. Silk top hats and gray or black tailcoats with jaunty carnations in the lapels contrasted sharply with the clothes of the ordinary London man. Silks and chiffons and fine straw hats bedecked with flowers looked incongruous beside women in jeans and T-shirts. And all around, Roland could smell the very scent of prosperity in wafts of expensive perfume and after-shave.

When he reached the central gates of the palace, which were only ever opened to let the monarch through, he paused and looked up at the rooftops, to where the red and gold and blue Royal Standard fluttered from the flagpole, signifying the Queen was in residence. His expression was impassive and his eyes showed no emotion. The police on duty barely noticed the neatly dressed young man with a pale face and pebble glasses. But Roland Shaw was deep in thought as he schemed and planned with formidable determination.

Jumping out of the hired car, Jackie Daventry hurried up the four shallow mottled gray marble steps of the main entrance of Buckingham Palace, so polished they reflected like mirror, and entered through the glass-and-mahogany double doors. Inside, footmen in scarlet and gold livery took her invitation from her with white-gloved hands and then ushered her forward into the vast and imposing hall that seemed as big as an aircraft hangar. Oceans of scarlet carpeting flowed before her in a sea of red, and overhead the crystal chandeliers blazed down like diamond dewdrops. A staircase, also carpeted in red, with gilded banisters, swept upward to the floors above, and all around there was the impression of a stage setting. This could be the final scene of *The Sleeping Beauty* or *Cinderella*, Jackie thought. All it required was for the corps de ballet to come tripping down the staircase to the music of Tchaikovsky, leading in the Fairy Princess to meet her Prince Charming, and the picture would be complete. Then Jackie grinned, remembering it was Princess Anne who had said she was no "fairy princess" and that the public had better accept that fact! It was true, of course, although on occasion she could resemble the clichéd image of how a royal princess should look. But mostly she was a down-to-earth practical woman who liked comfortable country clothes and had no pretensions.

More footmen were shepherding the guests into the garden now, because the royal family would be appearing shortly, and so Jackie moved forward, ascending another flight of shallow stairs, also carpeted in red, which led to the Bow Room. She had loved this room since her first visit to the palace with her parents, years before. It was oval-shaped, with glass doors that led straight onto the terrace, painted in delicate cream and gilt. Sparsely furnished with a few French chairs and sofas, it did, though, contain four built-in corner recesses in which were displayed a magnificent dinner service of Mecklenburg-Strelitz porcelain, made in 1763, which had been commissioned by King George III.

Some of the guests wanted to linger so they could get a closer look at the treasures, and she heard someone grumbling that her camera had been confiscated when she'd arrived, but officials kept everyone moving forward with friendly but firm expressions. There was no opportunity to loiter.

A moment later they were out on the terrace overlooking the sweeping lawns that covered forty-five acres, the lake with its collection of rare birds and pink flamingos, which were fed prawns so that their plumage would retain its pink color, and its trees and shrubs which would have done credit to a botanical garden. The herbaceous border, planted on the right, and directly under the Queen's bedroom window, was ablaze with the most perfect blooms Jackie had ever seen. It was so perfect, with not the hint of a weed or wilting leaf, that if she hadn't known better, she'd have said all the flowers were artificial. One of the guests had walked over to have a closer look, bending down to examine the roses and sweet-scented stock and begonias, but a policeman had walked up to her and politely requested she move back to the lawns.

Jackie frowned, puzzled, but then realized that security at the palace had to be very tight these days. With bombs being left in strategic places by the IRA, and more recently by the Animal Liberation Front, constant vigilance had to be practiced at all times. Members of the royal family, the armed forces, and the government were prime targets, and for all anyone knew, the woman might have been about to slip a plastic explosive device behind a rosebush, timed to go off later. After all, Jackie remembered how five years ago an intruder had got into the palace by scaling a drainpipe and had entered the Queen's bedroom at six o'clock in the morning. She'd been awakened by him sitting on her bed, asking for a cigarette. If that could happen, anything was possible.

Descending the stone steps that led down to the lawn, Jackie paused to take in the summer scene. Against the green of the grass, which had been crushed to a sweet perfume by thousands of feet, the women's dresses and hats contrasted in a profusion of colors from fondant pastels to rich strong patterns, while gray and black top hats bobbed about like animated chimney pots, and some of the men, from the back view, resembled penguins in their black tailcoats. The most exotic touch was provided by the African dignitaries in their traditional costume, while the most graceful were the Indian ladies in their brilliant saris.

In the distance, a long green-and-white-striped marquee, open down one side and fronted by a veranda, was already crowded with guests, but the other marquee, the much smaller and more exclusive-looking one, stood in readiness for the Queen. Here, little tables covered with white damask cloths and decorated with bunches of pink and white flowers were arranged around the entrance, while dozens of small gilt chairs stood in readiness. A little distance away on a bandstand under the trees, the band of the Royal Scots Guards were giving a brassy rendition of the hit tunes from *Carousel,* and Jackie thought she had never seen such a typically English scene. She could almost smell the roses and strawberries that epitomized an English summer, and the warm air, freshened by the recent rain, seemed to carry on its lilting waves the scents of the countryside. Only in England, too, would you see the upper-class way of life in action with well-dressed people executing a slow pavanelike promenade as they strolled up and down, to and fro, traversing the lawns backward and forward, acknowledging each other with restrained pleasure and a refinement of greeting they had perfected to an art form. Voices were modulated, shows of affection were confined to a cool peck somewhere near the cheek, hands were clasped for only a second. The scene was almost choreographed, a parade so stilted in its unique perfection it might have been painted by Lowry.

Cool and graceful in a suit of buttermilk-colored silk, with a large straw hat to match, Jackie took a deep breath before plunging into the crowds. In a moment she'd be surrounded by those who wanted to be mentioned in her column, and they'd give her no peace until she'd acknowledged their presence.

"Hello, Mrs. Daventry."

It had begun. Her foot had barely been planted on the spongy turf before a voice in her ear was wheedling her to pay attention.

Jackie turned, and found herself face-to-face with Lady Tetbury, a highly respected member of the nobility, whose husband was a regular speaker in the House of Lords.

"Good afternoon, Lady Tetbury," she replied.

Cold blue eyes looked into hers. The peeress was

not about to mince her words. "I wish you had let me know you were sending a representative to our party for Harry's twenty-first last week. I wouldn't have minded if you'd wanted to come yourself, although you know we hate publicity of any sort, but I really objected to that wretched young man who turned up, uninvited as far as I was concerned."

Jackie looked at her blankly. "What young man? I'm sorry, I don't understand."

"The young man . . . I've forgotten his name, who helps you with your column," Lady Tetbury replied testily.

"But I don't have anyone who helps me. I don't have outside contributors. I'm the only person who covers the party scene for *Society,* and I'm the only person who does the writing," Jackie protested hotly. "Are you sure you're not mixing me up with *Tatler,* or *Harpers & Queen,* or perhaps *Hello*?" They were the only other journals who ran a regular social-diary section, and sometimes people got confused between the various journalists who wrote for them.

The dark blue ostrich feathers on Lady Tetbury's hat stirred and trembled. "Of course it was your magazine," she retorted haughtily. "The young man said you were too busy to come yourself, but you definitely wanted him to write about it for the next issue. It put me in a very awkward position, as your parents were friends of ours when they were in England, but Harry said I should have sent him packing." Her voice dropped, becoming softer. "I know you need this job since you got divorced, so I didn't want to upset the applecart, but I do think you might have at least phoned me first to explain."

Jackie flushed with annoyance. So even the noble Lady Tetbury could be a bitch at heart.

"I assure you," Jackie said coldly, raising her chin, "that I know nothing about this. I repeat, I have no assistant. This man is obviously a gate-crasher. What was he like?"

"In his twenties, I suppose. Well-spoken and wearing a decent dinner jacket. He looked just like hundreds of other young men these days, but Harry had never seen him before."

"What was his name?"

Lady Tetbury shrugged. "My dear, I couldn't tell you." Her tone was still patronizing. "I was so annoyed by the whole thing that I ignored him all evening. I think he did tell me his name when he arrived, but I really can't remember what it was."

Jackie regarded her with grave blue eyes. "Well, I'm very sorry about this, and I shall try to find out who it was. It is a serious matter when people go around saying they represent a magazine. If he approaches you again, will you let me know, please?"

"Yes, of course." Then she seemed to thaw slightly. "You see, my husband says that in the present financial climate and with a general election only a year away, perhaps we don't want to be seen to be spending money on lavish entertaining. It gives Neil Kinnock and the Labor party cause to say the likes of us are profligate."

"Well, you can rest assured that your party will not be featured in *Society,* Lady Tetbury," Jackie retorted dryly.

"Thank you." The older woman had seen some friends in the distance, and without another word, moved away, almost dismissively.

Immediately Jackie was assailed by a middle-aged couple who were insatiable publicity seekers. It was obvious they were terrified Jackie wouldn't see them.

"Hel-*lo!*" they gushed. And "It's *so* good to see you." The woman's hat was like a red cock's comb under which her tanned and freckled face made her look like a speckled bantam.

Banal greetings exchanged, she cried: "We're absolutely thrilled to be here today. Isn't it a wonderful sight? I just can't wait to see the royals in the flesh!"

Jackie quickly suppressed a vision, conjured up by the woman's words, of the royal family strolling around the grounds naked. A moment later a debutante was being dragged up to her by a forceful mother, dislodging the other couple as she did so.

"You do know Fiona, don't you?" she said loudly, grabbing Jackie's arm. "She's so excited . . . aren't you, darling? . . . to have been chosen to represent English debs at a ball in New York next month. It's all going to be televised too! We've got to get you a really wonderful dress, haven't we, darling?" The mother kept looking at the daughter with a mixture of pride and adoration; in contrast, the girl looked silently and sulkily back. Jackie privately thanked God that her mother had never behaved like that, at least not in public.

By the time she'd moved twenty yards from the terrace, she'd been assailed by three more couples eager to be seen in such a smart setting, also a rich and powerful business tycoon, several mothers with daughters of marriageable age, for whom they were desperately seeking husbands, and a widow in her sixties who was also looking for a spouse.

The aristocrats, the true celebrities, and the people of real worth did not rush up to Jackie in order to secure a mention.

But then, she reflected, they didn't need it. Swiftly she made a mental list of the more genuinely interesting guests, when, as if by a secret signal, an excited ripple swept through the thousands of guests, stilling and silencing them so that they paused expectantly. All eyes turned toward the terrace. Quietly and without fuss, the Queen and her family had emerged from the palace and were standing informally grouped on the terrace. A moment later the band struck up "God Save the Queen."

With the eyes of a journalist, Jackie committed the tableau to memory: the royal princes and dukes standing rigidly to attention in their elegant morning dress, the Queen, her mother, Princess Anne, Princess Diana, and the Duchesses of York and Gloucester all wearing primary colors, from daffodil yellow to sapphire blue and soft rose pink and cool lime, so that they would stand out in the crowds. It was rumored that the Queen had once observed: "If I don't wear a bright color, nobody will know who I am."

With a final boom of drums and a clash of cymbals, the National Anthem came to an end, and as if a clockwork toy had been wound up and set in motion, the group started moving, breaking ranks, shifting apart, and walking toward the crowds with a stiffness which she assumed must be the result of years of regal bearing. Jackie had never seen a member of the royal family slouch or amble or lean against anything when on duty.

Moving toward the tea tent, she ran almost immediately into Lord and Lady Witley of Vauxhall. Elfreida bore down on Jackie with beefy determination.

"It stopped raining in time, huh? It good, no?" she enthused, pushing her face into Jackie's. "I say to Selwyn this morning, I think the party will be canceled, so it's good, huh?" Her turquoise grosgrain suit, with a matching hat which Freddie Fox had made specially for her, contrasted unbecomingly with her fair skin, making her look pasty-faced.

Jackie backed away from the face pressed so close to her own. "Yes, I'm glad it cleared up in time. Now, if you'll excuse me . . ."

Elfreida grabbed her by the arm. "Are you writing about the Mayfair Ball? Selwyn and I were there, you know. We took a table of friends."

"Yes, I know." Jackie looked purposely vague. "I'm not sure how next week's column is going to work out. We're so short of space, and there's so much on."

"Well, we're going to the White Dove Ball next week! You'll be at that? You'll join our table? We have a very nice time, with all our friends, huh?"

With a supreme effort Jackie curbed her irritation. "I don't think I shall have time to go to that," she said briefly.

"Come along now, Elfie."

Selwyn had spoken at last! He tried to pull his wife away, but she was determined to have the last word.

"You put in your column we are at the garden party today, huh?"

Jackie ignored the remark, determined about one

thing. She wasn't a snob and she didn't care what type of background people came from, nor what their color, class, or creed was, but there was one thing she couldn't stand at any price, and that was people who were publicity seekers. Those men and women who smarmed up to her, desperate for a mention in next week's column, willing to sell their souls for a flattering photograph of themselves splashed all over the page in order to impress their friends, their relatives, their neighbors. As far as she was concerned, those who clamored and cajoled and calculated in order to be written about were the ones who wouldn't get mentioned. And Elfreida Witley had definitely just become one of them.

Celia, with Hugo by her side now, hovered a few feet away from the Queen, watching, always watching, for the slightest signal that might mean: *I've spoken to this person long enough. Bring up someone else to be presented.* Or: *I think it's time we circulated a bit more.* The Queen was able to convey her messages with the merest flicker of her eyebrows or a change of expression in her blue eyes. When Celia accompanied her on public engagements, of course, the messages became stronger and more urgent. *Help me to carry all these bouquets. Give me my umbrella and raincoat—I'm getting soaked! Let's say good-bye and go, we've stayed long enough.*

In Celia's handbag she also carried a spare handkerchief, a pair of tights, hairpins and safety pins, and anything else that might be needed in an emergency, with the exception of aspirin or any form of medicine. The Queen did not believe in taking pills. Celia remembered she had even refused to take seasickness tablets when she had been on board the royal yacht *Britannia,* although she'd been very unwell.

Now, as the Queen moved from group to group, smiling, shaking hands, greeting old friends, she looked relaxed and happy in a way the general public rarely saw. Few realized she was not only a brilliant mimic but also had a great sense of humor. Now and again she caught Celia's eye and grinned broadly, implying she was enjoying herself and Celia should do the same.

"I don't believe it!" Hugo exclaimed suddenly in a low voice.

"What's the matter?" Celia looked across the royal tea tent to where he was staring. There, arguing with an official, was Elfreida, accompanied by Selwyn, who was looking extremely embarrassed.

"Oh, my God," breathed Celia. "I knew she'd try to get in here."

"I'll go and head them off," Hugo said. "I'll have a word with Selwyn. He won't cause any trouble."

"No, but she will." Visions of Elfreida charging across the crimson carpeting of the royal tea tent to say a pert hello to the Queen, which she was quite capable of doing, sent a cold chill through Celia. Not for the first time did she feel sorry for Selwyn. He'd been a fool to leave his wife for someone who was going to go through his money like a dose of salts, and cause him embarrassment at the same time, but Elfreida had been so clever, cunning almost, in seducing him that one could only feel sympathetic.

Celia watched as Hugo went over to the entrance of the tent and charmingly and diplomatically edged the Witleys away and back into the main mélange of guests, talking to them all the while and finally introducing them to some people he knew so they would not feel abandoned. Selwyn looked quite relieved, but Elfreida glowered at being denied the ultimate privilege. Celia watched as Hugo, with seeming reluctance, took his leave of them and headed back.

"You were brilliant, darling," she whispered. "Even Elfreida couldn't have been offended by the way you handled that situation."

"Don't you believe it," Hugo chuckled. "Poor old Selwyn. He's bitten off more than he can chew with that one!"

"I just wish it hadn't been in our house that he met her. I still feel responsible."

"Don't be silly, sweetheart. How were you to know

Selwyn was heading for the male menopause? He was ready to fall for anyone under twenty-five, and it just happened to be Elfreida."

Celia smiled ruefully. "Yes, I know. It wouldn't matter if only she wasn't so horrendously pushy! If she would only wait until people got to know her, she'd be all right. As it is, she's driving everyone mad in her desperation to be noticed."

"Watch it!" Hugo said, looking over her shoulder. "I think HM is about to head this way." Like a lot of people, he always referred to her majesty as HM. Likewise Princess Margaret was known by her circle of friends as PM.

Celia looked up and saw the Queen had a merry twinkle in her eyes. Had she perhaps noticed Elfreida's attempts to get to meet her?

Kip raised his hands in alarm. "Hey, wait a minute. I don't want to find myself bopping with a bunch of duchesses at some stately shindig!"

Jackie burst out laughing, stretching her toes as she kicked off her shoes and flopped down on the long white sofa in her living room. She'd had to walk back from Buckingham Palace to Knightsbridge because it was chaos being picked up by a car in all that scrum, and there were never enough taxis for all the guests as they poured out into the Mall at six o'clock. She had, however, left by the garden exit at Hyde Park Corner, which the majority of people didn't know existed, and so it had taken her only ten minutes to get home.

"I wasn't going to suggest anything so traumatic, Kip. This is the opera at Glyndebourne. You like opera, don't you? It's a performance of *Le nozze di Figaro* and I'd love you to come with me tomorrow night."

"But it's formal, isn't it? The full tuxedo and all that?"

"Go to Moss Bros. in the morning. You can hire everything from them, and it will be a wonderful evening, I can promise you." Jackie recalled the beautiful manor house in Sussex, where the owner, John Christie, had built an adjoining eight-hundred-seat auditorium in 1934 for his soprano wife, Audrey Mildmay. An evening at Glyndebourne was still one of the most elegant events of the summer season, unchanged since before World War II, with full evening dress compulsory. It was also a tradition to have a picnic in the beautiful grounds during the hour-and-a-half interval.

"I'll get Benjie to take us by helicopter," she cajoled. "As long as I mention his hire company in my column, he'll give us the ride for free."

Kip seemed to brighten. "One of the perks of the job? Okay, I'll escort you . . . but only because I like Mozart," he teased.

"Good. I'll also ask Fortnum and Mason to fix us a hamper in the morning. What do you fancy? Cold lobster, smoked salmon, fresh nectarines, washed down with some Dom Perignon?"

"Say, are you getting the hamper for free too . . . in exchange for a mention?"

Jackie shook her head, still laughing. "No such luck. Free dinners in restaurants, yes. Free flights, hotel accommodation, hired cars, yes. But I can hardly expect Fortnum's to donate a picnic supper!"

Kip's eyes twinkled. "Why not? You're the queen of the freebies, aren't you?"

"Only up to a point. If I wanted to, I could be dressed by several couturiers, have my hair done by a top salon, and probably deck myself with borrowed diamonds from a leading jeweller's, but I'd hate that. I once borrowed a dress from an up-and-coming designer to wear at Ascot, because they thought everyone would ask where I'd bought it and it would attract other customers, but I hated the outfit so much that I felt absolutely miserable. It taught me a lesson. Always wear what you feel comfortable in, even if it doesn't have a designer label. I want to be free, Kip, to look the way I want to look, and not be an animated advertisement for a bunch of designers."

"I don't blame you. You always look very nice anyway," he added as an afterthought.

"Typical brother!" Jackie snorted. "Shall I take you out to dinner, although you don't deserve it?"

"Somewhere quiet, where you don't know anyone and you won't be jumping up and down all night saying 'Hello, darling!' "

She looked indignant. "I'll have you know I never jump up and down saying 'Hello, darling!' to anyone. But I agree about going somewhere quiet. I've had a long enough day as it is, without running into people who'll ask me if I enjoyed the garden party this afternoon so that I'll know *they* were there." She rose, unbuttoning her jacket. "I'll have a quick shower and change and then I'll be ready. I know a divine Italian restaurant in Fulham that no one's discovered yet. We'll go there."

"Yet another freebie?" He was grinning.

She picked up a needle-worked cushion from the sofa and threw it at him. "Buzz off! I do pay, occasionally, you know, for my opulent life-style."

Kip picked up the cushion and threw it back at her. "You don't say!"

It was nearly seven o'clock before Selwyn and Elfreida got back to the Boltons, and by that time they were both in a very bad mood. Their car, on its way to pick them up from the garden party, had got stuck with a long line of other cars, all on the same mission, and so they'd had to hang about the hall of Buckingham Palace, with nowhere to sit, waiting for it to arrive. Listening intently as a loudspeaker called out the names of people whose car was approaching the main entrance, she sighed with loud and gusty irritability when no call came for them.

"How he so stupid?" she demanded, referring to their chauffeur. "I feel humiliated waiting here . . . suppose we are the last?"

"Oh, shut up," snapped Selwyn under his breath. He was longing for a strong drink and a cigarette, and his legs ached from standing three hours.

"He should have been here ages ago. Everyone

important has already gone. What shall we do if he doesn't come? I can't be seen *walking* away!"

Selwyn strolled away from her a few paces, under the watchful eye of a footman, and then with a strained expression walked back to her again. At that moment he didn't trust himself to speak.

At last the disembodied voice announced "Lord and Lady Witley," and with a gasp of relief Elfreida charged forward and into the waiting Rolls-Royce, which, on her insistence, now bore the number plate WOV 1. Sinking back onto the dove-gray leather seat, she regretted bitterly that her debut in royal circles had not been more successful. She'd hoped to make a social impact that would lead her to dizzy and enviable heights. *Do join us for tea,* the Queen had said in her imagination. *You and Lord Witley must come and stay with us at Windsor one weekend. . . .*

When they got inside the house, Elfreida turned on Selwyn with all the charm of a four-year-old who has just had her ice cream swiped from her hand by another child.

"That was terrible!" she stormed, bursting into tears. "Fancy being turned away from the royal tea tent like that! And in front of that bitch Celia Atherton too! How could you let Hugo lead us away like that? We might have got in if it hadn't been for Hugo!" Her smart Freddie Fox hat had fallen over her eyes, and in exasperation she tore it off and flung it across the room.

"You don't get admitted to the royal tea tent without a special invitation. I told you that from the beginning," Selwyn retorted, going straight to the black lacquered King Charles II cabinet that rested on a silvered carved stand in a corner of the drawing room and was always well-stocked with liquor. "We should never have tried to crash it! Christ, woman, I haven't got as far as I have in life without learning a thing or two. I may have been ambitious all my life, and God knows being the son of a Welsh miner I *had* to be ambitious if I was going to start my own company and end up a millionaire, but I always remembered something my mother said, and I've always kept it in mind. 'Sel,' she told me again and again, 'it's all right to be ambitious, and it's all right to be hardworking, and you can even be a bit sharp, but never, *never* be pushy.' "

Elfreida sniffed into her lace-edged handkerchief. "What has that to do with anything?"

He took a gulp of Johnnie Walker Black Label, neat and without ice.

"You're pushy," he said flatly.

She stopped sobbing as if an electric circuit had been turned off, and glared at him. "What you mean? I not pushy!"

"You're very pushy. Just relax and take things quietly, like I do. Be nice to everyone, be gracious and kind, do your hostess stuff and your charity work, and you'll see, in time everyone will grow to like you and you'll be accepted everywhere."

"But *when*, Selwyn, when?" The tears had started to flow again and her neck looked flushed and sweaty. "I want to be big success *now*! While I'm young. After all, I'm a titled woman . . . I'm rich . . . I'm pretty and well-dressed and I go everywhere. . . . Why does nobody care?"

Selwyn's normally loose mouth tightened. "You mean *I'm* titled and rich and successful, not you. You're merely my wife. You'll have to earn the respect of people in society, like I did. It's time you educated yourself a bit too. When I was your age I was reading all the time, teaching myself about things, learning everything I could, so when the time came I could hold my own with more educated people. And it paid off. Look at me now!"

"Yes, look at you now," wept Elfreida resentfully. "A tired old man who doesn't know how to have fun." Then she went over to him and knelt at his feet like a fat little girl with a blotchy face and her hair in a mess, quite unaware that her words had been hurtful. "I want to have fun, Selwyn," she said piteously. "I want to go dancing and have my picture in all the papers, like that Fergie. All I need is to be noticed.

Once I'm noticed, then I'm sure it will happen, but you've got to help me. You've got to push me forward.''

Selwyn rose creakily to refill his glass, wondering as he did so why he'd thrown away a comfortable marriage to an undemanding wife for a disruptive life with a fractious and willful child. Then he dismissed the thought immediately. Elfreida had him by the balls. Literally, in fact, for one night she'd waylaid him on his way to the lavatory when he and Helen had been dining with Hugo and Celia, and her subsequent manipulations had brought about a sudden and crashing orgasm, which had sent his mind spinning off into a frenzy of desire for her as he stood leaning against the cloakroom wall while she crouched before him.

He'd been insatiable for a while after that, meeting her in secret places, devoured by lust, so that in the end he'd left Helen and insisted on marrying Elfreida. Having sex with her had become like a drug—addictive and undeniable. Just when he thought the tide had finally turned and gone out forever, leaving him stranded on the dry beach of impotence and old age, she'd revitalized him and restored the wondrous and exquisite sensations of his youth. Unfortunately this pleasurable phenomenon had lasted only a couple of years. Now her strong hands and jaws and tongue were the only way he could recapture that earlier ecstasy, and he was having to pay a high price for it. On the other hand, he had to remember that Elfreida wasn't really getting it at all these days, and although she said she didn't mind, there were times when he felt a sense of guilt. He was, however, a very generous husband, but how many dresses and jewels did it take to equal a good fuck? he asked himself.

An hour later, exasperated by her complaining and weeping, Selwyn slammed out of the house, and walking the short distance to the Old Brompton Road, hailed a cab.

"Boodle's," he said briefly, clambering in and dropping heavily onto the bench seat.

He'd become a member of Boodle's in St. James's

Street the same year he'd been given his peerage—a double first, he was sure, for the son of a Welsh miner. Alongside White's, Buck's, the Garrick, Brooks's, Pratt's, and the Beefsteak, Boodle's ranked as one of the grandest and most snobbish gentlemen's clubs in the United Kingdom. You had to be approved of and sponsored, and the sponsor had to be seconded before you were even considered for membership. Within its hallowed walls a man of quality could feel cherished, though, and protected from the hoi polloi, and shielded most of all, perhaps, from women, for they were allowed in only by invitation and then confined to certain parts of the building. Menservants waited on the members with the same deference given the master of a private house, and so into this calming atmosphere Selwyn submerged himself on this summer evening, with a glass of whiskey in one hand and the *Daily Telegraph* in the other. Leather armchairs, as reassuring as a cradle to a child, and quiet, dimly lit rooms, as comforting as an old nursery in their much-loved familiarity, soon assuaged his irritability. He drank steadily and with deep enjoyment, ordering glass after glass of whiskey, which was served to him with willing solicitude, as if he were paying the club a great honor by just being there. At one point an old friend who had been a famous BBC sports commentator put his head around the door, saw Selwyn, and strolled over to chat to him.

"Nice to see you, Michael," Selwyn greeted him. "How are things?"

"Fine. Couldn't be better!" Michael Battersby was still handsome, although he was nearly seventy, with thick white hair and bright blue eyes that blazed with life. "Want a spot of dinner? Joan's away staying with her mother for a few days, so I thought I'd eat here tonight."

"No, thanks." Selwyn shook his head, knowing that although he was younger than Michael, he lacked the vitality that had once made the commentator a household name. Tonight he felt particularly old.

"Why are you still in your garden-party togs?" Michael demanded, glancing at the now rather creased trousers and tailcoat. For a moment Selwyn felt embarrassed, knowing it wasn't the "done thing," knowing it looked like showing off to be seen in morning dress hours after the party had ended.

"Actually, I forgot!" he confessed. "I had a bloody row with Elfreida and I stormed out of the house, I'm afraid. Better be getting home, though, I suppose." Regretfully he looked at his empty glass.

"Have one for the road. I'll join you, old chap," said Michael with sudden understanding. More whiskey was ordered. The two old men started talking politics: Was Mrs. Thatcher's insistence on a poll tax going to lose the Conservative party the next election? . . . How could Neil Kinnock have any credibility when he kept changing the Labor party's manifesto? . . . Would inflation continue to creep up? . . . Would the new education reforms work? More whiskey was ordered. It was nine o'clock. Ten o'clock. Michael ordered some ham and some cheese sandwiches to go with the next lot of whiskey. Suddenly it was eleven-thirty, and still as bright and sparkling as ever, he rose and said he must be going, as he had an early start the next morning.

"Eleven-thirty?" Selwyn echoed. "I'd better be going too. Elfreida will wonder where the hell I am." Shakily he rose to his feet, aware that he had consumed great quantities of alcohol during the evening but was nevertheless still in command of his faculties.

"We go different ways, otherwise I'd have given you a lift in my cab," Michael observed as they came out of the charming eithteenth-century building and into St. James's Street. In the darkness the traffic surged past, while the men kept a lookout for taxis.

"Let's have lunch one day next week," said Selwyn. He'd enjoyed the evening so much, away from the usual round of parties and away from Elfreida's incessant wishing to be everywhere but where she was, that he thought it would be nice to continue the political debate with his old friend.

"Good idea," agreed Michael. "I'll ring you on

Monday to see how you're fixed. We might go to Wheeler's Oyster Bar, eh?"

Selwyn's mouth watered at the thought. Suddenly he felt very hungry. The idea of a dozen Whitstable oysters, washed down with a bottle of Bollinger, was irresistible.

At that moment two available cabs appeared in the distance, coming up the one-way street at high speed. Both men waved, and the cabs drew up to the curb with a flourish. Good-byes were exchanged, with much pumping of hands and hearty slaps on the back, and then Selwyn was being whisked back to the quiet residential streets of Kensington and the Boltons, where not a breath stirred and where the white stucco houses surrounding the central garden, with its nineteenth-century church, stood in silent splendor under a deep violet night sky.

Selwyn glanced up at his house when the taxi drew up at the high wrought-iron gates. All the lights were out, and he realized with thankfulness that Elfreida must be asleep. Giving the driver a five-pound note, indicating with a nod of his head that he didn't expect any change, he pushed open the gates, and treading lightly, entered the small paved garden from which a shallow flight of white steps led up to the front door. Selwyn had paid more than six million pounds for this imposing mansion, with six reception rooms, and eight bedrooms, all with bathrooms *en suite,* and at moments like this he could only hope it was a good investment. Certainly it wasn't a home. Built in 1850 and listed as a building of historic interest, it was a showpiece, a setting for entertaining and impressing, an edifice to his success and a symbol of financial prosperity. Perhaps when bank interest rates dropped again and the property market recovered, he'd sell up and move to a nice service flat. Meanwhile all he wanted was to creep up to bed and go to sleep in the Napoleonic *lit à la polonaise* in his dressing room, so as not to disturb Elfreida. It had been a very long day and he'd had enough.

On tiptoe now, he crept stealthily up the front steps,

reaching for the key in his trouser pocket. Softly, so that not even the faintest tinkle of metal would disturb the still air, he slid the Banham key into the lock, and turning it gently, pushed open the heavy door.

Peep-peep-peep-peep sounded the warning signal of the burglar alarm. *Peep-peep-peep-peep* it repeated loudly from the control box, which was halfway up the hall on the right, in a hidden alcove just beyond the dining-room door. *Peep-peep-peep-peep!*

"Oh, shit!" Selwyn muttered under his breath. The beastly thing bleeping away like a time bomb had startled him, and now he couldn't find the light switch. How was he going to turn off the bloody alarm if he couldn't see what he was doing?

"Bugger it!" he exclaimed, bumping into a table and hurting his knee as he groped and fumbled for the brass light switch that Elfreida had wanted because it was a "dipper" switch. His hand caught the frame of a painting, nearly bringing it off the wall. *Peep-peep-peep-peep* . . . Panic began to make him sweat. He must find the switch. He must turn off the alarm. Any minute now Elfreida would wake up, and then there'd be no peace for the rest of the night.

Suddenly blessed relief flooded over him. He'd found the switch! He turned it on. Dazzling light from the fifty-six high-wattage electric bulbs that Elfreida had insisted be installed in the chandelier nearly blinded him. With eyes screwed up against the glare, he stumbled along the hall until he came face-to-face with the glass control panel of the alarm system. All he had to do now was press the numbers that formed the secret combination.

With hands that were sweating and shaking as the *Peep-peep-peep-peep* nearly deafened him by its close proximity now, he reached out to press . . . to press . . . His hand faltered and dropped.

"Fuck it!" he shouted, glaring at the panel. He reached forward again, brows furrowed, bleary eyes trying to concentrate on the little gray squares on which were numbers from one to nine, plus a naught.

"Fuck it! Fuck it! Bloody fuck it!" he swore in desperation.

The fact was that, having got to the control panel just in time to switch the alarm off, he'd forgotten the combination. Was it 5-9-3-2 . . . or 9-5-3-2? Or could it be 3-2-9-5? He racked his brains, knowing the last few seconds of the *peep-peep-peep-peep* would be ending and then . . . 2-3-5-9? 2-5-3-9? He jabbed frantically at the numbers which lurked so cunningly embedded in the sheet of glass, defeating him totally as they kept their mystery to themselves.

"Cunt!" he roared. He'd spent five thousand pounds having this goddamn alarm system installed, and now he couldn't even remember how to turn the fucking thing off! A second later he bent double, his hands clasped over his ears as the siren, fitted to the front of the building, screamed into action, splintering the silent night in two.

Selwyn sank down onto the floor, overcome at last by tiredness, whiskey, and now the awful and powerful wailing that seemed to be filling the sky and the night and the whole universe.

"Selwyn! Selwyn!" It was Elfreida, pounding down the stairs, naked. "What happen, Selwyn?"

He buried his head in his hands, defeated. There was worse to come, and he knew it wouldn't be long in arriving.

"Why you not turn off alarm when you come in?" Elfreida yelled, trying to make herself heard above the din. "We wake up neighbors!"

More than the neighbors will have been awakened by now, he thought miserably.

A moment later the shrill whine of police sirens speeding through the empty streets added to the cacophony of noise. The insurance company had insisted that Selwyn's alarm be wired directly to the local police station. The police were now on their way to the scene of action.

3

"You must find out who this impostor is and put a stop to his activities, Jackie," Bertram Marriott said, concern making his voice harsh. "He could do us untold damage by saying he works for *Society*. What type of person is he?"

It was the morning after the garden party and Jackie was in Bertram's office. He sat behind the empty sweep of oak, his cuffs brilliantly white, his fingertips pressed fastidiously together.

"All I know is, he's youngish, well-educated, and well-dressed. Just like a couple of hundred other young men on the scene. Lady Tetbury didn't remember his name, though, so it's not going to be easy." Jackie felt impatient with Bertram. It was all very well for him to say "do this" and "do that" from the safety of his desk. Why didn't *he* do something positive for a change, instead of delegating everything to other people, while he kept himself metaphorically and physically clean? There was something old-womanish about him that irritated her at this moment, when her workload was heavy and she didn't have time to play detective.

Bertram pursed his thin lips. "How many parties has this chap gate-crashed in this way?"

Jackie shrugged. "It's hard to say, but three that I actually know about. There was Lady Tetbury's party for her son, and then when I got to my desk this morning I found two messages from hostesses wanting to know if my 'assistant' had all the information he needed to write up their parties for the column. He's obviously preying on certain people's desire for publicity."

Bertram flicked away a speck from the polished surface in front of him. "And none of them know his name? They must have asked him who he was, surely?"

"They told me, when I spoke to them just now, that they'd forgotten. Frankly, I don't believe they ever bothered to ask. Apart from Lady Tetbury, these particular hostesses are only interested in promoting themselves. They don't care how they do it. If a mass rapist turned up on their doorsteps and said he'd give them half a page in *Society,* they'd roll out the welcome carpet and shove a glass of champagne into his hand."

Bertram wasn't amused. "Don't exaggerate. This is serious," he told her sternly. "We can't have someone running around London saying he's representing us when he isn't. He might upset some people, if he hasn't already done so."

"I know," Jackie replied crisply. "And in some cases it sounds like he and certain hostesses could deserve each other."

He looked shocked, his yellowish eyes staring at her.

"What do you mean?"

She sighed inwardly. Bertram did not share her dislike of people who hustled for publicity. He regarded them instead as loyal readers who must be pandered to and satisfied by what appeared on the glossy pages of the magazine. But then, she reminded herself, he didn't really know what it was like. He didn't have to face a daily bombardment from ambitious hostesses, all clamoring for attention. He remained behind his bare desk, taking a vicarious pleasure in the antics of society without having any real knowledge of what some of the people in "society" were like.

It was her phone, not his, that started ringing at half-past eight some mornings, and as late as midnight some nights, with people calling up to make sure she had the dates of their parties in her diary. It was her desk, not his, that was stacked up each morning with invitations, most of which were unsuitable for her column. Worst of all, it was she who had to endure the endless sycophantic gushing of a bunch of people whose sole aim in life seemed to be to get their names in print.

Jackie leveled her gaze at him, however, determined to be frank. "If you knew what some of these hostesses are like, you'd realize it might teach them a lesson to wine and dine someone because they thought he was going to write about them, only to find they'd entertained a confidence trickster."

"But that's awful! How can you say a thing like that? They must be so disappointed when they find there's nothing about their parties in *Society*. I don't like that, Jackie. I don't like that at all! We don't want to risk alienating readers, you know, and if someone has spent a lot of money giving a party, the least we can do is mention it."

"But it has to be a party in keeping with the whole style of the magazine," Jackie protested. "You should see some of the invitations I get! They'd be totally unsuitable."

"You mean they're from the wrong class of person?"

"No, I do not mean they're from the wrong class of person. I mean they're *boring* parties given by *boring* people! We have to feature dazzling events, amusing and glamorous people, functions that sparkle, and more than anything, amuse and titillate the thousands of readers who do not go to parties every night!" Jackie spoke with conviction. "Who wants to read about Mrs. Bloggs and her dreary friends having drinks in a flat in Fulham? Who is interested in a bring-and-buy sale given by the local church, no matter how worthy the cause? What the readers want is escapism. They want to read about balls at Buckingham Palace and receptions at the Ritz. They want to know how duchesses dress, what debutantes do, and who's who on the social scene at the moment. We have to make the social diary exclusive, Bertram, or there's no point in doing it."

He still looked upset. Unable, even after all these years as a successful publisher, to distinguish between the real aristocracy, who never sought publicity, and the nouveaux riches, who sought nothing else, Bertram maintained a naive illusion that they were one and the same. His deep-rooted shyness allowed him to be a voyeur of society only, and secretly he was in awe of the whole social scene. This had made him unable to distinguish any difference or to understand what Jackie was saying. She was making him feel nervous now by the glib way she was talking about the "right" sort of function to feature, and her attitude struck him as too casual.

"We mustn't offend people, you know," he observed pickily. "We don't want them to think their function isn't good enough for us. We don't want to be accused of being snobbish."

"Snobbery has nothing to do with it," Jackie protested hotly. "I don't give a damn who people are, as long as they're amusing and invite us to write up newsy, fun, well-organized dos. Otherwise it's no good. Our circulation will fall, and once we feature tacky events, we're finished. I'm always aware we're in competition with *Tatler* and *Harpers & Queen*, and I want *Society* to be the best, and to my way of thinking, the higher the standard of social function we publish, the higher the standard of function we'll be invited to." She paused, wondering if she'd gone too far. To anyone listening, it might sound as if she were the editor in chief instead of merely the social editor, and it wouldn't serve any purpose to put Bertram's nose out of joint. She leaned forward and spoke earnestly.

"It's just that the magazine means so much to me, I want to do everything I can to make my column good. But I can assure you I'm very careful never to offend anyone. If I don't want to feature a certain party, I tell the hostess with great regret that I've no space in the next issue. There's no argument and no recriminations that way, and I promise you I always sound very sad at not being able to go to their parties."

"Just so long as you don't offend anyone," he replied, slightly mollified.

"Of course not." She gave him a reassuring smile. "And I'll find out who this gate-crasher is and tell him he must stop saying he's representing me."

"Please do, and threaten him with an injunction and legal proceedings if he tries it on again."

Jackie looked startled. "I don't think it will come to that," she said reasonably. "He's probably a university undergraduate who's missed out on getting his name on this year's list of young men. If all his friends are doing the round of parties and debutante dances, he probably wants to get a few himself."

"Maybe he was left off for a very good reason," Bertram observed darkly. "After all, the mothers who compile the list for the debutante season have to be very careful. They don't want undesirables dancing with their daughters."

Jackie suppressed a smile at his old-fashioned phraseology. "Don't worry, I'll put a stop to it." She rose to go back to her own office. "By the way," she added, pausing in the doorway, "I think I'm making good progress on the feature about Charles and Diana. I've been ringing around this morning and I've come up with some good contacts. People who are prepared to talk, too."

"Good." He sounded as if it was no more than he expected.

Back in her office, which was piled high today with a variety of exotic hats which Rosie was about to have photographed, Jackie called up some of the young men and debutantes she knew were in the midst of "doing the season" and were going to balls, receptions, dinners, and cocktail parties every night. She had so little to go on, such vague details of the impostor to describe, that all her inquiries drew a blank. No one seemed to have heard of a young man purporting to be her assistant. No one seemed to have noticed an interloper in their midst. After a while she gave up. With any luck, she thought, having had his little fling, he might not be heard of again.

Celia glanced down at the references Robertson and Short had sent her about Roland Shaw, and had to admit she was impressed. While she did not known the various parents who had employed him personally, she did know some of them by name. There were a Scottish duchess, two county ladies, a professor, and a foreign princess, whose reference was written on heavily crested writing paper. They all described Roland Shaw as "dedicated," a "patient teacher," and a "good companion" for their offspring. Celia decided to phone a couple of them, and they were most expansive on the subject.

"We were very pleased, Lady Atherton," one of the county ladies gushed. "My husband and I were delighted with the way he handled our sons, and we had complete confidence in him."

"He was a good teacher too, was he?" Celia asked.

"Excellent, I think. One can't be too careful whom one has in one's home, either, can one?" she added primly. "We took to him right away."

Professor Arthur Rouse, when she phoned him, went even further.

"I am a widower," he explained. "My son is twelve and rather backward. Roland Shaw was absolutely wonderful with him."

"How long did he stay with you? He lived in, didn't he?"

"Yes, I'm at work all day at the Shawley Nuclear Experimental Station, just outside Andover, and we have a house nearby, so he stayed with us for the Easter holidays. Usually Tom is here all by himself, except for my housekeeper, but this time he was kept fully occupied by Roland Shaw and he benefited greatly."

"Thank you, Professor Rouse, you have been most helpful."

"My dear lady, it's been a pleasure." He sounded

more like a courtly old-world gentleman than a professor of nuclear physics.

Professor Arthur Rouse belonged to a generation who put women on a pedestal, and his late wife, Mary, had been no exception. He had adored her from the moment he'd set eyes on her, and when she died of cancer, when Tom was small, Arthur Rouse had insisted the old rectory in which they lived be kept exactly as it was when Mary had been alive. He'd never had the heart to look at another woman either, preferring to have a housekeeper who came in daily to look after things. Sometimes Arthur Rouse worried that Tom was missing out, not having a mother, but Tom seemed happy enough in his own way. Usually he stayed with his aunt during the holidays because she maintained he needed the rough-and-tumble of "real family life," as she described it, but last Easter Arthur Rouse had decided to keep Tom at home, in the care of a tutor, who would hopefully help Tom with his studies. Looking back, he realized what a success it had been. Roland Shaw proved to be just what Tom needed—a stimulating force who encouraged him to work and gave him confidence, and at the same time provided the individual attention he required. It was as if Roland identified with the boy in some way, and the professor came to the conclusion that they'd both had learning problems, but for different reasons. Tom because he was slow, Roland because he came from a background where "learning" was sometimes jeered at and hardly ever encouraged. Roland's patience with Tom was remarkable, and the professor had tried to persuade him to return for the long summer holidays, but Roland had refused.

"It's not that I don't like it here," he explained, "and I get on very well with Tom, but I'd planned to be in London for the summer." And so these coming holidays Tom would be with his aunt in Somerset and other boys would be benefiting from Roland's tutorage. Arthur Rouse glanced at his watch, realizing it was later than he thought. His conversation with the charming Lady Atherton had distracted him and he was due at the Shawley Experimental Station in ten minutes. Luckily it was only six miles away. Stuffing his papers, which were stamped "TOP SECRET," into his briefcase, he glanced around the study to make sure he hadn't forgotten anything. Not that Mrs. Mulroy, as she dusted, would know the difference between blueprints for a new fridge-freezer and blueprints for an atom bomb. Copies of his most highly secret designs were kept locked in the safe, of course, although that was strictly against the rules. Sets of plans and blueprints were supposed to be kept under lock and key at Shawley, but sometimes the professor liked to work at night, and he found it useful to keep an extra set at home.

For the past two years he'd been working on a new type of nuclear warhead, deadlier than a Scud missile, resistant to Patriot interceptors. There were foreign powers who would give anything to get hold of his designs. The burden of having invented such a lethal weapon sometimes weighed heavily on him. Slowly he left his study, calling out to Mrs. Mulroy that he was off to Shawley and wouldn't be back until the evening.

Perhaps, he thought hopefully, he could persuade Roland Shaw to come and spend Christmas with them. Tom would like it; they might even try to make it a proper Christmas, with a tree and everything. Making a mental note to ring up Robertson and Short to see if he could book the tutor for December, he got into his car and headed for Shawley.

Celia was sitting at her desk in the cozy book-lined study, compiling a shopping list for the dinner party they were giving the following night, when Mrs. Pinner announced in her broad cockney accent that a Mr. Shaw had arrived to see her.

"Oh, my goodness! Is it ten-thirty already?" Celia exclaimed. She'd been trying to decide whether to give the guests roast lamb with red currant *tartlettes* or poached salmon with hollandaise sauce, and she'd lost track of time.

"Shall I pop him into the drawing room, m'lady?" Mrs. Pinner asked.

"Yes, and could you bring us some coffee, please?" Celia glanced in the mirror, thankful she wore hardly any makeup so that it didn't take her hours to look presentable. From her handbag she produced a small brush and flicked it through her fair hair, cut short in a style very similar to Princess Diana's, so that it was neat at all times. Then she hurried up to the drawing room on the second floor. When she entered the room, she saw Roland Shaw standing by the window, looking down at the street below.

"Good morning." With outstretched hand she went forward to greet him, taking in the pale regular features, the tilt-rimmed pebble glasses that magnified his hazel eyes, and the neatly cut brown hair. Of slim build, and not very tall, he was wearing a well-pressed gray suit and polished black lace-up shoes.

"Lady Atherton?" he inquired, smiling.

"Hello. Come and sit down." Celia indicated the sofa facing the carved pine mantelpiece, in front of which stood a low glass tabletop supported by four gray stone lions. Books, magazines, flowers, and several Chinese lacquered bowls filled with colored marbles and rose-scented potpourri were arranged on it with artful informality.

"Let me tell you something about the job," she began, "and I'll try to describe Colin and Ian, although I suppose they're typical of the average thirteen- and fifteen-year-old." As she talked, Roland Shaw listened with interest, making comments from time to time, and agreeing with Celia on several points about the boys' education.

"As I see it," she concluded, "my husband and I are so busy we need someone who can keep the boys amused during the school holidays and also help them with their studies. Maybe you could interest them in a holiday project too?"

Roland Shaw replied without hesitation, showing slightly crooked teeth.

"That's no problem. As you will see from my references, I'm accustomed to having teenage boys in my charge, and although it's easier if they live in the country, the one thing about being in London is that there's always plenty of things to do."

"Yes, they need to be kept occupied, otherwise they get very bored."

Roland nodded understandingly. "We can go to the many museums there are, the Science Museum is always the most popular. Then there are lots of exhibitions on during the summer, and I expect they like to go swimming and play tennis. I'm sure I can think of ways of keeping them amused."

Celia picked up the folder in which she'd placed his references and glanced at them again, as if for final reassurance. Professor Rouse's letter lay on the top, and looking at his neat handwriting, she came to a decision. Roland seemed to be exactly what she and Hugo were looking for, and at this stage, with Colin and Ian breaking for the holidays in a couple of weeks' time, she felt she'd left it too late to start interviewing other possible candidates.

"Could you start in two weeks' time?" she asked.

"Yes, that would be fine." He spoke easily, as if he'd expected to get the post. "I usually arrive at nine-thirty in the morning and stay with my charges until six. Will that be all right?"

Celia was just about to agree when the phone rang.

"Excuse me," she murmured, rising and going over to the table by the window to answer it.

"Hello. Oh, good morning. How are you?" It was one of the Queen's assistant private secretaries calling her to discuss a detail of her attendance on her majesty at a royal gala film premiere the following week. While Celia made notes, her back to the room, she did not notice Roland Shaw looking around with deep interest. It was an L-shaped drawing room with windows both ends, decorated in champagne creams and gold, with a tapestry rug that glowed with muted colors on the polished floor, antique velvet and needle-point cushions piled on the brocade sofas and chairs, and a fine assortment of family portraits on the walls.

Rockingham, Dresden, and Chelsea china figurines and bowls and vases were displayed on the mantelpiece, and in one corner the Atherton collection of cranberry glass, which dated back to 1720, sparkled ruby red in the morning light. It was a jewel of a room, containing all sorts of valuable *objets d'art* and rare bibelots, scattered enticingly about, and Roland's eyes darted to and fro like a magpie's, not a single jade or ivory carving or porcelain ornament escaping his gaze. What made the room unique and exceptional, though, especially when most people relied on interior designers and decorators to tell them what to do, was that Celia had done it all herself. As a result, it reflected her personality, being an eclectic mixture, rich with memorabilia of past experiences and exciting finds, of objects inherited, collected, gathered, or acquired—indeed a medley of unexpected discoveries, colors, textures, and tones of light and shade, a veritable cornucopia of treasures garnered over the years and overlaid with a patina of antique shabbiness so beloved by the English aristocracy.

Not a trinket eluded Roland's notice, and yet when Celia put down the receiver and turned back toward the room, he was flipping through a copy of *Country Life*.

"I'm sorry about that," she said briefly. She resumed her seat. "Now, I think we've discussed everything, don't you?" They'd already fixed his salary and she knew the agency would send her an invoice for their fee. "Keep a list of all the expenses you incur," she reminded him, "and we'll settle that at the end of each week. I know when I take the boys out it costs me a fortune, so don't forget. By the time you've paid to get into all the museums and exhibitions, not to mention the bus and tube fares, and an absolutely vital visit to McDonald's, it will have added up to pounds!" She smiled. "It may sound indulgent, but I do like the boys to have a good time when they're on holiday. We miss them very much when they're away at school, although we know it's best for them, and then I suppose I feel guilty at not being here all the time to look after them when they are home."

Roland Shaw looked at her knowingly. "Yes, I suppose you're at the palace a great deal," he said.

Celia blinked, slightly taken aback. She'd never mentioned she was a lady-in-waiting, and she certainly hadn't told Robertson and Short.

"Yes, I am," she replied briefly.

Roland leaned forward. "That must be very interesting."

"It's quite hard work," she said, rising briskly, hoping he wouldn't pursue the subject. It was a known fact among her friends that she couldn't talk about her work. She was not allowed to say what it was like Waiting on the Queen, and she was forbidden to repeat any conversations she might either overhear or have with any member of the royal family. To disobey their wishes for complete privacy within the walls of their own homes, and to display disloyalty by revealing what went on, would be to incur banishment from court. "Being put in purdah" was the expression used when a courtier was indiscreet, and Celia knew that the Queen's wrath could be formidable on such occasions. She was capable of freezing someone in his tracks from fifty paces away, with blue eyes that blazed with anger if she was displeased, and many a strong man had wilted under her icy gaze of disapproval.

Roland had risen. "Well, I must be going," he said, shaking her hand. "I'll look forward to meeting Colin and Ian."

Celia relaxed. He obviously knew the form. Gratefully she smiled at him. "I'm sure that they will look forward to meeting you too."

Elfreida and Selwyn slept late. It had been three o'clock in the morning before they'd finally gone to sleep, having assured the police that the house had not been broken into, and they were exhausted. Elfreida had, however, recovered from her disappoint-

ment at the garden party and seemed all set to
conquer London afresh.

"I have a wonderful idea," she told Selwyn as they
dressed after a late breakfast in their room. "We
should give a ball! A summer party, with a marquee
in the garden, and we ask everyone we know and we
get all the press to come. Is that not a good idea,
huh?"

Selwyn, thankful that she wasn't nagging him
about staying out late the previous night, grunted
noncommittally.

"Could we get some real celebrities to come, d'you
think?" she continued. "The press are more likely to
come if we have Michael Caine and Ivana Trump, and
maybe Elton John."

"God, you are a fantasy queen, aren't you?" Selwyn
grunted, tying his dark blue silk tie with care. "We
don't know any of those people, so how can we invite
them? Now, I know plenty of businessmen and their
wives, and several bankers and politicians. We could
even invite Mrs. Thatcher; now you can't get a bigger
celebrity than that!"

Elfreida pursed her lips. "I suppose not, but I want
the evening to be glittering. The Conservative party is
not very glittering, is it?"

As Selwyn owed his life peerage to the goodwill
of the Conservative party, and to Mrs. Thatcher in
particular, he bristled as if someone had criticized his
own family.

"Don't be ridiculous," he snapped. "I wouldn't be
where I am today if it hadn't been for the Tories and
the encouragement they give to entrepreneurial talent.
If you want to cut a dash, it's a damned sight better
having some of the Cabinet to a party than a lot of
show-biz people."

Elfreida remained unconvinced. "That Fergie—she
has show-biz people to her parties!" she protested.

Selwyn, who would have preferred Elfreida to
model herself on Princess Diana rather than the Duchess of York, remained silent, but the idea of giving a
party had begun to grow on him. It could be good for

business, and God knows he might as well do *something* with the large house and garden he'd lumbered himself with. Then he realized with a pang that it would also be the first party he'd given without Helen.

"When would we give it?" he asked cautiously.

Elfreida was looking radiant now, her blond hair curling around her face, a broad grin making her rosy cheeks bulge.

"The end of July! Before everyone go away. Oh, Selwyn! We make it the ball of the season!"

He consulted his pocket diary. "How about Thursday the twenty-sixth? It doesn't give us long to get the invitations out, but if we don't do it then, we'll have to wait until everyone's back in town after the summer, and that would mean October."

"Let's have it on the twenty-sixth," Elfreida replied instantly. "I get the invitations printed right away—"

"You know how to word it correctly, don't you?"

"What? . . . Oh, Lord and Lady Witley of—"

Selwyn shook his head. "No, no, you know you must put only the wife's name on an invitation card, never the husband's, unless it's an invitation to attend their daughter's wedding. That's the only time the man's name is used. You must put 'Lady Witley of Vauxhall' and then on the line below, 'At Home' and below that, the date. Then you have RSVP at the bottom-left-hand corner with our address beneath it, for people to reply to—"

"And the telephone number," Elfreida reminded him excitedly.

He shook his head more violently. "You must *never* put the telephone number, except on a commercial invitation."

"Commercial?" She looked at him blankly.

"Yes, commercial," he replied, "like the opening of a hairdressing salon or a shop."

Elfreida digested this newest lesson in etiquette with interest. Selwyn was always teaching her what to do. And then she said, "I go to Harrods. They print our invitations."

"No, you go to Smythson's in New Bond Street,"

he said firmly, "and you go to Pulbrook and Gould for the flowers, and you go to Searcy's for everything else—the food, drink, cutlery, glass, and the waiters. Tell them how many people we're having and leave everything to them." Selwyn checked his sapphire-and-diamond tiepin and turned to leave the room.

"How you know these things, Selwyn?" Elfreida called out admiringly after him.

He paused in the doorway, a reedy man with a tired face. "Helen knew what to do," he replied quietly, avoiding looking at her. "I learned everything from Helen."

Elfreida's chin rose and her eyes flashed. "I bet I make more glamorous hostess," she declared defiantly. Then, in a softer, more conciliatory tone, "Selwyn, couldn't we invite one of the royal family to our party?"

He snorted, turning on his heel. "Don't be so bloody silly!"

Undeterred, Elfreida set about making plans. This was going to be the best party London had seen for years. This would really get her noticed and her picture in the newspapers. She started drawing up lists of guests, wondering how quickly Smythson's could have the invitations ready. One thing was certain, the first batch to be mailed would be the ones to the press. All those photographers and journalists who had so persistently ignored her since she'd married Selwyn . . . well, they wouldn't be able to ignore her now, because whatever Selwyn said, she fully intended to have a member of the royal family present . . . and to make certain of getting one, she reflected it would be a good idea to invite them all.

As Roland Shaw hurried up Sloane Street, back to his flat above a shop in Knightsbridge, he glowed with excitement. To have secured the post of holiday tutor to the Atherton boys, with the family's royal connections, was the best position he'd been offered so far. Even better than working for the Scottish duchess; far better than working for that dreary Professor Arthur

Rouse, looking after his son last Easter. This was the next-best thing to being asked to tutor Prince William and Prince Harry. And who knows? he thought to himself. Lady Atherton might even recommend him to Princess Diana if the need arose.

With quickening step he paused outside a pet shop, in the window of which were two cheeky-looking Pekingese puppies. Then, taking a key out of his pocket, he entered the building by a side door.

Roland had lived here for seven years, and those who were impressed by the address—86 Hans Crescent, Knightsbridge—had no idea it was a rent-controlled building and that he paid a nominal amount to the landlord for the privilege of being there. In fact, the address was 86 B, because he occupied only the third floor, and there was another flat below him and a third one above, but on his expensively printed writing paper he dropped the B. It gave the game away, he thought. Let people think his abode was grander than it really was. He never invited anyone there in any case.

At thirty-one, Roland Shaw was beginning to feel his life was going the way he wanted, and for the first time he experienced a sense of satisfaction. If he didn't succeed in his wish to improve himself, it certainly wouldn't be through lack of effort.

Roland had been born a few miles outside Nottingham in a bleak little village called Faxby. His father, who had been killed in an accident when Roland was twelve, had worked on the railways—a large rough-spoken man who had little use for the weakling only child his wife had given birth to fifteen years after they'd been married. Roland had been quite glad, in a detached sort of way, when his father died; happy that he and his gentle mother could be alone together in the small stone house near the sidings, which the railway company allowed her to live in for the rest of her life; and content to read all the books he could borrow from the public lending library in his thirst for knowledge. Without realizing it, Roland had set out on the steep path of self-education and self-improvement.

While his mother tended the stunted and puny plants in the small backyard, perpetually smothered under a layer of coal dust that covered everything and caused her hands to be blackened by the simple act of weeding, Roland, weak and feeble like the plants, swotted over his school lessons at the kitchen table, half-listening to his mother as she talked in grandiose terms. In her mind Roland was as capable of becoming another Einstein as her wizened oxygen-starved flowers were capable of winning prizes at the local horticultural show. Her attempts to inspire, though, led Roland to grow discontented with his lot as he visualized horizons as yet unknown to him. He wanted to escape the poverty, the boredom, the dullness of life, and most of all that dreadful sticky black dust that clung to every surface like a film. By the time he was sixteen he couldn't wait to get away.

Always clever at school, he saw studying as a means of escape, and when one of the teachers took a special interest in him, telling him that if he continued to study hard there was a chance he might win a scholarship to university, Roland threw himself into his work. The result was that he got into Caius College, leaving behind his mother and his home without a backward glance.

He learned a lot at university, but not just about English and history, which were his subjects. He learned about the Good Life too, and now nothing less would do.

Kip had left to go back to Boston, and Jackie suddenly found the flat unbearably quiet and empty without him. It was always the same. Just when she thought she'd become used to living on her own, even to luxuriating in a sense of freedom and independence, a member of her family or an old friend from the States would come and stay, and when the visit ended, she'd realize what she'd been missing. How had she ever imagined she was happy and fulfilled, having those big empty rooms to herself and an even more empty bed at night? How could she have thought that it was fun to be able to come and go when she liked and not have to worry about anyone else? Richard had left a great black hole in her life when he'd walked out, and she thought she'd got used to it, but at moments like this the gaping void seemed larger than ever. It threatened to engulf her in waves of depression so that there were moments when she wondered if she wouldn't admit defeat, pack her bags, and return to the warmth and welcome of her parents' home in Boston. A part of her longed to be comforted and petted again, as she'd been when she was a little girl; she longed to be told everything was going to be all right, that everyone ended up living happily ever after, and that there was a pot of gold at the end of the rainbow. But then the mature woman that Jackie had become would laugh through her tears at her own childishness and know that she had to go on standing on her own two feet. Big girls didn't go running back to Mom and Dad.

She got to the office early that morning, knowing that to throw herself into work was the best way of coping with her sudden sense of loneliness and loss. For once she was quite glad she had a busy day ahead of her, with two cocktail parties in the evening, followed by a ball at Syon Park; but first there was the mail to open.

Apart from the usual stack of invitations, asking her to everything from a ladies' lunch to the opening of a new nightclub, there were letters from hostesses asking advice on where and when to hold their parties, a request from a mother to put her daughter's name on next year's list of debutantes, and an invitation to a smart wedding in Hampshire. Jackie grimaced. Functions outside London were very time-consuming, and usually she refused unless they were going to be very special in some way.

Finally she came to three letters marked "Personal," which she read with growing concern. They were all from hostesses whom she had never met but whose names were familiar. They all wrote in the same vein, saying that they were disappointed not to have seen her in person at their various parties but were delighted she had sent her assistant, and were looking forward to seeing the write-ups in a future copy of _Society_.

"I don't believe this," Jackie exclaimed aloud. "It's happened again!"

Rosie looked up from sorting out a batch of fashion shots.

"What has?" she asked. Rosie was as intrigued by Jackie's job, which seemed to consist of a constant social whirl, as Jackie was by the world of fashion.

"Someone's taking my name in vain and I don't know who it is," Jackie replied, rising from her desk and going over to Rosie, the letters in her hand. She told her briefly what had been happening. "None of them say who he actually is," she added in frustration. "Why doesn't anybody give me his name?"

"It can't be difficult to find out," Rosie reasoned. "Haven't you always said the social scene in England is so small that everybody knows everybody else?"

"Yes, it is. I'm going to call up these people and question them closely and also put them right about my not having an assistant. This has got to stop. Bertram is already doing his nut in case this man brings disgrace on _Society_, and if he hears there have been more incidents, he'll go crazy."

Half an hour later she was still as nonplussed as ever. Nobody seemed to know who she was talking about, and if they did, they couldn't remember his name. A lot of young people floated in and out of the social scene in the summer. Most were after a good time and some free drinks. Very few had ever proved harmful.

Jackie left home shortly before six-thirty that evening, already changed for the long night ahead, her real day's work just beginning. From the many evening dresses hanging in her wardrobe she'd chosen a low-cut, full-skirted red satin ball gown that enhanced her pale skin and black hair. Applying a brilliant red lipstick, she slipped into the matching high-heeled sandals and then stood looking into the long mirror to get the full effect. She had to admit she looked fabulous. The color gave a vibrance to her face so that her skin looked almost luminous, and her hair, which was taken back into a loose chignon, shone glossily.

Reaching for her jewel case, she clipped on sparkling crystal-and-pearl drop earrings, and then wound a long necklace that matched around the base of her throat. Then she picked up her red purse and took a final look at herself. For someone who had woken up in a state of depression that morning, she certainly looked as if she'd made a dramatic recovery.

Hurrying out of the apartment block, she found the chauffeur-driven car waiting for her. "The Cavalry and Guards Club in Piccadilly first, please," she told Pete, who was the driver the car hire company always sent to take her around in the evenings. "I have to go on to Claridge's after that, and I'd like to be there by seven-fifteen, because you're going to have to pick me up at eight o'clock again; we've got to get to Syon Park by eight-thirty."

"Very well, madam." Pete, in his gray uniform and visored cap, held the door open while Jackie climbed into the back of the black Jaguar.

The first party was being given by a General Sir Ralph Andrews and his wife, and the club was packed, as Jackie had known it would be, with retired top brass, all reminiscing and drinking whiskey and greeting each new arrival with loud heartiness. Lady Andrews slipped several sheets of paper, covered in her large round handwriting, into Jackie's hand.

"I thought you'd find this useful, my dear," she said in a low voice. "It's a list of guests with all their ranks and everything, so I hope it will save you time when you're writing your piece."

Jackie took it gratefully. She never carried a notepad because she had a photographic memory, and as long as she knew the guests, she could recall their names and faces, even what they said or were wearing,

for months and sometimes years afterward, but tonight she knew hardly anyone, and had accepted the
party only because it would be a good contrast to the
other functions she was covering.

"Thank you very much," she replied, slipping the
list into her purse. At that moment a middle-aged
couple pounced on her, almost blocking her way.

"We're absolutely thrilled," the wife began eagerly,
"that you're going to feature our drinks party in your
column. I'm Betty Wilkinson, and this is my husband,
Mike."

Jackie racked her brains, not even remembering
having received the invitation.

"Your drinks party?" she inquired politely. "I don't
believe I know when it is."

The heavily made-up face quivered and the eyes
blinked rapidly. "It was ten days ago! You'll be putting it in your next edition, I gather?"

"No-o-o," Jackie replied, drawing out the word
slowly, guessing what was coming next. "I only write
about the parties I've attended."

The head jerked in agitation. "But your assistant is
doing it! He asked if he could come, and of course
we were delighted. Absolutely so!"

Whoever this young man was, Jackie reflected, he'd
been busy. How many other parties had he crashed
on the pretext of being her assistant? He was probably
wining and dining all over town, using *Society* as an
entrée.

"What was his name?" she asked urgently. Her tone
made the woman suddenly anxious and her voice rose,
edged with hysteria.

"You *are* going to put our party in your paper,
aren't you?"

"I'm sorry, but we have a policy that the only parties that are included are the ones I've actually attended myself. Who is this person? Do you know how
I can get hold of him?"

Outrage and disappointment showed on the faces of
the couple.

"No," croaked the woman. "He may have told us

his name, but I can't remember it. Do you?" She turned to her husband, who had remained silent so far. He shook his head, and then they looked at each other almost accusingly. It was clear to Jackie that they hadn't cared who the hell he was as long as they got their party into *Society*.

"That's a pity," she said. "There's isn't much I can do if I don't know who he is."

"But our party!"

"I'm very sorry, but there really is nothing I can do," Jackie apologized as she graciously excused herself.

For the next half-hour she mingled with the guests, sipping a glass of orange juice and keeping an eye on the time. Pete was once more waiting for her outside when she slipped away at five past seven.

The party at Claridge's, London's grandest hotel, where kings and princes and presidents always stay, was an altogether different affair. The host was a leading French industrialist who had married a member of a minor European royal family. That had not precluded him from inviting the *crème de la crème* from all over the Continent, and within the first few minutes Jackie spotted King Constantine of Greece with his wife, Queen Anne Marie, Queen Sofia of Spain, Prince Bernadotte of Sweden, Prince Tomislav of Yugoslavia, and Princess Margarita of Baden. Several photographers were flashing away, including a young free lance called Tom Quincy, whom she'd commissioned on behalf of *Society*.

"Everything all right?" she asked him as he frantically reloaded his camera between shots.

Tom nodded, looking rather overwhelmed. "They're all here tonight, aren't they?" he replied breathlessly. "Are there going to be any members of our royal family dropping in too?"

Jackie grinned. "The royal family don't exactly 'drop in,'" she reminded him. "Prince Philip is expected, so try to get a shot of him arriving and being greeted by our host, but otherwise concentrate on who is here and try to get them talking to some of the

English guests, otherwise it will look as if the party
was held in Paris or Rome instead of London."

"Right!" Flushed with excitement, he sped away,
deeply impressed by both Jackie and the assignment
she'd sent him on.

The host and hostess continued to stand in the entrance of the ballroom, receiving the guests, while
their two grown-up sons circulated around the room,
carrying out introductions. One of them guided Jackie
over to a group of people, whom he proceeded to
present to her in a rush of names and titles, which she
tried to commit to memory, as they were all new to
her. Like herself, many were already in evening dress,
and they were discussing where they were all going on
to.

"I'm off to Covent Garden to see *Turandot*," said
one, glancing at her diamond wristwatch. "In fact, I
ought to leave now."

"Lucky you," remarked another. "I'm dining with
my in-laws."

"Well, we're going to a party for my godson's twenty-
first birthday," said a third. "It's being held at the
Savoy, so at least the food should be good."

"And where are you heading for?" Jackie heard
someone ask, and turning, she found herself face-to-
face with a tall, strongly built man whose smile was
charmingly wicked. He was looking directly at her.

"Syon Park," she replied.

He raised dark eyebrows and his smile deepened.
"Syon Park? So am I. What a coincidence!" Then he
hesitated for a second before asking: "How are you
getting there?"

She blinked, taken aback by his direct manner.
She'd lived long enough in England to know that at
first most men hedged and hinted but rarely came out
with what they really wanted to say. No Englishman,
for instance, had ever asked her if she was on her
own. They'd shift from foot to foot, fiddle nervously
with their gold cufflinks (even Prince Charles did that
at times), and then finally ask in a strained voice as

they looked around the room: "And which one is your husband?"

Here, however, was an Englishman emanating a powerful persona, who not only seemed to sense she was on her own, but was obviously about to offer her a lift.

"I've got a car," she replied, and then instantly regretted saying so. This was one of the most attractive men she'd met in a long time and she wondered who he was.

"What a pity. Never mind, I'll see you there," he replied. At that moment someone came up to claim his attention, and with a final nod he drifted away. As Jackie watched him mingling with the other guests, she was also aware there was a strong sexuality about him that she found both exciting and disturbing. When Richard had left, she'd made up her mind about one thing: she was never going to let a man hurt her again. She would protect herself behind a friendly but breezy facade that would keep men at a safe distance, and she would not allow herself to get involved. It was all very well for Kip to say she should remarry; he'd never been hurt, and he had no idea what it was like. But she knew . . . she'd experienced the tearing agony, as if someone had scooped out her innards and left her bleeding and raw; she knew what it was like to lose confidence, feel humiliated, brokenhearted, and despairing. Never, she resolved, would she risk going through all that again. And yet . . . another part of her quivered on the brink of longing for love, wanting an amorous adventure, especially at moments like this, when she felt dangerously vulnerable and lonely after Kip's departure.

She continued her circuit of the room, meeting many old friends but always aware of a dark head towering above everyone else's and never more than a few feet away.

It was nearly eight o'clock. Pete would be double-parked alongside the Rolls-Royces and Bentleys in Brook Street. Jackie said good-bye to her hosts and gave a final look around the room. The stranger was nowhere to be seen. At that moment she realized she didn't even know his name.

Jackie walked slowly up the long wide gravel path to the marquee, marveling at the effects created to welcome the three hundred guests to the coming-out ball of Bunty Lawson, already dubbed by the press "Debutante of the Year." On either side, and forming an avenue, were high pillars topped by ornate stone urns, out of which billowed clouds of curling red smoke, as if the route were bordered by glowing fires. The reflected glow cast a warm light on the faces of the laughing, jostling guests as they made their way to the marquee, the young girls in drifting groups of white tulle and lace and chiffon, the older women in rich satins and brocades and a blaze of jewelry.

Intrigued, Jackie stood to one side to take in the spectacle. Bill Glass, her favorite photographer, joined her.

"Clever stuff, eh?" he remarked jovially. Bill attended on average six hundred parties each year, and he never let anything faze him. At all times he could be relied upon to be cheerful, good-tempered, and delighted by everything he saw. More important to Jackie, he was also punctual, took good pictures, and delivered the finished prints on time.

"How is it done?" she asked, watching the fiery red smoke curl and twist as if it had a life force of its own.

Bill also had a prosaic streak. "Easy," he chuckled, adjusting the strap of his camera. "They've put red electric light bulbs at the bottom of each urn, then something like a wire cage or wire netting to protect the bulbs, and then, on top of that, lumps of dry ice."

"That's brilliant."

He nodded in the direction of the marquee. "Wait until you see that lot in there! Talk of decorations! It must have cost a packet."

"Does it look wonderful?"

"It's a blooming stage set. They had a top theater designer do the whole thing, and the theme is 'A Summer Dream.' "

Jackie's eyes widened. Bill was always full of useful anecdotes and bits of information.

"Anyone interesting arrived yet?" she asked.

"Not yet, but I'm on the lookout. Quite a few big nobs are expected." As he spoke, a beautiful woman in pale blue, with a dazzling sapphire-and-diamond tiara and necklace to match, walked past, escorted by a good-looking tall man. "There's a case of ti-ara-boom-di-ay!" Bill sang the old music-hall song in a soft voice. "They'll all be wearing them tonight, not just the Countess of Atherton."

"In that case, I'm going to feel thoroughly under-dressed," Jackie laughed. "I suppose she was wearing family jewels? That tiara really is something, isn't it?"

"Yes, and a very nice lady she is, too." If Jackie had learned who everyone was during the years she'd lived in London, Bill had known them all since before World War II. Most of the aristocracy had been photographed by him as children, and then he'd done their coming-out parties and eventually their weddings, and finally he'd been invited to photograph their babies' christenings. Some of those children now had children of their own, but Bill was still going strong, still snapping away at every party and celebration and anniversary. There were probably more of his pictures displayed on the grand pianos of England than any other photographer's.

"I'm going to see who else is here," Jackie told him. "This is obviously going to be the best ball of the season and I don't want to miss a moment of it."

"The champagne bar is on your right as you enter the marquee," he informed her knowledgeably.

"Thanks. I've drunk so much orange juice this evening, I could do with a proper drink."

Jackie continued up the path and under an archway festooned with Michaelmas daisies and white satin ribbons. Then she entered the marquee, and standing in front of banks of white flowers stood Bunty Lawson, receiving the guests with her parents.

"Good evening." Bunty greeted Jackie enthusiastically. "How nice of you to come." She was a tall girl with an intelligent face, who'd professed an ambition to become a barrister, but meanwhile was enjoying a year's sabbatical from studies in order to "do the Season," as she told her friends who weren't debutantes, with some embarrassment. "It's all Mummy's idea, really," she'd assured them earnestly. "It's frightfully boring, actually."

Boring or not, the year had been planned with the precision of a military operation, as her mother attended and gave luncheon parties throughout the previous October and November in order to get to know all the other mothers. By February and March, Bunty was going to and giving tea parties every day, and getting to know all the other girls; by April the cocktail parties had started, when the young men were introduced onto the scene. Now, with July in its zenith there were dances and balls several nights a week, many of them taking place on a Friday or Saturday night at someone's home, in the country, with all the guests being put up by friends and neighbors in large house parties. Most of the girls looked upon the whole thing as a chance to have fun before they settled down to studies and an eventual career, but there were a few others who seemed to think it was a way of life; it was what happened to you when you grew up, and they were the ones that came down to earth with a terrible bump when the year ended. Bunty looked as if she had her head screwed on, though, Jackie thought as she greeted her.

"You look lovely. That's a beautiful dress," she told Bunty.

"Oh, do you like it? I'm so glad." Bunty did a little twirl, so that the flowing white muslin crinoline swirled out around her feet, reminding Jackie of when she'd been seventeen herself and her mother had bought her a white dress for her first dance. It seemed like such a long time ago now, almost as if it had happened to another person.

Jackie quickly stifled a sigh and shook hands with Bunty's mother and father. She was thirty-four, and there were moments when she looked at a young girl like Bunty and felt every day of if.

A waiter moved forward and offered her a glass of champagne. Over a hundred guests were already seated at small candlelit tables on a flower-filled veranda built up around three sides of the dance floor. White trellis arbors decked with climbing roses divided the veranda into intimate sections, and above, a dark blue silk sky was spangled with hundreds of tiny white fairy lights, so that it resembled the Milky Way on a summer's night. Never had Jackie seen such magnificent decorations or such a total effect of a fantasy garden. As Bill had said, it must have cost a packet.

Making her way up the steps of the veranda, she found a spare seat at a table where Celia and Hugo Atherton were sitting with some other friends of hers, Sarah and Roger White. They greeted her with a chorus of delight as she joined them.

"How's the social diary going?" Celia asked immediately in her usual direct fashion, her candid gray eyes looking directly into Jackie's.

"Fine," Jackie replied. "Hard work, though."

Celia nodded. "I like your column, because you never say anything nasty about people like some of the other gossip columnists."

"I suppose that's because mine isn't a gossip column as such, but a straight reportage of events. My mother also brought me up to believe that if you can't say something nice about a person, you shouldn't say anything at all!" Jackie laughed.

"Quite right too," agreed Celia, smiling. Her magnificent diamond-and-sapphire tiara glinted in the candlelight, and Jackie hoped Bill had got a good picture of her.

Waiters hovered around their table, topping up their glasses with champagne while the heady scent of roses and gardenias wafted on the warm candlelit air. In one corner a small band played softly, and looking around, Jackie felt a sudden empty ache of longing. This was altogether too wonderful a night to spend alone. There was something sensuous and languorous in the atmosphere, and for a moment she closed her eyes, absorbing the sounds and the smells and the feeling of heat on her bare shoulders. It had been so long since anyone had loved her. The yearning inside her swelled and grew, spreading all through her veins so that she felt weak.

When she opened her eyes a second later, she was not in the least surprised to see the tall dark man she'd met at Claridge's leaning over Celia and greeting her with a kiss on the cheek.

"My dear Gerald," Celia exclaimed, smiling up in delight into the strong-featured face. "What a lovely surprise! When did you get back from New York?" She turned to her husband. "Hugo, look who's here!"

"My dear chap!" Hugo shook Gerald's hand. "Good to see you."

Introductions were quickly made and an extra chair pulled up so that Gerald Gould could join them.

All at once Jackie felt perfectly calm and relaxed as he sat down beside her. This is fate and I was meant to meet him, she told herself with a strange feeling of assurance. In due course we will fall in love and have an affair. The thought slid into her mind with all the naturalness of an everyday event. She did not even pause to rationalize her feelings or to consider that she'd never experienced an emotion quite like this before. In a way, almost as if she'd had a premonition, she felt that this meeting was predestined. She'd been meant to meet this man whose name she now knew to be Gerald Gould, and it didn't matter that she knew nothing about him. There was time enough for that. While the party went on around her, she smiled and talked, joining in the general conversation, but her mind was floating on a wave of inner contentment, and it was as if she'd found the answer to everything at last.

Then she heard Gerald asking her to dance.

"I'd love to," she replied. With a sense of unreality Jackie walked with him the few yards to the dance floor, where several couples were already swaying and clinging to each other.

This is like a scene from a film, she thought, a 1930's movie set in an artificially contrived garden, while an orchestra, cunningly concealed in the bushes, plays a slow romantic number and I drift about in my *Gone With the Wind* ball gown! Her mouth twitched. It was all absurdly funny, really. Even the stars above were fake. She wondered what this man with the wicked smile was thinking.

Then he put his arms around her and pulled her close, while the music throbbed in the background.

I don't believe this is happening, said a small voice in her head. The pressure of his arm was like a vise squeezing the breath out of her body. She could feel his thighs, hard and muscular, brush against hers as they danced. Silently, almost gritting her teeth, she found she was fighting the overwhelming feelings that were starting to envelop her. She wanted this stranger and she wanted him more than anything else in the world; but then she dismissed the idea as impossible. She'd never been promiscuous, or gone to bed with anyone on a first date, and she didn't intend to start now. And yet the feeling of heat was surging her along dangerous channels and she couldn't help pressing closer. As if he sensed her feelings, he looked down at her, smiling gently.

"You're quite something, aren't you?" he said softly. "The minute I saw you tonight I knew we would be good together."

Jackie's breath caught in her throat, echoing the sudden lurching sensation of her heart. She made one last resolve not to give in too quickly.

"Maybe," she said weakly.

Gerald smiled. "Yes, in time," he said, as if he understood.

Looking up into his eyes, she knew his desire was as strong as hers, and her head swam for a second as she tried to imagine what it would be like to be made love to by this man who exuded such strength, such power, such vitality. Is this love at first sight? she asked herself, struggling to hold on to her sense of humor. She'd never felt like this about Richard, not even at the beginning, so perhaps this was just over-whelming chemistry. How the hell did one tell the difference, though?

They danced a little longer, his cheek only a fraction away from hers but close enough for her to feel the warmth of his skin. In unison they moved around the crowded floor, and there was no need for words. It seemed to Jackie as if they'd known each other for a very long time and her horizon was now filled by the touch and the sight and the smell of Gerald. How long, she wondered, could she hold out against the demands he would surely make?

At last the music changed, quickened, and the younger couples broke apart to do energetic solos, the girls tossing their hair and wiggling their hips, the young men stomping as they undid their black bow ties to prove they were real ties and not made-up ones on elasticized neckbands. Jackie and Gerald looked at each other, and laughing, decided to rejoin the others on the veranda. Almost at once Celia started chatting to Gerald again, and it was obvious they were old friends. Lulled into a sense of well-being, Jackie sipped her champagne, only half-listening to their conversation until she heard Celia say:

"Gerald, you must come to dinner one night. When is your wife coming over from the States to join you?"

4

*I*n a charmingly furnished sitting room in Buckingham Palace, which doubled as an office and meeting place for courtiers when there was business to be discussed, Celia sat facing one of the Queen's equerries as they went through the final details of the Queen's engagements for the coming week. It was eleven o'clock in the morning and all around the atmosphere was charged with activity, from the Changing of the Guard in the forecourt, which was being watched by thousands of tourists, to the kitchens, where the chef and undercooks were preparing the food for a lunch party. In the office wing, three hundred secretarial staff were dealing with the usual vast amount of mail as well as the administrative running of the palace, Windsor Castle, Balmoral, and Sandringham, while in the stables horses were being groomed, in the gardens lawns were being mowed, and in the garages the Queen's fleet of Rolls-Royces and Daimlers was being polished.

The Queen herself, Celia knew, was up on the second floor in one of the many large reception rooms, receiving various Commonwealth delegates who were in London for a conference. Prince Philip was conducting a meeting in another part of the palace, in connection with the World Wildlife Fund, of which he was president, while in another private sitting room that doubled as an office, Princess Anne was planning her list of engagements for the next six months with her own entourage of secretaries and ladies-in-waiting.

Keeping tabs on everything that happened was James Ireland, head of public relations. From the press office in the palace where he worked, assisted by two upper-class young women, Jean Hopkins and Phoebe Walsh, employed because they "knew the ropes" about royal protocol, it was his job to supervise all press and television coverage of public appearances made by all the members of the royal family. He had to make sure they had a good press too; no pictures were to be taken of either Princess Diana or the Duchess of York revealing too much thigh or cleavage; they were never to be photographed while eating or drinking either. Every day James Ireland received hundreds of inquiries about the movements of the royals, and all the time, helped by his two assistants and backed by a team of secretaries, he had to answer the questions politely, while at the same time giving nothing of a personal nature away. It was an exacting job, demanding great diplomacy, and only on rare occasions, thinking he was taking evasive action, did he in fact score a home goal and cause more furor than would otherwise have happened. This was highlighted when a newspaper was handed some very personal letters from an equerry to Princess Anne, which had been stolen from her briefcase. As it happened, the newspaper decided not to publish the story and they returned the letters to the palace, but not before the press office, in a panic, had not only admitted the story but also given the name of the equerry.

It did not surprise Celia, therefore, that the Queen referred to the palace as the "office," while all her other residences, especially Windsor Castle, which was her favorite, were looked upon as "home."

"Shall we go through everything now?" Commander Alan Copeland asked. He'd been seconded from the Royal Navy for a two-year period to be an equerry to the royal family, and he was privately longing to return to command his frigate in the Mediterranean. Meanwhile, he was staying in a house the Queen had bought privately, in Victoria, with several other equerries, who all kept normal office hours at the palace.

Celia faced him across the baize-topped table, which was stacked with transparent folders, each headed with a different date and function. She picked up the top one and skimmed the neatly typed itinerary for the coming week with a practiced eye.

"We are going to be busy, aren't we?" she remarked.

The reasons Celia had been invited to be one of the Queen's ladies-in-waiting were manifold. Not only was she efficient and professional in her approach to her work, but she also possessed all the other unique qualities required for such a post: she was wellborn and well-educated, "speaking the same language," literally, as the royal family. She also had a great sense of humor, looked smart and neat but never glamorous, was discreet and friendly, and could be relied upon to behave impeccably, no matter what the circumstances. Her reputation was spotless, she was respectably married to a very nice man, and she knew how to make conversation—excluding talk about politics, religion, money, sex, illness, and servants while "on duty."

"At least we're coming up to the summer break," Commander Copeland observed. There was a touch of weariness in his voice.

At this time of year the "back-room boys" at the palace were exhausted from all the work that went into organizing the official royal diary, as well as attending dozens of appointments when the Queen was receiving visiting diplomats and other dignitaries. From the moment the Queen emerged from her suite of rooms on the second floor, overlooking the gardens, at half-past nine each morning, until she retired to watch television and have her supper on a tray in the evening, which she usually did alone, every move was planned, timed, typed and duplicated, and then circulated to those concerned. People she was to meet were listed with a short biography, so she would know something about them beforehand, and if she was inspecting a regiment of which she was colonel-in-chief, or a factory that manufactured electronic devices, there would be a brief prepared so she would know the background and could then make the appropriate comments. Then there was security to be arranged, which the Queen insisted be kept to a minimum. Time also had to be allowed for her to go through the red leather dispatch boxes which were delivered every day, full of highly confidential state papers.

Celia had soon discovered that the work was not as glamorous as she'd supposed. The palace was a cross between a regimental headquarters, a production company that staged massive theatrical extravaganzas with a cast of thousands, and a five-star-hotel empire. The task of organization was endless and the effort put into the arrangement of minutiae unrelenting. And all the time, all of them, from the Queen down, had to be diplomatically charming to everyone they came in contact with from morning till night.

It was no wonder the royal family was looking forward to spending two months in Scotland.

"Are you getting away for a rest too?" Celia asked Alan sympathetically.

"I'm hoping to go to Spain for a couple of weeks when the Queen goes to Balmoral. What about you?"

"When my spell of duty ends here, we might go and stay with my parents in southern Ireland. The boys love it there and I'm hoping I can persuade the tutor we've taken on to come with us. He can keep Colin and Ian amused while Hugo and I have a bit of a break."

"Sounds nice and relaxing."

"It is. Kilfrush is a small village not far from the sea. We love it there." Modestly, she did not add that her mother and father, Aileen and Ernest Smythe-Mallin, owned a large mansion set in hundreds of acres of lush countryside and that the village of Kilfrush nestled on the edge of their estate like a straggling collection of pretty dolls' houses, with only one small general store and a pub. Her eyes strayed back to the typed sheets on her knee, trying to digest all the detailed arrangements.

"Tuesday is going to be the worst day," Alan Copeland observed. "Several government ministers have an audience with the Queen in the morning, and at eleven-thirty she is bestowing the Insignia of a Companion of the Most Distinguished Order of Saint Michael and Saint George on the Ambassador Extraordinary and Plenipotentiary at Quinto. As you will see, his wife is coming with him. Then the Queen and Prince Philip have another of their meet-the-people luncheon parties, and in the afternoon the Minister for the Environment has an audience, and of course the Prime Minister will be coming for her usual Tuesday-evening meeting."

Celia nodded, privately wondering, as she so often did, how these two women, the Queen and Margaret Thatcher, got on with each other. They were the same age, they were both wives and mothers, and they both had demanding jobs; but there any similarity ended. Their backgrounds were so tremendously different, one so privileged from birth and the other brought up within the rigid confines of a Methodist home, where, if money was not exactly short, it was never spent on frivolities or luxuries. One wondered what they could have in common. Only perhaps that each served her country to the utmost, although in the Queen's case it was by inheritance and in Mrs. Thatcher's case by choice.

Even Celia, though, who was at times privy to the Queen's private thoughts and views because she was so trustworthy, did not dare ask such a leading question as "How do you get on with your Prime Minister?" Their meetings, held at six-thirty every Tuesday evening, were conducted in strict privacy in the Queen's study, and although the conversation was supposed to be informal, they worked from a joint agenda prepared by their private secretaries. Topical subjects were discussed over drinks, and the meetings lasted about forty-five minutes, after which Mrs. Thatcher, with a final curtsy, would leave the Queen's apartments and be ushered back along the red-carpeted corridors by a liveried footman to her waiting car. No one knew what had been said, and no one ever would. The meetings were confidential and there were those who surmised they were sometimes strained.

"I don't think their relationship is so much strained as awkward," a courtier once confided to Celia. "They are both women who are more used to dealing with men than they are with other women. Apart from which they have very different interests—the Queen loves being in the country, out in the open in all weathers, surrounded by her dogs and horses . . ."

"While Mrs. Thatcher is a city person, into power dressing, and also a workaholic," added Celia with sudden understanding. "Yes, I can see why they're not bosom buddies."

She turned the page of the itinerary. "Wednesday is a heavy day," she remarked, a hint of dread in her voice. Like everyone else, she was feeling the strain and longing for the summer break. On Wednesday she was accompanying HM on a trip to Glasgow. They were going in a Silver Andover of the Queen's Flight, taking a specially created flight path for the occasion. These were known as the "purple airways," and all other aircraft were forbidden to enter the ten-mile-wide flight path or enter within one thousand feet above or below the royal aircraft. The first appointment of the day was to open a new school; then there was lunch with some local dignitaries, followed by a visit to the new wing of a hospital, where the Queen would unveil a plaque and plant a tree commemorating her visit. The distances between engagements were farther than was really comfortable, and the royal chauffeurs and police outriders were going to have to keep up to schedule or the day's plans would be wrecked. Celia also had to ensure that the Queen's "walkabout" outside the school and hospital did not run on for too long. Sometimes things could be controlled to the minute, but small children pressing posies of flowers into the Queen's hands was something that could not be ignored in order to stick to a planned timetable.

"You've been up to Glasgow to 'walk the course,' haven't you?" Alan asked.

Celia nodded, consulting her notes. "I've also had a meeting with the local organizers at both the hospital and the school, and answered their usual queries, so I think everything's under control." The first query was always about the royal bouquet: "What color should the flowers be? We don't want them to clash with the Queen's clothes!" To which Celia always gave the same reply: "A mixed bouquet is best, but please don't wire the flowers into a stiff arrangement, as the Queen likes to put them in a vase when she gets home."

The second query was always: "What refreshments should we offer?"

"A cup of tea if it's an afternoon engagement, and Indian tea, please, as the Queen is loyal to the Commonwealth," Celia would reply.

"Not champagne?" people would exclaim, surprised.

"The Queen will only have a glass of wine with lunch or dinner, otherwise she prefers English spa water." Celia knew that only in her own home did the Queen enjoy an occasional gin and tonic before dinner. Alcohol did not flow freely in any of the royal households. Champagne was served only on special occasions, and most of the younger members of the family were teetotal.

Celia and Alan spent another half-hour going through everything for the coming week, and then it was twelve-fifteen, time to freshen up before helping to look after the guests who were coming to lunch with the Queen and Prince Philip that day. She slipped into a cloakroom near the offices, powdered her nose, applied some pink lipstick, and checked her hair. Apart from wearing the right clothes when she was Waiting, she'd also realized that a simple hairstyle that stayed in place and looked right with a hat was another requirement for the job, along with shoes that didn't pinch, belts that weren't too tight, and fabrics that didn't crease. "Props," the Queen called them, wishing that she could live in the country tweeds and woolens she so loved.

Celia gave her appearance a final check in the mirror and hurried along to the 1844 Room, where a fantastic clock, known as the "Negress Head," which showed the hours in one eye and the minutes in the other, was displayed alongside many other interesting works of art. Here the guests would gather before lunch, having been escorted on their arrival by a liveried footman down hundreds of yards of red-carpeted corridors.

It was then up to Celia and several other members of the household to offer them drinks and put them at their ease. She'd already studied the list and noted that as usual they were all high-flying achievers, drawn from every walk of life. Today's guests included Simon Levene, chairman of the Manchester Building Society, Sir Alan Whitton, the explorer, the actor David Smedley, who had recently been in a television series, the well-known BBC war correspondent Malcolm Everett, who had recently returned from the Middle East, a pop star who went under the stage name of Bold!, and the famous romantic novelist Deanna Lancaster.

Husbands, wives, and lovers were never invited, and so this diverse collection of people, whose only link with each other was success, were thrown into close proximity with their soverign and expected to be interesting and amusing. For some it was a nightmare. Celia, aware of nervousness and knowing some of the guests were awestruck by the magnificent surroundings, strove to get them to relax by carrying out introductions, offering drinks, and jollying them along.

"What do I call her?" whispered Bold!, who had forgotten to bring the brief list of instructions the palace had sent him.

"Ma'am . . . rhymes with Spam," Celia replied, adding, "The Queen likes everyone to act naturally, though, so don't worry about it."

"Yes, but I was told that when I was first presented to her, I had to call her something else," he persisted, a thin film of sweat forming on his face, a face that normally stared raunchily from the sleeve of his latest record, to the delight of his teenage fans, but that now looked positively wretched.

"Your Majesty," Celia prompted gently, "but honestly, don't worry about it. Just be yourself."

"I think it's only Princess Diana who likes my records," he observed dolefully, accepting a vodka and tonic.

Deanna Lancaster sidled up to Celia. Her pale blond hair was teased so that it looked like cotton candy, and her portly shape was encased in shiny pink silk. She smiled in a genteel fashion.

"How deep a curtsy should I make?"

"A little bob will do fine," replied Celia in a matter-of-fact voice.

"Will that be all right? Oh, I'm so glad they said I didn't have to wear a hat. I hate hats." She patted her spun-sugar tresses and simpered. "Shall I keep on my gloves until after I've been presented?"

"That's not really necessary. Just relax and enjoy yourself. The Queen likes these occasions to be very informal, you know. It's her one opportunity to get to know people."

"Oh, dear, I don't think I shall be able to eat a thing." The novelist sipped her sherry, leaving a bright pink lipstick smear on the glass, which she tried to wipe off surreptitiously with her gloved thumb.

All around the room the tension was building. People stood in twos and threes, talking in hushed voices as if they were in church, while glancing discreetly at their watches every now and again. They'd been asked to arrive at twelve-forty-five, and had been told lunch would be at one o'clock. Some were watching the paneled door apprehensively, starting visibly when it opened for the arrival of another guest.

Celia counted heads. At least everyone had arrived now, which was a relief. To turn up after the Queen was to drop the biggest social brick of all, and was considered unforgivable.

Bold! was looking around anxiously. "Why is this

called the 1844 Room? Is it after some battle or something?"

"No. Nicholas I, the Emperor of Russia, stayed at the palace in 1844 and used this room, so Queen Victoria decided to call it after him."

"Nice." He looked around again, gazing up at the ceiling. "Very nice."

"Does the Queen give many of these luncheon parties?" inquired Sir Alan Whitton, joining them. His eyes had a haunted look about them, as if he'd find it much easier to trace the source of the Amazon than to take lunch with his sovereign.

"About a dozen times a year," Celia replied. "They've become part of the regular calendar. In total, though, I suppose the Queen entertains about fifty thousand people one way or another.'"

Deanna Lancaster's mouth fell open and she stared with eyes filled with incredulity in which panic was also displayed. *"My!"* she gasped. "Each year?" Then she retreated into silence.

Sir Alan spoke again, his voice quavering slightly. "Will the Queen just walk in through those doors?" Those who heard him turned to watch the doors, not waiting for Celia's answer. In fact the whole atmosphere in the room had tightened, become heavy with a mixture of excitement and trepidation, as the hands of the clock neared one. Guests had lapsed into speaking in disjointed sentences as their concentration went and they became distracted by what was about to happen. They were also assailed by sudden fears that had never occurred to them before. Which knife and fork should I use? What glass do I drink from? The worst thought of all struck fear in several pounding hearts: Suppose I'm offered a dish I can't eat? The fact that everyone had been contacted discreetly by a palace secretary two weeks before, to check on any special dietary requirements, did nothing to alleviate frayed nerves at this moment.

What a pity, thought Celia, watching the group, who would normally have been completely in command of the situation, that the Queen gets to meet her subjects only when they've become transformed into either gibbering morons with bulging eyes or overbearing buffoons who talk too much. There were moments when the Queen must wonder if any of her subjects were normal and rational. It wouldn't be until the coffee stage that these particular guests, especially Bold!, were sufficiently relaxed to act naturally.

"Is she due yet?" breathed Deanna Lancaster.

Celia, who knew exactly to the second when and through which door the Queen would make her entrance, smiled. They wouldn't have long to wait now.

A moment later the double doors sprang wide and into the room bounded half a dozen corgis, tumbling and tripping over each other. They then proceeded to streak around the room, dodging in between people's legs and the furniture, barking their heads off in a joyful explosion of golden-brown fur and cold black noses, their foxy faces set in a permanent grin. Startled, the guests watched the charging pack with amazement, almost missing the entrance of a small neat woman in a bright blue-and-white patterned dress, standing in the doorway. She was grinning too, and holding a handful of dog biscuits.

"Here, Fable! Come on! Diamond! Good boy, Spark!" The dogs swarmed around her now, jumping and begging in an excited cluster at her feet.

"There you are! Down, Kelpie! Down, Myth! . . . Good girl! Good girl. There . . ." Her clear, almost girlish voice, calling out the dogs' names, was filled with amused warmth, and as they began to settle, sniffing the priceless silk rugs for any crumbs, Prince Philip appeared behind the Queen and one of the equerries began to make the introductions.

Only Celia knew that the business with the dogs was a cleverly planned ploy to help break the ice and put guests at their ease.

"May I present . . ." One by one the guests bowed or curtsied. Then the Queen came level with Celia, and greeting her, leaned forward to kiss her on the cheek. Responding, Celia then dropped into a deep and graceful curtsy, smooth from so much practice,

perfected because she'd first been taught how to make
a court curtsy, with knees crossed, at the age of six.
For a moment the two women exchanged pleasantries,
which deeply impressed Deanna Lancaster, and then
the Queen moved on.

Introductions completed, the conversation was general and Sir Alan found himself standing beside the
Queen, who still had the dogs prancing around her
feet, hoping for more biscuits. One of them had recently been in the news for nipping a palace sentry on
the ankle.

"Which is the one that bites, ma'am?" he inquired
for want of anything better to say.

The Queen turned to him, smiling radiantly. Her
blue eyes twinkled.

"Oh, they all do!" she replied brightly.

A few minutes later, smoothly and as if prompted
by some secret signal, everyone was being gently ushered into the adjoining room for lunch. At this point,
Celia and the other courtiers stood to one side, their
job done. The party was now in full swing and the
royal couple would entertain the guests on their own.
The menu would be simple. Tartlets filled with quails'
eggs in aspic, roast chicken stuffed with lamb, with
some simply cooked vegetables, and a raspberry sorbet with fresh raspberries that had been sprinkled with
a squeeze of lemon juice. It was well known that the
Queen did not like elaborate dishes or rich sauces,
and that in all the royal households the food was
wholesome and plain. "That's why they are all so
healthy," Celia commented to Hugo one day. "Most
of the food is organically grown, simply cooked, and
consumed with just a little wine and a lot of mineral
water."

Hugo had made a grimace. Something of a gourmet,
he loved French cooking, great wines, and old brandies.

Outside in the corridor Celia glanced at her watch.
It was eight minutes past one. The Queen would
emerge from the lunch party at precisely two-forty-
five, long enough for Celia to join the rest of the
palace staff for a quick lunch in the household dining

room and then attend to some correspondence on behalf of the Queen, who received hundreds of letters each year—"fan mail," Celia called it—mainly from small children and old people. These letters were always given special treatment, being answered by ladies-in-waiting rather than the secretaries. Using the thick cream writing paper, which was embossed in scarlet with the Crown of England and the words "Buckingham Palace," Celia thanked the sender for writing, adding that the Queen had been very interested in the letter.

Then Celia had an audience with the Queen at three o'clock in her private sitting room, when they would go through any further details for the coming week. It was also possible that the Queen, unable to shop in public places because of security and the crowds her presence would attract, would be giving Celia a list of personal shopping to do. This usually meant a quick trip to Harrods for books, maybe games to take on holiday to Scotland, occasionally some records or tapes, and perhaps a present for someone. The last time Celia had been on one of these expeditions, putting the goods on her own account and later being repaid by the Privy Purse office in the palace, she had bumped into the Duchess of Kent in the men's clothing department, buying a navy-blue woolen dressing gown for the Duke, and then up in the "hospitality" department she'd spotted Princess Diana stocking up on Batman paper plates and funny hats and streamers for Prince William's birthday party. The rest of the royal family could slip around London, mingling with shoppers and tourists unnoticed and without drawing attention to themselves, but for the Queen it was different. One's face could not appear on every postage stamp and every coin or note without being recognized at a hundred paces.

Elfreida insisted on arriving early at the Golden Ball. This was an annual charity event, held in aid of leukemia research, at the London Hilton, and according to Elfreida when persuading Selwyn to buy

ten very expensive tickets, a social "must." Everyone
attended. This year the guests of honor were Prince
and Princess Michael of Kent, so that meant all the
press photographers would be there in force.

"You see I haf good table?" Elfreida had asked the
ball organizer, her English even less fluent than usual
in her agitation to be well-seated. Selwyn didn't worry
about that sort of thing, so long as they weren't sitting
too close to the band, because then, he said, you
couldn't hear yourself think. But Elfreida worried; she
fretted desperately. It was vital to be near the top
table, in close proximity to the dance floor, somewhere near the middle of the ballroom. Once they'd
been given a table near the kitchens, and her chair
had been bumped by the swinging doors every time a
waiter passed through bearing loaded trays precari-
ously balanced over Elfreida's head. The next day she
had kicked up a terrible fuss and had told the organizer she felt deeply insulted, humiliated, and would
never patronize the occasion again. "You will regret
treating me like this!" she'd shouted into the phone.
"My husband powerful man."

But on this occasion the organizer, who had heard
all about Elfreida's behavior if she wasn't treated like
minor royalty, was too terrified to do anything but
allocate them a table in a good position.

"And we get to meet Princess Michael?" Elfreida
demanded.

The organizer blanched. This was the moment she'd
been dreading. "The reception room is so small that
we are able to present only twenty people to their
royal highnesses," she began carefully, "and we have
been instructed by Kensington Palace to keep the
numbers down too, otherwise it takes too long. That
being the case, we have restricted it to the chairman
of the ball, Lady Buchanan, and her hardworking
committee."

Elfreida bristled. "Why am I not on the committee?
I buy a lot of tickets."

"You and your husband are listed as patrons in the
program," it was tactfully explained to her.

"But patrons don't get to meet royalty! I tell you something"—Elfreida managed to sound both aggressive and persuasive at the same time—"if you put me on committee or give me something important to do . . ." At this point even she hadn't the gall to ask to be the chairman on the next occasion. ". . . I will do a lot for the charity. A lot! We buy fifty tickets. My husband, he will give a large donation. I persuade my friends to give good prizes. I might even be able to get a car to raffle! Huh? What you say?"

The organizer couldn't think of anything to say, so she smiled patiently and murmured something about another year, perhaps.

Now, as Elfreida and Selwyn entered the ballroom of the Hilton, she rushed to the noticeboard where the guests and their table numbers were listed. Her eyes flicked down the list until she got to the W's. Lord and Lady Witley of Vauxhall. Table number twenty-three. That in itself didn't mean a thing. It all depended on *where* the table had been placed. She shot across the bar area, where waiters were preparing trays of champagne in readiness for the arrival of the six hundred guests, and yanked open the door to the ballroom, colliding with a waiter who was coming out at that moment.

"Shit!" she swore, annoyed. "Why you no look where you're going?"

Apologizing humbly, he sidled away, but with a backward look of loathing. Then Elfreida marched into the ballroom, scanning the vast area, trying to locate table twenty-three among the sixty tables set with gleaming candelabra and pink candles and flowers and sparkling arrays of cutlery and glass.

The banqueting manager, David Irving, who was checking on the final details, came forward with a pleasant smile on his face. Guests were not admitted into the ballroom until dinner was announced, and he was just about to point this out when, on seeing her belligerent expression, he decided tact was required.

"Can I help you?" he asked graciously.

"I'm Lady Witley. I want to know which is my

table." She tried to hide her fear at having to deal with someone who would recognize a lady when he saw one.

"Ah, and your table number is . . . ?" He raised inquiring eyebrows.

"Twenty-three. If it's not in a good position, you must change it."

"I'm afraid that would be up to the organizers, Lady Witley. They arrange the seating plan." He led her to the center of the ballroom. "Here is twenty-three. It's in a very nice position."

"Where are the royal party sitting?"

David Irving indicated a long table, set for twenty people, only a few feet away.

"That is the top table? Very good." Elfreida flushed with pleasure, looking quite pretty for a moment. Then, without another word she turned on her heel and strode out of the ballroom, without even thanking him.

Selwyn, who was already imbibing his first glass of champagne of the evening, was sitting quietly by the bar. He looked more haggard than usual.

"Do you want a drink?" he asked.

"I have orange." She helped herself from a tray held by a waiter.

"That's bucks fizz, you know," Selwyn pointed out. One of the good things about Elfreida was she hardly drank at all. Even he couldn't imagine the awfulness of what it would be like if she did.

"I know," she snapped irritably. She hadn't known at all. She'd presumed it was plain orange juice. Now she must force herself to drink it rather than show her ignorance. "Where is everyone? Our guests should be here by now!" They'd invited a Belgian banker and his wife, two of Selwyn's directors with their wives, and a bogus princess and her boyfriend to make up their table of ten.

"It's barely eight o'clock. We got here far too early," Selwyn remarked.

"I wanted to make sure everything was all right." She leaned toward Selwyn and whispered, "They give us wonderful table. Right beside the Prince and Princess."

"Well, I hope it's a long way from the band."

"Oh, come on, Selwyn! Tonight's going to be fun! I know it is. You like my new dress?"

Belleville Sassoon had made her a beautiful gown, elegant and stylish, in ice-blue taffeta. It contrived to disguise the more rounded of her curves as it flowed into a slight train at the back. With it she was wearing the pearl choker with the aquamarine-and-diamond clasp Selwyn had given her as a wedding present, with the earrings to match.

"You look very nice, my dear," he replied equably.

Elfreida squeezed his bony hand and her smile sparkled with genuine satisfaction. She was really going to enjoy herself tonight. This was the type of occasion that delighted her most and afforded her an opportunity to dress up, meet the "right" people, eat a good dinner, and be photographed. Good-looking men might flirt with her, but that side of it no longer interested her. She'd got what she wanted—a husband with money and position, a lovely house, a Rolls-Royce, and closetfuls of clothes—and she fully intended hanging on to all of it. Nothing would distract her now as she set out to become one of London's leading socialites. Sex, after all, was a mechanical act which she knew she was good at performing but which gave her no personal pleasure, and so the advances of other men did not interest her. There were far more enjoyable things to do than writhe around in a bed anyway! Like buying clothes, and getting invited to the best parties, and getting one's picture in the papers. Anyone could have sex! Being a society hostess was something else.

Their guests arrived, a boring collection as far as Elfreida was concerned, but Selwyn said it was good for business to include them in their social life. More champagne was ordered, introductions were made. The bar area was now packed with partygoers greeting each other in loud voices, forking out money for raffle tickets, and shrieking with delight if they won a good prize on the tombola. Taffeta and brocade, silk and lace rustled against each other as the ladies clustered together, eyeing each other's jewels and exclaiming how nice everyone looked.

"It's bloody hot in here," Selwyn grumbled, wiping his face, which was now flushed to a rich shade of peony. A party of new arrivals was crushing him and his guests into a corner and he was beginning to feel claustrophobic.

"Let's get nearer the exit," Elfreida suggested. "It's not so crowded there." The blue taffeta was sticking to her back and the dress now seemed so tight she could hardly breathe.

They moved forward, just as the Prince and Princess were arriving. Elfreida could see the roped-off area where, behind silk-covered screens, the committee and their husbands were lined up ready to be presented.

Without another word, Elfreida grabbed Selwyn's arm and dragged him forward. Security had been tight, she knew. No one had been allowed into the cordoned-off section without a special invitation. Earlier she'd overheard a woman telling her friends how she'd almost gate-crashed the VIP reception area by mistake and how three security guards had pounced on her. The point now, as Elfreida was quick to appreciate, was that everyone was already assembled and all eyes were on the royal couple.

Keeping a firm grip on Selwyn and smiling sweetly, she linked up with the special detective and the lady-in-waiting who were following behind, in such a way that they presumed she was one of the ball organizers. Then, resplendent in her ice-blue taffeta, she proceeded forward. It was at that moment that the ball chairman, Lady Buchanan, saw what was happening.

In the wake of Prince and Princess Michael of Kent, and about five feet behind them, the Witleys were also shaking hands with the lineup, who in turn presumed they were a part of the royal party. Frantic signaling ensued. It was important the royals should not be embarrassed. On the other hand, the Witleys had no business to be there. The organizer stood dumbfounded, her mouth open. Lady Buchanan looked on with growing consternation. The committee watched, perplexed, as many of them had met Elfreida, and none could remember her having been mentioned in connection with the royal couple's attendance tonight. So what was she doing, arriving with them? Would she expect to sit at the top table? Confusion and dismay reigned. Meanwhile Elfreida continued to shake hands with gracious condescension, her chin held high, while Selwyn, appearing wretched and mortified, looked as if he wished a hole would appear in the floor into which he could forever disappear.

Lady Buchanan made a swift decision. There was no point in making a scene that would attract the wrong type of publicity for the ball. This was her pet charity, and if the Witleys had gate-crashed the VIP reception, she knew how to deal with it. And next year she'd make sure Selwyn Witley paid the price for this privilege in the form of at least a five-thousand-pound donation.

"May I present . . ." she said with a gracious inclination of her head, "Lord and Lady Witley?"

Prince and Princess Michael of Kent shook hands, while Selwyn bowed and Elfreida genuflected in triumph. In fact, she was so thrilled she could have kissed the carpet. A few minutes of precious conversation that she couldn't even recall later, a couple of flashes from a nearby photographer, and her evening was made. Afterward she was to curse herself because in the heat of the moment she'd forgotten to issue an invitation to the party she and Selwyn were giving, but she consoled herself with the thought that now she'd actually met the Prince and Princess, they would remember her and hopefully accept to come.

Dizzy with delight and drunk on achievement, she held on to Selwyn's arm until they eventually made their way to their own table, where their guests were already seated, wondering what had happened to them.

"We had to be presented, you know," Elfreida said

loudly, her face flushed, her manner flustered. Their
friends looked impressed.

"Yes, they are such a charming couple. We hope
to see them at our party," she continued.

If Selwyn looked startled, nobody noticed. The
toastmaster was asking everyone to be upstanding as
the Prince and Princess made their entrance and the
band began playing the National Anthem.

So began Elfreida's evening of exultation. She'd
pulled off a great coup. She noticed that people were
looking and even pointing at her, and she felt it had
been a master stroke to get into the VIP reception
with the royals. Nothing was going to stop her now.
She was on her way, at last!

Toward the end of dinner a young man came up to
their table and spoke to her with deferential humility.

"Lady Witley . . . I do apologize for butting in like
this, but I work for *Society,* and I hear you are giving
a big party?"

Elfreida's eyes widened at the mention of the magazine. "Yes, that is right," she replied. "In two weeks'
time. It going to be the best ball of the season."

"A ball? Really?"

"Yes, with many, many people." She spoke confidently. "Royalty too."

"Really? And you are holding it in your own
home?"

"Of course! Three hundred people will come. My
husband and I wouldn't want to give a party in a hotel.
That is only for this sort of thing." She glanced
around, shrugging, as if she were witnessing a down-
market social event. "What do you do on *Society*?"

The young man cleared his throat and smiled ingratiatingly. "I write the social diary."

"I thought that was written by someone called
Jackie Daventry."

His smile deepened and he gazed into Elfreida's
eyes. "She doesn't do it single-handed, though. I write
up most of the parties. I'd be delighted to come along
to your ball and write a nice account of it for our
readers, if you'd allow me to. There are so few splen-

did private functions nowadays, and the editor always gives them extra space. We could take some photographs too."

Elfreida drew in a tremulous breath. It really *was* all happening for her. This was the very first time a journalist had approached her. It was usually the other way around.

"Of course! That would be good." She reached for her silver beaded evening purse. "I will send you an invitation."

"Thank you, but there's no need. I know your address. I'll look forward to seeing you on the night."

A bouquet of deep red roses arrived the first morning, with a note that read: "Please let me explain. I want to see you. Gerald." At the bottom he'd written his phone number.

As far as Jackie was concerned, there was nothing to explain, and nothing to forgive either. It had been one of those things. The meeting of a man and a woman in which the chemistry between them explodes on sight and they are consumed by a crazy notion that they were meant for each other. Well, she and Gerald weren't meant for each other, unfortunately, and that was that. He'd tried to explain at the ball about having a wife. As soon as Celia Atherton had asked when she was coming over from the States, he'd turned to Jackie and said swiftly, "I'll tell you all about it later."

But Jackie hadn't waited to hear. Feeling sick with disappointment, although she told herself it was absurd to react so strongly because she'd met Gerald only a few hours before, she slipped away to the powder room and then went in search of Pete and the car. She found him eventually, chatting to some other chauffeurs in a corner of the car park. He looked surprised to see her and glanced at his watch, wondering if he'd mistaken the time.

"I've decided to leave now, Pete. I've got all I need and I'd like to go home."

"Very well, madam." He straightened up quickly,

ground his cigarette out under his heel, and went to open the car door for her.

On the journey back to Knightsbridge, through the darkened but still busy streets of London, Jackie thought about the evening and wondered why Gerald Gould had made such a deep impression on her. She knew it had been mutual too. From the moment they had set eyes on each other there had been something magnetic between them, an electric charge that was almost tangible. It was as if something strong and binding had drawn them together, making words superfluous. There was a sense of knowing, too, as if they had been together in some past existence. Closing her eyes in the dimness of the car, Jackie tried to shake off the spell that seemed to have been cast over her, but she could not rid herself of the image of his face, his smile, the expression in his eyes. It was as if he were in the car beside her.

Back at her apartment, she took off her red silk dress and put on a peach silk nightgown. It slithered sensuously against her bare skin. Then, pouring herself a glass of Evian water, she got into bed. But sleep didn't come. Thoughts of Gerald filled her mind: the memory of his searching looks, so piercing she felt they could perforate her soul; his hands, with well-kept nails and tanned fingers; his mouth, full-lipped and seductive; his tall lean frame and muscular thighs . . .

With a groan, Jackie turned on the light again, and climbing out of bed, went next door to the living room. At least she could find out exactly who he was. There could be no harm in that.

Lifting the most recent copy of *Who's Who* off the shelf by her desk, a publication she found so useful she had a copy at the office as well as at home because she must never spell a name wrong or put a title incorrectly in her column, she flipped through the fine ricepaper pages until she got to Godley . . . Goldstone . . . Gough . . . Gould. There were nine Goulds listed, but running her finger down the columns, she quickly came to Gerald Solomon Gould; born 1944.

Settling herself on the sofa with the heavy volume on her knee, she started to read. His biographical notes were both fascinating and revealing. She had imagined him to be an aristocratic Englishman, probably an Old Etonian, and maybe in some high position—perhaps in government. What she read was very different. Gerald had been educated at Oldbury Grammar School in the north of England, and then he'd won a scholarship to Leeds University. The only son of Harold and Rachael Gould, he'd entered the clothing trade by joining the men's department of a leading London store as a trainee, before going on in 1967 to Goray's, manufacturer of men's clothing with a chain of shops throughout Great Britain. Jackie gasped when she got to the bottom few lines. He was now chief executive and managing director of the Goray Group, a member of the CBI Marketing and Consumer Affairs Committee, a member of the Institute of Directors and the Monopolies Commission, and a leading figure on the Clothing Export Council. He was also an outside name of Lloyd's of London.

Jackie's admiration grew. Her knowledge of the United Kingdom was good enough for her to realize that Gerald's achievements were fantastic for someone from an underprivileged background in the north. No one got to his position without a mixture of brilliance and hard work. And charisma too, of course. That was what had impressed her most. Then she paused, frowning, and skimmed some of the other entries in *Who's Who*. They all stated whether the person was married or not and whether there were any offspring. No such details appeared in Gerald's entry, which meant one thing only. He must have married since this edition of the directory had been published, six months before.

Sleep came late and fitfully to her that night, and the next morning she found herself still brooding. Annoyed at being so obsessional, she was just about to leave for the office when the red roses arrived.

Putting them in water, she slipped the card into her purse and set off for Berkeley Street. There was work to be done, and anyway, the more she thought about it, the more she realized it would be a mistake to see Gerald again. If you played with fire, you got burned, and she didn't intend to let that happen. Gerald was married, newly married, and Jackie never forgot the advice her mother had given her when she'd started out. "If you can't get a man of your own, darling," she'd admonished, "don't take someone else's." It was a rule she'd always adhered to.

On the second morning, a bouquet of cream roses was delivered, their centers tinted a delicate shade of pink, their stems long and straight with all the thorns removed. With them was another card: "I await your call with hope and longing. Please let me explain? Gerald."

Jackie arranged the exquisite blooms that reminded her of Dresden china in their fragility and delicacy, and felt torn between longing to see him again and fear of what she might be getting herself into if she did.

On the third morning Jackie, who had been half-expecting more flowers or a present, was taken by surprise. A comical card arrived in the mail, and she opened it eagerly. When she saw the drawing of a sad little elephant trying to pin a red heart to his sleeve, with the caption: "Can you fix this for me?" she burst out laughing.

Gerald seemed to know exactly how to appeal to her, and she loved the unpredictability of his style. She wavered in her resolve. Wasn't she being rather absurd in refusing to telephone him? Surely the least she could do was hear what he had to say? Perhaps she'd call him from the office. She glanced at her watch. It was half-past nine and she had a meeting with Bertram at ten o'clock. Maybe she'd ring Gerald later.

"How are you getting on with the article on the Waleses?" Bertram asked as soon as she entered his office.

Jackie took the seat opposite and opened the file she was holding. "Fine. It's going well. I've found out exactly how they spend the average day, and Princess Diana's is by far the more interesting. Charles seems to have meetings from morning until night; he is involved in so many projects to do with underprivileged young people, the homeless, intercity problems, the architecture of new buildings, and of course raising money for the Prince's Trust, which finances so many of these projects. It isn't until the evening that he gets a chance to relax. The pattern of his life is very similar to the Queen's in that it seems to be all work and no play, except at weekends of course. Then he's at Highgrove, pottering in the garden or playing polo."

"What is Diana's day like, then?" Bertram asked.

Jackie consulted her notes. "She rises early, shortly after six, leaves Kensington Palace and drives herself, sometimes without even a bodyguard, to Buckingham Palace. There she swims twenty lengths in the indoor pool before going back to KP as they call Kensington Palace. While Prince William and Prince Harry have breakfast, she has a cup of tea and then drives them to school. I've got several pictures of her wearing jeans with her hair hidden under a baseball cap, seeing them into the building. Then it's back to KP once more, where her hairdresser is waiting for her. From then on it's a round of public duties; she visits AIDS clinics, you know, and hospitals and old people's homes. It's a real 'hands-on' operation. On the days she doesn't have any public engagements, she meets girlfriends, and sometimes her brother, Lord Althorp, for lunch at either Ménage à Trois or San Lorenzo, in Knightsbridge. She might also do some shopping in the afternoon before the boys come home from school. She likes to have tea with them and play with them before they go to bed, and when he can, Prince Charles joins them in the nursery too. I am building up a picture," Jackie added reflectively, "from all the various people I have spoken to, of a very normal but very hardworking married couple with a couple of kids. They do all the things other parents do at the weekend—have picnics when they're in the country, ride bicycles, buy sweets from the local shop if the boys have been good, and generally behave like an ordinary upper-class family."

"But they're not an ordinary upper-class family; he's the future King of England," Bertram protested. "Surely their lives are very formal, with servants around all the time?"

"They are formal when they have guests," Jackie explained. "When they give a dinner party, evening dress is worn and butlers and footmen wait on them; but when they're on their own, I gather they do their own thing, apart from the presence of private detectives, of course. Diana often goes into the kitchen and raids the freezer or makes some sandwiches. She also loves making custard, which she eats last thing at night because she says it helps her sleep, and she'll even do some washing-up if she feels like it. We have it on good authority that she is very house-proud and particular. Before she married Charles she insisted on washing up after a dinner party and clearing everything in the apartment she shared with two girlfriends before she'd go to bed."

"Extraordinary." Bertram shook his head. "You'd think she'd get other people to do everything for her."

"Apparently most members of the royal family show great consideration for their staff. Someone told me that Princess Margaret got into trouble once, when she was young, by bringing back a couple of dozen friends from a ball and then waking up the Buckingham Palace kitchen staff to cook them all eggs and bacon at three in the morning. Her father, King George VI, was furious!"

"What else have you got on Charles and Diana? Do you know where she shops? What she buys? They say the royal family never carry money. Is that true?"

Jackie sighed inwardly. She'd thought Bertram would be pleased that she'd found out as much as she had, but he was never satisfied. She consulted her notes again.

"Princess Diana does go to Harvey Nichols, which is just opposite where I live in Knightsbridge, in the early morning if she has no engagements. She has charge accounts at big stores like that, but otherwise her private detective or one of the bodyguards pays with a credit card, chargeable to the Duchy of Cornwall, which is the estate owned by Prince Charles. As you know, he owns thousands of acres of land in Cornwall, which he rents to farmers and which brings him in an enormous annual revenue. Diana also shops a lot in the High Street, near Kensington Palace. She'll think nothing of pushing a trolley round Sainsbury's supermarket or popping into one of the smaller shops for clothes and books and toys for the boys. She even pops into Marks & Spencer to buy some of her underclothes."

Bertram looked stunned. "That can't be right."

Jackie grinned. "I promise you it is. I met someone who saw her buying lots of bras and panties; peach is her favorite colour."

"At Marks & Spencer? But I thought they were only for . . . only for . . ."

Jackie laughed. "You're behind the times, Bertram. Everyone goes to Marks & Spencer! It's frightfully smart to shop there these days."

He looked pained. His illusions about the royal family were being fast destroyed, and he didn't like it. Quite crossly he asked, "What about her proper clothes? Don't tell me Diana buys them from Marks & Spencer too?"

"No. She goes to a collection of couture designers. All in all, I've worked out she spends about a quarter of a million pounds a year on clothes, hair, accessories, and that sort of thing."

Bertram looked quite relieved. "That's more like it! That's the sort of thing we want for the article—glamour . . . exclusivity! The last thing we want is for you to make them sound just like some of our readers."

Jackie suppressed the retort that in many ways they were exactly like *Society*'s more aristocratic and rich readers.

"I'm having lunch with Celia Atherton tomorrow and I'm going to see if she can help with my research," she continued. "She is one of the Queen's ladies-in-waiting, so it may be difficult for her to talk, but I'm hoping she can point me in the right direction."

"I don't see why not."

"It's not as easy as that. I believe people who join the royal staff have to sign forms promising never to reveal anything they have seen or heard, and that includes conversations with members of the royal family or what they may say to each other," Jackie explained. She was pretty certain Celia Atherton was going to clam up, but as a journalist she couldn't resist trying. "I'm sure it will be a most useful lunch," she added, trying to sound confident in order to impress Bertram.

Back in her own office, the phone rang almost immediately.

"It's a Mr. Gerald Gould," the girl on the switchboard informed her.

Jackie's heart began hammering in her rib cage as she heard the click of his call being put through. When she replied to his greeting, she felt quite breathless.

"How are you, Jackie?" He sounded warm and friendly, as if they were already old friends. "What are you doing for lunch today?"

"Well, I'm a bit tied up. We're frantic here, getting ready for the next issue . . ." Suddenly she was all stumbling tongue and jangling thoughts, confused now that she'd heard his voice again.

"Then what about this evening?"

Jackie thought quickly. "I've got to go to a drinks party and then the opening of a new restaurant."

"Will you be dining at the restaurant?"

"I don't know, I'm not sure . . ." She was floundering now, desperate to see him again and yet fearful of what would happen if she did. She wished she didn't have to speak to him until after she'd lunched with Celia Atherton tomorrow, her real reason for the meeting being to find out as much as she could about Gerald Gould and not the royal family. Forewarned was forearmed; she'd been depending on Celia to tell her everything she knew about Gerald.

"Tonight is a bit difficult," she added.

"Why?" he asked blandly. "I know what we'll do. Why don't I pick you up from this restaurant at nine o'clock, and then we can go to the Savoy Grill for dinner. I really want us to talk, you know, Jackie."

"Yes. Well . . ."

"Please? We needn't be late if you don't want to be, and I'll book a table in a quiet corner so we won't be disturbed." His voice sounded persuasive now, but as if he was sure she was going to agree.

Jackie felt as if she was sinking into a deep vat of warm treacle, so sweet she couldn't resist, so binding that escape was impossible.

"All right," she heard herself say in a small voice. "What's the address of this restaurant?"

She told him, wondering all the time what she'd wear tonight. Her sexy black organza? The yellow-and-white silk dress? The cool linen suit with the long jacket, worn with big gold earrings?

"I'll see you tonight," Gerald was saying.

When she'd hung up, she sat at her desk gazing into space, wondering if she'd done the right thing in agreeing to see him again, feeling the cold shadow of a dark premonition obliterate her moment of excited elation. Gerald Gould had a wife. Anytime now, according to Celia Atherton, that wife would be arriving in England from the United States. Those were the facts, and nothing was going to alter them.

5

"You haven't forgotten, Selwyn?" Elfreida's voice filled the study, where Selwyn had taken refuge after a busy day of business meetings. His bald head was just visible over the back of the wing chair in which he lurked, and on a small table by his side a half-filled tumbler of whiskey glowed amber in the early-evening sunlight that streamed through the windows. The last thing he wanted right now was to have the peace and quiet of the room shattered by the presence of his young wife.

"You drink already?" Elfreida continued, going over to him. "I told you we go to a cocktail party tonight. You'll be drunk before we even get there."

His voice snapped coldly. "No, I won't. Why do we have to go anyway?"

"Because it's important. The Tregunters know everyone. It's the sort of party we can't miss."

"I can," he retorted, closing his eyes.

"Oh, Selwyn! My sweetness!" She dropped onto her knees in front of him, all coaxing winsomeness now, her mouth pouting, her eyes misty. "My angel," she cooed, pushing her face into his. "You come to the party with your little girl? You not let your baby go alone?"

Selwyn's eyes opened so suddenly she recoiled, startled. He glared at her.

"For Christ's sake, Elfreida, be your age. Why can't you go to the party on your own?"

"You're not afraid of me having too good a time?" Her tone was sly.

"I couldn't bloody care less."

"What?" She sprang to her feet, offended. "You don't mind if I have a good time without you? You don't mind my meeting other men?"

At that moment a dozen thoughts flashed through Selwyn's mind. To have another man go off with Elfreida would be very humiliating; on the other hand, it would be a way, and an inexpensive way, of unloading her. He'd be able to act the wronged husband, suffering his public hurt with stoic courage, and then he could get himself a nice little apartment where he could spend the rest of his life in peace. On the other hand . . . Another thought, less comfortable, struck him. Who else would want her? Only another old fool like himself, he supposed. And then *she* wouldn't be interested, unless the man was even richer than he was.

Elfreida was regarding him speculatively, her eyes thoughtful. Then she dropped to her knees again, her hands diving swiftly for his fly this time, her strong thick fingers lifting out his limp and reluctant manhood.

"You love your little girl, you know you do," she simpered, getting a grip on him. "It's naughty to tease me, you bad boy!" Then she dropped her head, and taking him in her mouth, sucked greedily.

For a moment nothing happened, and then, to Selwyn's amazement, he felt a flicker of life stirring somewhere in his depths. Was it only the memory of past sexual triumphs? A mere shadow of what had been, when he'd been young and virile and thought nothing of making love three times a night? . . . Or was the awakening in his loins a momentary spasm? Surely his wizened body had enjoyed its final fling after he'd first met Elfreida . . . when his mind had become dazed by rediscovering his sexual drive as climax after unexpected climax had shuddered its way through his being?

Selwyn closed his eyes and gripped the arms of the

chair, wondering if Elfreida could possibly work her magic on him once more. Ten minutes later, he could feel the buildup beginning, growing, gathering in a surging heat that made him gasp with pleasure. My God, it was going to happen! Clutching at every sensation as Elfreida's tongue flicked and curled, wet and teasing, around and around, and her strong jaws sucked expertly, he thought: Oh, Jesus Christ, it's going to happen! That wild ecstasy was almost within his reach now. His hands tightened their grip on the arms of the chair as a man will hold on to the sides of a boat that is about to capsize. He squeezed his eyes tightly shut. It was almost upon him now, that soaring exquisite searing pleasure as he neared the peak, driven on by the escalating feeling of desire.

"Oh, yes, Elfie . . . oh, God, yes . . . yes . . . oh . . . oh!" he roared. Then a flooding explosion erupted from his tired body so that he flew for a moment on the wings of youth again.

There was a heavy silence in the room, broken only by his labored breathing, when Elfreida asked coyly: "You enjoy that, huh?"

He sat there drained and spent. "Yes. Oh, yes."

"You come to the party with me now?"

Selwyn closed his eyes and wondered how he was ever going to move again. He felt a hundred years old and so weak he wasn't sure he could even stand.

"Pour me another drink."

Obediently she went over to the drinks cabinet and refilled his glass with more whiskey. When she handed it back to him, her expression was thoughtful.

"We have to discuss the final details of our party too. It's only one more week and there are still a lot of arrangements to make."

"What arrangements?" Selwyn's hand shook as he raised the glass to his lips.

"I think we should have a red carpet laid on the pavement outside the house, leading up the steps to the entrance. We should also get livery for the waiters. They always look so dreary and ordinary in black. Why don't we dress them in dark green velvet edged with gold braid, like the stewards at Royal Ascot? They always look so smart."

Selwyn looked at her with barely concealed astonishment. "What are you trying to do?" he demanded. "Create a scene from *The Merry Widow*, for God's sake? You're being absurd, Elfreida. We'd be the laughingstock of London if we dressed the waiters in livery."

She looked stubborn. "I don't see why! The Queen's servants wear scarlet-and-gold livery; why shouldn't we dress ours in green and gold?"

"Because this is not Buckingham Palace and you are not the Queen," he said firmly.

It was the usual gushing crowd at the Tregunters' cocktail party. Elfreida, instantly in her element, joined the melee as they guzzled champagne and greeted her and each other with the usual accepted and inane collection of clichés.

"My dear, how lovely to see you."

"Hel-*lo*! How are you?"

"You look great."

"Wasn't it a good party last night?"

". . . two nights ago?"

". . . last week?"

"Is it true you've got royalty coming to your dance?"

To this last question Elfreida simpered and smiled mysteriously. "Wait and see!" In truth, she'd only heard so far from three of the ladies-in-waiting, replying on behalf of Princess Margaret, the Duchess of Kent, and Princess Anne, and in each case they had declined her invitation, politely but firmly. That still left the Queen, Prince Charles and Princess Diana, the Gloucesters, and Prince and Princess Michael of Kent, and she was keeping her fingers crossed. There was still a chance they'd attend, she thought, though now she wished she hadn't made such a fuss at the hairdresser's within earshot of the Duchess of Gloucester.

She awaited each delivery of mail with a mixture of excitement and apprehension, looking anxiously for the thick cream envelope bearing the royal coat of arms in red, which would signal it was from Buckingham Palace.

Selwyn had slunk away, over to the bar, where he stood in conversation with an old crony. Elfreida, looking around the room swiftly, assessing who was there and who would be useful to talk to, spied Jackie Daventry with a group of people at the far end by the windows. They'd met only a few times and Jackie had never been overfriendly, but Elfreida felt confident tonight. After all, *Society* magazine had offered to cover her party.

"Jackie! Hello! How are you?" Elfreida greeted her, ignoring the others. "This is a good party, huh?" Without waiting for introductions to the others, she continued. "I'm Lady Witley of Vauxhall. How do you do." Everyone shook hands politely with her and there was an awkward silence. She turned back to Jackie.

"I'm so glad you send your young man to write about my ball. He will bring a photographer, won't he?"

"I'm sorry . . ." Jackie hesitated.

"My party! The young man who write your column. He said he would do a big write-up about my party. Of course, I hope you'll come too. You must both come! It's going to be the most glorious night London has seen for a very long time."

Jackie spoke slowly and clearly. "I don't have 'a young man' who contributes to my column."

"What do you mean?"

"I mean that I'm the only person who writes the social diary in *Society*."

Elfreida looked flushed and upset. "No, there is a young man, a charming young man," she insisted. "He asked me if he could do it, and I said yes. He promised me half a page. What's the matter? Can't you both come? Can't you both write a piece?"

"It would be very clever if we could, but this man, whoever he is, is a fraud. He is going around gate-crashing whenever he can, on the pretext of being a journalist. I'm sorry you've been taken in like this. What is his name? Can you tell me where I can get hold of him?"

"But my party!" Elfreida looked ready to weep. "Can you write about it, then? I do so want to get it into your magazine. This young man, he promised. Pleasc, you come intead?"

For a moment Jackie felt quite sorry for this woman with plump cheeks and anxious eyes.

"We're very short of space, but I'll see what I can do," she replied gently.

"Oh, please! It would mean so much to me!"

Gerald Gould arrived at the Caviar Bar just before nine o'clock, his large frame filling the doorway, his dark eyes sweeping the room so that Jackie was instantly aware of him. Suddenly her heart started to hammer, and with legs that had unaccountably turned to jelly, she made her way through the crowded restaurant toward him.

"Hi, there!" Somehow she managed to keep her voice steady as she looked up at him.

"Hi, there."

Gerald was even more attractive than she remembered.

"Are you all done here?" he asked.

Jackie glanced around the packed restaurant, seeing but not seeing the black-and-white-and-silver decor, noting but not noting the jostling guests as they sampled small square canapés of red and black caviar set out like a chessboard on platters, and sipped ice-cold Dom Perignon.

"Yes," she nodded. "I'm done here."

Gerald slipped his hand under her elbow, guiding her to his car, which was parked right outside the restaurant. Neither of them spoke. There seemed no need. It was as if everything had already been said and now it was only left to them to reach out and link together the invisible bonds that already seemed to be binding them to each other. In the confined space of the dark green Jaguar, which he drove with the same ease with which he seemed to do everything, Jackie tried to collect her thoughts, but was only aware of the close proximity of this sensual man. His hands, resting lightly on the steering wheel, were well-kept and strong-looking. The curve of his thigh, encased in dark blue pinstriped trousers, looked powerfully muscled, and she could just smell his after-shave, tantalizingly sharp yet musky. He turned to smile at her.

"Had a good evening?"

Jackie smiled back. "An interesting one," she replied. "It's a busy time of year and I shall be glad when the Season's over, but of course my work doesn't stop just because the London parties end. I've got to go where the in crowd go, whether it's the Red Cross Ball in Monte Carlo or grouse shooting in Scotland."

"Is it fun? Do you enjoy yourself?" he asked curiously. It was a question Jackie was used to answering, and the people who asked it were either full of envy at what they thought must be a glamorous existence, or, like Kip, horrified at the prospect of going out all the time.

She shrugged. "I did at the beginning," she admitted truthfully, "but eventually the novelty wears off, and there are times when I feel that if I have to go to another cocktail party or charity dance, I'll scream. Eventually I want to do interviews and write features, but meanwhile I am getting good experience on the magazine."

Gerald nodded as if he understood. "Why don't you go free-lance?"

"I might in time," Jackie replied, "but right now I rather like the security of a regular salary."

He chuckled. "I can understand that. There's nothing as reassuring as a regular paycheck."

Jackie looked at him; a man who exuded wealth, had the trappings of a rich man, and who probably owned an impressive portfolio of stock. Her mouth twitched. It must have been a long time since Gerald Gould had been dependent on a regular paycheck.

When they arrived at the Savoy, Gerald handed the car keys to the doorman and then he led the way to the opulent and yet understated elegance of the Grill Room. Almost every table was occupied, and there was a low-key buzz of excitement caused by the euphoria derived from good food, fine wines, excellent service, and the presence of several celebrated faces. Jackie spotted Luciano Pavarotti with a party of friends, Elaine Stritch deep in conversation with an attractive-looking man, and Ivana Trump, stunning in red satin and diamonds.

They were shown to a table in a corner, taking their places side by side on the gray velvet banquette seating. The maître d', bowing and scraping with deference, handed them large cream folders containing the menu.

Expertly Gerald gave their order and chose the wine with care. Sitting beside him, Jackie experienced a frisson of pleasure. She was sitting next to one of the most attractive men she'd ever met and they were about to enjoy an evening together, getting to know each other better, and she felt full of anticipation. At some point, driving to the Savoy, she knew she'd lost the inner battle to control her feelings. Whether Gerald was married or not, whether she ever went to bed with him or not, she knew he would fill her thoughts and dominate her emotions for a long time to come. It was something she could not deny; not to herself, and in time, not to Gerald either. Never before had she felt so committed to the impossible. She looked at Gerald, wondering what he was going to tell her about his marriage, wondering what explanation he'd come up with about his wife—if there *was* an explanation.

As if he knew what she was thinking, he said, "I'm so glad you've given me this opportunity to talk to you. There's so much I want to say, and I want you to know what's happening in my life."

"What *is* happening in your life, Gerald? You're married, and that's that," she replied, trying to sound cool and assured.

"It's not as simple as that."

"It rarely is." Her tone was dry. Had Richard gone

into lengthy explanations to Stella when he'd decided to have an affair with her? Had there been secret dinners when Jackie thought he was working late? Had he told Stella he was unhappily married? . . . misunderstood? . . . bored, even? Jackie felt a pang, remembering the hurt she'd felt when Richard had finally announced he was leaving. How she'd hated Stella then, hated her so much there had been moments when she felt she could have killed her. Tormented by doubt, she'd lost all confidence in herself for a while, and it had been a long tough haul to get back on her feet again. Was she now about to inflict that same pain on another woman? For the first time in her life she suddenly knew the real meaning of temptation. Never before had she wanted a man so much; never before had she felt justified in doing something she knew, from her own experience, was basically wrong and harmful.

"But we have to talk," Gerald said urgently.

Jackie took a deep breath, feeling slightly sick. "Do I really want to know all this?"

"I *must* tell you about my wife." Then he paused, frowning, as if in pain.

Jackie looked down at her slim hands, bare except for the antique emerald-and-diamond ring Richard had given her, which she still wore because it was so beautiful.

"I know that your marriage ended some time ago," Gerald was saying.

She looked up sharply. "How did you know that?"

Gerald smiled knowingly. "I know everything about you. Celia Atherton was very forthcoming, and flattering too. She likes you a lot. I checked with her about you, because I wanted to make sure I wasn't treading on anyone else's toes."

"I see."

"Do you like being on your own? Why haven't you remarried?"

"Because I haven't wanted to," she replied truthfully. "I suppose it's also a case of 'once bitten . . .' "

"I don't feel like that at all." Gerald spoke positively. "You were married for . . . how long? Ten years?"

"Nine years, and I thought we were supposed to be talking about you," she replied crisply.

He grinned, and deep laugh lines formed around his eyes. "So we were, but I'd much rather talk about you."

"How long have you been married?"

"Four months."

"Four *months*?" Jackie's mouth opened wide in amazement. "Four months? I don't believe this. You haven't even given it a chance, for God's sake."

"It never stood a chance."

"How can you say that?" For a moment she felt angry. She'd been married for nine years before it went wrong, and for a while those years had been good. Even if they hadn't been, she'd never have thought of walking out after a mere few months. "Where is your wife now?" she demanded.

"She's over here, but we're not living together. She arrived from New York, where we were married, a few days ago."

"Have you talked to her?"

"No way," Gerald replied shortly.

Jackie sat still, waiting to hear more. Waiting to hear all the cruel clichés from a disaffected husband who would try to justify what he was doing. Her lips tightened nervously, and her already pale skin was almond white now as she clenched her fists in her lap. A part of her wanted to run away, blot out this whole scene before it got uglier, put her hands over her ears so that she might never hear his excuses for falling out of love with a woman he'd been married to for only four months. But another part of her wanted to stay and listen to some miraculous explanation that would make everything all right between them. She averted her head, unable to look into his eyes because the closeness of him was like an oppressively demanding force she knew she would be unable to resist much longer. The wine waiter refilled their glasses, causing Gerald to hesitate in what he was about to say, and

then, at that moment, out of the corner of her eye,
Jackie became aware of a swish of white chiffon and
a flash of jewels and a sheen of golden hair crossing
the restaurant to go to a table in the far corner. A
group of tall young men in dinner jackets seemed to
be floating and hovering around this heady vision, and
just as Jackie was vaguely wondering if it was some
celebrity she ought to know, she felt the grip of Gerald's hand on her arm.

"What's the matter?" she asked.

Gerald was looking horrified. "Get out of here as
quickly as you can," he muttered urgently. "Go . . .
go now, I'll follow in a moment."

"Why? What's wrong?" Jackie had never seen anyone's manner change so quickly. He looked tense and
angry now as he urged her to hurry.

"It's my wife," he replied harshly. "Go quickly, or
she'll see you."

Jackie arrived at the offices of *Society* early the next
morning, her thoughts still in a turmoil after a sleepless night. Of course she hadn't waited for Gerald to
leave the restaurant after her. His explanations were
of no use now, his excuses irrelevant. At the moment
his wife had entered the Grill Room, he'd made it
plain that Jackie's presence was an acute embarrassment to him, as it would be to any man who had
been married for only four months and was found
dining out with another woman. He'd wanted Jackie
out of the restaurant and he'd wanted it fast, before
his wife spotted them together. And then what had he
done? Gone over to her and said he'd been dining
with a business colleague? Or slunk out himself, fearful of being seen?

She hadn't waited to find out. Rushing to the lobby
of the Savoy, she'd charged out into the front courtyard, where luckily there was a line of empty cabs.
Once home, she'd taken the phone off the hook and
gone to bed, consumed with rage and misery that she
knew was out of all proportion to what had actually
happened. After all, she wasn't having an affair with

Gerald, so why should she mind so much, she argued to herself as she tried to get to sleep. On the other hand, who the hell did he think he was, for God's sake? He'd begged her again and again to meet him and listen to the story of his marriage, and when she finally agreed to, he'd hustled her out of sight when his wife appeared, like some servant girl down the back stairs.

Anger kept Jackie awake most of the night. In the morning she switched on her answering machine so she wouldn't have to take any phone calls herself, and she also resolved to get the girls on the switchboard at *Society* to say she was unavailable if Gerald called her there.

Pale and grim-faced, she sat at her desk now, contemplating her diary.

When the phone on her desk rang, she started nervously, then picked up the receiver with caution.

"Yes?"

"Jackie, there's a call for you," the operator said.

"Who is it?"

"Lady Atherton."

"Put her through."

There was a click and she heard Celia's voice, warm and friendly, on the line.

"My dear Jackie, you know I wouldn't do this unless I absolutely had to, but I've had an unexpected call to go to the palace early this afternoon, and so I'm terribly afraid I'm going to have to cancel luncheon today."

Unexpectedly, Jackie felt relieved. She wasn't ready to talk about Gerald at the moment, and Celia would have been sure to bring him up in the conversation, because she'd introduced them.

"That's fine," Jackie replied. "I'm snowed under with work anyway."

"Will that be all right? I'm really sorry."

"Don't worry about it," Jackie assured her. "Let's make it another day instead."

"That would be lovely. How about Friday, the twenty-seventh?"

"Perfect." Jackie scribbled a note in her diary. "Are you going to the Witleys' dance the night before?"

She heard Celia chuckle. "No. Elfreida sent us an invitation, but we were . . . shall we say . . . otherwise engaged that night!"

"Of course. I'd forgotten the trouble you had. Well, I'll just have to tell you all about it," Jackie replied, laughing.

"Oh, do, please," Celia begged. "I can't *wait* to hear every detail. Someone told me they're having a fireworks display."

"Not only a fireworks display . . . but a red carpet laid on the pavement outside the house, ten thousand pounds' worth of flowers decorating the marquee, waiters in velvet livery, and a fountain in the middle of the dance floor, spouting pink champagne."

"My God! It will make the banquets at Buckingham Palace pale into insignificance by comparison," Celia joked. "Hugo will be sorry we refused the invitation!"

There was no mistaking the urgent appeal to Gerald's voice as he begged to be allowed to see her again. Jackie listened to his recorded voice on her answering machine when she got back to her apartment that evening. In spite of herself, she found her heart pounding uncomfortably. She played it back a second time. He certainly sounded sincere, she thought, and rather distraught too.

"Why did you run away like that," he demanded, "without giving me a chance to explain?"

Jackie shrugged, feeling a flash of bitterness for errant husbands' "explanations," because she was sure Richard had been a master at that game too. Gerald could try to explain all he liked, she told herself, but she was no longer listening. "In fact," she said out loud as she undressed and slipped under the shower, "I've had it up to here." She waved her hand above the top of her head and glared at her own reflection in the bathroom mirror. "Up to *here,*" she repeated fiercely.

The evening loomed long and relentlessly before

her; two cocktail parties, a reception at the Mansion House, hosted by the Lord Mayor of London, and then she had to drop in to a charity ball at the Dorchester around midnight. Jackie closed her eyes, letting the warm water ease away the tense ache in her shoulders, and she wished she could stay at home. Oh, what heaven that would be! To make herself some scrambled eggs on toast and then curl up on the sofa and watch television and then go to bed with a good book until sleep overcame her. The prospect was so enticing that she contemplated, just for a moment, canceling all her arrangements. After all, she hadn't missed a single party or dance or reception or premiere since she'd started writing the social diary. Surely one evening off wouldn't be so dreadful? But then she thought about the people who would be disappointed if their functions weren't written up. Until she'd taken on this job it had never occurred to her that seeing one's name in print in a glossy magazine could mean so much to someone. People planned the dates of their parties and compiled the guest lists with such care that she knew a lot of it was done for her benefit; the smarter the guest list, the more likely she was to write up the party, they surmised, and of course in a way they were right. Given the right ingredients, like an interesting location, a glittering collection of guests, and perhaps an amusing theme, she was the first to agree it would make good copy.

Sighing, Jackie got out of the shower, wrapped a large terry bath sheet around herself, and decided she couldn't let tonight's hostesses down. They had a right to expect her to do a professional job once she'd accepted to attend, and so she sat at her dressing table brushing her hair and deciding to make the best of it. She must try to get home early. But a voice at the back of her mind kept asking: What am I doing with my life? What sort of madness is this, that takes me to four or five parties every night of the week, on a constant whirligig of socializing? She never had time to see her real friends, much less form new relation-

ships, and the whole essence of her life seemed to be
one of total superficial banality.

Dispiritedly she put on her black satin-and-lace bra
and panties and a pair of gossamer black tights, and
then she chose an emerald satin dress, against which
her skin looked marble white. Looping her hair up
loosely, so that wisps and tendrils fell about her ears
and at the nape of her neck, she started to apply her
makeup, all the while getting herself psyched up for
the evening ahead.

As far as she was concerned, the young man who
was gate-crashing parties was welcome to her job at
this moment!

Jackie was still feeling ruffled when she arrived at
the first party of the evening, in a lovely old house in
Chelsea, overlooking the Thames. Almost immediately she bumped into Bill Glass, busy taking pictures
of the host and hostess receiving their guests.

"How are things going?" he asked conversationally,
taking a break to reload his camera.

"The gate-crasher is still up to his tricks and I can't
find out who he is. I don't even know what he looks
like, but if you hear anything, let me know, will you,
Bill?"

Bill pursed his lips, his jovial face serious for a moment, his kind gray eyes scanning the room full of
people.

"I certainly will," he promised. "It shouldn't be difficult to spot him at a party. People who don't belong
always stand out like a sore thumb."

"Do they, Bill?" she asked curiously. There were
still things about English society that intrigued her,
but Bill had been around so long he knew the scene,
with all its quaint nuances, like the back of his hand.

"Yes, because nobody knows them and they don't
know anybody either," he replied.

"You're taking pictures for us at Lord and Lady
Witley's dance on Thursday, aren't you?"

He cast his eyes comically to heaven. "Lady Witley
booked me to go the day she decided to give it. It
wouldn't be worth my life not to attend."

Jackie burst out laughing. "I know what you mean. That lady is certainly hoping for press coverage that night, in everything from the glossy magazines to the gutter-press tabloids. I have a feeling our gate-crasher might show up too."

Bill let out a long low whistle. "Then we're in for a bit of fun, aren't we!" he observed cheerfully.

"Kip! How wonderful to hear from you! How are you?" Jackie felt a surge of elation at the sound of her brother's voice the following afternoon.

"I'm fine, but utterly pissed off."

"Why? What's happened?"

"I've got to fly back to London tomorrow. I thought I'd tied up all the loose ends on this export deal I'm doing, but something has come up and I've got to return for another week." He sounded tired and irritated.

"That's a bore for you, but it means you'll be staying here with me, doesn't it?"

"If that's all right."

"Kip, you know it will be more than all right. I've been missing you since you left. What time are you landing?"

"Nine-forty, your time, tomorrow night. I should be with you by eleven. Will you be in?"

"I'll be sure to be in," Jackie promised. "I'm going to the first night of *Manhattan Starlight,* but I'll be back in good time."

"That was a big hit on Broadway last year," Kip remarked. "Not that I go to the theater much, but Mom and Dad insisted we go with them, and it was really good."

"Don't I know it. It's being hailed here as the greatest musical of the decade, but it remains to be seen if English audiences are equally crazy about it."

"Is Candy Wyldman still the star of it?"

"As far as I know," Jackie replied.

"Good, because she *is* the show. Without her it wouldn't be the same. Well, have a good time, Jackie, and I'll see you later."

"See you, Kip." Jackie hung up, greatly cheered by the impending arrival of her brother.

The next night she arrived at the Drury Lane Theater, to find the foyer packed with celebrities, members of the press, and two television crews. Princess Anne was expected, as the evening was in aid of charity, and already she could see celebrities such as Michael Caine and his wife, Shakira, Roger Moore, Sean Connery, Jane Seymour, and Michael Douglas. Flashbulbs blinded Jackie as she struggled through the crowd, making a mental note of who was there, seeing the cream of London society mingling with the cream of show-biz glitterati. They were all reluctant to take their seats until the last moment, because this was their one chance, having paid a small fortune for their tickets, to see and be seen and to enjoy the party atmosphere that filled the foyer. Soon the area would have to be cleared for the arrival of the Queen's daughter, but meanwhile everyone was determined to have a good time.

Jackie pushed her way through to the stalls bar and almost immediately bumped into Jasper Klein, a fellow American whom she'd known most of her life.

"Jasper!"

"Jackie! It's great to see you." He gave her a brotherly bear hug.

"It's great to see you too. I didn't know you were in London." Jasper was a successful New York lawyer, in his mid-thirties, but he rarely had time to travel or take vacations.

"I'm over here on business," he explained, grinning.

"I might have guessed it," Jackie replied. "How long are you staying? Kip arrives tomorrow for a few days."

Jasper shook his head. "I'm off again tomorrow. Can I get you a drink? I'm with someone, but she's gone to powder her nose."

Jackie looked over to the bar, where the crowds were five deep, all clamoring for drinks before the curtain went up.

"I think I'll give it a miss," she replied. "So how is life?"

Jasper was just about to reply when a pale elegant woman with blond hair and an exquisite silver beaded dress slid up to his side. He turned to her immediately, smiling welcomingly.

"Hello, Morgan. Can I introduce you to . . ." he began.

Jackie held out her hand to the other woman. "It's Morgan Lomond, isn't it?" she asked.

Her hand was shaken gravely. "Yes," the woman replied quietly.

Jackie remembered her well, the beautiful American heiress who had married the Scottish Duke of Lomond. The marriage had been a disaster and she'd heard that Morgan had returned to the United States with a nervous breakdown a couple of years ago.

"It's nice to see you again." Jackie smiled reassuringly.

"And you too," Morgan replied.

Theater ushers were beginning to urge the crowd to take their seats.

"Let's meet for a drink in the interval," Jasper suggested, shouting above the hubbub of voices. The pushing and shoving had become worse as dozens of people began squeezing into the aisles to get to their seats. At last Jackie reached hers and found that the organizers of the gala had given her a press ticket with an excellent view of the stage.

Manhattan Starlight was a frothy, lively production, with glamorous sets and costumes, and as Act One proceeded, Jackie relaxed in her seat, letting herself be carried along on a wave of sheer delight. Kip had been right about one thing too: the leading lady was superb; blond and dainty, she played the part of a jilted bride, with a voice as delicate as a choirboy's one moment and with all the raucous pain of the gutter the next. Moving around the stage with grace and beauty, she captivated the audience. As the curtain came down at the end of the first act, the applause was almost hysterical in its enthusiasm.

Jackie glanced at her program again before joining

Jasper and Morgan for a drink. Candy Wyldman's biography was impressive. She had starred in several Broadway hits, done cabaret in Las Vegas, and had been in the film version of *Alice Through the Looking Glass*. It wasn't until Jackie got to the last line that the full impact of what she was reading hit her like a hammer blow to the heart:

"Candy was recently married in New York," ran the blurb, "to English businessman Gerald Gould."

Roland Shaw arrived early on his first morning with the Athertons, bringing with him a list of suggestions to keep Ian and Colin occupied.

"Hi, boys." His manner was relaxed and easy, his light gray flannel suit and pale blue shirt and tie eminently suitable for his position. "Shall we do a couple of hours' work and then go along to the Science Museum; they've got a wonderful exhibition of electronic equipment at the moment. I think you'll enjoy it."

Ian and Colin nodded in agreement. Shy at first with people they didn't know, they remained silent. Celia appeared at that moment to greet Roland.

"Good morning, how are you?" She shook his hand warmly. "As I've got to use the study, would you and the boys like to work in the dining room? We never use it during the day, so you won't be disturbed."

Roland replied enthusiastically. "That would be great. I'll spend this morning assessing their progress and I'll see if there are any books they need for their studies. We can begin work in earnest tomorrow morning, can't we, boys?"

They nodded again.

Then Ian asked, "What are we doing for lunch, Mummy?"

Celia looked at him in mock horror. "Lunch? It's only nine o'clock and you've barely finished breakfast, and you're already talking about lunch?" There was hidden laughter in her voice as she ran a hand across the top of Ian's blond head.

"Perhaps some biscuits and a drink in an hour or so would stave off the hunger pangs before we fade away altogether," Roland Shaw teased. He looked merrily at Celia, who smiled back.

"I'll see what Mrs. Pinner can do," she promised, "and as I'm going out later, she's very kindly cooking lunch for you."

"Good-ee!" said Colin, swinging on the staircase banister.

"You'll be all right, then?" Celia asked Roland.

"Absolutely fine," he assured her. "We're going to be really busy in the next few weeks. I've got lots of plans."

The boys looked at him expectantly and Celia could see she'd chosen wisely. Roland looked as if he was going to be a big hit with Ian and Colin, and if he kept them interested and amused during the long summer holidays, she'd be eternally grateful.

"I'll leave you to get on with it," she said. "If you have any problems, I'll be in the study, so just come and ask."

"Don't worry." Roland sounded confident and assured. "We're going to be fine, aren't we, boys?"

For the first time they smiled broadly.

"Sure," said Colin, disengaging himself from the ornamental balustrade and heading for the dining room.

"Yup," said his brother, following him.

Gerald Gould was an imposing figure as he sat at the head of the long polished table in the boardroom of the Goray Group. Around him the directors watched and waited to hear the announcement he was about to make. As the up-and-coming king of the retail business, he'd already acquired on behalf of Goray half a dozen struggling businesses, building them up until they became highly profitable. They included Young Casuals, Best Buys, New Style, and a clothing store called Blacketts. Now it was obvious to them all that he was about to suggest they make another acquisition. It would be a brave step in a recession, but then, Gerald was known for his business boldness. Failure was something he didn't acknowledge, and

fear was unknown to him. In the past few years he'd
turned Goray from a small unfashionable menswear
group into an empire owning shops and businesses up
and down the country. Goray had so far been his life,
and he didn't care how hard he worked to build it up.

There was a distinct glow about him today, and his
dark eyes gleamed with anticipation, indicating to the
board he had something up his sleeve. They didn't
have long to wait.

"Gentlemen," he began, and those who knew him
well could sense the suppressed excitement in his
voice. "We have an opportunity to buy one of the
best stores in the country."

There was an expectant hush.

"We are in a position to buy Roddick's," he continued, beaming triumphantly at the assembled company.
"The price is five hundred and fifty million pounds,
and I recommend we go ahead."

There were sharp intakes of breath, and one of the
younger directors was heard to gasp: "Wow!" Then
everyone started talking at once.

Gerald leaned back in his chair, well-satisfied. It
would be a big challenge, but one that he looked forward to. Roddick's was the most prestigious store in
London, and his next plan would be to develop a mail-
order company, under the Roddick's label, for teenage clothes.

When the meeting came to a satisfactory conclusion,
he rose and strode out of the headquarters of Goray,
which were just off Oxford Street, and hurried along
to the underground garage where he kept his Jaguar.
Preferring to drive himself rather than have a chauffeur, he headed for Marble Arch, aware that he had
a business dinner to attend that evening. If only . . .
His mind drifted to Jackie Daventry as it had done
night and day, ever since he'd met her. Their evening
at the Savoy had been most unfortunate, an absolute
disaster, in fact, and somehow he was going to have
to get her to listen to his explanation, but meanwhile
he longed to see her again. He might have been a
workaholic all his life, but now, for the first time, he

felt a great yearning to relax and enjoy a relationship. And as far as he was concerned, Jackie was the only woman who had ever made him feel this way.

"I wish I'd never set eyes on the man," Jackie said to Kip that night as they sat drinking coffee in her drawing room. The French windows were open, and from the stillness of the trees in Hyde Park below, the warm night air filtered gently into the room.

"I'm so sorry," Kip said sympathetically. He was sprawled on the sofa, surrounded by business papers.

"I suppose when he took me to the Savoy he thought she would be rehearsing or something," she continued. "I tell you, Kip, I feel sick. I had no idea Candy Wyldman was his wife."

"Would it have made any difference if you had?"

She shrugged. "I suppose not."

"I must say, he doesn't sound like the best news to me." He yawned and stretched his arms above his head.

At once Jackie said contritely, "Oh, God, Kip, I'm being selfish keeping you up like this. Let's go to bed. I'm going to forget all about Gerald Gould. Life's too short to have all this aggro; as if I hadn't had enough with Richard as it is!" She rose and started turning off the lights. Kip groped in his hand luggage.

"Here. I bought you these." He handed her a bottle of duty-free gin and a casket of Baryshnikov's Mischa.

Jackie kissed him on the cheek. "Thanks, Kip."

"Do you have an early start tomorrow?"

"Not particularly. And you?" She closed the windows for the night.

"My first meeting is at ten, in the City."

"Good. We'll have breakfast together. Sleep well."

"You too."

"So, how did your first day with your new tutor go?" Hugo asked Colin and Ian as they all sat in the dining room having supper. Mrs. Pinner had prepared the boys' favorite dish, shepherd's pie, and Celia had served it with a salad, followed by baked apples drip-

ping with honey and a sprinkling of cinnamon. These
were the evenings the Athertons loved best, when
they could all be at home together, sharing the ordinary delights of family life.

"It was great," Colin said, helping himself to more
salad. "He's a good bloke."

"What did you do?" Celia asked.

Ian cocked his head on one side, knife and fork
held upright in his fists.

"Hrrrr-hrrm . . ." Hugo cleared his throat pointedly, indicating the position of the cutlery.

Ian looked blank for a moment, then nonchalantly
laid his knife and fork down, crossed, on the plate.
"Sorry!" He took a swig of water and then dabbed
his mouth with his table napkin. Hugo nodded in
approval.

"We started off by going over what we were learning during this half, and then he drew up a plan for
studies during the holidays," said Ian. "He says I'm
weak at maths."

"So what's new?" Colin exclaimed. "You've been
weak at maths since you were six."

"I have not!"

"Yes, you have! You were bottom of your class at
Ludgrove, and you're bottom of your class now."

"No, I'm not! Rudgewick's boy is bottom. I'm one
up from the bottom."

"Who's Rudgewick's boy?" Celia inquired.

"Lord Rudgewick. You know, the Honorable Tom
Western. Lord Rudgewick's his father. He's the next
heir," Colin said knowledgeably.

"Nothing changes over the years," Hugo laughed.
"We used to call the present earl 'Rudgewick's boy'
when *we* were at Eton together!"

"Was there a 'Robbie m'boy' in your day too,
Dad?" Ian asked. "We have a 'Robbie m'boy' in our
house whose father was at Eton. His real name is
Robert Vane-Moncrieff-Urquhart."

Hugo nodded. "*His* father was always called 'Char-
lie m'boy.' "

Ian looked relieved. "It's nice, isn't it," he confided. "The continuity, I mean. I wonder what my son will be known as, when he goes?"

Celia's mouth twitched. "What do they call you?"

Ian looked slightly sheepish. " 'Wickets.' "

"Why 'Wickets'?"

"Because I like being the wicket keeper in cricket."

"Do you have a nickname, Colin?" his father asked.

"Yes. Sometimes." He paused, going slowly red.

"Well? What is it?"

" 'Atherton's heir,' " he said in a low voice.

Hugo burst out laughing. "Nothing *has* changed! That's what I was known as too."

"Coming from the wilds of Ireland, I seem to have missed out on all this sort of thing," Celia observed. "Girls are much more mature anyway. We always called each other by our proper names."

"Were you never given a nickname?" Ian asked wonderingly. "And may I have some more shepherd's pie, please?" He held his cleanly scraped plate toward his mother.

"Of course, darling. No, I was never known by a nickname. Mummy and Daddy had pet names for me, but that was all."

"Are we going to Grandpa and Grandma these hols?" Colin asked.

"Yes. As soon as I've finished my term of Waiting, we're going to Kilfrush for a couple of weeks. It'll be at the beginning of August, and I'm going to ask Mr. Shaw to come with us."

Ian pulled a face. "Do you have to?"

"Why not? I thought you liked him."

"Oh, I do, but will we have to do schoolwork all the time we're at Kilfrush? Me and Colin want to—"

"Colin and I," Hugo corrected him.

"Sorry. Colin and I want to go fishing and riding, and can we do some rabbit shooting, Dad?"

"Of course you can. We thought it would be fun for you to have Roland Shaw as well, though, and I'm sure he won't make you study too much. After all, these are the holidays."

"I'll make sure he doesn't," Celia promised them.

"Now, how about some baked apples? There's some clotted cream in the fridge too, if anyone wants it."

"Me! Me!" cried the boys, racing off to the kitchen.

"I'm sure your mother doesn't need you both to fetch it," Hugo called mildly after them.

Celia chuckled. "It's good to have them home again, isn't it, darling?"

"Great. I'm looking forward to staying with your parents too. The holidays should be fun." Hugo thought about the lovely old house in Kilfrush, set in acres of lush fertile countryside, where Celia had taken him just before they'd got engaged. There was a solitary peace about the place, and a haunting isolation that appealed to Hugo after the hurly-burly of London. At Kilfrush he could relax and recharge his batteries and let the cool clean air blow over him like a cleansing benediction. It was at Kilfrush that he had proposed to Celia, the most beautiful and gentle girl he had ever met, and it was at her home that her parents, Ernest and Aileen Smythe-Mallin, had blessed the idea of their union. Never had Hugo felt so welcomed into the bosom of a family; never before had a future son-in-law experienced such affectionate cordiality.

"I'll ask Roland tomorrow if he can come with us," Celia added, spooning a large juicy apple onto a plate.

"Oh, he'll say yes," Colin observed, prizing open the tub of Cornish cream. "He said today he likes staying in other people's houses."

Hugo nodded to Celia in approval. "We've certainly struck lucky this time, haven't we, darling?"

When Roland arrived the next morning, his reaction at being invited to Ireland was, as the boys had predicted, one of delight.

"When do we go?" he asked eagerly.

"I'd planned to leave on August 3," Celia replied.

He consulted his pocket diary. "That would be great. Do we fly from Heathrow?"

"No, Luton. My old home is near Limerick, on the coast overlooking the river Shannon."

Roland looked interested. "Has your family always lived there? I love old buildings."

"Kilfrush has been in my mother's family for several generations." She rose, gathering up her handbag and gloves.

"Are you off to the palace again?"

"In a few minutes," she replied shortly. Then she kissed Colin and Ian good-bye. "Behave yourselves," she chided teasingly. "I'll be back by six o'clock."

" 'Bye, Ma," they chorused.

When she left the room, Roland turned to the boys with his most charming smile. "Do you sometimes go to the palace too?" he asked.

Ian, who had been doodling with his new fountain pen, drawing a series of little overlapping boxes, shrugged. "Sometimes," he replied noncommittally.

"For parties?"

"Yes, we were invited . . . Ouch! Colin, why did you kick me?" Ian demanded crossly of his brother. "That jolly well hurt!"

"Sorry. My foot sort of slipped. Are we going to the Natural History Museum today, Mr. Shaw?" Colin shot his brother a warning look before turning politely to the tutor. "You were going to show us the exhibition of prehistoric mammals."

A frown flickered across Roland's brow and he took off his glasses and started polishing them again.

"When you've filled in all these historical dates on this chart, we'll think about it," he replied almost crossly.

Bill Glass watched closely as the dancers bopped and stamped to the vigorous music of the Dark Blues at yet another debutante's party. Over the years it had become a habit with him to study the faces of the guests, always on the lookout for a celebrity, or at least someone who would be known to the readers of *Society*. Faces sold copies; the more familiar the face, the more people rushed out to get their weekly edition.

"Remember, Bill," Bertram Marriott had told him

when he'd first joined the magazine, "for every photograph we reproduce of a well-known socialite, we sell eight copies of the magazine. They're snapped up by all the friends and family of the subject. In the same way, for every name Jackie Daventry mentions, we sell six copies."

Bill had done a quick calculation and come up with a distribution figure of around three hundred thousand. It made sense.

Now, as he took a shot of Bunty Lawson, who was still hanging on to her titles of Deb of the Year and Most Photographed Girl of the Season, Bill felt a tap on the shoulder. Turning, he saw Lady Tetbury standing imperiously, her steely gaze fixed on someone who was dancing.

"Good evening, Lady Tetbury," he said, inclining his head with old-world chivalry.

Lady Tetbury didn't look at him. "Over there," she said, ignoring his greeting. "That young man."

Bill followed her fixed look. All he could see were a hundred young people gyrating energetically, the girls' dresses swirling out around their gold-slippered feet, the young men clean-cut with shining hair, faces flushed with heat.

"Which young man?" Bill asked.

"*That* young man! Dancing with the gel in the off-the-shoulder blue dress." Lady Tetbury's aristocratic accent pierced the air above the pounding beat of the music.

Bill searched until he found the couple she was referring to and looked closely at the young man. He shook his head.

"I'm afraid I don't know who he is, Lady Tetbury."

For the first time she turned to glare at him angrily. "You *must* know! You take pictures of everyone . . . you go to all the parties. You must find out *exactly* what his name is."

For a moment Bill wondered if he'd slipped up. Was this young man a member of some foreign royal family? An eligible bachelor whom every girl was chasing? *Should* he know who it was? He scratched his head absentmindedly and felt humbled in front of this overbearing peeress.

"No, I'm sorry. I don't know his name."

"I don't know it either, and that's the problem," she replied tartly. "That's the dreadful young man who is going around gate-crashing all the parties. I told you, or at least I told Jackie Daventry, he got into our party by saying he was on your magazine."

Enlightenment came to Bill in a flash. He checked his camera to see how much film he had. "Thank you very much, Lady Tetbury," he said, swiftly moving forward into a better position. Then, focusing, he took several flash shots of the young man and his partner as they shimmied on the edge of the dance floor. Then he got out his notebook and pencil and moved in for the kill.

Smiling at the pretty girl in blue, whom he knew to be a debutante named Vanessa Petre, he turned to the young man, pencil poised, a disarmingly friendly smile on his face.

"Can I take your name please?"

The young man seemed to flinch, hesitate, and for a moment Bill thought he was going to refuse.

"I need it for the caption, you know," Bill added encouragingly.

"I really don't think . . ." Again he hesitated, chin raised, eyes suddenly cold.

Vanessa chipped in. "Oh, Bill, you know who this is! His name is Roland Shaw." Turning, she hugged Roland's arm and looked up smilingly into his face.

"Thanks very much, Bill," said Jackie when he phoned her the next morning. "Now I know what to do."

"It was a bit of luck, really," Bill replied modestly. "I've probably seen him a hundred times, but he looks so like all the others that I never spotted him. Blows my theory that an outsider can't infiltrate the social scene, though, doesn't it?"

"Umm. Perhaps he's not such an outsider as we thought. Probably he's a quite respectable young man, without any money, who just wants to get to all the best parties and doesn't care how he manages it."

"His address is good," Bill conceeded grudgingly. "Mind you, if I hadn't taken Vanessa Petre to one side afterward, I'd never have found out where he lived. He was most secretive about himself."

"He would be, with you, because you know he's a fraud, and the others don't."

"Will you let me know what happens? I can't wait to hear his reaction when you tackle him."

Jackie laughed at the relish in Bill's voice. "You bet I will." A few minutes later she had acquired his telephone number from directory inquiries. When she got through, a woman with a cockney accent, whom she took to be the cleaner, answered.

"May I speak to Mr. Roland Shaw, please?" she asked politely.

" 'E's out, luv. D'you want to leave a message?"

"When will he be back?" Jackie did not want to say who she was and put Roland on his guard.

"I dunno. I never knows when 'e's comin' back."

"Thanks. I'll try later."

"Ta, luv."

Kip was opening a bottle of wine in the kitchen when Jackie returned home at half-past six that evening.

"Hope you don't mind, sis," he said breezily as he drew the cork out of the bottle with a gentle pop. "I'm making myself a spritzer. Want one?"

"Yes, please." She kicked off her shoes and gave her brother a friendly hug. "Am I glad to be home. God, it's so hot, and for once I've been stuck in the office all day, doing the research for my Charles-and-Diana article."

"Is it going well?" Kip added ice cubes to the wine and soda water and handed her a brimming glass.

"Not bad. I've nearly finished it, in fact, which has certainly helped keep my mind off Gerald." Her tone was dry.

"Heard from him again?"

She shrugged. "The usual calls at the office. I wish he'd been honest with me from the beginning."

"He never lied to you," Kip pointed out.

"I know, but why did he have to show interest in me when the situation was impossible? Anyway, I'm refusing to speak to him, and in a way, I hope he'll soon stop pursuing me. Meanwhile"—she rose and went over to the phone in the kitchen window, "—I've got an important call to make."

"You sound mysterious. Anyone I know? A new lover, perhaps?" Kip's grin was mischievous.

"That I should be so lucky," she retorted. "No, this is the infamous gate-crasher." Quickly she told him about Roland Shaw.

"Before you phone him take my advice on one thing," said Kip.

"What's that?"

"Make a tape of your conversation with him."

Jackie wrinkled her nose. "Isn't that a bit sneaky?"

"Isn't what he's doing more than a bit sneaky?" he protested. "Come on, sis. Wise up. You may need to prove to your editor that you actually tried to put a stop to this man saying he's on *Society*. Otherwise, it will be his word against yours."

"I suppose you're right." She still sounded doubtful.

"You can record conversations on your answering machine, can't you? Then do it; cover yourself, for heaven's sake."

"Stop bullying me, Kip! Okay, I'll go and do it now." Laughing, they went into the drawing room, and Jackie dialed the number.

"Hello?" The phone was answered immediately.

"Is that Roland Shaw?"

"Roland Shaw speaking." The voice was easy and relaxed.

"This is Jackie Daventry from *Society* magazine."

There was a stunned silence. Then he snapped: "Yes?"

"It has been brought to my attention, on several occasions," she said clearly, "that you are gaining entry to a variety of parties by saying you write the social diary in *Society*."

"So?"

"I'm afraid I must ask you to stop," she continued. "I am the social editor, the only person who attends functions and compiles and writes the diary. We have *no* outside contributors, and your promising to write up people's parties for them is causing both distress and embarrassment."

"I don't see why." Sullen now, his voice had completely lost its original charm and taken on an aggressive tone.

"Because it happens to be untrue," Jackie replied bluntly. "You do *not* write for *Society*, and I can assure you my editor is very angry that you are going around saying you do. He has instructed me to tell you it must stop. So many people are upset at having been misled by you, and disappointed too."

"I haven't had any complaints," Roland said arrogantly. "People are always delighted to see me, and if you'd publish my accounts of the parties I go to, everybody would be happy."

"I'm afraid that isn't possible. I have been appointed to write the diary, and that's the way it is."

"Then I'll get on to Bertram Marriott direct. The more people who contribute to the social diary, the better it would be."

"You will do no such thing," Jackie said hotly, thinking how furious Bertram was going to be if she didn't handle this relatively simple matter by herself. If Roland started ringing up the editor directly, there really would be hell to pay.

His voice rose to a higher key, so that it became almost squeaky. "Don't you talk to me like that! I happen to be a free-lance journalist and I've been contributing to magazines and newspapers for years. I don't see why I shouldn't contribute to *Society*. Who the hell do you think *you* are?"

"A staff member of *Society*, which you are not," she retorted. "Good-bye, Mr. Shaw. I trust I shall not be hearing from you again." She slammed down the receiver, infuriated.

"Well?" Kip was looking at her expectantly. "What did he say?"

"What a prick!" Jackie exclaimed. "I'll play back the tape and you can hear for yourself." Still fuming, she sat listening to the playback. "Did you ever hear anything like it?"

At that moment the phone rang, and thinking it might be Roland calling her back, she snatched up the receiver. "Yes?"

A moment later her knees had turned to jelly and her hands were shaking. "Gerald," she croaked.

"Oh, Jackie." He sounded relieved at being able to talk to her, and she could imagine him, broad shoulders hunched over the phone, dark eyes eager and intense. "I've been trying to get hold of you for days; why won't you take my calls? I've got to explain so much to you, and you're not giving me the chance."

"Listen, Gerald." She was resolved to put a finish to this nonrelationship right now. She'd had enough of sleepless nights, waiting to hear something that made sense from him, to let it go on any longer. I don't need this, she told herself. Did I learn nothing from my divorce from Richard? Like self-preservation? Like knowing when to quit?

"Listen," she repeated. "There is nothing to say. You're married, you've been married four months, and your wife is in town starring in a hit show. End of story. I'd rather not see you again, because I happen to disapprove of two-timing husbands, having had one myself, and so I'm going to say good-bye and I really would be very grateful if you wouldn't try to contact me again." It was a long speech for her, and she barely paused for breath as she delivered it. Inside, though, she was quivering so much she felt sick.

"But, Jackie—"

"No, Gerald. Honestly. No." Quietly and firmly she replaced the receiver.

* * *

In spite of her resolve to put him out of her mind, their conversation kept coming back to her the following day as she lunched at the Savoy for a charity event attended by Princess Diana and then went home to write her copy for the next edition. That night she and Kip dined quietly at home before she set off for a private party in the Orangery in Holland Park.

Several times she thought she saw Gerald's dark head towering above the other partygoers, but it always turned out to be someone else, and each time her heart gave a little lurch of disappointment. Damn the man, she thought, leaving the dance at midnight. And then she was struck by a sudden thought. Gerald hadn't realized, when he'd spoken to her the previous evening, that she knew his wife was Candy Wyldman. Not that it made any difference; and she chided herself angrily for ever allowing her feelings to overcome her good sense.

Jackie awoke late the next morning, not having fallen asleep until nearly five. Struggling out of bed, she called out to Kip.

"Put on the coffee, will you, Kip? I'm running late. I'm supposed to be at the office in thirty minutes."

"Okay," he called back.

She didn't hear the ringing of the phone as she showered and washed her hair. Neither did she hear Kip's startled reply when he answered it. Leisurely and luxuriously she wrapped a towel around her head and then put on her terry bathrobe.

"Jackie?" Kip's voice, coming from the corridor outside the bathroom, sounded urgent. "Are you in there?"

"Where else would I be?" she demanded mildly.

"That was Roddick's Stores on the phone."

"So?" She opened the door and saw him standing there, a shocked expression on his face. He looked at her strangely.

"Kip, what's the matter?"

"You haven't, by any chance, acquired a manservant called Raphael that I know nothing about?"

Jackie grinned. "Give me a break! This isn't April Fools' Day, is it? What are you talking about?"

Kip drew a deep breath. "Well, you may be interested to know that Roddick's funeral department have just phoned to say your manservant, Raphael, has informed them of your death, and ordered, on behalf of your distraught family, your coffin, a hearse, and five cars to take people to your funeral next Monday."

6

*E*lfreida had invited the guests for eight o'clock, but by six-thirty she herself was ready. Hair fluffed out in a tangle of blond curls, her body encased in bright pink satin so that she resembled an overstuffed bedroom chair, and her manner so fraught she seemed to be driven by an overcharged battery.

"Selwyn!" she screamed at intervals, as she rushed about the place, checking on every detail no matter how trivial. "Selwyn!" she yelled, when she realised how much amplification equipment the Dark Blues Band was setting up on the stage at one end of the marquee. "Why do you need all this stuff?" she demanded. "It looks ugly!"

Selwyn, half dressed in his black evening trousers but with a silk robe over his evening shirt, tried to keep his temper.

"You should have hired a string quartet if you didn't want loudspeakers," he retorted. "Maybe you should have, anyway. This lot is going to keep the neighbors awake half the night." Then a slow smile of malice crossed his face. "Serve the buggers right for being such pompous asses."

It had already been a long day for Selwyn, who felt—given Elfreida's excitable frame of mind that morning—that he'd better stay at home to make sure nothing went wrong. He wished now he'd gone to his office, where it would have been quiet and peaceful by comparison. From the moment the caterers had arrived with the first consignment of tables and chairs for the marquee, which they'd erected two days before, Elfreida had been like a person demented by anxiety. Were there enough chairs? Where were the tablecloths? The silver candlesticks? The flowers? What had happened to the champagne glasses she'd ordered? The silver platters for the whole salmons they were serving? The ice buckets? Oh, God . . . her wail rang out around the kitchens . . . where were the ice buckets and the ice? They couldn't serve warm champagne.

It wasn't until noon that the real crisis arose. Elfreida couldn't remember where she'd put the place cards. A secretary had come in the previous day and written out all the guests' names in beautiful italic handwriting, ready to be put on the tables.

"Write out some more," Selwyn grumbled, already into his third whiskey by now.

"I haven't any more." There was barely suppressed hysteria in her voice.

"What do you mean, you haven't any more?"

"I *haven't* any more cards to write people's names on."

"Oh, for God's sake, go to the stationer's and *buy* some more. Send the chauffeur round to Harrods and let *him* buy some more."

"I can't." Elfreida looked ready to burst into tears as she rummaged in the drawers of the drawing-room desk where she was sure they'd been put.

Selwyn's eyes flashed dangerously. "And why can't you?"

"They were special cards. I know I should have ordered more, but I thought . . ."

Selwyn's voice cracked dangerously now. "What was so special about them?"

She started to sniff, and a tear fell with a plop onto her bosom. "They had a little coronet . . ." Her mouth drooped at his expression. "Oh, Selwyn, just a *little* coronet, in gold, at the top, in the middle of each card. They looked so sweet. So smart. Oh, they must be somewhere . . . I must find them."

Touched by her distress, Selwyn put his arm around

her shoulder. How could one be cross, he thought, at the vulgarity of this buxom child who knew no better?

"I'll help you look."

"Oh, yes, please, Selwyn, you find them."

Finally, after much searching, they were discovered in the kitchen, where the secretary had left them the previous night, in readiness to be put out on the tables by the hired servants.

Elfreida's relief was short-lived. What had happened to the red carpet she'd wanted laid on the pavement outside the front door? Why hadn't Selwyn informed the local police, so that they could help regulate the flow of cars that would descend on the Boltons at eight o'clock? On and on she went, and now it was nearly time for everyone to arrive and she felt strung out and exhausted. In a short time three hundred guests would be there, filling the drawing room, dining room, library, study, sitting room, morning room, and marquee with their exotic presence and . . .

"Selwyn! Are there hand towels in the gentlemen's cloakroom?" she shrilled as she raced across the gleaming dance floor that had been laid on the lawn. "There must be plenty of hand towels in there."

"For God's sake, calm down, everything's going to be all right." Selwyn himself felt quite calm now. A slow but steady intake of whiskey since eleven o'clock that morning had done much to steady his fraught nerves, and now he felt fatalistic about the whole evening. They'd hired the best people to look after everything, and there was nothing more they could do. If it went well, that was great, and if it didn't, he'd wasted fifty thousand pounds, which he was sure his lateral-thinking accountants would make tax-deductible, so what the hell! He refilled his glass from the heavy cut-class decanter on the sideboard and regarded his wife with mellow eyes.

"You look very nice, my dear."

"I do? You think this dress is all right?"

Generously, he didn't ask her how much it had cost. "It's fine, Elfie."

She clasped her hands, encased in long white kid

gloves, and looked at him beseechingly. "Do you think everyone will come? We never heard from Prince and Princess Michael of Kent or Princess Anne. Do you think they will come after all? Oh, I pray they come. I'm so nervous, Selwyn. Suppose no one comes?"

"Then we'll be living on quails' eggs and salmon for a long time."

"How can you joke at a moment like this?" She looked around wildly, as if begging the hovering waiters to produce guests out of thin air. "We should go into the drawing room now. That's where we are receiving everyone. The toastmaster in the red jacket, he will be announcing the names."

Selwyn looked at his watch. "I hope you've got Bryn Williams. He's the best toastmaster there is. He'll see the party runs smoothly."

"Yes, I've already talked to him about the celebrities we are expecting." Side by side, Elfreida and Selwyn left the marquee and entered the house from the gardens.

"Then you've nothing to worry about."

Elfreida drew a deep and heartfelt breath. "That is, if anyone comes."

A waiter glided forward, carrying a silver tray on which stood a dozen crystal glasses already filled with champagne.

"Would m'lady care for a drink?" he asked courteously.

Although she didn't drink, it was just what Elfreida needed at that moment. Her confidence flowed back in a surge of euphoria. She gave her fluffy hair a final pat, pulled in her stomach, and took one of the proffered glasses.

"Thank you very much," she said, and smiled. Her Big Night was about to begin, and Selwyn was right. They'd hired the best people to see to all the arrangements, and there was nothing more she could do now except try to enjoy herself.

It was nine-thirty before Jackie arrived at the Witleys', a determined expression on her face. The day had been taken up in endless consultations and discussions with her lawyer, and Bertram Marriott, and Kip, and the undertaker at Roddick's funeral department.

"Are you sure it was this Roland Shaw who ordered you a funeral?" Bertram demanded as they sat in his office discussing the matter. "It seems a very extreme way to behave. After all, you only told him he couldn't go around saying he was working for *Society*."

"I don't see who else it could be. As far as I know, I have no enemies, and this is such a sick thing to do. I'm convinced it's him."

Bertram leaned across the desk toward her and spoke in a confidential voice. "Would your ex-husband do anything like this?"

Jackie started, shocked. "Richard? Of course not! Why would he want to, anyway? He may not have been the most perfect man on earth, but he'd never in a million years do a thing like this."

Bertram flushed slightly. "I'm sorry, but I felt I had to ask. We must eliminate all other possibilities before we go accusing Roland Shaw. After all, we've no proof it was him."

"I hope to have proof later on today."

"How?"

"When I spoke to him on the phone, I made a tape of the conversation. I'm going to take that tape to Roddick's and play it to the undertaker he spoke to. I'm hoping he will be able to identify the voice."

"Is that likely?" Bertram sounded unconvinced.

"Roland has a very distinctive voice, quite high-pitched for a man—once heard, never forgotten . . . I hope."

"What will you do if it is him?"

"I'm getting advice from my solicitor. I look upon it as a very serious matter, Bertram." Jackie spoke gravely. "It's a horrible feeling having someone order one's funeral. It's creepy. It's also very nasty to realize anyone could hate me so much as to actually wish me dead."

"I think it would be prudent to play the whole thing down, though, don't you?" He pulled his snowy shirt cuffs down a fraction so that exactly one inch showed beneath the sleeve of his navy-blue pinstripe suit. "We don't want *Society* involved in any unpleasantness or bad publicity. It wouldn't do the image of the magazine any good, and it could attract all the wrong sort of interest."

"I don't agree!" Jackie replied, outraged. "I'm damned if I'm going to let him get away with this. How would you like it if someone ordered your funeral, Bertram?"

"We have to think of the magazine, though," he replied primly.

"To hell with the magazine. This is my life we're talking about, or rather," she added recklessly, "my death! I propose to pursue this to the limits. One can't allow someone to go around informing funeral parlors you're dead and do nothing about it!"

A pained look flickered across Bertram's face. "I've just thought of something. We may not be able to hush this business up. Oh, dear. This is all very unpleasant." He clucked accusingly, almost as if it was all her fault.

"What do you mean?"

He reached for the phone on his desk. "I'm going to call up the *Times* and *Telegraph,* just in case."

"Just in case of what?"

"In case this joker has decided to put the announcements of your death in the newspapers. Anyone can do it, you know. You don't have to produce a death certificate or anything. All he would have to do is call up the 'Births and Deaths' column and give them the details."

"Oh, great! That's all I need!" Jackie had visions of her parents in Boston hearing about her 'death'; of all her friends in London, and how shocked they'd be; even of Richard's reaction. And then there were the readers of *Society*! Suppose they started swamping the funeral parlor with floral wreaths?

A moment later Bertram was being put through to

the *Daily Telegraph*. Jackie listened as he asked if they'd received the details of her demise.

"Thank goodness for that," she heard him say at last. And then he added: "If anyone calls to notify you about the death of a Mrs. Jacqueline Daventry, will you please get in touch with me at once?" When he came off the line he looked relieved.

"I'll get on to the *Times* now, but I think it's okay. He'd have to leave his name and phone number so they could confirm the details, and he wouldn't dare do that; it would be far too incriminating."

Jackie nodded. "Let's hope you're right."

A few minutes later Bertram put down the phone with a satisfied expression. "Okay. We've no problem there. Now, shall I come with you to see your lawyer?"

"There's no need, thank you, Bertram. My brother, Kip, is coming with me, but first we've got to see the undertaker who was given the instructions," Jackie replied, rising and preparing to leave his office. "I'll let you know what happens."

"Please do, and try to keep *Society* out of this business as much as you can." Bertram's hands were folded neatly on his desktop and once again his mouth was set in prim old-womanish lines.

"Damned magazine," Jackie said to herself as she left the building to catch a cab to Roddick's. "That's all he cares about."

The undertaker, Mr. Phillips, had a surprisingly breezy and cheerful demeanor. Dressed in black out of respect for the bereaved customers, he was nevertheless a fresh-faced young man who smelled of Chanel after-shave and sported a trendy haircut.

"I was horrified to find we'd been tricked into believing we had to supply our funeral services for you," he said immediately, ushering Jackie and Kip into his pleasant and comfortable office. "We've never had anything like this happen before. We are taking a very serious view of the matter, I can assure you."

"I'm sure you are," Jackie replied. She had already

told him over the phone that she had a tape recording of the suspect's voice. Now, as she laid her cassette recorder on Mr. Phillips's desk, she said: "I hope you'll be able to identify this man from this tape."

Mr. Phillips looked expectant. Jackie pressed the On switch.

". . . *I happen to be a free-lance journalist and I've been contributing to magazines and newspapers for years. I . . .*"

"That's the voice," Mr. Phillips cut in eagerly. "I'd know it anywhere. It's quite a high-pitched voice, isn't it? Almost squeaky."

Kip and Jackie looked at each other, nodding. Then Jackie asked Mr. Phillips: "You're absolutely sure that's the man?"

"Absolutely. He called himself 'Raphael' and said he was your manservant. He said your family were too upset to call us and had asked him to do it. There's no question of it, that's the voice."

"Thank you very much. That's all I needed to know," Jackie replied, slipping the cassette back into her bag. "His name is Roland Shaw and he has a grudge against me, but I never thought he'd go to these lengths."

"What are you going to do now?" Mr. Phillips asked.

"I'm taking legal advice."

"Very wise, and if I can be of further assistance, please let me know."

They shook hands, and Jackie got another whiff of Chanel. She smiled. "This is a strange job for you to be doing, isn't it?" she asked. "What made you want to become an undertaker?"

Mr. Phillips smiled back. "My father has a company that manufactures coffins," he said blandly. "It seemed like a good idea to keep the business in the family."

Jackie and Kip took a taxi to Lincoln's Inn, where her lawyers had chambers in a sixteenth-century building, shared with several other law firms. It was on the third floor, and reached by flights of steep stone stairs lit only by small mullioned windows. Kip, who was used to the plush modern splendor of American law offices, was intrigued.

"It's like something out of *Great Expectations,*" he whispered as they waited on hard chairs in a drafty corridor to see Mr. Heering, who had obtained Jackie's divorce for her.

"In England," she whispered back, "the more prestigious the law firm, the more antiquated the premises." She indicated the stone floor, worn in places so it resembled the patterns left on sand when the tide has gone out. "This place probably hasn't changed much since the reign of Henry VIII."

"Imagine lawyers back home putting up with these conditions," Kip replied, chuckling. "No central heating, no air-conditioning, no double glazing. It's all very quaint, but I should think damned uncomfortable to work in. Do you suppose they heat the offices with coal fires in the winter?"

Jackie tapped her foot on the hard floor. "I don't know, but they could do with some heating right now, even if this is July. All this stone and these thick walls make it cold even at the height of summer."

At that moment Mr. Heering's assistant appeared to take them to his private office. Jackie and Kip followed along more narrow stone corridors, coming finally to an oak door set in a deep wall. It suddenly opened with a flourish, and there stood the colorful Mr. Heering, a well-known and flamboyant personality in legal circles, waiting to greet them.

"My dear, how delightful to see you again!" He planted a damp kiss on Jackie's cheek and then ushered them to seats facing his vast and cluttered desk. "Tell me all about this business now, my dear. What a terrible thing to happen! How very distressing for you." He turned to Kip. "And for you too! Dear, dear, what a nasty shock it must have been."

Mr. Heering lowered his large bulky body into a strong-looking chair and regarded them with eyes filled with sympathy.

"Tell me everything, my dears. Have you any idea who carried out this dastardly trick?"

Jackie explained quickly and briefly, while Mr. Heering sat like a large and benign Buddha, nodding and listening and sticking out his bottom lip in a way that reminded Kip of pictures of Winston Churchill.

"What type of person is this Roland Shaw?" he asked at last.

"I don't know. I've never met him, although I half-expect to at a party I'm going to tonight," said Jackie.

"You see . . ." Mr. Heering picked up a fine gold fountain pen that lay on his desk, smoothing its length with large but gentle fingers, "this may be a trap."

"What kind of trap?" Kip asked.

"Let me explain. There are certain people in this world, evil people in my opinion, who do something nasty in order to get sued!"

Jackie looked taken aback. "A nut case, you mean?"

"Far from it. In a court of law your recording of this man's voice, and the subsequent identification of it by the undertaker, will not stand up as proof of his guilt." He paused dramatically.

"So?" Kip looked expectant.

"So, my dear fellow, he counterattacks by suing *you* for defamation of character and demanding financial compensation to make up for the damage done to his reputation." He laid the gold pen down again with loving care.

Jackie looked at him, astonishment widening her vivid blue eyes.

"Are you serious?" she blurted out.

Mr. Heering regarded her with a kindly smile. "I'm very serious, my dear. This Roland Shaw might try to sue both you and the publishers of *Society* in order to obtain damages."

"But he *did* order a funeral for me! He's as guilty as hell!"

"The greater the truth, the greater the libel . . . have you never heard that saying? Believe me, my dears, I know what I'm talking about. At this very minute your evil prankster is probably hoping against hope that you are going to slap an injunction against him or something." Mr. Heering leaned forward suddenly and addressed them fiercely.

"Be very, very careful. Don't even go around saying this man carried out this dastardly trick or that he is a fraud or a pretender or anything. I've got a feeling there's a purpose behind his actions, and that is to collect damages from anyone who says a word against him."

"What is my sister supposed to do, then?" Kip demanded.

Mr. Heering waved a large hand in the air with an expansive gesture. "Ignore him. Pretend he isn't there. Rise above his petty behavior and horrid pranks."

"That isn't going to be so easy," Jackie conceded, "but I do see your point. Until we know more about this man, it probably is wiser to do nothing. After all, he may just be a university undergraduate who wants to go to a few parties and is plain angry because I've told him he can't use the magazine as a means of gaining entry."

"We shall see, we shall see. Meanwhile, keep in touch with me, my dear. You know I am always at your disposal, and I will do anything I can to help you." He inclined his head gallantly, and a few minutes later they were being ushered down the corridor again, which seemed completely blocked by his portly shape as he led the way.

"What a character!" Kip whispered as they made their way down the stone stairs and out into the open.

"Isn't he amazing!" Jackie agreed.

"And you're going to do as he suggested?"

She shrugged. "We'll see."

"What do you mean by that?"

"If Roland is at the Witleys' ball tonight," she said with a wicked smile, "I'm going to have a bit of fun."

"Be careful, Jackie."

"Don't worry. It takes more than some cranky gate-crasher to scare me."

*   *   *

The phone was ringing in Jackie's apartment when they got back an hour later. Swiftly, before the answering machine could connect, she picked up the receiver.

"Hello?"

"I'm sorry to bother you at a time like this, but I wanted to confirm that you'd like brass handles on the coffin we are preparing for the late Mrs. Jacqueline Daventry?" The man's voice was cockney, with an attempt at refined overtones, and he was speaking with gentle sympathy.

Before she could stop herself, Jackie said incredulously "But this is Jacqueline Daventry speaking. Who are you?"

The voice on the other end of the phone changed completely, becoming very agitated and reverting to a strong East End accent.

"If this is a practical joke, it is no laughing matter! This is very serious. We can't have people going around ordering funerals when there's no body!" he snapped.

"But who are you?" Jackie demanded.

"We, madam, are Messrs. Davies, of Cross Road, Balham, South London. We are a firm of undertakers and we don't like having this sort of trick played on us!"

"Hey, wait a minute," Jackie retorted hotly. "This is not *my* doing. I'm as much a victim in all this as you are."

Kip grabbed the phone from her hand. "Here, let me take it," he said, guessing what had happened. While he gave an explanation to Messrs. Davies, Jackie went into the kitchen to make coffee. Damn this Roland Shaw, she thought angrily. Ordering one funeral was bad enough, but two! Mr. Heering might have told her to be careful in what she said, but nothing was going to stop her approaching Roland Shaw at the Witleys' ball tonight.

Now, as she strode along the strip of crimson carpeting that lay across the pavement and up the front steps to the large white stucco house in the Boltons, she felt a certain relish at the thought of baiting Roland Shaw. He wouldn't be able to retaliate either, without giving himself away.

Jackie did a circuit of the ground-floor rooms, assessing who was at the party and admiring the magnificent arrangements of flowers as she sipped a glass of chilled Pol Roger. Selwyn Witley had spared no expense, she reflected, in decorating and furnishing his home, and the color schemes were restrained and in excellent taste, the furniture antique, and the paintings chosen by a connoisseur. Nearly a hundred guests were already standing around talking and drinking, while others had already moved on through to the marquee where dinner was to be served.

As half a dozen photographers flashed away at every new arrival and Elfreida and Selwyn posed with each guest, Jackie stepped out through the French windows of the drawing room into the garden. Here a wide carpeted path, sheltered by an awning, led to the marquee. Rosebushes in terra-cotta urns lined the path, garlands of flowers and fairy lights festooned the poles supporting the awning, and beyond, the entrance was framed by an archway of summer flowers and greenery. In the marquee itself, round tables for ten had been arranged under crystal chandeliers which seemed to float, suspended only by garlands of flowers, while hundreds of candles glowed softly in silver candlesticks, and more flowers in small crystal bowls gave off a sensual perfume which pervaded the warm night air.

Jackie stood for a moment, taking it all in, committing to memory the yellow-and-white silk drapes that decked the walls, the dark green carpet, laid to prevent delicate evening sandals from getting spoiled, and finally the guests themselves: exquisite women in expensive ball gowns and dazzling jewelry, men who exuded wealth and power. Unwittingly, she found herself searching for Gerald Gould's face among this group of the metropolis' leading personalities, but there was no sign of him. She wasn't surprised. He obviously wasn't a regular socialite because she'd never seen him before the night of the ball at Syon House, and she hadn't seen him at a party since. Somehow she had an idea he had better ways of spending his time than flitting from function to function, night after night. No doubt, now that his wife was in England and in a West End show, he'd be picking her up at the stage door every night and taking her out to dinner, she thought with a pang of jealousy.

At that moment Elfreida came skimming across the marquee, her cheeks almost as pink as her dress, a smile spread across her face.

"I'm so glad you come to my party," she said, kissing Jackie effusively on both cheeks again. "Now I find a lovely table for you to sit at! We must find a handsome man for you to talk to!" she added coyly. Then, grabbing Jackie's hand, she set off at a fast pace across the floor. They came to a table where there were still a few vacant seats, and pushing Jackie onto one of the gilt chairs, Elfreida carried out voluble introductions in such excited broken English that no one could understand a word. A moment later she'd gone again, heading off in the direction of the house to greet more guests.

Laughing with polite indulgence at their hostess, Jackie and the other people introduced themselves. By the time the waiters had served supper, which consisted of beluga caviar, lobster served with an exotic variety of salads, and then wild strawberries and cream with brandy snaps, everyone had become very friendly, and to her surprise, Jackie was enjoying herself. Elfreida had been amazingly shrewd in her choice of guests, mixing young and old, the newly rich and the newly poor, businessmen, aristocrats, politicians, and designers, all of which led to a very stimulating mix, she reflected. Only one thing was unusual about the evening, and that was that nobody really seemed to know Elfreida!

"Have you known her for long?" they all asked each other at Jackie's table.

"I can't think why we've been asked," whispered one couple. "We've never met her until tonight."

"Neither have I," said the man opposite.

Everyone started talking in low confidential voices, while Jackie listened.

"I've seen her name on charity-ball-committee lists," observed a middle-aged woman whose hair had been dyed a startling shade of brassy auburn.

"Where did she come from? She's not English, is she?"

"Where do they get their money from? They must be loaded to give a party like this."

"Who was she before she married Selwyn Witley?"

"She hasn't been around for long, has she?"

Jackie excused herself on the pretext of going to look for Bill Glass. She found Bill sitting on a garden bench eating a peach and drinking a glass of mineral water as he surveyed the scene.

"Is this your idea of having a good time?" Jackie asked, sitting down beside him. He nodded cheerfully.

"Never drink alcohol, and fruit clears the system," he replied succinctly. He wiped his bushy white mustache with a silk handkerchief. "How's everything going with you?"

As briefly as she could, Jackie told him about the two funerals ordered for her by Roland Shaw.

Bill turned his usually merry eyes in her direction, and she could see how angry he was.

"That's disgusting!" he exploded loudly. "How could he have done such a thing? You won't let him get away with it, will you?"

"My lawyer has advised me against taking him to court, but if he's here tonight I'm going to say something to him. I want him to be aware that I know what he's done."

Bill pushed his peach stone neatly into the earth of a nearby flowerbed and then covered it over with the soil. "That's my bit of gardening for the week," he remarked, wiping his fingers on the grass. Then he rose. "I'll keep my eyes open for Roland Shaw and let you know if he's here tonight." He looked around.

People were merrily drinking and dining and talking, and a few had begun to dance. "You're staying on for a bit?"

Jackie nodded. "I'll check with you before I leave. Maybe I'll ask Elfreida if he's here, then she can point him out to me, although," she added, "she does seem a bit distracted."

The twinkle returned to Bill's eyes. "I hate to think what she'd have been like if royalty *had* turned up." He chuckled.

Reentering the drawing room, Jackie joined the other guests—some standing by the fireplace, others grouped on sofas and chairs—and all the time she was wondering which might be Roland Shaw, always supposing he'd turned up, of course. All she knew about him was he was thirty-something, had brown hair and glasses. An awful lot of men seemed to fit that description tonight.

Suddenly there was a lot of activity in the hall and the photographers were gathering like moths around a flame. Selwyn and Elfreida hurried forward to the open front door, where security men and two policemen were hovering, and, intrigued, Jackie moved closer to see what all the commotion was about. Someone special was obviously arriving, judging by the frantic efforts of the press, and at that moment Jackie saw a blond head, beautifully coiffured, emerging from a Daimler. Popping flashbulbs exploded in the darkness of this quiet residential area, and then Selwyn stepped forward, a delighted smile of welcome on his face.

"Mrs. Thatcher," he exclaimed rapturously as the Prime Minister came up the steps, followed by Denis Thatcher.

"Good evening, Selwyn," she replied, and then they kissed warmly on the cheeks.

"How very good of you to come," he said. "You know my wife, Elfreida, of course."

Elfreida, quivering like a full-blown rose with excitement, came forward and practically curtsied. "Good evening," she said breathlessly. "Welcome to our little party."

Smiling graciously, Mrs. Thatcher turned back to Selwyn as he led them through the house to the marquee. "I'm sorry Denis and I couldn't get here sooner," Jackie heard her say. "We had to go to this dinner, you know, and some people make speeches that are far too long."

Selwyn was nodding and agreeing with her, while Elfreida prattled on to a bemused-looking Denis Thatcher, who was walking with his hands clasped behind him, like the Duke of Edinburgh.

As they disappeared into the crowded marquee, the Dark Blues Band launched into a rendering of "Red Roses for a Blue Lady" in honor of the Conservative party, whose color is blue, and Jackie saw Elfreida signaling wildly to a waiter to bring them drinks. A buzz of excitement spread through the guests and everyone began talking at once.

"Of course he owes his title to her," she heard one man remark.

"I wonder how much it cost him?" another asked cattily.

The wave of distaste Jackie felt at the remarks of these freeloaders made her want to go home to get away from it all. It was typical of the social circuit, of course, she reflected, to be sycophantic to people's faces and then bitchy about them behind their backs. Not until she left *Society* would she know who her real friends were, and in some cases not even then. There would still be those who'd continue to fawn over her, just in case she thought they'd been nice to her only because of her job in the first place.

"Damned ridiculous," she muttered to herself under her breath.

"First sign of madness, you know," quipped Bill, coming up behind her, camera still slung around his neck. "Interesting conversation with yourself?"

Jackie spun round, laughing. "Fascinating!"

"Your little friend is here. I've just seen him."

Jackie started. "Where is he? What does he look like?" She glanced around expectantly.

Bill shrugged, hitching his camera higher on his shoulder. "Bloody nondescript little bugger," he said shortly. "He's on the dance floor at the moment, with the ex-Duchess of Lomond."

"How convenient. I know her. Thanks, Bill." Jackie edged nearer the dance floor, keeping an eye on the couple. Morgan Lomond looked pale and bored, but Roland Shaw was talking with great animation. Then the band slipped into a smoochy number and Morgan seemed to push Roland gently but firmly away. He laughed and they turned to leave the dance floor. Jackie moved swiftly forward.

"Hello, Morgan! How lovely to see you again." She stood blocking their way, and was aware of Roland shifting uneasily from foot to foot.

Morgan's face lit up. "Hello, Jackie!"

Jackie turned and looked directly into Roland's face. "Ah, Raphael!" she said pointedly. "How are you this evening?"

Roland blushed furiously. "My name's not Raphael."

Jackie pretended to look surprised. "Oh, surely it is? Yes, I *know* your name's Raphael."

"I tell you it's not!" He looked quickly over his shoulder, as if to find an escape route.

"But of course it *is*!" Jackie insisted smoothly. She was smiling now, enjoying her little game. "I have it on the best authority that your name is Raphael."

Morgan Lomond was looking at them both with a puzzled expression. When she spoke, her voice was soft, her American accent pronounced. "But this is Roland Shaw."

Jackie shot her a wicked look. "Tonight, I believe it is. But the other day he was definitely calling himself Raphael! One of your middle names, is it?" she inquired sweetly as she moved away.

When she found Bill again, she told him what had happened.

"Good for you," he chortled. "I expect that's the last we'll hear of him."

"Somehow I don't think so," Jackie replied thoughtfully. "In fact, I have a strange feeling that my association with Roland Shaw has only just begun."

Celia arrived first at Claridge's the next day, for her lunch with Jackie. She'd booked a table in the Causerie, much loved by the Ladies Who Lunch because it is intimate, elegant, and has an excellent buffet so those who are diet-conscious can choose what they eat with care. The maître d' came forward to greet her with deference; the Countess of Atherton was one of his favorite clients and in his opinion belonged to the Good Old Days before money changed hands, when only members of the aristocracy darkened the hallowed portals of Claridge's and the crowned heads of Europe swept down the grand staircase into the marble lobby, where a real fire in a carved fireplace glowed welcomingly in winter and great vases of flowers exuded perfume in the summer.

Everything had changed now, and not for the better, as far as he was concerned. A pop star had even tried to enter the restaurant the other day in an open-neck shirt . . . and refused to wear the tie that was offered him too! The maître d' shuddered at the memory. King Constantine of Greece had been lunching at the time and must have noticed the commotion, as the pop star raved and ranted at not being allowed in.

"I trust you're keeping well, m'lady?" he inquired, showing Celia to one of the "special" tables in a prime position by the windows, which he kept for his best clients.

"Very well, thank you," Celia replied. "And yourself?"

"Fine, thank you, m'lady." He gave the hint of a bow. "May I get you something to drink?"

"I think I'll wait until my guest arrives . . . Ah, here she is!" Celia jumped to her feet again as Jackie entered the restaurant. Today her black hair was tied back with a becoming cream silk bow that matched her suit and accessories, and she looked stunning. Several heads turned as she made her way over to Celia, and one older man, lunching with his daughter, grinned in obvious approval.

"How lovely to see you." The two women kissed, and resuming their seats, decided to order gin and tonics.

"Terribly wicked," Celia laughed, "but I've got a long day ahead of me and I need something to perk me up."

"I've had a long night behind me, and I definitely need something to perk me up!" Jackie rejoined. "What are you doing today?"

A veiled look crossed Celia's face, as if she didn't want to talk about it. "There's a ball at the palace tonight for the diplomatic corps. It means getting ready early and having my hairdresser come to the house at five o'clock to fix my tiara." She laughed. "The boys refer to it as my 'fender,' and I must say it does weigh a ton! Now, tell me about the Witleys' ball last night; was it fun?" Swiftly and diplomatically she'd changed the topic of conversation, and Jackie took the hint. There was no way Celia was going to talk about her life at court.

"It was quite entertaining," Jackie replied. It was her turn to be reticent now. She longed to tell Celia the saga of Roland Shaw, but her lawyer's words kept coming back to her: Don't give him any reason to sue you for slander by telling the story of the two funerals. Pretend he doesn't exist; ignore him completely. She hadn't quite done that at last night's party, but she hadn't given him grounds for suing her.

"Mr. and Mrs. Thatcher came, which somewhat mollified Elfreida for not having a member of the royal family, but all in all, it was a good party. I've come to the conclusion that Selwyn is a very nice man."

Celia responded immediately. "Oh, he's a fabulous person. Hugo and I admire him a lot. He's achieved so much in his life and he's very caring and kind. Helen, his first wife, was so nice too; I shall never forgive myself for letting Elfreida anywhere near him." She shook her head. "I should have seen what she was up to. The whole thing broke Helen's heart, you know. She'd stood by Selwyn through all the hard times when he first started in the building trade, and it was thanks to her that he did so well."

"What's happened to her now?"

Celia sighed. "She lives in the country with her sister, somewhere in Hampshire. We keep in touch, but Elfreida ruined our friendship. It's really a very sad situation, especially as I don't believe Selwyn is happy."

They went to help themselves at the long buffet in the center of the restaurant. Celia chose a little underdone beef with salad, and Jackie had some large Dublin Bay prawns with garlic mayonnaise.

There was something Jackie was longing to ask Celia, but she kept losing her nerve because she was afraid she'd sound like a lovesick teenager. At last she could bear it no longer.

"Have you seen Gerald Gould lately?" she inquired, trying to keep her voice light.

Celia looked surprised. "Do you know him? Oh, of course, we all met at that party at Syon House, didn't we! I saw him a couple of nights ago, dining at the Ivy. It's very hard for him to lead a normal social life with a wife who's on the stage; he likes to dine at a normal hour, but she doesn't get away from the theater until nearly eleven o'clock. She's in *Manhattan Starlight*, you know, that smash hit that's just come over from America."

"So they must lead rather separate lives," Jackie said carefully. "And they haven't been married for very long, have they?"

"No, not long. Hugo and I were so surprised, actually. We'd always looked upon Gerald as a confirmed bachelor, and suddenly he comes back from a business trip to New York and announces he's married. He did admit it was pure impulse on his part, but he seemed very thrilled anyway."

"I'm sure." Jackie tried to sound noncommittal, and Celia continued.

"In many ways Gerald reminds me of Selwyn, although of course he's over twenty years younger, but both come from underprivileged backgrounds, both have worked hard to get where they are today, and both are successful self-made men."

Jackie nodded, wishing she didn't have this cold ache in her chest. It was so absurd; she hardly knew Gerald, and yet she was as drawn to him, as much in love with him, as if she'd known him for years. The feeling of bitter disappointment that he was married was as acute as if they'd already been lovers, and with the perversity of someone who cannot resist probing a painful tooth, even though it makes the agony worse, she asked: "His wife . . . is she nice?"

"I've never met her. She began rehearsing as soon as she arrived from America, and since the show opened I've heard she's out on the town every night, but at a rather later hour than Hugo and I," she added, smiling. "We're early birds if we have the choice."

Jackie could not help her persistence. "She looks very pretty. I went to the first night, and she certainly stole the show."

Celia shrugged. "I'm not really into theater and show-biz people myself. Opera is my scene, and Hugo's too, but no doubt Gerald finds her fabulous."

Jackie let the subject drop. She'd found out what she wanted to know, and no matter what Gerald said now, she definitely wouldn't be seeing him again.

Celia was looking at her wristwatch. "Heavens! Is that the time? Will you forgive me if I rush? The boys have a tutor for the holidays and he's taking them to play tennis this afternoon. I promised I'd pop along to Regent's Park to see how they're progressing."

"I must go too," Jackie agreed. "My brother, Kip, is over here again, and we're going shopping. He's got two small daughters and his wife has asked him to get some classical English-style clothes for them. Naturally, of course, he doesn't know where to begin!"

Celia laughed. "Naturally! There's one thing to be said for boys, they're not interested in clothes. As long as they've got someone to play sports with, they're as happy as anything."

"And you've got a private tutor for them?" Jackie asked. "I don't think we've anything like that in the States."

"Oh, it's great. He stays all day, helps them with their studies, and keeps them amused. It's not a cheap option, but it certainly helps me," said Celia enthusiastically. "We were lucky to find the most perfect young man for the job."

Roland Shaw had spent the day in such a paroxysm of pent-up fury that he could hardly contain himself. As Colin and Ian did their studies in the morning, seated at one end of the dining-room table, he ground his teeth in silent anger and frustration. *That bitch Jackie Daventry! That goddamn cunt of a bitch.* His hatred of her knew no limitations. Not only had she put a block on him going around saying he wrote for *Society,* but she'd also guessed he'd ordered the funerals for her. *How the hell had she known? And how dare she call him Raphael at the ball last night?* Maddened with rage, he sat staring out the window, almost unaware of the boys' presence, consumed by his desire to destroy Jackie Daventry. *Stuck-up American whore! A pity she wasn't dead!* He clenched his fists until the nails dug deep into the palms of his hands. One of the worst parts was that she had made a public fool of him. Soon everyone would know he didn't write for *Society.* They'd laugh at him for being a fraud, these people he had so wanted to be accepted by but who had turned out to be false heroes, consumed by their own importance, blinded by their innate snobbery. *Fuck the lot of them!* He didn't need them. Thoughts of revenge burned hot chunks out of his mind, setting his brain on fire. If he couldn't be accepted, then he would destroy! But to destroy, he had to have power and money. They were the only answers. He looked around the Athertons' beautiful dining room with its pale yellow walls hung with the paintings of their ancestors, and he hated them almost as much as he hated Jackie Daventry.

Meanwhile, he had to minimize the damage Jackie might have done to his reputation. He thought quickly and decided to call Elfreida. Although she was coarse, and of course not a lady, he felt a certain kindred spirit in her; perhaps because they'd both come from nowhere. It was important, though, to get his side of the story over to Elfreida before she heard the truth, because she was London's resident motormouth and she could do him a lot of harm if she started talking.

"I'm going to make a call to confirm we have the tennis court booked for this afternoon," he announced pleasantly to Colin and Ian as he left the dining room. "I shan't be long."

"The court was confirmed by Mum last night," Colin observed.

"It's still a good idea to check," said Roland firmly.

He closed the door behind him and hurried into the study. Celia was out and Mrs. Pinner was upstairs wielding a vacuum cleaner. With any luck he'd be undisturbed.

"Can I come and see you this evening?" he asked when he got through. "I won't keep you for long."

"What's the matter? What do you want? Jackie Daventry says you're not on *Society* magazine! She says you don't write the diary!" Elfreida sounded both cross and querulous, making Roland wonder if he wasn't too late in getting across his side of the story.

"I did write for *Society* . . . until she made mischief with the editor and had me sacked," he replied tartly.

"She had you sacked?" Elfreida repeated in a stunned voice.

"I've been very badly treated by that magazine. Jackie made up all sorts of lies about me, and the editor, who is an old man, believed her! Can I come round for a short while to explain?" said Roland, pressing his point.

"But you won't be able to write about my ball last night, will you?"

"I won't be able to write about it for *Society* . . . but

there are other publications, and I've had an idea—a way to get you lots of very good press coverage."

"You have?" Her manner changed completely, becoming friendly and gushing. "Why don't you come by at about six-thirty? The house is still a mess after last night, but we can talk, huh?"

"That would be delightful. I'll see you later," Roland replied.

As he went back to Colin and Ian, his head was full of plans. Elfreida's husband was a very rich man. The arrangement he was going to suggest to her could be both useful and lucrative for him.

It was three days since Gerald had spoken to Jackie on the phone; three days and nights of misery as far as he was concerned. He couldn't concentrate on his work, was short-tempered with everyone around him in the head offices of the Goray Group, and had even snapped at his elderly mother when she phoned to invite him and Candy to visit her on the weekend.

"Candy performs on Saturday nights, she can never get away for a weekend," he said, not really wishing to discuss his wife, even with his mother. "People in the theater keep quite different hours from the rest of us," he added crisply.

Rachael Gould hadn't pursued the matter, sensing instinctively that her son was unhappy about something; he would tell her in good time. He always did. The mother-and-son bond was a close one.

"Very well, Gerald," she replied soothingly. "You just let me know when it's *convenant*."

"Yes, I will." Now he felt guilty. He'd have to make it up to her later. But first he had to see Jackie. He had to explain. If he didn't, he felt he'd become unhinged. This was the first time in his life a woman had caused him to become obsessed, and it was driving him crazy. Suppose he lost her before he even had her? The thought was unthinkable, unbearable. If only he'd met her before he'd met Candy! Gerald closed his eyes, feeling a rush of something that resembled panic coursing through his veins. The trouble was, he'd concentrated on work with such intensity and for so long that he was unfamiliar with strong personal emotions, and now that they were carrying him along on a torrent of feelings, he was desperate to tell Jackie how much he loved her. Several further attempts to talk to her on the phone had come to nothing; there was only one thing left for him to do, and that was to go to her flat and try to see her in person.

At five o'clock that afternoon he went around to where she lived, but she was out.

"I don't know when she'll be in," the hall porter told him.

"Is it all right if I wait?" Gerald asked.

The porter looked around the lobby. "There's no-where to sit," he said doubtfully.

"I don't mind standing."

"It might be hours before the young lady's back. She's often very late."

Gerald opened his slim briefcase and drew out a copy of the *Financial Times*. "I can wait," he replied firmly.

An hour later Jackie came through the main street door, her laughter filling the air, her arms full of parcels. A tall dark-haired young man was by her side. She stopped in her tracks, startled.

"Gerald! What are you doing here?"

Tiredness had etched a fine cobweb of lines around his eyes and mouth. He smiled at her wistfully.

"I came to see you," he said simply. Then he glanced at the man by her side. Jackie intercepted the look.

"This is my brother, Kip," she said quickly. "Kip, this is Gerald Gould."

Gerald stepped forward to shake hands, and for a moment it seemed that Kip hesitated, but then he moved forward also, and the two men greeted each other formally.

"You'd better come up," Jackie said, pressing the elevator button. There was no need to ask what he wanted. He looked as if he hadn't slept for nights, and there were dark hollows under his eyes. Towering

over both her and Kip, he followed them into the
elevator, and in silence they glided up to the fourth
floor.

As soon as they stepped into her hallway, Kip said
with the tact of a diplomat's son: "I'm going to fix
some coffee," and with that he disappeared in the
direction of the kitchen, leaving them alone.

"Come through," Jackie said, leading the way into
the drawing room, which was bathed in late-afternoon
sunshine. She dumped the parcels on the table in the
window, and unbuttoning her jacket, took it off and
placed it over the back of a chair. Beneath it she was
aware that her cream silk blouse clung to her body,
outlining the contours of her breasts, and almost pro-
tectively she folded her arms.

Without waiting to be asked, Gerald sat on the sofa,
his strong hands resting on his knees, while Jackie
dropped into an armchair nearby. Then she looked at
him expectantly, hoping he wouldn't see the thumping
of her heart, for it felt as if it was pulsing visibly
through her blouse, and hoping her hands would stop
shaking. He was the first to speak.

"I really do have some explaining to do, Jackie.
That's why I had to come here today—in hope of
seeing you, since you won't take my calls."

"What explanation is there?" To her surprise, her
voice was cool and clear, as if she was in complete
possession of her senses.

"I want you to know that my marriage is far from
what it seems. Whatever happens, I owe you that.
That's why it was imperative I see you." His voice,
rich and deep, almost broke as he spoke.

"Well, I'm listening."

"And you'll hear me out?"

Jackie nodded solemnly. "I'll hear you out, Gerald,
but I think you ought to know that I don't like cheat-
ing husbands. Mine cheated on me and ended up running off with one of my best friends. I'm a bit
allergic"—she gave a wry smile—"to the sort of line
he no doubt gave her, so please don't give me the
neglected-misunderstood routine."

Gerald leaned forward, anxious to explain. "It's nothing like that, I promise you. Nothing like that at all."

She met his eyes. "Good," she said as evenly as she could.

He took a deep breath. "I hadn't married until earlier this year because I'd always been too busy, working too hard to give any relationship a real chance. Suddenly I was forty-six! My friends were all married and had children, and there was I, still a bachelor, with a string of fairly unimportant affairs behind me, and basically lonely. I think I panicked. Anyway, when I was on a trip to New York last year, I met Candy Wyldman. Being an actress, she was great fun to be with and she introduced me to the whole show-biz scene." He shook his head, as if he couldn't quite believe it himself. "I suppose I was star-struck or something. Coming from where I do, and always having worked so hard, I've never come into contact with such sheer glamour. The whole business of theater entranced me, and I thought everyone in it was amusing, talented, and great company."

Jackie smiled in spite of herself. He sounded like a young man who'd suddenly discovered that life could be fun.

Gerald continued: "When I flew back to England, we corresponded a bit and spoke on the phone quite often. Candy would call me in the middle of the night, after her show, because she said she was lonely and missing me." He paused, as if remembering something. "In all honesty, she pursued me more than I pursued her, but that was fine by me. Why not? She was beautiful, talented, and any man would be proud to be associated with her."

Jackie looked away, past him, finding his explanation even more painful than she'd expected.

"I flew over to spend last Christmas in New York, and we had a few days in Acapulco, and that was great, and then I dropped her off in New York again on my way home. January was a very busy month for me, I had one hell of a lot of work on, and problems

with exports, and amazing as it may seem, I hardly
had time to give Candy a thought." His voice had
lowered and become husky.

"In February I had a call from her." He paused
heavily. "You can probably guess what happened
next. She said she was pregnant and that she wanted
to keep the child and that we must get married."

Jackie sat very still, taking short shallow breaths,
wanting to hear what was coming, yet dreading it too.

"So," Gerald continued, "I flew over as soon as I
could. It wasn't until the end of February because I
couldn't get away, and she was in a show she couldn't
leave, but we got married as soon as we could at a
quick secret wedding. She said she didn't want the
public to know exactly when she'd married, as they'd
realize in due course that she must have been pregnant
at the time. That suited me fine; I didn't want a big
wedding either. There was no time for a honeymoon,
but she told me *Manhattan Starlight* was transferring
to London and we'd be together then, in any case. I
was delighted, of course, although I wondered how
she was going to cope with being in the show while
she was pregnant." He paused, remembering again.
"I bought a house in Cheyne Walk and had a decora-
tor do it up, including turning the top floor into a
nursery, and I planned everything for her arrival in
England, down to the last detail. It was the thought
of the baby that thrilled me most. I'd always planned
to have children one day, but now that there was one
on the way, I was over the moon, fantasizing about
having a son and heir and all that stuff." His voice
was self-mocking, and nervously he ran his hand over
the crown of his head.

Jackie spoke softly. "And she lost the baby?" It was
late July. If Candy had announced she was pregnant
in February, she certainly wouldn't be high-kicking
her way through *Manhattan Starlight* now!

A painful, awkward silence hung between them,
and Jackie wished she hadn't said anything. It was
obvious from his face that the loss of the child had
hurt him deeply.

Gerald rose and went and stood with his back to the fireplace, towering over her as she sat curled up in the armchair, but the look of sadness had gone from his face, and instead his eyes glittered with an emotion she couldn't fathom.

"I flew over to New York for a weekend in May to celebrate her birthday, and I planned to arrive at her apartment in the early morning with all the usual corny clichés, like red roses and champagne and a piece of jewelry. I meant to surprise her, but it was I who got the surprise."

Jackie looked up sharply.

"She was still in bed when I arrived," Gerald continued, "only she was not alone. It was then that I found out she'd never stopped having an affair with a New York artist with whom she'd been living for five years."

"But . . ." Jackie gasped.

"There never had been a baby."

"Then why . . . ?"

"Candy was desperate to star in the London production of *Manhattan Starlight*, but being an American, she couldn't get a work permit and Equity had forbidden her to perform in England. The only solution was for her to marry an Englishman and become a British national. And that is exactly what she did. Since she married me, she can perform legitimately in this country. Her boyfriend has come over with her and they're living at the Grosvenor House Hotel."

"But where does that leave you?" Jackie asked, stunned.

"It leaves me free," he replied quietly. "I'm seeking a divorce."

"Then why did you hustle me out of the Savoy Grill the other evening when she turned up?"

"Because she's a greedy little bitch and if she thought she had grounds for divorcing *me*, then she would, and demand half of everything I possess. As it is, she's after a settlement that my lawyers are fighting like hell. *I owe her nothing*," he added bitterly, pronouncing each word heavily.

"So, in the meanwhile, you've got to be careful?"

Gerald nodded. "For the time being, yes. I've put the house in Cheyne Walk on the market and I'm living in a service flat in Rutland Gate while I keep a low profile."

He sat down again, close to her, and reached out for her hand. Automatically and unquestioningly she gave it to him. "I had to see you to explain all this, Jackie." His eyes searched hers. "I wanted you to know exactly what was going on and why I'm having to be secretive at the moment."

"Yes, I do understand," Jackie said slowly. It was such an unexpected twist to what she'd imagined that it would take a little time to come to terms with the situation.

"Can I see you again, now that you know what's going on?" he asked tentatively.

She half-nodded, but then said, "I think I need a little time to take it all in. It's such an astonishing story . . ." Her voice drifted off as she thought how she'd imagined he had been double-crossing his wife.

As if he sensed her need for breathing space, he squeezed her hand and then rose to leave.

"I understand," he said softly. "I'll ring you tomorrow. Will you take my call? Will you speak to me now?" The wistfulness had returned to his face and his eyes looked anxious.

Jackie smiled tremulously. "Yes, I'll talk to you now."

Gerald leaned forward and kissed her on the cheek, a thoughtful, loving kiss that lingered a moment before he stood upright again.

"Thank you for telling me everything," she said.

"It was the very least I could do. I hope very much . . ." He broke off, as if afraid of saying more.

"Yes." She nodded quickly. "We'll talk tomorrow."

When he'd gone, Kip came bounding into the room, a quizzical look on his face.

"Well?" he demanded. His tone was brotherly and protective. "What did he have to say for himself?"

*   *   *

"So where will you write about my party?" Elfreida demanded, patting the sofa beside her for Roland to sit down. "I hope Jackie Daventry do it for *Society*, and there were photographers here last night from all the other magazines and newspapers. I was hoping there would be something in the *Evening Standard*, but they do nothing." There was a disappointed whine in her voice.

"Not even the Londoner's Diary?" Roland asked.

She shook her head. "Nothing." Then she added more hopefully: "Perhaps they will do it tomorrow."

Roland looked around the drawing room, better able to see it than at last night's ball, and noted a Monet, a Constable, and a John Singer Sargent hanging on the walls. Selwyn must be worth at least a hundred million, he reflected. And this blowsy bimbo not only had access to that money but was also ripe for the picking. Deliciously, juicily ripe. He smirked as he looked at her and knew she could be a steady source of income to him.

"I was thinking," he began, putting on a tentative manner in order to get her initial interest, "I was wondering . . ."

"Yes?"

"The people who are photographed wherever they go, and are reported on whatever they do . . . well, Lady Witley, it doesn't just happen by accident."

"How you mean?"

"It is *organized* publicity. Nothing is left to chance. These people *arrange* to have publicity."

Elfreida's eyes brightened and her bosom, encased in a black chiffon blouse, rose and fell alarmingly. She drew in a deep breath. "Ah-h-h! So they *pay* to have themselves put in the newspapers?" It was as if she'd seen the light, as if the mysteries of heaven and earth had been revealed to her in all their wondrous glory. "I understand what you say!"

"They don't pay the newspapers or magazines," Roland corrected her carefully. "That isn't allowed."

"Then who do they pay?"

"They engage a public-relations person to promote

them, and it is up to the public-relations person to make sure they are properly featured."

"I never knew that! Why did Selwyn never tell me that? Is that really true? Can one have someone who will make sure that when I go to a big party, it will be reported in the *Daily Mail* the next day? Or *Tatler* the next month?"

Roland nodded vigorously. "Of course! Publicists issue press releases, make sure you are photographed, and supply little stories and angles of interest to the press; why else do you think certain people are in the papers all the time, while others never make it?" He watched Elfreida closely. The basis of what he was saying was gleaned from an article he'd read about public-relation companies in the *Independent*. He'd no idea how true it was, but at the time he'd thought this sort of knowledge might come in useful one day. Now it looked as if he'd hit the jackpot.

"So-o-o!" Elfreida drew out the word as if all the problems of life had been solved in one fell swoop. "*That* is the answer, then! I can't understand why Selwyn didn't know about all this."

"I'm sure his construction company employs a public-relations firm," said Roland soothingly.

"Yes, to promote bricks, no doubt!" she snorted. "Who could promote *me*?"

This was what Roland had been working up to ever since he'd phoned her earlier. He tried to look modest and self-deprecating, and taking off his glasses, polished them with a white handkerchief.

"Before I became a journalist," he explained earnestly, "I was in public relations."

"Oh! Then that is perfect." She clasped her pudgy hands together. "If you no longer journalist, you become public relations—for me," she added almost fiercely. "Only for me. I wouldn't want you promoting other people as well."

"I had thought about going back to it," he said with seeming reluctance, "but I'm not sure about doing it for only one person. I was thinking more in terms of joining a big company, such as a chain of restaurants or hotels."

"Why can't you just work for me?" The whine had returned to her voice.

Roland cleared his throat and dropped his voice conspiratorially. "Because it would be very expensive."

"How expensive?"

"Well . . ." He seemed to be working something out in his head. "If I was taken on by a large public-relations company, I would of course be paid an annual salary, but if I was to do it privately, I'd charge on a daily basis, because of course there would be times, like when you were away on holiday, when you wouldn't need a PR."

"That is fair . . . and true," she agreed approvingly.

"So, on a daily basis . . . ?" He appeared to make rapid calculations, mouthing figures silently as he gazed up at the ceiling.

"Well? How much?" she demanded eagerly.

"A hundred pounds a day."

"A hundred—"

"Plus expenses."

Elfreida put her head coquettishly on one side, pretending she was thinking about it, although of course she'd made up her mind to have him do it the minute he'd started talking about PR.

"I think that quite okay," she said at last. "Do you mind cash? Selwyn always give me cash, for housekeeping, and so it would be easier that way."

Roland felt a hot flush of triumph rising up his neck, suffusing his face, leaving him sweating. "That's quite all right," he murmured smoothly, hoping she hadn't noticed.

"When can we start?"

He thought rapidly. "It's too late to do much about your ball last night," he said regretfully. "If that dreadful Jackie Daventry hadn't got me the sack because she's so jealous of me, I would have seen to it that you had a whole page of pictures . . ." His voice trailed off, suggesting all sorts of wonderful opportunities that had been lost.

"However," he continued briskly, "this gives us time to plan for the autumn and winter. The parties start again in October, so why don't I work out our campaign when I return from staying with the Earl and Countess of Atherton in Ireland?"

Elfreida looked shocked. "You stay with the Athertons?" she asked suspiciously. "Why you stay with them? How you know them?"

Roland smiled slyly. "They're very old family friends. My father and the previous Lord Atherton knew each other at school; Eton, you know," he lied coolly.

Alarm was etched on every plane of Elfreida's rosy face. "But you don't tell them what we are doing? This arrangement between us is secret?"

"Of course, Lady Witley. There's no question of it. I am the height of discretion." He smirked self-deprecatingly. "If I wasn't, I could give you the names of all the people who are well-known today and always in the newspapers, because, well . . . because I put many of them there. This job is as secret as the confessional."

"Very good." She looked relieved.

"When I get back from Ireland in mid-August, shall we meet? And shall we go through your diary for the next three months so that I can get everything organized?" He plucked a wild idea out of the air. "It would be nice to get *Vogue* to feature you, in a couture dress, in this wonderful house of yours." He looked around appreciatively.

"Oh, that would be marvelous," she breathed, already seeing the page in her mind's eye—herself in a Caroline Charles creation, sitting on one of the gilt French chairs, with the flower-filled room stretching away behind her. . . . Everyone would see it. She beamed at Roland. Their secret partnership was going to work very well, she thought.

The next morning Roland arrived early at the Athertons' in order to help Colin and Ian with their packing. Celia wanted them to continue their studies while on holiday, and she'd asked him to make sure they had all the right books with them.

"Of course," he replied breezily. Now, as he picked out what they needed, a plan began to form in his head. As soon as he returned to London, he would be receiving a weekly source of income from Elfreida Witley; more money than he'd ever earned before on a regular basis; enough money to do a little entertaining in restaurants, enabling him to invite the "right" people. With money would come the one thing he also craved—social power.

When he joined Celia for a midmorning cup of coffee while the boys collected their sports gear from where they'd left it scattered around the house, he broached the subject with what he thought was the right amount of subtlety.

"I'm thinking of giving a dinner party for my birthday in November," he began, knowing she had no means of finding out that his birthday was actually in February. "I'd be very pleased if you and Lord Atherton could attend. I'm planning to hold it at Claridge's, just an intimate dinner in one of their private dining rooms, for about a dozen people or so." He paused and looked up at the ceiling as if idly reflecting. "I'll probably invite Princess Isabella of Liechtenstein, Lord and Lady Tetbury, Crown Prince Gustaf of Luxembourg, maybe Lord and Lady Ravensbrook . . . They're friends of yours, actually, aren't they?"

Celia seemed to freeze and withdraw. "Goodness!" she exclaimed lightly. "You do know some grand people!"

Roland felt himself bristling, hot and angry. It was obvious she didn't believe a word he'd said.

"Not really," he replied coolly. "They're all friends of my family, and I've recently inherited some money from a great-aunt, so I thought it would be nice to give a little party." He looked directly at her, challenging her to call him a liar, which of course he knew she was far too well-bred to do.

Celia's fixed smile was polite as she stared back at him.

"I'll let you have the date as soon as I've fixed it," he continued. "I know Prince Ivan of Russia is longing to meet you too, and of course his cousin, the Queen. He's been living in America for so long he's lost all contact with his European relations." Roland paused and sipped his coffee. It was true that Prince Ivan had recently come to England from California and was in fact staying at Claridge's. It was also true that he was related to the British royal family, through the late czar, but it wasn't true that Roland knew him or had even met him. This wouldn't be the first time he'd introduced people to each other while not actually knowing either side, but he had never attempted it on such a dazzling scale before. However, his system always worked. He would telephone A and say he was giving a dinner party for B, whom he knew A wanted to meet. Then he'd call B and say the same thing. Usually both parties accepted and thanked him for effecting the introduction as well! And that wasn't where it ended either, he thought smugly. Time and time again his "dinner parties" were paid for by someone else, either because he had embarrassed them into it or because it was their "fee" for being introduced to A and B.

"Perhaps you could have a word with the Queen about Prince Ivan?" he suggested boldly. "The dinner party could be absolutely private and discreet; I mean, heaven forbid the newspapers should get wind of it! If you were to tell the Queen that it was a small, very exclusive dinner . . ." He paused, seeing Celia's increasingly cold expression.

"Mr. Shaw," she cut in formally, and her voice was icy, "I'm afraid it's quite out of the question for me to approach Her Majesty on such a matter, or any other member of the royal family. If Prince Ivan wishes to make contact, he must do so through his embassy."

Roland regarded her stonily, his eyes like polished marble through the lenses of his thick glasses. He sat there tight-lipped, hands clenched, unable to speak through his anger at the patronizing way she was talking to him.

Celia continued: "You must realize it puts me in a very embarrassing position if it were ever thought you were using me in order to meet the Queen. I think, under the circumstances, it would be better to keep our relationship a professional one. You are an excellent tutor and I'm delighted with the way you are handling the boys, but I think it's better to keep business and pleasure separate, don't you?" she added coolly.

Roland gave a sickly smile in an effort to hide his chagrin.

"There would be no harm in effecting a little introduction, though, would there?" he said with persistence. "In fact, why don't we make it *your* dinner party? Yours and Lord Atherton's? It wouldn't cost you anything, I'd look after that side of it, and you could invite the Queen and I could invite Prince Ivan, and between us we could select a small gathering of people who would be acceptable to both."

Celia's eyes sparkled dangerously. Part of her job was to be protective of the Queen and to make sure people like Roland Shaw didn't cause any embarrassment.

"It's out of the question, Mr. Shaw. Please try to understand—"

"But I've already spoken to Prince Ivan," he interjected. Of course he'd done nothing of the sort, but how was Celia to know that? he reflected, hoping this last threat would be his trump card. "He's not going to think it very nice if his cousin the Queen refuses to have anything to do with him, is he?"

Celia rose imperiously. If Roland hadn't been such a good tutor, and if they hadn't been about to go to Ireland, she'd have asked him to leave immediately. His cheek and pushiness were intolerable. She was struck by a sudden nasty thought: suppose Roland got on to the Queen's private secretary behind her back and told him Celia had suggested he approach the Queen about Prince Ivan?

"It is out of the question, Mr. Shaw," she repeated firmly.

Roland had risen too. This was the nearest he was ever likely to get to meeting the Queen, or any of her family, and something near to panic filled him as he saw his big chance slipping away.

"Could we perhaps work it another way, then?" he asked.

She paused in the doorway, looking back regally over her shoulder. "I refuse to discuss this any further."

Roland pranced forward. "But if I could meet the Queen on some occasion . . . if you could perhaps introduce us . . . maybe you could get me invited to Buckingham Palace for a garden party or something . . . then I could invite her myself?" A part of him knew he was almost gibbering in his desperation, but he couldn't stop. His desire to be a part of the aristocracy, to be accepted and treated as one of them, was so strong it was as if he were about to drown in a sea of middle-class mediocrity, and only Celia Atherton could throw him the lifeline that would help him to rise above it. That would make him *belong*, where he so craved to be. Through a red mist of longing that was as strong as sexual desire, he heard her speak again.

"Everyone wants to meet the Queen, so I understand how you feel, but I'm afraid it is impossible for me to arrange it. I'm in a position of great trust, you see," she continued, "so really, Mr. Shaw, if you are to remain as Colin and Ian's tutor, you must desist from pressuring me about this. I can arrange absolutely nothing for you when it comes to meeting anyone in the royal family." Then she was gone, her stubborn back disappearing up the stairs to her bedroom.

Roland was beside himself with wrath, so maddened and infuriated that he vowed then and there to have his revenge on Celia. Jackie Daventry had stood in the way of his going to all the best parties; now Celia Atherton was stopping him getting to know the best people. Fucking patronizing bitch! Well, fuck her and fuck her job as a lady-in-waiting. By the time he'd finished, she wasn't going to be able to *show* her face at Buckingham Palace. He'd find a way to discredit her; he'd see her social standing in ruins; he'd see her humiliated and disgraced. He hated people like Celia, with their hypocrisy, and he hated the way she was too snobbish to accept him as a friend, because he hadn't come from a similar background, and he hadn't been to Eton, and he'd had to have elocution lessons in order to speak with the "right" accent. As never before, he now hated the condescension of the upper classes, with their cliques and elitism. What made them think they were any better than he was? he asked himself as his rage bit deep and his bitterness increased.

As he paced to and fro across the rich tapestry carpet of the Atherton's drawing room, his towering passion reached its peak, then seemed to explode in his head before subsiding into icy, calculating calm. He wasn't sure how he'd get his revenge for the way Celia had snubbed him, but that didn't matter. If he couldn't find a way, he'd invent one. That method had worked before, and it would work again. He sat down to finish his cup of coffee, remembering the Beautiful Boy. He'd had to invent something in order to punish him for not accepting his advances.

The Beautiful Boy, the Honorable Anthony Markham, son and heir of the Earl of Eddington, had been one of his pupils. He was a fresh-skinned, blond-haired young man of seventeen, with gentle blue eyes and a sweet smile. One day Roland had inveigled him to come to his flat for tuition, planning all the while to seduce him, thinking how easy it was going to be. The youth, trusting and easygoing, had agreed, and as he sat in Roland's living room, head bent over his books, Roland had fantasized about what would happen when the lesson was over. The Beautiful Boy had thighs and wrists that drove him crazy, and the soft fair down on his cheek made Roland's longing to kiss him almost desperate.

At last the lessons came to an end, and all the pent-up desire that he'd been feeling for the past two hours made him act rashly, crudely, as he at first put his hand on Anthony's back, before letting it slide down to the small tight buttocks encased in tight blue jeans.

Anthony's eyes seemed to widen in complete astonishment as he turned to look at Roland, and at that moment Roland pulled the boy toward him, murmuring: "Oh, God, you're so beautiful. I want you desperately. Let's go to bed."

A moment later Roland found himself sprawled back in his only armchair, while the Beautiful Boy, his cheeks flaming, yelled angrily, "I'm not a bloody faggot!"

As Roland heard Anthony's feet thunder down the stairs of the building and the front door slam, a mixture of frustration and rage overcame him so that he burst into tears. He had wanted that boy more than he'd wanted anyone for years, and his erection was still hard and painful, denied relief except from his hot and sticky hand. As he brought himself to a miserable lonely climax, he planned how he would get even. By the time he'd finished, the Beautiful-bloody-cock-tease-Boy wouldn't be around to torture him anymore.

A swift call to a local police station, informing them he could identify the thief who had broken into a neighbor's flat the previous day and stolen some valuable snuffboxes, led to the Honorable Anthony Markham's arrest. From then on it was his word against Roland's, and the judge who heard the case believed Roland's version of what had happened. Guilty only of rejecting his tutor's advances, the boy was put on remand, to the mortification of his family, who went to great lengths to hush the whole thing up.

Roland rose now, calling calmly to Colin and Ian, asking if they'd collected all their sports things to take on holiday. From now on he'd keep his eyes and ears open, seeking the best way to wreak his revenge on Celia or even on one of her family.

7

The village of Kilfrush, picturesquely situated at the foot of the highest and wildest mountains in Southern Ireland, overlooked St. Finan's Bay and the Atlantic beyond. Isolated and insular, its twisting lanes and worn steps divided the closely built waterfront houses, and at dawn, before the sun rose to clear the mists, the cobblestones were slippery from the damp and salty air.

Below and beyond the village, to the right, a pretty beach led to the headland, where gannets and gulls nested on the steep cliff face and where, in summer, wildflowers grew in profusion. To the left there was a small harbor encircled by a high wall, protection against the sea, which at high tide could cause the water to rise by as much as twenty feet. For five thousand years the Irish have lived surrounded by the lush green beauty of the countryside, and the village of Kilfrush was like a perfect jewel set in a band of gems, and the outside world was as remote to the small community as the movements of the planets. They had no use for television, seldom listened to the radio, and only occasionally saw a newspaper. Life revolved around the only pub, Ryan's: a tot of Irish whiskey or a glass of Guinness, and a turf fire to sit by in winter. Dependent on the fruits of the sea and the land for sustenance, the people of Kilfrush minded their own business as they went about their daily tasks, contented with their lot.

They did not even show much interest in the elderly

couple who lived up at the "big house," which was
set apart from the village on a higher plateau of land,
but then, the Smythe-Mallins had lived for so long at
Kilfrush House, they were like a part of the landscape;
familiar as the heather-covered hills, commonplace as
the glens and moors. The only visitors were Oonagh,
a sweet young girl from the village, who cleaned
every morning, and the delivery boy from the local
general store, who took supplies to the Smythe-
Mallins every week. Otherwise they lived in splendid
and self-contained isolation, as if they did not need
other people.

The Mallin family had originally built the large gray
stone mansion in 1827, and set it in an Italian-style
terraced garden with its main rooms facing the sea.
They had been rich landowners and importers of merchandise brought by ship from Spain and put in to
port at the nearby Derrynane harbor, while the Spanish fishing fleets moored overnight at Valentia Island,
farther along the coast. The ties with Spain were
strong in this part of Ireland in the early days, and
the trading brisk. Declan Mallin, the head of the family, had made a fortune, but by the time his great-
great-grandson died in 1932, most of the money had
been squandered on high living, and only the house
remained. This, and the surrounding land, were the
only monument to a glorious past that Aileen Mallin
inherited from her father when she was twenty-three.
She took one look at the bare rooms and the exqui-
sitely melancholic view of the Atlantic from the long
windows and decided to shut the house up and go to
live in England, where her cousins lived. Kilfrush
House remained empty during the war, while Aileen
joined the Women's Army Corps and got married to
a Royal Air Force fighter pilot. When he was killed
in the Battle of Britain, she stuck out the remainder
of the war in England, but on her release from the
WAC she returned to Ireland, feeling like some poor
animal that had been mortally savaged. All she
wanted was to be left in peace so that she could come
to terms with the tragic loss of her husband. There

was also the enormous house to cope with. She was loath to sell the Mallin "family seat," but on the other hand, how was she going to do it up and furnish those depressing bare rooms, which echoed hollowly when she entered them? It was then she met Ernest Smythe. He was a widower who seemed both to be rich and to possess the most remarkable collection of works of art.

Living in a small hotel in Derrynane, with his possessions in storage, he pursued her with persuasive arguments about two lonely people being less lonely if they shared their lives. When he asked her to marry him, Aileen, tired after six years of war and all the pain it had caused her, accepted. What in fact resulted was more a marriage of a house and its new contents rather than the union of two human beings. It seemed that Kilfrush House had been designed and built to provide a fit setting for the collection Ernest brought with him, and as the heavy wooden crates and packing cases revealed a wealth of paintings, French furniture, marble statues, bronzes, porcelain, gilt, silver, and tapestries, the house seemed to come alive and glow with a warmth and happiness that were almost palpable. Ernest also paid to have new curtains made throughout, and even managed to trace a large stock of prewar brocade in shades of deep rose and gold and green that complemented the paneled rooms. Soon the rooms were like a series of jewel boxes leading off each other, a veritable cornucopia of treasures that were beyond normal domestic insurance policies.

That was when the Smythe-Mallins, for they had decided to link their names together as well as their respective properties, drew about themselves a cloak of tight privacy, so that few ever entered their house, and fewer knew what it contained. Remotely situated, and reached only by a winding lane that bypassed Bolus Head, the deserted peninsula west of Kilfrush, there was no passing traffic or tourists to disturb them or disrupt their lives.

When their only child, Celia, was born, she was educated at the tiny village school until she was seven, and then Aileen sent her regretfully away to boarding school in Dublin, because that was the only way she would get a good education. At twelve, Celia was then sent to England, to be based with her mother's cousins, the Mallins, while she attended Benenden, the exclusive public school which, two years later, Princess Anne was also to attend. Celia was quite happy with the arrangements, but for Aileen it was a heartbreaking wrench. Ernest had insisted, however, saying it would teach their daughter to be independent and stand on her own feet, and so from then on Celia was only to visit her family once or twice a year. Aileen cherished these visits, knowing she must not stand in her daughter's way, and in time of course the rewards had been evident. It was unlikely, if Celia had remained at Kilfrush, that she'd have met and married Hugo Atherton.

Now, as Aileen opened up the drawing room and dining room and library, because when she and Ernest were on their own they used only the study and a small adjoining morning room, she felt a rush of happiness at the thought of seeing her daughter again. Celia and Hugo would be arriving with Colin and Ian tomorrow, and staying for two whole weeks. It was something she had been looking forward to ever since they'd announced their visit, and long after they'd gone she would still be remembering each moment with an afterglow of pleasure. Already she had arranged for extra supplies to be delivered from Waterville, food she knew her grandsons would like but which the local store did not carry, and the larder was now stocked with enough to feed a small army. The cellar was always full, of course. Years ago Ernest had laid down some fine Bordeaux, and there was no shortage of Irish whiskey either. Oonagh would be bringing up freshly caught fish from her Uncle Ben, the local fisherman, and fresh vegetables were always plentiful, if limited in choice. They would do well, Aileen reflected happily. For a short while she would try to forget her problems and enjoy herself; she owed that to Celia. Her daughter must never know that things were less than perfect. Celia must be protected at all costs; especially now. Especially since she'd become the Queen's lady-in-waiting.

Going to one of the long French windows of the drawing room that overlooked the neglected terraced garden, Aileen looked out to sea. With misted eyes she searched for the band of silvery light that marked the horizon, looking to see if she could spot Great Skellig today. It was a massive offshore rock that rose seven hundred feet out of the water and boasted the ruins of St. Michael's Church and a monastery built a thousand years ago but uninhabited since the thirteenth century. On a good day she could still make out the shape of the tiny rugged island, but when the light was dim and the sky overcast, the view was hazy, like a Monet painting. She liked to think it was the mist that veiled Great Skellig, but in her heart she knew it was cataracts creeping stealthily across the pupils of her eyes, slowly blotting out all but the boldest objects. At seventy-nine, she supposed, things were bound to go wrong. Her joints hurt when it was damp, which it was for ten months of the year, and she slept badly too. Not like Ernest; at eighty-two he still seemed to have the good health of a man in his sixties and wouldn't hear of them going to live in Limerick or Cork and handing over Celia's inheritance to her now.

"This is my home and I'm staying here until I die," he declared when Aileen suggested they move to a place that would be easier to run.

"But suppose one of us is ill or has a fall?" Aileen reasoned. "Who will look after us? We'd be much safer in a nice flat in town, near all the shops and near a good doctor too."

But Ernest wouldn't listen. Stubbornly he refused to even discuss the matter. Ever since they'd married, Aileen had realized he was an obstinate man, but she'd never felt strong enough to stand up to him. Besides . . . She drew in her breath sharply, trying to banish from her mind the knowledge that had hung over her like a dark shadow for over forty years. That was why Ernest wouldn't leave Kilfrush, of course. Not until they carried him out in his coffin, and then it wouldn't matter; at least for him it wouldn't.

She turned slowly away from the windows. *Don't think about it,* she reflected, not realizing that in old age she sometimes spoke aloud, voicing in quite clear tones what was on her mind, and then she went upstairs to make sure Oonagh had made up the beds. The family were bringing a holiday tutor with them and Aileen had put him in the small blue room that looked inland to the distant mountains. *Forget what you found out all those years ago.* She patted the white Irish linen coverlet and checked on the number of towels Oonagh had put out. But the thought kept coming, she couldn't forget; it was impossible. Something like that couldn't be swept under the carpet, it stayed with you, eating a great black hole in your mind for the rest of your life. Why did she suddenly feel particular unease today? she asked herself. It was entirely unreasonable, with Celia and Hugo and the boys coming to stay. What could go wrong? *It need never come out.* . . . Although she knew that was true, her Celtic blood ran cold with premonition. So much so that as she went downstairs again to make herself and Ernest a cup of tea, she almost wished her daughter's visit was already safely over.

"Dad, can we go fishing this morning?" Colin asked as they all sat around the kitchen table having breakfast. It was all hustle and bustle at Kilfrush now they'd arrived, the old house echoing to the sound of voices and laughter, the aroma of nourishing Irish stews permeating into the hall and the chink of whiskey glasses coming from the study. It was the second day of the holidays and at last they'd all recovered from the exhausting journey, flying by Ryan Air from Luton airport in Hertfordshire, to Farranfore, near Tralee, before hiring a car for the long winding drive that took them through Killorglin, Glenbeigh, Cahersiveen, Portmagee on the edge of the sea, Ballynahow, overlooking Puffin Island, and finally to Killonecaha and Kilfrush. It was a beautiful route, especially at this time of year, but they were always glad when it was over and they arrived at Kilfrush House, because then it meant the holidays had really started.

Celia, in blue jeans and a white Arran sweater, able to forget for a while the refinements of life at Buckingham Palace, stood by the Aga cooker, wielding a large wooden spoon as she stirred the porridge. She'd already given Aileen breakfast in bed, because her mother had seemed so tired since they'd arrived, and then she'd asked Oonagh to get on with the cleaning while she made breakfast.

"Yes, let's go fishing. Perhaps we can hire a boat from old Sean," Ian suggested, "that is, if he's still alive," he added cheerfully.

"Really, Ian," Hugo laughed. "Sean isn't that old."

"He's *ancient,* Dad," Colin replied. "He must be at least sixty!"

"So, what does that make me?" Ernest inquired dryly from his place at the head of the scrubbed table. He was a tall thin man with a long angular face and deep-set eyes. Even in casual country clothes, such as he wore now, his whole demeanor was elegant, the cavalry-twill trousers pressed to a razor-sharp crease line, the blue shirt and brown sweater immaculate. His brown lace-up shoes were polished so that they almost twinkled, and his white hair was brushed smooth and thick. He had been forty when Celia had been born, and although he had not basically changed, she could still just remember him as having thick fair hair and dazzling blue eyes. She also remembered sitting on his knee while he told her fairy stories that scared her to death.

Colin giggled, undaunted by his austere-looking grandfather. "You're as old as God," he quipped.

"Don't be cheeky," said Celia. She turned to her husband. "Hugo, why don't you take the boys and Roland down to the village after breakfast and see if you can hire a boat?"

"Good idea," he agreed. "Is that porridge ready? I'm starving."

She spooned a generous helping into a bowl and set it down before him. "Roland, do you like fishing? It's deep-sea fishing around here, although we'll be going upstream to fish for salmon at some point before the season ends."

Roland took off his glasses and polished them rapidly. In casual trousers and T-shirt, he looked quite different, she thought, from when he was dressed in a formal suit or evening dress. "Undistinguished" was the word that sprang to mind. One would not have guessed at the high level of education and culture he'd achieved, or that he had a degree from Oxford.

"I don't actually fish myself, but I'd be interested to watch," he said with forced enthusiasm.

"You don't have to," Ian said bluntly. "Dad usually takes us fishing."

In case Roland took it the wrong way, Celia cut in. "When you're not actually taking the boys for study sessions, you must do as you like. There are some lovely drives around here, and if the weather's calm, you can take a boat over to Great Skellig."

"There's the remains of a monastery there," said Colin, longing to show off his knowledge. "You have to climb six hundred and twenty steps to reach the ruins . . . and the steps are so worn and crumbly that one slip and you'd fall into the sea and be killed. It's a drop of a hundred and twenty feet," he concluded dramatically.

"And a very spooky place it is, too," Hugo remarked, sprinkling brown sugar on his porridge.

Roland raised pale eyebrows. "It does sound interesting. I might go and have a look at it one day. Meanwhile, I'm very happy just pottering about the house, you know." He turned to Ernest Smythe-Mallin with an ingratiating smile. "You have such beautiful things, it's a pleasure just to look at them."

Ernest knit his brows fiercely together and didn't reply at first. When he spoke his voice was sharp.

"This isn't a museum, you know."

Celia looked embarrassed. There were times when her father could be irascible and offend people.

"Daddy, I'm sure . . ."

"What's wrong, Grandpa?" Colin asked.

"He's not one of the Great Train Robbers!" Ian exclaimed, thinking he was being very witty. "He's not going to run off with all the silver spoons!"

"Don't be silly, Ian," Celia snapped, seeing Roland's expression of growing displeasure and guessing he sorely lacked a sense of humor.

Ernest's frown deepened. "This is a private house. I don't like people poking around."

"It's all right, Daddy. Roland's just interested in antiques," Celia said to soothe her father, although she didn't know whether it was true or not. She glanced quickly at Roland, hoping he'd say something to lighten the sudden atmosphere that had been cast over the breakfast table, but he was toying with a bit of toast and she couldn't gauge what he was thinking.

When breakfast was over and they were on their own in the kitchen, Ernest turned to Celia with irritation.

"I don't know why you brought that young man here," he complained testily. "What do you know about him?" A faint accent and the way he sometimes phrased a sentence were the only trace left of his Austrian antecedents.

"We've got excellent references," Celia assured him. "I spoke to several people who had recommended him, including Professor Arthur Rouse, who I've since discovered is a very famous nuclear scientist, and he said Roland was wonderful with his son."

"Humph! What does some professor know? They all live in another world; I've never known a learned professor yet who wasn't as vague as hell. I tell you, Celia, there's something about Roland Shaw I don't like."

"Oh, Daddy, I'm sure you're wrong. You're just afraid someone is going to pinch your valuables," she laughed. Having been brought up surrounded by great works of art, she took them for granted; like the marble statues in the hall, by Todolini and Fabi-Altini; the bewitchinig dark pond of lilies which was one of a series by Monet; the Louis XV marquetry commodes and writing table; and the bronze horses, virile-looking and rampant, by Fremit, Barye, and Bonheur. She was unable to think of them in terms of monetary value. They were as much a part of her childhood and her life as Kilfrush House and her parents.

Ernest remained silent and obstinate-looking. "I still wish you hadn't brought him."

Later that day, as Celia sat on the terrace with Aileen, looking out to sea at the Great Skellig, her mother echoed Ernest's misgivings.

"It would have been better if you'd come on your own, like you usually do, darling. How do you know you can trust this man?"

Celia turned to Aileen in surprise. "Really, Mother, what do you mean? He comes through Robertson and Short, who used to provide tutors for Hugo, and he's got excellent references. He's a bit pushy, socially I mean, but so are a lot of people. The minute they know I'm a lady-in-waiting, I get all sorts of people wanting introductions or to be invited to a garden party."

Aileen nodded, understanding. Even she never asked Celia about the private life of the Queen, or what went on behind the golden gates of Buckingham Palace.

"Well," she conceded, although she still looked doubtful, "I'm sure you know what you're doing, darling, but keep Roland out of your father's way as much as you can. Daddy really hasn't taken to him."

"Oh, dear," Celia sighed. These two weeks were supposed to be a rest and an opportunity to relax, but now it looked as if she was going to have to spend most of her time keeping the peace. "I'll do my best, Mother, but I do assure you Roland is a perfectly harmless young man, in spite of his social-climbing aspirations."

"Very well, dear." Aileen rose. "I'm going to make

us a cup of tea while the boys are out and we have a bit of peace."

"Shall I do it?" Celia looked at her mother. She seemed so much frailer than she had the previous summer, and her eyes had a cloudy look.

"No, you sit in the sun. I'll do it." Aileen hurried off to the kitchen, happy to be able to do something, however small, for her beloved daughter.

Nothing must be allowed to affect Celia's life now. Aileen put on the kettle, murmuring to herself. *If I had known forty-five years ago . . . if I'd realized . . . Oh, my God, if I'd realized that Ernest . . .* She got out the teapot, the pretty white one with the pink roses, and put it on a small tray with two cups and saucers and a small milk jug. *The sins of the fathers . . . Oh, dear God, dear God, the sins. How can he have lived with himself all these years?*

Out on the terrace, overlooking the sea that sparkled like variegated sapphires in the afternoon sun, Celia sat peacefully, thinking Kilfrush to be paradise on earth.

Professor Arthur Rouse always slept badly. He felt fortunate if oblivion stole over him for three consecutive hours. Sometimes he lay awake until four or five in the morning, his overactive brain continuing its endless seeking for answers to the problems his work created; at other times he fell almost immediately into a deep slumber, only to awaken two hours later as if some inner alarm had been triggered.

Tonight he suddenly found himself alert, heart pounding, mind seething, at two o'clock in the morning. He'd gone to bed at midnight, and rolling over in his narrow monastic single bed, he groaned aloud. He was so tired, and yet he couldn't sleep. What the hell had caused him to wake up now, jangled and feverish?

For a little while he lay there in the darkness, thinking about his late wife, whom he still missed; thinking about Tom, away at a boarding school that specialized in backward children. He missed Tom too.

By three o'clock the professor had decided sleep would elude him altogether; better to get up and make himself a warm drink, and perhaps take another look at those blueprints. The warhead was soon to go into production, but there were final adjustments he wanted to make. Now, he decided, would be as good a time as any to do some work. He certainly felt alert enough, he reflected wryly.

Going to the kitchen, he made himself a cup of Horlicks, sniffing appreciatively at the comforting aroma as he did so, and then he went to the study. It was a cozy room, book-lined and with a partner's desk set in front of the long windows that overlooked the garden. Drawing the dark green velvet curtains, he turned on the lights and went to open the safe. Earlier in the year, he remembered, he'd worked during the early hours on many occassions, with very useful results. In recent months, though, he'd tried to resist the temptation. One could get too close to a subject to be able to see the forest for the trees.

Opening the safe, he reached for the familiar blue folder in which he kept the designs. His hand touched other papers, documents of a personal nature, his passport . . . insurance policies . . . share certificates . . . but no blue folder. Little darts of fear prickled through his veins. He always kept the blueprints on the top shelf. Perhaps he'd put them at the bottom of the safe? It must be three months at least since he'd taken them out, and so he couldn't be sure . . . but why hadn't he put them in the usual place? Panic took hold of him now as he rummaged around, pulling out the contents.

Gold cufflinks fell onto the floor with a copy of his will; tax papers and a valuable George III cream jug quickly followed. Soon there was a pile of papers and trinkets at his slippered feet, but still no folder containing his blueprints.

Professor Rouse sat down rather suddenly, his face gray, his eyes pools of anxiety. If those secret plans for a deadly missile had been stolen, he would feel responsible for whatever the terrible consequences might be. Suppose some foreign power were to get hold of them? Wildly he looked around the study, as if hoping to see them lying on a table or stuck into a bookshelf. His heart was almost choking him now, pounding sickeningly in his chest, and his hands were clammy with horror. This was catastrophic. The blueprints must be somewhere. The house hadn't been burgled and he'd been visited by no strangers. Desperation at the consequences of their not being found forced him to struggle to his feet on shaking legs. Then he started to search the entire room. Books were pulled out of shelves, drawers were tipped out onto the floor, their contents scattered. In a growing frenzy, tinged with despair, he ransacked the study, turning over everything, again and again.

"Dear God, what has happened to them?" he kept repeating, his voice catching in a dry sob. Bathed in sweat and exhausted, he stood to survey the scene of devestation he had wrought. It looked as if an army of burglars had torn the place apart, tossing books and papers around in some sort of demonic frenzy.

It was five o'clock in the morning, and the first melancholy gray light of dawn showed through the gap in the curtains, where the professor had not quite pulled them together. Slumped at his desk, his head in his hands, he had spent the last hour wrestling with his conscience. He had two alternatives. One was to say nothing to the director of operations at the experimental station, who didn't know the professor had made an extra set of blueprints to keep at home; in fact, it wouldn't enter his head because it was strictly forbidden. The second option was to make a clean breast of the whole thing. Admit the loss of the secret designs and face the consequences. It was such a serious breach of security that MI5 would be brought in, of course, and there would be endless inquiries, questions would be asked, his own integrity put in doubt.

The professor looked around his study and wondered what his housekeeper would say when she saw the mess, and then he thought: What a ridiculous thing to worry about at a moment like this. Someone had stolen his plans, which might already have been sold to one of the Middle East countries.

Or maybe they'd been taken by someone who would make financial demands for their return. Whatever had happened, he knew he had no choice but to tell the director of operations. The burden of knowing he would be held personally responsible for the possible consequences was more than he could stand.

At nine o'clock that morning, Professor Rouse went to his superior to tell him what had happened.

Bill Glass's normally cheerful face looked woebegone and his silvery mustache drooped. Nothing like this had ever happened to him before, and he felt quite shaken. Over the years he'd built up a good relationship with the elite section of society whose activities he photographed, and they trusted him and they respected his work; most important of all, they liked him and treated him like a friend. And now this! He looked at Jackie as if hoping she could offer a solution to his predicament.

"My God, Bill, this is getting very nasty," she exclaimed.

Bill nodded. "I only told about half a dozen people to beware of Roland Shaw and not to have him to their parties if he said he was on *Society*, and what happens? The bugger takes out a writ to sue me for slander! I should have listened when you told me to be careful what I said."

They were in her office and she was going through the contacts of the photographs he'd taken at the Witley party, marking the ones she wanted to reproduce in her diary.

"What are you going to do, Bill?"

Bill spread his hands expressively. "What can I do? I got onto a lawyer and he said that if Roland Shaw could produce some evidence, then technically I *am* guilty of slander."

Jackie thumped her small clenched fist on the desk. "Oh, this is so unfair and I'm so sorry you've got involved. You were only warning people for their own good, not to let this man gate-crash their parties."

"I know, and all that's happened is I've landed myself in trouble."

"What sort of evidence has Roland Shaw been asked to produce?"

"A list of people that I'm supposed to have warned, together with places and dates; people, I was told, who would be willing to go to court and give evidence."

Jackie looked at Bill anxiously. "Can you remember whom you spoke to?"

"I think so," Bill replied, although he looked doubtful. "But you know how it is—you're at a party and something comes up in the conversation, and you tell someone something, and then you can't be sure whom you've told."

"Someone you've talked to about Roland Shaw must be a friend of his. Otherwise, how did it get back to him?"

"Unless it was someone who refused him admission to a party, saying I'd warned them not to let him in."

"Oh, God, Bill, what a mess!" She got up from her desk and went over to the coffee machine in the corner, her movements restless, her eyes troubled. "We've got to get him, you know. We can't take this lying down, hoping it will go away. Coffee, Bill?"

"Thanks. Have you seen him at anything during the past week?"

Jackie returned to her desk with two mugs, which she put down carefully. "I haven't seen him since the Witleys' party, when I accused him of being called Raphael." Suddenly she chuckled. "If it wasn't so serious, it would all be quite funny, wouldn't it?"

"I'll see the funny side when I'm assured I'm not going to be taken to court and that this business is not going to cost me a packet." Bill sipped his coffee thoughtfully, his usual bonhomie vanished.

"I am sorry, Bill. If there's anything I can do, you'll let me know, won't you?"

"Yes, I will." The ghost of a smile shimmered

across his face. "I might need a character reference from you!"

"You'll get it, Bill," she replied, smiling.

They talked for a few minutes longer as they went through the list of forthcoming events. Bill was off to the Isle of Wight to cover the Cowes Regatta and all the balls and parties that took place during the week.

"Here are your invitations and entry tickets," said Jackie. She placed them one by one on the desk in front of him. "There's the Royal Yacht Club Ball at the Squadron, the Royal London Ball, the Bembridge Ball, a reception on board the royal yacht *Britannia,* and several parties every night. I'll be coming down on the Monday for the one at the Squadron, but I'm leaving on Thursday to fly to Paris for a race meeting."

Bill picked up all the tickets and press passes and put them in his briefcase. "I enjoy Cowes week," he admitted, looking more cheerful. "If the weather's good, it'll be great."

"Then we'll be working together again at the Oban Ball and Highland Gathering, won't we, before going on to the Braemer Games," Jackie continued, consulting her diary. "You'll get some good shots of the royal family at that. Then I'm going to the opening of the Edinburgh Festival before I fly south again." As she spoke, she picked up a photograph of the Queen, taken at the opening of a new hospital.

"Oh, why does she look so dowdy, Bill?" she exclaimed. "Just look at this picture of her! I can never understand why she hasn't changed her hairstyle in sixty years! Or why she never paints her nails, or wears high heels? She's got the best designers in the world for her clothes and hats, and yet she still goes out looking like a provincial housewife who hasn't got a clue about elegance or smartness."

Bill seemed to bristle. His loyalty to the royal family was equaled only by his loyalty to his own wife and children. "You're an American, Jackie," he said as mildly as he could. "You don't understand the Queen *is* the Queen, and above all the fripperies of glamour and high fashion. It wouldn't do."

"Why not?" Jackie demanded, although her eyes twinkled. She could always get a rise out of Bill by criticizing any member of the royal family, and it amused her to see him coming to their defense. "Think how wonderful she'd look if she had a face lift. And her hair tinted and restyled. And her face done by an expert makeup artist."

If she'd suggested the Queen should get in a rocket and go to Mars, he couldn't have looked more shocked.

"That would be dreadful!" he protested. "She's the monarch, the sovereign, head of the Church of England . . . not some film star from Hollywood!"

Jackie burst out laughing. "I'm only teasing, Bill, but I'll tell you one thing. I'm prompted to write an article about the Queen and her image."

Bill looked cagey and suspicious. "What do you mean?"

"How do you suppose she feels," she continued thoughtfully, "surrounded by other women, all of whom are upstaging her?"

"Who?" he demanded.

Jackie started counting on her fingers. "First, her daughter-in-law, Princess Diana, the most beautiful young woman in the world; elegant, charming, an inspiration to all other young women. Second, her mother, Queen Elizabeth the Queen Mother, charismatic at ninety, still pretty, stylish, amusing, and adored by the nation." She was watching Bill's expression of growing concern as she talked. "Third," she continued, "her Prime Minisiter, Mrs. Thatcher. And look at the difference. The Prime Minister is vibrantly alive and alert-looking, sharply dressed, and looking ten years younger than she is, while the Queen looks plain old-fashioned and dull in every way."

"But the Queen's a much nicer woman," Bill protested.

"Who says?" Jackie asked. "I've heard the Queen has a terrible temper and doesn't suffer fools gladly."

"Neither does Mrs. Thatcher," Bill argued. "I've photographed people who have served in Cabinet with her, and if someone hasn't done his job properly, she bites his head off."

Jackie's mouth twitched. "While the Queen gets her corgis to do it for her, you mean?"

Bill grinned reluctantly. "I hope you don't write an article on those lines, Jackie."

She grimaced. "Chance would be a fine thing. Can you see Bertram allowing it? He's as much in awe of the royals as you are." She sighed gustily. "No, I suppose I'll have to wait until I leave *Society* to write the type of features I want to write, which I reckon, being an American, I can do with impunity."

"In olden times you would have been clapped in the Tower of London for expressing such treasonable thoughts." But he smiled at her, his good humor restored. "And that would have served you right!"

In the small blue bedroom at Kilfrush House, Roland sat writing in his diary, making meticulous notes in his tiny black handwriting about everyone and everything he came into contact with. He'd been doing this for years, at first because he wanted to be able to look back on all the places he'd been and all the people he'd met. Then, as the years passed, he discovered this "diary," composed of little memoranda as much as a list of social engagements, became increasingly useful as he infiltrated the upper classes. For one thing, it meant he could talk with certain knowledge on various topics: theater, "in" restaurants, art galleries, stately homes, the latest fads and fashions, the old families of Great Britain. It was a way of learning to *talk the same language*, something that divided the various classes more than anything, and something that he felt had made his inferior background very apparent when he'd gone to Oxford. It was a fine dividing line, though, as he'd quickly discovered, but it became a gaping chasm when he wanted to form friendships with people who had been to schools like Eton or Harrow. A chasm that became apparent when he talked about "dinner" instead of "lunch," confessed he liked Cliff Richard, used the wrong knife and fork, and said things like "cheerio" and "posh."

Nowadays, apart from having improved his accent, he could hold his own with anyone, and in fact he'd become more cultured and knowledgeable than many of his aristocratic contemporaries.

Today he was making a list of some of the more recognizable treasures displayed at Kilfrush House. This was from general interest, but also because he was sure there was more than met the eye about the works of art that filled the main rooms so that they resembled a museum. When he returned to London, he decided he'd do some research because, for example, what was the provenance of the *Still Life with Flowers* by Dutch artist Ernst Stuven? Or the incredible *Portrait of a Girl in a Hat* by Renoir? Then there were the Utrillo, depicting the Sacré-Coeur de Montmartre, Boldini's painting of a park scene at Versailles, and a small but exquisite Corot of a harbor at La Rochelle. Carefully Roland listed them, together with some of the most notable pieces of furniture, Sèvres china, and a collection of carved jade that ranged from smoky lavender to sparkling apple green. The contents of Kilfrush House had to be worth millions. The question was, where had it all come from? And why did Ernest and Aileen live in such seclusion, hiding themselves and their treasures away from the world and living the meager lives of paupers?

Roland looked out the window across St. Finan's Bay, to Great Skellig, which stood crystal clear on this fine morning, so near it seemed one would be able to reach it by boat in a few minutes instead of an hour. The more he thought about it, the more he became certain that here, within this Aladdin's cave of treasures, he could find the source of Celia's downfall. He *must* find something, he thought bitterly, the bile of rejection tasting sour, the humilation of not being considered as good as "them" distorting his senses until at times he felt he would go mad. Every family, however noble, had its skeletons hidden away, whether an illegitimate birth, a tax fiddle, a prison record, or a case of unrecorded insanity.

He flung open the sash-cord window and leaned out, breathing in the tangy air of the Atlantic, filling his lungs until he felt quite dizzy. Then he took off his glasses and polished them on the tail of his shirt. Celia deserved to be ruined for the way she'd talked to him, he reflected darkly, not stopping to consider that there might not be anything in Celia's background to be ashamed of. She deserved to be humiliated as she'd humiliated him, and he hoped with all his heart he could bring about her downfall.

He took a final deep breath before closing the window, thinking how sweet would be his revenge on the snobbish Celia. How delightful to see her punished for treating him so churlishly. After all, he was as good as any of them.

Jackie was dining with Gerald that night, having returned from the Isle of Wight that morning, where she'd attended several balls and dances as part of the Regatta week of festivities. Tomorrow she was flying to Paris for the races, but tonight she was free of engagements for the first time since he'd told her about Candy, and so they'd arranged to have dinner in the private upstairs room of the English House in Chelsea. Furnished on the lines of an opulent private drawing room, it was usually hired out for stag and dinner parties, but tonight there would just be the two of them.

"This way we can relax and no one can disturb us," Gerald explained on the phone that morning.

"I think it's a beautiful idea," Jackie agreed. Very romantic and clandestine too, she reflected. There was no doubt in her mind now that their attraction was mutual, and that once he'd got his divorce, they would be able to go about publicly together, but in the meanwhile there was something very exciting about meeting in secret.

"I'll come by to collect you at eight o'clock," he said.

"I'll be ready," she promised.

Now, as she slipped into a summery dress of hyacinth blue that matched her eyes exactly, she felt a frisson of anticipation. Much as she had yearned for Gerald, and had longed for the feel of his hands and his body close to hers, she suddenly felt nervous and strangely inexperienced.

Jackie had been to bed with a couple of boyfriends in her youth, before she'd married Richard, and she considered herself to be fairly experienced, but for some unaccountable reason, this date with Gerald was making her feel as shy as a girl in high school. The last time she'd felt like this, she'd been seventeen, living in Boston, and getting ready to go to a dance with a guy called Tom.

Feverishly she brushed her hair so that it hung long and loose, and then she applied a little light makeup. At eight o'clock the front doorbell rang, and as soon as she opened it, her heart gave a little upward flip. "Powerful" was the first word that sprang to mind when she saw Gerald standing there. Strong and powerful, as if nothing would faze him; as if he could carry the world on his broad shoulders and take everything that was presented to him in his stride.

"Hi!" she greeted him, her legs suddenly weak.

He looked happy and relaxed tonight, his smile eager and his dark eyes shining. "Are you ready?"

She picked up her purse from the hall table. "I'm ready."

"Let's go, then." With his hand under her elbow, they walked to the elevator in silence, and as she had realized before, she was conscious that small talk wasn't necessary between them. It was as if everything had already been said and they could enjoy the companionable silence of complete understanding.

In the intimacy of his car, which smelled of leather and cologne, he turned and smiled at her.

"I've been looking forward to this evening so much, Jackie."

"So have I," she admitted, looking into his eyes. Their gaze held for a long moment and she felt her cheeks growing hot under his scrutiny. Then the lights changed and they drove on, his proximity making her feel claustrophobic as the car whizzed down Sloane Street. The companionable silence had suddenly become replaced by crackling tension.

"Have you been busy?" she asked in desperation. The hot flush had spread from her cheeks to all over her, and reaching out, she pressed the down button on the car window.

"Frantic, but there's nothing new in that. And you?"

Glad to have something to say, she told him about Roland Shaw issuing a writ for slander against Bill Glass.

Gerald listened intently, turning to glance at her from time to time as he drove along the King's Road.

"Is there anything I can do to help?" he asked at last. "I mean, my company have a first-class legal firm who represent us, which, thank God, isn't often, but I can put you onto them if you like?"

"I might take you up on that," Jackie replied.

When they arrived at the English House, they were shown up to the private room, where gleaming paneled walls, fine paintings, antique furniture, and brocade chairs and sofas were arranged as in a private house. Vases containing exquisite flowers stood on the side tables, and the room was softly lit by candles. A Sheraton table set for two stood at the far end, its centerpiece a pyramid of fruit arranged in a crystal bowl.

"Dinner will be served in fifteen minutes, madame, monsieur," the manager told them smilingly. He indicated a table of drinks by the window. "Meanwhile, everything you might require is there." Then he withdrew, leaving them alone.

Looking around, Jackie realized Gerald had gone to a lot of trouble to arrange the evening. Decanters of liquor and a bottle of champagne stood ready, and there were several platters of canapés, including her favorite quails' eggs, arranged on the coffee table. As if he knew what she was thinking, he said:

"I hope you like the dinner I've ordered. I had to take a chance, but I have a feeling we probably like the same things."

"You're doing very well so far," Jackie responded, suddenly feeling immensely happy. She looked at the plates of hors d'oeuvres. "You must have guessed I was hungry too!"

Suddenly he caught her hand and held it tight. "I hope this is the first of many evenings we will have together."

Jackie looked earnestly into his eyes, and her own were clear and candid. "I hope so too," she replied softly.

Then he leaned forward and kissed her very tenderly on the lips. It was an undemanding, considered kiss; more a gesture of promise than of desire; more a token of commitment than an expression of passion. Jackie, as she kissed him back, wanted to prolong the moment and savor it, knowing it would never happen in quite this way again. Once their mutual feelings were released, there would be no turning back. Once they gave way and surrendered to their desire, nothing would ever be quite the same. This was the lull, the calm, the stillness before the storm broke, the moment when they committed themselves to each other in silent dedication, and as she felt his lips pressed gently to hers, she realized how much she loved this man.

When they drew apart, Gerald poured champagne into two fluted glasses.

"Here's to us," he murmured, raising his glass.

Jackie held his gaze. "Here's to us," she repeated.

When they had toasted each other, he took her by the arm and led her to the sofa, drawing her down beside him.

"I'm thankful you know everything now," he said, his voice low and husky.

"I wish I'd known from the beginning. I was so sure you were a philandering husband." Jackie smiled ruefully. "I suppose I was branding all men together with Richard."

"It's easy to mistrust, especially when you've been

hurt. I don't blame you. In your place I'd have jumped to exactly the same conclusion."

At that moment a waiter slid unobtrusively into the room, carrying a tray through to the adjoining dining room.

"Come on, let's eat. I only had time for a cheese sandwich at my desk for lunch," he remarked, grabbing her hand, pulling her laughingly to her feet, and leading her to the dining table. For the time being the spell was broken, fragmented into a lighter vein with sparkling facets of conversation as they sat down to a dish of smoked quail, the tiny birds arranged on a silver platter, surrounded by wedges of lemon and thin brown bread and butter.

Jackie sipped her wine, tinglingly aware of Gerald as he sat opposite her, and of his ready smile and easy conversation. The next day, she had no idea what they talked about, except that the time had flowed effortlessly by as they exchanged views and experiences and opinions, seeming to agree on everything.

A dish of lobster tails served with a mango hollandaise sauce was brought in next by the young waiter, who seemed to glide on silent feet as he set finger bowls before them, filled with warm water and a scattering of white jasmine petals floating on the surface like snowflakes on a dark pool.

As they talked, telling each other about their youths, it was as if they were cocooned in a candlelit oasis, far away from the mundane world. This is a magic night, Jackie thought as she listened to his description of his childhood.

"But you were obviously born with the proverbial silver spoon in your mouth," Gerald remarked in a teasing voice.

Jackie traced the circle of petals in the water with her forefinger, pushing them below the surface and watching them rise again. "Kip and I were very lucky," she admitted. "Because of Daddy being a diplomat, we always lived in grand houses with lots of staff, and of course when he became an ambassador it was red carpets all the way! As I said to Kip the other day, we'll never have it so good again.''

"You may, you know," Gerald said, suddenly serious, and Jackie could guess what he was thinking. He was an exceedingly rich man, and if she were to become involved with him, she too could enjoy the benefit of his self-made wealth.

"I'm not sure I'd want to be really rich," she replied, serious too now. "There's wealth and wealth, of course; it's all relative, but I do believe the trappings of great wealth can be a burden. Imagine having to look after half a dozen mansions and palaces all over the world, like the Sultan of Brunei. One would spend one's time flying from one property to another, making sure the staff in each place were doing their job properly. Think how unsettling and exhausting that would be."

"I wasn't talking mega-bucks," Gerald replied, his eyes twinkling. "Just big bucks!"

Jackie grinned back at him. "Oh, I see. Just a small private jet and a medium-size yacht."

"That sort of thing," he agreed easily. "And a house in London and an apartment in New York, and maybe villas in Greece and France . . . nothing too grand, you know."

She knew he was teasing her and she suspected he didn't like a glitzy life-style any more than she did. "Is that all?" she asked flippantly. "My goodness, and I thought you were a man with big ideas!"

Gerald's eyes bore into hers. "They can be as big as you want them to be. Where I come from, an indoor lavatory was considered a luxury, and the only running water in our house was through the roof when it rained."

She knew that in spite of the lightness in his voice, what he said was true. He had an appreciation, she'd realized for the good things in life, because he'd been deprived of them as a child. "Were you really that poor?" she asked softly.

He nodded. "Church mice were in the upper income bracket compared to us. Looking back, I don't know how my mother coped with the five of us. She was a seamstress, you know, in a factory. When more money was needed, she made clothes for the neighbors—those that were better off than us, that is. She'd sit sewing all night sometimes, and then be making breakfast for us the next morning, seeing us off to school and my father off to the quarry where he worked." He smiled cheerfully in spite of a lingering look of sadness in his eyes. "The clothes business is in my blood, you see, through my mother."

"Are they still alive?"

"My mother is. I bought her a house in Yorkshire, where she spent her childhood. She's amazingly fit for her age. My father died some years ago." There was rough pain in his voice.

"He would have been very proud of you." She thought about the entry in *Who's Who:* chief executive and managing director of the Goray Group, a member of the CBI Marketing and Consumer Affairs Committee, a member of the Institute of Directors and the Monopolies Commission, and a leading figure on the Clothing Export Council. If his background had been as poor as he'd said, then that made his achievements all the more remarkable.

"Do you see much of your brothers and sisters?"

"No, not much. I want to help out, keep in touch, you know, but we've grown apart over the years." He turned his glass of wine by the stem, twirling it slowly to and fro. "They're proud, especially my brother, and they think I've grown too big for my boots, as we say up north. They're not comfortable with me anymore, which is a pity." He shook his head. "I can't force them to be friendly if they don't want to be, but I hope they realize I'm here if I'm needed."

A wave of admiration and compassion swept through Jackie as she looked at him, sitting so elegantly in his handmade Savile Row suit and silk tie, as if he'd been born to a life of riches. The dinner he had ordered, and the wines, were in perfect taste too.

"You've come a long way," she said with sincerity.

"And I've loved every minute of it," he replied

promptly. "For one thing, I'd never have met you if I'd stayed up in Oldbury."

The mood had changed back to one of gaiety. Jackie glanced at the menu, handwritten in italic lettering, and saw the next course was "A Symphony of Sorbets, Splashed with French Champagne."

Gerald leaned across the table and took her hand again. "Are we going to make it?" he asked in a voice so low she had to strain forward to catch what he said.

"I hope so . . . I think so," she replied slowly.

"So do I, darling."

It was the first time he had called her that, and the way he said it made it sound as if he really meant it, that it was a special endearment.

"Can we spend the night together?" He asked the question directly, and his eyes were even more direct.

From the moment she'd accepted to go out to dinner with him, she'd known how the evening would end, and her earlier nervousness vanished. She had no doubts now, no fears, not even the faintest flicker of reluctance.

"Yes."

He reached across and gripped her hand, and the urgency and longing showed in his eyes now.

"Oh, yes," she repeated.

Jackie hardly remembered leaving the restaurant, or getting into Gerald's car, or the drive back to her place. In a daze, she seemed to float, feeling that this was the most wonderful night of her life; a night she would always remember, no matter what happened in future.

When they arrived at her apartment, where she'd left on all the lights so the rooms were bathed in a peachy glow, she opened the French windows, letting in the sultry night air. It was so warm and still, the trees in the park below stood motionless, as if becalmed, outlined under a dusky sky that reflected a million city lights, and far away the roar of traffic was dulled to the gentle rumble of distant surf.

Jackie indicated a tray of drinks. "What would you like?" she asked. "Whiskey and soda? Brandy?"

He came up behind her and slid his arms around her waist, pressing his cheek against hers. "Only you, my sweetheart, it's only you I want."

Jackie leaned back against him for a moment, her head on his shoulder so that he supported her weight. She could feel the strength of his body as his arms held her tightly, and the hardness of his manhood. Excitement shot through her, filling her veins with heavy languor. It seemed as if she could hardly breathe, and then Gerald turned her around so that she faced him, and holding her closely, he kissed her again. But this was a very different kiss; this was hungry and demanding, a kiss that spoke of his urgency and desire, a kiss that was filled with love and longing. Responding, she felt his tongue, incredibly soft and probing, enter her mouth, flipping the tip of her tongue, compelling in its persistence. Jackie clung to this big man as someone who is drowning will cling to the only thing that will provide her salvation, and knew that she was lost to the world of mundane things forever. Her marriage to Richard seemed as nothing now, a mere interlude that had passed and left no trace, an experience that might well have happened to someone else.

Gerald's voice was husky. "Let's go to bed."

In silence, for she feared words might break the spell, she led the way down the corridor to her bedroom. Dimly lit, the mounds of white lacy pillows at the head of the bed looked like little drifts of crisp snow, and in a room decorated in delicate shades of rose, with a moss-green carpet, the bed seemed to float in the semidarkness like a large white lily on a pond, inviting and tempting.

But now the moment had come, Gerald was in no hurry. He kissed her lingeringly again, holding her close before drawing her down beside him on the bed. As they looked into each other's eyes, their hands started to explore each other's bodies with aching slowness. She ran her fingers along his jawline and down his neck; he traced the line of her ear with his thumb and squeezed her earlobe gently. She let her hands slide down his shoulders until she could feel the hard muscles of his upper arms; he ran the tips of his fingers down her throat until they came to rest, momentarily, between her breasts. Inch by inch, with infinite care, they made their discoveries. Gerald kissed the inside of Jackie's wrists, and found her skin to be incredibly soft and scented; Jackie cupped his hand to her cheek and found it to be strong and comforting. Still with their clothes on, they became more adventurous; he skimmed the tips of her breasts with a feather touch, making her tingle; she slid her hands down to his hips and thighs, so that he shuddered with desire. Then, as if they had all the time in the world, she stroked his back while he kissed her eyelids and temples and lips. Finally he clasped her tightly, straining her to him so that, helpless, she clung around his neck, wanting him so much it hurt.

Then with a swift movement Gerald stood up and started to undress, his eyes silently begging her to do the same. By the time her hyacinth-blue silk dress lay in a little heap on the floor, he lay naked on the bed, his hands outstretched toward her. Never before had she seen such a perfect physique in a man. Gerald's broad shoulders and narrow hips were perfectly proportioned, his arms and legs muscular. It was the body of a man who works out every day and keeps himself in perfect shape.

"You're even more beautiful than I'd imagined," she heard him whisper as, kneeling on the edge of the bed, she leaned forward to kiss him. "I've never seen such incredibly white skin."

He traced the outline of her breasts, her stomach, her thighs, his hands dark and tanned beside the alabaster paleness of her body. Trembling beneath his touch, she sank down beside him among the downy pillows, and her hand reached for where it yearned to be, fondling him tenderly, stroking his tumescent manhood until he groaned and shut his eyes in ecstasy. His hands had found her too, and probing gently, he explored deep inside her, so that she moved her hips to let him plunge still deeper.

"Gerald . . ." His name caught in her throat, "Please . . ." But he was intent on making this moment, before they came together, last as long as possible, and so he knelt beside her now, his tongue exploring where his hand had been.

"I want you," she gasped, closing her eyes and biting her lips until they almost bled. It had been such a long time since anyone had loved her like this, an age since she'd burned with a longing that felt as if it was going to consume her.

"Oh, please, darling," she cried out, almost in anguish.

As if he could not wait a moment longer either, Gerald turned, and swiftly lowering himself onto her, thrust himself inside her with the passion of a man who had waited all his life for this moment, whose very being was intent on making this woman his forever.

"Jackie!" Her name was wrenched from his throat. "Oh, God, Jackie, I love you so much." Then rockets of searing pleasure rose within her, bursting in a million dazzling tremors, blinding her, binding her, coursing through her in a series of licking flames, so that she could only cling helplessly in total surrender and wonder why she'd never felt this sense of belonging to anyone before. Richard had never . . . But that was in the past. Now, as she lay in Gerald's arms, glowing and invigorated by his love, she knew with deep certainty that she'd met the right man at last.

8

The holiday in Ireland was nearly over, and as Hugo took Colin and Ian on a fishing trip on their last day at Kilfrush, Roland sat once more in his bedroom, black diary in hand, his mind spinning with blacker thoughts. It had been a fluke, of course, that he'd found out why Ernest and Aileen Smythe-Mallin lived in such seclusion. An incredible fluke that had stunned him for a full twenty-four hours after his discovery. At most he'd hoped to find a way of discrediting Celia by being able to reveal that her father's art collection had been obtained by doubtful means. On his return to London he'd intended doing some research at the Courtauld Institute into the provenance of the paintings, hoping they would be able to trace the history and the original ownership of the Renoir and the Monet, the Utrillo and the Corot. Paintings of that caliber couldn't remain hidden and unknown; someone would be able to tell him if Ernest had inherited them or bought them, and Roland had a gut feeling they'd been dishonestly acquired.

One day, when the family had gone for a walk and he'd pleaded a headache so that he could stay behind, he'd slipped into the main rooms and taken photographs of everything, the pictures, the furniture, the bronze and marble statues, the Fabergé diamond-and-green-enamel egg that opened to reveal a miniature carriage drawn by two horses, in gold, and the collection of carved jade. Some of these items must surely have been acquired by dishonest means, he told himself. Many of them were museum pieces. There was another factor which convinced him that something was not quite right. It was obvious that neither the Athertons, for all their nobility, nor the Smythe-Mallins were rich. Celia and Hugo lived relatively simply in London, without live-in servants, and although they couldn't be described as poor, there didn't seem to be much spare cash around, and this was not surprising if they hadn't inherited money from Hugo's father. As for the Smythe-Mallins, Roland reflected that they were definitely short of money. Not only was Kilfrush House crumbling into a moldering ruin, with damp coming through his bedroom ceiling and flaking paint in the hall, but there was a smell of poverty about the place, as if they had only just enough to live on. Celia, he noticed, had been buying all the food and drink since they'd arrived, and her parents accepted this without demur. So why, he asked himself, didn't they sell even *one* of the paintings? Or a Louis XIV chair . . . or the Fabergé egg?

One evening when he'd been talking to Hugo in the study and they were on their own, he'd broached the subject, but Hugo had shaken his head regretfully.

"I wish they would, Roland," he'd replied. "For their own sakes I wish they'd sell, not just the odd thing, but this whole pile, and come and live in London, or even move to Cork or Limerick, with someone to look after them; but they won't hear of it."

"I suppose your wife will inherit all these treasures one day?"

Hugo shrugged. "Presumably, she's their only child. But meanwhile they're living in genteel poverty and I think it's absurd. This house is too big for them, and in winter it's so cold all the pipes freeze and there isn't even any water."

"Have you suggested to your father-in-law that they sell some of the treasures?"

"Often," Hugo replied succinctly, "but he explodes with rage at the idea, and that's the end of that."

Something about the way he spoke made Roland suddenly realize that Hugo didn't like Ernest very much. It had never been apparent before in front of Celia and the boys, but now there was a definite, if faint, tone of hostility in Hugo's voice.

"How did he come to have all this stuff?" Roland ventured to ask, trying to keep the deep interest out of his voice. Maybe Hugo would have something revealing to say.

"I think he inherited most of it," Hugo replied vaguely.

"Could it have belonged to your mother-in-law's family?" Roland persisted, struck by another thought. "This was her family home, wasn't it?"

"Yes, but I remember Celia saying that all the stuff was her father's."

Roland tried to question Hugo further, but, as if he'd already said too much, the earl withdrew behind a copy of the *Times*, taking refuge in reading the "hatched, matched, and dispatched" columns and leaving Roland fuming with frustration. They were all the same, these fucking aristos! They'd be friendly for a few minutes, then remember they were speaking to someone inferior, and so curtail further intimacy, but with such graciousness there was no reason to accuse them of rudeness. Roland's mind worked furtively as he sat pretending to read a book. If, when they got back to London, his visit to the Courtauld Institute revealed nothing out of the ordinary about Ernest's collection, then his revenge would have to take the form of introducing Colin and Ian to drugs. Or maybe drugs and sex. The little blighters had shown no sign of interest in their own sex so far, but under the influence of drugs . . . Roland smiled to himself as he thought of their fair young bodies. Anything could happen.

But then . . . Early the next morning something happened to wipe from his mind all thoughts of the boys and how he could get back at their mother through them; all thoughts of trekking off to do research on the art collection. He overheard Aileen talking with such urgency he thought she was quarreling with someone, until he peered round the dining-room door and found she was alone, putting away the silver cutlery in the sideboard drawers. She was shaking her head in obvious agitation. Something seemed to have happened to make her angry, and then Roland recalled hearing Ernest yelling at her earlier that morning when he'd gone to the bathroom.

"Shut up, you bloody fool," he'd heard Ernest shout. And she hadn't seemed to reply, but now, as Roland strained forward, all her pent-up aggression seemed to be coming out as she carried on a conversation as if Ernest had been in the room with her.

"Swine!" she was muttering. "It would serve you right if . . ." And then Roland heard her say something so incredible that for a moment he couldn't believe it. Straining desperately, praying that neither Ernest nor any of the Athertons would appear to catch him eavesdropping at that moment, Roland stood in the dining-room doorway while Aileen continued to talk quite loudly at moments, totally unaware of what she was doing. It was a one-sided conversation of epic proportions and it told Roland all he needed to know to get even with Celia. It all made sense and explained the strange discrepancies of Kilfrush House that had been puzzling him for days.

Elated and unable to believe his luck, he slipped away down the corridor to the kitchen as soon as he heard Colin and Ian coming out of their rooms on the second floor. By the time they joined him he was putting on the kettle and smiling with sly cheerfulness.

"Good morning, boys. Did you sleep well?" he asked. Then, as soon as Hugo had taken them off on the fishing trip, Roland had gone to his room to write down what he'd overheard, lest he forget a word of it. Not that he would, of course. The feverish mutterings of Aileen Smythe-Mallin would be imprinted on his mind forever, and then, when the time was right, he'd earn himself a nice little fee as a stringer by selling the story to one of the newspapers.

That was all it would require to bring about the total downfall of Celia Atherton.

* * *

Although Celia was not officially Waiting when she returned from Ireland, it did not mean her contacts with the Queen had ceased until her next spell of duty. Regarded as friends of the royal family, she and Hugo frequently found themselves being invited to private dinners and parties, of which there were many more than the general public ever realized. Those connected with the palace kept their counsel about such matters, and so the private functions went unreported and anyone breaking the rules was never invited again.

The telephone call came through from the Queen's private secretary at the beginning of September; her majesty would like them to fly up to Scotland, in a plane of the Queen's Flight, to spend a weekend at Balmoral Castle with her and the Duke of Edinburgh. Celia consulted her diary. The timing was perfect. Colin and Ian would be returning to Eton a few days before, so she and Hugo would be free to go.

"That would be delightful," she told the secretary. "Please thank the Queen very much and say we'd love to come."

"Good. I'll send you all the details. The shooting is wonderful this year, so don't let Hugo forget to bring his gun. We've got more grouse than we know what to do with."

"He'll love that," Celia laughed.

"We'll look forward to seeing you, then."

Staying at Balmoral was something that Celia particularly enjoyed. There was an informality about the place that didn't exist when one stayed at either Windsor or Sandringham, although Celia knew Windsor Castle was the Queen's favorite home. She'd once told someone she "loved every stick and stone of the place." But Balmoral was fun, especially if the weather was fine, with picnic luncheons on the heather-covered hills and some amusement every evening, which took the form of charades, or word games, or watching a film, with canasta or Scrabble for older members of the party, while the younger ones enjoyed a game of Trivial Pursuit or Monopoly.

"It's the royal family with their collective hair

down," Celia once told her mother, "and you haven't seen anything until you've seen the Queen mimicking someone, quite brilliantly, while Princess Margaret plays the piano and sings and does her impersonation of Ethel Merman!"

With her usual efficiency Celia drew up a list of the clothes she and Hugo would need: thick tweeds and woolens, warm boots and gloves and scarves, plaid skirts for her and plus-fours for Hugo; and then of course evening dress for both of them, for the Queen and her family changed for dinner every night, a custom Celia enjoyed because it made each evening more of a festive occasion than it would otherwise have been.

They were due to fly up on Friday, arriving in time for tea, which, in Scotland after a day's shooting, would consist of scones and jam, rich Dundee cake, and shortbread biscuits, eaten before a blazing log fire, while the Duke of Edinburgh and the other men, who often included Prince Charles, discussed the day's bag.

"I'm so looking forward to it," Celia told Hugo that night as they lay in bed together. "We always have such a good time when we stay at Balmoral, don't we?"

The beginning of September also saw the start of Elfreida's PR campaign, helped by Roland, to get herself written about in as many periodicals and newspapers as she could. What annoyed her was the fact that she hadn't thought of getting herself a public-relations person before. Why hadn't Selwyn suggested it when he saw her floundering around the social scene like a desperately small minnow in a large pond, streaking and zigzagging this way and that in her efforts to be noticed? She must have looked so undignified, she thought with a pang. It was also of great consolation to her to realize that it took proper planning to get yourself publicized, and that it didn't happen by chance. It made her feel that there was nothing wrong with her, after all.

Now, as she pored over the *Tatler, Harpers & Queen, Hello!,* and *Society,* she studied the photographs in a quite businesslike way and made a note of who had taken them so she would know which were the photographers to cultivate. No longer would she go about trying to get publicity in a haphazard way; as Roland Shaw had said, you had to have a properly planned campaign and go about it the right way.

Elfreida had a meeting with Roland that afternoon, which she'd told Selwyn was to do with a charity ball she was helping to arrange. Roland was coming to tea, and she hoped they could get down to making real plans for her future. At four o'clock he arrived as arranged, but Elfreida was dismayed to see he had a young dark-haired woman with him. Surely their arrangement was to be strictly private and confidential!

"Do you know Princess Ada of Bavaria?" he asked conversationally as he guided his companion into the hall.

The two women shook hands, and Elfreida wondered if she was supposed to curtsy.

"So kind of you to invite me to tea," said the Princess shyly.

Roland strode purposefully into the drawing room, as if he were the host, and before Elfreida could say anything, he gushed:

"Do sit down, Princess." Then he seated himself opposite her and turned to Elfreida.

"This is the Princess's first visit to London. Her parents own the magnificent Schloss Waxenstein, as you probably know, one of the biggest castles in Bavaria, but they thought it would be nice for her to meet the English aristocracy and make some friends over here. I thought you and the Princess would like to get to know each other."

Pink with delight, and deeply flattered, Elfreida extended a warm and welcoming smile to the Princess, making up her mind to be evasive about her own Swedish background if asked. Bavaria's royal family, although officially deposed by the communist regime, were one of Europe's oldest and most noble families, and to be able to count Princess Ada among her friends would indeed be an honor.

Tea was served and Elfreida presided over the silver tea tray as if to the manner born. The Princess said little, but Roland kept the conversation rolling breezily along while the two women eyed each other surreptitiously behind masks of politeness.

"More tea?" Elfreida asked. The genteel clink of fine bone china and silver was the only noise in the room until Roland suddenly spoke again, as if he'd just had a wonderful idea.

"Elfreida, why don't you give a party for Princess Ada? Then she could meet all your friends."

Having just given a very large and expensive party, which didn't seem to have advanced her socially at all, Elfreida hesitated. What on earth would Selwyn say? The bills were still coming in from their dance, and he would be furious if she suggested they give another party. On the other hand, how could she refuse with the Princess sitting there?

As if he knew what she was thinking, Roland said hastily: "Just a drinks party, I mean. Forty or fifty people, that's all." He looked around the tastefully furnished drawing room. "This is a perfect room for little parties. It shouldn't be any trouble, really." His final remark held a note of reproval which was not lost on Elfreida. She did not wish to appear mean in front of the Princess, and anyway, it would be a social cachet to give a party in her honor.

"That would be fine. No trouble at all," she said sweetly.

"Have you got your diary?" Roland said persistently. "Let's fix a date now."

"But so many people are away on vacation," Elfreida protested. "We give a party now and nobody come."

"I was going to suggest the beginning of October, when everyone's back, but the invitations should go out now," Roland explained.

"Oh, I see." Like an obedient child, Elfreida fetched her diary from the study next door. Giving this party for the Princess must be Stage One of Roland's public-relations plan for her.

The date was fixed, the time arranged for six-thirty to eight-thirty, and Elfreida promised to draw up a list of guests.

"I might be able to help you with that," Roland informed her, with the merest hint of a wink when the Princess wasn't looking.

"Very good," Elfreida replied quietly. This hadn't been quite what she'd expected, but Roland obviously knew what he was doing because, as he'd said, he'd helped make so many people prominent in society and he'd promised to do the same for her.

As he and the Princess were departing, Elfreida whispered to him: "I see you soon? Later this week? When do we meet again?"

Roland looked embarrassed. "Er . . . I'll ring you, Elfrieda, all right?" With a faint inclination of his head, he tried to convey the message that they couldn't talk in front of the Princess.

"Oh, yes, of course." She nodded understandingly. But when she hadn't heard from him for three days, she phoned him at his flat, catching him just as he was going out.

"What's happening?" she demanded. "I've not heard from you since you bring the Princess to tea. I've made a list of guests, but I want to know what we do about the press. Are you getting the top photographers to come? I thought we'd arranged to start my public-relations campaign now, but nothing happen." Querulous, and aware she had agreed to pay him one hundred pounds a day, not forgetting expenses, she was anxious to know what he was doing, if anything.

"Everything's under control," Roland replied reassuringly. "I've been doing a lot of work behind the scenes for you, setting up interviews, getting your name onto some of the lists so you will be invited to all the best parties in London this autumn, and arranging for you to meet certain people. But it all takes time, Elfreida. Rome wasn't built in a day."

"But it is going okay? When do I have to do anything?"

"Don't worry. I'll let you know. I spent the whole of yesterday on your behalf, mostly on the phone, getting the ball rolling."

"But I thought you teach the Atherton boys during the day."

There was a momentary pause, and then she heard Roland say smoothly: "The holidays are nearly over and they return to Eton next week. I only go for a couple of hours in the mornings now."

"Yes, okay, but when do I see you again?"

"I'll ring you, Elfreida. All right?"

"Yes." She still sounded doubtful. "And you let me know about the special guests you ask to the party to meet the Princess?"

"Don't worry about a thing. I'll let you know. So far, Prince Ivan of Russia has agreed to come, and as I'm about to arrange for him to meet the Queen, who is related to him, and other members of the royal family . . . well, no promises, but I might be able to persuade one of them to come and meet Princess Ada too."

Entirely mollified by the dazzling prospects he was dangling before her, Elfreida felt a great rush of gratitude.

"That is wonderful, Roland." She could see it all. Her home could become the center of royal European society! All those kings and queens and princes and princesses, many of whom were related to the British royal family, would find in her a rich benefactress whose soirees brought them all together again and gave them the recognition and dignity they'd been denied in their own countries.

"That is wonderful," she repeated, "thank you very much."

So far she'd only told Selwyn that she was lending their house for a party to launch a charity ball. How amazed he'd be when he found he was actually entertaining half the crowned heads of Europe!

*   *   *

The director of operations at the Shawley Nuclear Experimental Station sat facing Professor Rouse, his lean angular face grave and solemn. During the past few weeks he'd been kept informed by the Ministry of Defense on their progress into tracing the missing blueprints, and as Professor Rouse predicted, MI5 had been brought into the picture, with all their usual cloak-and-dagger tactics.

"On your own admission," the director, whose name was Hartly Woodcroft, reminded the professor, "the only people who could have had access to your study were your housekeeper, your young son, and your son's tutor. Naturally, the first two were quickly ruled out, which leaves the tutor." He paused, his bushy black eyebrows raised inquiringly.

"Did Roland Shaw steal them?" Professor Rouse asked. "It's hard to believe—"

"I've been informed by MI5 that he's under surveillance. That's all they've told me. We shall have to wait and see."

The professor sighed fretfully. "It seems so unlikely it was him. I don't know . . . he wasn't a sophisticated young man. He was a serious person who had worked hard to get an education, and I'd say he was more interested in improving himself than getting into espionage." Suddenly the professor gave a dry mirthless laugh. "The idea is absurd, in fact. If Roland Shaw had his head buried in anything, it was a history book."

"That doesn't rule out the fact that someone, knowing he was staying in your house, bribed him to steal those blueprints."

"But no one, and I repeat, no one, not even Tom, knows the combination to my safe," the professor protested.

"Are you absolutely certain, without a shadow of doubt, that they were in your safe?"

Professor Rouse hesitated. He'd racked his brains for the past few weeks, trying to remember exactly when he'd last seen the designs. The more he thought about it, the less sure he became. It was now assuming the aspects of the did-I-turn-the-gas-off-or-not syndrome, and the more he dwelt on it, the more he was filled with doubt.

"I'm sure they were," he replied uncertainly.

The director looked at him with a pained expression. In his opinion, the professor was a genius and also a blithering idiot; one minute, head in the clouds, designing weapons that could wipe out a continent, and the next minute, so dreamy you could barely trust him to post a letter. Hartly Woodcroft, who had responsibility for the administrative side of the experimental station, found it hard to be patient at times, and he was deeply angry that Arthur Rouse had dared keep a copy of the blueprints in his home. He rose abruptly, bringing the meeting to an end. "I'll keep you informed," he said curtly. "Meanwhile, we can only hope Roland Shaw hasn't sold the designs to an enemy state by now."

Bill Glass's expression was grim as he strode into the offices of *Society*. He'd been summoned by Bertram and he knew exactly what it was about. Jackie was at her desk when he arrived. Jumping to her feet, she rushed over to him.

"I'm so sorry about all this, Bill. I'll go with you to see Bertram," she said as soon as she'd greeted him. "I hear our mutual friend has been stirring things up again."

"Too right he has. He's provided the evidence for suing me for slander—a list of people, including when and where I spoke to them and told them to have nothing to do with him. I've got a feeling I'm going to get it in the neck now." He sighed heavily.

"Then let's get it over with. Bertram's in his office."

Briskly Jackie led the way across the reception area and knocked on the editor's door. Bertram was sitting as usual at an empty desk, his cuffs pristine white, his hands folded in front of him. Inviting them to sit down, he began talking in a voice heavy-laden with disquiet.

"This is a very serious matter, and if we are not

careful, it will bring *Society* into disrepute," he began, looking accusingly at both Jackie and Bill. "I have had this wretched little man Roland Shaw on the phone threatening me—"

"Threatening *you*?" Jackie broke in.

"Threatening me *and* the magazine. He says that between you, you have slandered his reputation, and unless he is paid damages he will sue *Society*. He didn't have to point out to me that such a case would be deeply damaging to the magazine. That is why he is prepared to settle out of court, not that I have any intention of giving him a penny if I can help it."

"Ah . . ." The significance of what Roland was doing dawned on Jackie.

"But I don't think he has a case," said Bill tentatively. He had some papers in his hands, which he rolled into a tube, and he was tapping his knee nervously with it.

Bertram looked at him sharply. "But you have been going around warning people against letting him into their houses, haven't you?"

"Yes, but the list of so-called witnesses he's sent to my lawyer means nothing to me." He unrolled the papers and handed them to Jackie. "There you are. Never heard of any of them," he repeated.

Jackie studied the list, frowning.

"I'd like to see that after you, Jackie," Bertram intervened.

"Yes, of course." She handed it across the gleaming expanse of wood toward him. "Something strikes me as odd about that list."

Both men looked questioningly at her.

"Wasn't it hostesses you warned, Bill? The women who give the parties, rather than, say, their husbands?" she asked.

"Yes."

"Then why are all the names he's provided male? There's not one woman among them. Doesn't that strike you as strange? Who are all these men? They certainly aren't the people giving the parties."

Bill nodded thoughtfully. "That's a point."

"What do we actually know about this man?" Bertram demanded crossly. "It seems quite absurd that an unknown from nowhere can cause all this unpleasantness."

"He's a boys' tutor," Bill volunteered.

"How did you find that out?" Jackie asked.

"Because he taught Lady Molton's sons, and apparently got them through A levels. She said he was brilliant."

"Humph." Bertram digested the information sourly.

Jackie had a sudden thought. "I bet these are the names of some of his pupils."

"But I don't know any of them," Bill protested. "I don't know any of his pupils, except Lady Molton's sons, and they're not listed."

"Why would his pupils be prepared to act as false witnesses anyway?" Bertram asked. "What's in it for them?"

Jackie spoke with care. "Roland Shaw might have something on these young men that they'd rather their parents didn't find out about; maybe he is blackmailing them into agreeing to perjure themselves in return for his silence."

"Oh, dear, oh, dear. This is all very unsavory." Bertram handed the list back to Bill. "You must sort this out as quickly as you can with your lawyer. I do not intend *Society* to become involved in any way. It would be very bad for our image. I told Roland Shaw none of this had anything to do with me," he added self-righteously.

"But we are going to back Bill, if this gets to court, aren't we?" Jackie protested. "I'm as much to blame as he is, for crossing swords with Roland Shaw, but I did do it in order to protect the magazine. I think *Society* must stand by Bill now, because none of this is his fault."

"If he can prove these are false witnesses, then he's nothing to worry about," Bertram replied. "The whole thing will be flung out, of course, but our first priority must be to protect the magazine. We've never been sued and I don't intend to let us get involved in any unpleasantness now." His manner was crisp and final. In silence they left his office, shutting the door with meticulous care behind them. Then Jackie exploded.

"Son of a bitch," she seethed under her breath as they made their way back to her office. "All he cares about is his damned magazine." She turned to Bill with a look of sympathy. He didn't have much money; society photographers never earned the large amounts enjoyed by fashion or commercial photographers, and he could ill afford heavy legal fees.

"I'm going to get onto a friend of mine. He's already offered to help if he can. His company has a very good firm of lawyers and I'll talk to him tonight, Bill."

Bill still looked anxious. "But they will be expensive, won't they? Or perhaps I qualify for legal aid? I'm not sure."

"I'll find out everything tonight and let you know. This friend . . . well . . ." Jackie's eyes suddenly lit up and she smiled. "Between you and me, this friend is the new man in my life. When I told him about Roland, he said he'd do anything he could to help."

Bill's face softened, dissolving some of the worried lines that had gathered around his eyes. "Oh, I'm glad, Jackie. You deserve someone nice. Do I know him?"

"I'm not sure, and until he gets a divorce, I'm afraid I can't say who he is, but he has definitely promised to help."

"Thanks, that's wonderful."

"It's the least I can do. I feel I've got you into this mess by telling you about Roland in the first place, and when you think of it, you were only doing your duty by warning people he was a gate-crasher and not a bona fide journalist."

"We've cramped his style, Jackie, that's the trouble. He's going to find it almost impossible to continue freeloading around London now."

"I wouldn't be too sure of that, Bill. I think he's determined to get in on the social scene."

"He'll never succeed."

Jackie looked thoughtful. "I don't think we should underestimate him, though. You know how the British close ranks when things get difficult; I believe they'd rather swallow him up in their midst than let him loose, issuing writs all over the place. I think he's going to get away with a great deal more before he's finished, and I think he'll be difficult to stop."

Bill was later to remember Jackie's prophetic words.

Throughout the summer of 1990 the weather in the British Isles had been so hot and dry that everywhere the grass was brittle yellow, rivers and streams ran low and shallow, and the earth crumbled dustily underfoot. Even Scotland, normally so damp and lush, with its purple heather and emerald bracken, sweltered under a cloudless sky for weeks on end, while the vegetation on the mountains shriveled and even the deep lochs were warm enough to go swimming in.

As the flight from Heathrow touched down at Dyce Airport, just outside Aberdeen, Celia looked out the window and saw the landscape transformed from previous Septembers. Dried-out bracken cloaked the mountains in muted shades of cadmium, gold, and saffron, while small burns trickled over sparkling amber pebbles under a white-hot sky. Thankful that she'd repacked at the last minute, substituting many of the heavy tweed and woolen garments for linen and cotten, she alighted from the plane with Hugo and walked across the tarmac to the small terminus building.

"Isn't the air marvelous?" she remarked, taking a deep breath. "It makes one realize what muck we're breathing in London."

Hugo sniffed appreciatively. "It *is* good, isn't it? I wish we could afford a place in the country."

Celia slipped her hand through his arm. "We can't have everything, can we? And at the moment we have to be in London because of your work and mine."

He nodded. "Perhaps we'll retire to Ireland one day. Would you like that . . . to live in your old home eventually?"

"Maybe." She hugged his arm. "In the meanwhile, I'm really very happy as we are." She smiled up at him.

"So am I," he replied contentedly, smiling back.

The Queen had sent a car to meet them, a sturdy Land Rover into which the driver stacked their luggage. Then they set off along the A 93 to Balmoral Castle, a winding road through magnificent countryside, with mountains divided by deep glens and streams, and forests of pine and birch trees.

At last, in the distance, Celia spotted the turreted gray castle with its square clock tower, standing rock-like and welcoming. Then the Land Rover was swishing up the gravel drive, past acres of smooth well-kept lawns to the porticoed entrance, flanked on either side by traditional crenellated towers. Compared to the other castles and palaces, Balmoral was considered modern, having been built in 1855, but Celia loved its solid Victorian atmosphere and its typical Highland architecture.

As soon as she and Hugo climbed out of the car, the master of the household came out of the main entrance to greet them. He was a retired Army colonel and an old friend of the Athertons.

"My dear Celia." He kissed her on the cheek. A dapper figure in kilt and tweed jacket with silver buttons, he'd been a member of the household for several years. He turned to shake Hugo by the hand.

"Hugo, my dear fellow. How are you? Did you have a good flight?" He led them into the entrance hall. "The guns will be back soon, but in the meanwhile the Queen has asked me to take you along to the drawing room to join her and Princess Margaret for tea." Without waiting for a reply, he asked: "Do you want to wash and brush up first?"

Through years of royal training, Celia and Hugo had already taken the opportunity to "wash and brush up" on the plane before it landed, and so they went straight to the drawing room. This, like all the main rooms at Balmoral Castle, remained much as it had been during the reign of the Queen's great-grandmother,

Queen Victoria. Tartan fabric and tartan wallpaper, tartan fitted carpets, and even tartan curtains dazzled and decorated every surface. A fine collection of Landseer paintings, several stuffed stag heads sporting a forest of antlers, and bowls of heather confirmed Victoria's obsession with anything Scottish. As always, when the royal family were in residence, a log fire smoldered lazily in the large stone fireplace, because even in a heat wave the thick stone walls of the castle caused the rooms to be chilly.

"How lovely to see you," exclaimed a young girlish voice as they entered, and the Queen came forward to meet them, her arms outstretched, a vivid smile on her face. Dressed in a plaid skirt and a cherry-red twin set, she kissed first Celia and then Hugo before inviting them to sit down and have some tea. Around her feet pranced an assortment of dogs, some hers and some belonging to Princess Margaret, who had also come forward to greet them.

"Your Royal Highness," Celia murmured, curtsying, while Hugo bowed.

"Come and sit down beside me and tell me all your news, my dear Celia," Princess Margaret drawled. She waved a hand that held a cigarette in a long ivory holder. Hugo joined the Queen on the opposite sofa, and soon they were all laughing and chatting in a relaxed way as the Queen poured out the tea from a Georgian silver teapot. Suddenly she asked:

"Has either of you seen the film *Shirley Valentine*?"

"The one with Pauline Collins? No, Ma'am, I haven't," Celia replied.

The Queen clasped her hands together in delight. "Marvelous! Then we'll watch it tonight after dinner."

"But you've already seen it about six times, Lillibet," Princess Margaret protested, drawing deeply on her cigarette. When in private, the Queen was always known by her pet name, although only her immediate family would dare use it.

"I know, but I love it," replied the Queen amid laughter. "It's my favorite film at the moment."

"I think we've gathered that!" her sister riposted.

After tea, Celia and Hugo were shown to their room, which was simply furnished in an old-fashioned way, and extremely comfortable. As in most of the royal establishments, though, it did not have the luxury of a bathroom *en suite.* Celia well remembered her first visit to Balmoral, several years before, when she'd been so terrified of getting lost among the labyrinth of long corridors between their bedroom and the nearest bathroom that she'd dropped little fragments of cotton wool at regular intervals along the floor. Of course when the servants had cleaned the next morning, they'd swept away her little trail and she'd had to start all over again, much to Hugo's amusement.

A maid had done Celia's unpacking while they'd been having tea, and in the adjoining dressing room a valet had laid out Hugo's evening clothes. Celia knew that each room would have been inspected by the Queen herself before their arrival, because, like any hostess, she wanted to ensure her guests were comfortable and had everything they wanted. On the bedside table was a typed card giving the times of meals; in the desk, stationery, envelopes, postcards, and postage stamps had been provided, and Celia even noticed some recent publications had been placed on a table by the sofa in the window. There were a couple of novels, a biography, and a book on Highland birds. Beside them was a tray with a bottle of mineral water, two glasses, and a tin of oatcake biscuits.

"She seems in very good form," Hugo murmured *sotto voce* as he sat on the bed a little while later, watching Celia apply light makeup. They had both bathed and changed, and as he saw her lean forward to examine her face in the dressing-table mirror, he was struck by how pretty she looked tonight, with a soft glow in her cheeks and the healthy bloom of a happy and fulfilled woman.

"Yes, she does," Celia whispered back. "I'm so amused she likes *Shirley Valentine* so much. I hear there are a few lines that are quite risqué, including a reference to stretch marks!" She applied a light pink lipstick which matched her long pink silk evening skirt, with which she wore a cream lace blouse. It was a simple outfit, but very much in keeping with the understated dressing required when staying in Balmoral. Nearly all the royal ladies wore long skirts and pretty tops in the evening, and of course the minimum of jewelry. To be overdressed would have been an embarrassing faux pas; to be wearing more jewelry than the Queen would be considered the height of vulgarity.

Hugo was laughing. "But of course the Queen, and the rest of the family for that matter, are as broadminded as the rest of us, if not more so."

"That's probably because they watch television," Celia agreed. "There's nothing Colin and Ian don't know nowadays, because of the dreaded box."

Hugo shrugged. "I still think it educates more than corrupts."

"Have you discovered who else is staying this weekend?" She gave her hair a final pat before putting on her pearl stud earrings.

"The Prime Minister and Denis Thatcher are arriving in the morning, but otherwise, apart from the Queen and the Duke of Edinburgh, Princess Margaret, Prince Charles, and the Princess of Wales, there's only Lord and Lady Tetbury and that architect Prince Charles likes so much . . . what's his name?"

"Thomas Findlater."

"Yes, that's it, plus of course Prince William and Prince Harry and their nannies."

They talked quietly, because one never knew who might be passing in the corridors, but they always referred to every member of the family by correct title, a tip Hugo had given Celia when she'd first become a lady-in-waiting.

"Never talk about them when you're in private as 'Margaret' or 'Diana' or 'Charles,' " he'd advised, "because the chances of your saying it in front of them, by mistake, can be enormous. But if you make a habit of referring to them properly, you'll never go wrong."

When they went down to the library, the other guests, together with members of the royal household, were waiting for the arrival of the Queen. There was a long refectory table at one end of the room on which stood every imaginable type of liquor. Bottles of gin, vodka, whiskey, brandy, and vermouth stood among bottles of Campari, pernod, sherry, with every sort of mixer, and a jug of orange juice. Considering that most of the royal family were very light drinkers, or even completely teetotal, this always surprised Celia. A guest who was under eighteen, of course, was offered only orange juice and not even allowed wine with dinner. Celia remembered the story of a certain young girl whose mother was a lady-in-waiting, and, knowing she would not be offered any alcohol during her stay at Balmoral, took a large medicine bottle filled with whiskey that had a label saying "To Be Taken Three Times a Day." The girl kept disappearing up to her room to have a quick swig, while in front of the Queen she was seen to be sipping fruit juice with great decorum.

The conversation was light and inconsequential, as everyone gathered on this balmy late-summer evening; the men talked about the day's shooting and how enjoyable it had been, while the women talked about their favorite programs on television.

"I love *Emmerdale Farm*," Princess Diana giggled, "and of course *Coronation Street*. I can't bear to miss an episode of that."

It is impossible, Celia thought, watching her, not to be bowled over by the sheer charm and freshness of this young woman who would one day be queen. In the flesh she was even prettier than in her photographs, and there was a sweetness and compassion about her that were irresistible.

At that moment the Queen arrived, and having curtsied to her earlier in the day, no one curtsied now, and would do so only when she finally bade them good night.

"I've been listening to the weather forecast for tomorrow," she announced brightly, accepting a gin and tonic served to her by one of the footmen, on a small round silver tray. "They *say*"—she accentuated the word while her eyes twinkled—"it's going to be another fine day, so I thought we'd have a picnic instead of using the shooting lodge for lunch."

While everyone agreed, Hugo remarked: "If this wonderful weather is the result of the hole in the ozone layer, I can't say I'm complaining." Then he looked sheepishly at Prince Charles, knowing he had openly declared himself "green."

The Prince laughed. "But we can all do our bit trying to prevent the hole getting any bigger," he replied with an amused expression that reminded everyone how much he resembled his mother. They had the same clear blue eyes that could turn cold one minute and warm the next.

"It is a serious problem," Hugo admitted. "I shouldn't be flippant about it."

"My problem," Prince Charles continued with mock seriousness, "is trying to suggest an alternative to hair spray. I'm having a devil of a job trying to stop Diana using that lacquer in one of those aerosol cans."

All the women nodded understandingly, and Diana laughed.

"I wonder what we all did before lacquer was invented, sir?" Celia asked. "I have to say it has proved invaluable at times when it's really windy and one's trying to control one's hair."

"Sugar and water," announced the Queen.

Everyone looked at her in amazement.

"I beg your pardon, ma'am?" Hugo asked.

Enjoying the general reaction, the Queen continued:

"Yes, in the old days people used to make a paste with sugar and water, rather like icing for a cake. It kept the hair perfectly in place."

"Is that true?" asked Princess Margaret. "It must have been very sticky. How did one apply it?"

"I suppose one combed it in! Anyway," the Queen continued with relish, "the story goes that Queen Alexandra pasted up the back of her hair with this mixture before a particularly windy garden party, and every wasp and bee within a ten-mile radius of Buckingham Palace descended on her in swarms and followed her around all afternoon!"

Shrieks of laughter filled the room.

"You're joking!" said Princess Margaret. "Great-Grandmama was far too clued-up about beauty and fashion to do a thing like that."

"Well, that's the story I've always heard," said the Queen.

"It's probably a myth, like her emeralds," the Duke of Edinburgh cut in.

Celia spoke with care, knowing anything to do with the late Queen's uncle was a delicate subject in the royal family. "The emeralds that were supposedly left to the Duke of Windsor?" she asked cautiously.

"Yes," replied the Duke. "He's supposed to have either flogged them or given them to Wallis Simpson, who swapped them for other stones; but we don't believe they ever existed."

"That's right, and you have to remember," confided the Queen, "she wore a lot of costume jewelry too, as well as the real stuff."

"And not a lot of people know that," Princess Margaret remarked dryly.

"Quite. I think all those emeralds she used to wear were just bits of green glass." Her sister beamed.

Celia glanced at the brooch the Queen was wearing tonight on her simple dark green blouse. It was a diamond-and-emerald brooch with a teardrop emerald an inch long. *That,* she knew with certainty, was no fake. The Queen's collection of jewelry was magnificent, and worth millions of pounds. She was not at all interested in it, though, and regarded it as one of the "props" of the job, only really liking the solitaire diamond ring the Duke of Edinburgh had given her when they'd got engaged.

Dinner was announced, and the Queen led the way to the dining room, escorted by Hugo. Glancing at the seating plan, which was in a leather frame on a table just inside the doorway, Celia saw that tonight Hugo had been given the place of honor on the Queen's right, and she, likewise, was on the Duke of

Edinburgh's right. Every night the plan would change, giving everyone a chance to sit next to someone different.

Celia, at the other end of the table, watched the Queen through a forest of flowers and silver candlesticks, in order to follow her lead, because during the first course she always talked to the person on her right, not turning to the person on her left until the second course. Provided everyone followed her, this meant there was never some unfortunate person sitting isolated with no one to talk to.

The Duke of Edinburgh turned to Celia and started the conversation by asking Celia about Ian and Colin and how they were getting on at Eton. As they talked, white-gloved footmen served quails'-egg tartlets in aspic, garnished with watercress. A light Riesling was poured into the crystal glasses; the Queen nearly always had German wine rather than French.

When the second course, which consisted of poached salmon with some lightly cooked vegetables, was served, Celia turned to her other dinner companion, Lord Tetbury, whom she'd known for years. He was a rich landowner and lived in a house built in 1765 in Hertfordshire. The Tetburys also owned a string of racehorses, which was why they had become friends over the years with the Queen, whose abiding passion was both horses and racing.

John Tetbury, delighted to have been placed next to Celia, immediately plunged into gossipy conversation. There was nothing he enjoyed more than a bit of womanish chitchat, and before Celia had time to say anything, he remarked with smiling maliciousness; "You weren't at your ex-nanny's shindig the other night?"

"No, we were not," Celia replied, "but I gather the rest of London was there!"

He shrugged theatrically. "Café society, my dear; Nescafé, in fact! No one very grand except perhaps for some of Selwyn's political friends."

"But you were there?"

"Yes, we went." He sounded faintly apologetic. "I

didn't really want to," he continued swiftly, "but Julia was dying to see the inside of their house. Bloody magnificent it is, too, I must say. Selwyn's spent a packet; not a good investment these days, though, with the bottom dropped out of the property world."

"Poor old Selwyn."

"That awful little squirt was there too," he continued, "the one who gate-crashed the party we gave for our Harry's twenty-first."

She looked inquiringly at him. "Who is that?"

"Oh, you know, Celia . . . that creepy young man who's been gate-crashing everybody's party this summer . . . says he's on *Society* magazine. I saw that nice American gel who writes the diary, Jackie Daventry, going up to him at Elfreida's party, but he just slid away, laughing at her behind her back. I believed he ordered two funerals for her the other day, because she'd told him to get lost."

Celia still looked blank. "I've never heard of him, John. He certainly hasn't tried to gate-crash anything I've given . . . not that we've been entertaining much, mind you." She laughed. "I was too busy Waiting until the end of July to give any parties."

"I'm told he's quite a nasty bit of work. That photographer chappie, Bill Glass, told Julia never to let him into our house again. Apparently he's up to all sorts of dirty tricks."

"Really? Well, thanks for the warning, John. What's his name?"

John Tetbury furrowed his brows for a moment, and then his face lit up with recollection. "Shaw," he said triumphantly. "That's it. Roland Shaw."

The eerie wailing of bagpipes being played by a kilted Highlander under Celia's window awoke her with a start at eight o'clock the next morning. She had slept badly, worried by what John Tetbury had told her the previous evening. It was deeply disturbing to think they'd employed an unsavory character to look after the boys.

Hugo slid out of bed, and going to the window,

pulled back the crackling chintz curtains. Sunshine flooded into the room.

"What a perfect day," he observed.

Celia sat up in bed, propping the pillows behind her. One of the house rules, except on Sundays, was that the Queen requested all the women guests should remain in their rooms until noon, while the men were shooting. Breakfast would be brought to her on a tray by one of the maids, plus several newspapers, and she wouldn't be expected to join the others in the hall until they all set off for the picnic.

"Well, I'm looking forward to a lovely lazy morning," she remarked, stretching her arms above her head. "Isn't this bliss, Hugo?"

He came back to the side of the bed and leaned forward to kiss her. "It certainly is," he agreed affectionately. "I'd like to spend the morning with you, but I'd better get ready to join the others."

Celia caught the lapel of his blue silk pajamas. "I wish you could spend the morning with me too," she whispered. There was a hint of desire in her candid eyes as she gazed up at him.

Hugo kissed her again. "Wicked woman, trying to tempt me," he teased. "There's always tonight!"

She giggled. "Don't exhaust yourself on the moors, then."

"I won't," he promised.

While he bathed and shaved in some distant bathroom, Celia thought again about Roland Shaw. In the morning light of normality, what John Tetbury had said now sounded less serious. Maybe she'd been worrying unnecessarily. That's what happened when one couldn't sleep, she reflected. Everything became exaggerated in one's mind. Nevertheless, it was horrible to think he'd ordered two funerals for Jackie; that was the action of someone with a sick mind.

When Hugo returned to change into plus-fours and a checked vyella shirt with the thick shooting socks and garters she'd given him last Christmas, she brought up the subject again, although they'd talked about it late into the night.

"Do you think I should tell Robertson and Short?" she asked.

Hugo frowned thoughtfully. "I suppose so, but how reliable a source is John Tetbury? He's an awful gossip, you know. I sometimes wonder at the Queen letting him into the inner circle, like this weekend."

"Oh, she knows what he's like," Celia assured him. "She also knows how he values the privilege of being invited up here. He'd rather cut off his right arm than fall into disfavor with her, and he realizes full well that one indiscreet word about what goes on in the royal family means sudden death to him."

Hugo grinned. "Being 'put in purdah,' you mean. I think I'd check out this story, though, before you go rushing off to Robertson and Short complaining about Roland. Why not ask Jackie Daventry what happened? She's very reliable."

"You're right, darling. And Colin and Ian never complained about Roland, did they? If anything had been seriously wrong, they'd have told us, I'm sure."

At that moment a maid arrived with Celia's breakfast tray, and while Hugo went down to breakfast, she luxuriated in bed reading the newspapers. This was such a civilized idea, she thought, though she knew the real reason was that the Queen wanted the house to herself in the mornings after the men had gone off shooting. With the red boxes to go through, she preferred to be undisturbed and not have to play hostess. She also liked to spend time with her grandchildren, and she'd already mentioned to Celia how thrilled she was to have William and Harry staying at Balmoral this weekend.

Just before noon, Celia made her way down to the stone-flagged hall, where those who hadn't gone shooting were gathering. A dozen dogs, it seemed, charged excitedly about, while the footmen lifted the wicker picnic baskets, as big as trunks, into the backs of two Land Rovers, and Prince William and Prince Harry dodged around people's legs, shrieking with laughter. Prince Charles had left early to go shooting, and Princess Diana had gone swimming and would join the party for the picnic, but meanwhile their young sons were romping around having a wonderful time.

Lady Tetbury, in a cotton skirt and an anorak over her shirt, came up to Celia. "I wonder when they'll stop being so energetic?" she whispered plaintively. Now that her children were grown up, she found the young princes very exhausting.

Celia grinned at her. "Well, Ian and Colin are thirteen and fifteen, and I haven't noticed the activity level dropping yet!"

"Oh, dear me . . ." She raised her eyebrows. "No wonder Princess Diana doesn't want any more," she hissed.

They all moved out into the drive while waiting for the Queen to join them, and just as Celia was about to climb into one of the Land Rovers, Prince William went crashing down, grazing his knees on the gravel. Shakily he stood up, and Celia, being nearest, went over to help him.

"Are you all right, William?" she asked anxiously. Blood poured from one knee.

His lower lip quivered. "I want Gary," he said, trying to fight back tears of pain.

"Gary?" Celia looked around, puzzled. Which member of the household staff was called Gary? She turned hopefully to a young footman who stood nearby.

"I want Gary," Prince William repeated.

"Very well," Celia said placatingly, thinking the best thing was to lead him back into the house, where he could at least be cleaned up. At that moment the Queen emerged, bundled up in a headscarf, a dark green quilted puffa, ankle socks, and sturdy walking shoes, worn with her calf-length plaid skirt.

"Gary!" Prince William cried, flinging himself at her. "I hurt my knee!"

As the Queen scooped him up in her arms, she grinned sheepishly at Celia. "He couldn't say 'Granny' when he was small, and 'Gary' seems to have stuck," she admitted. "Think what the press would make of *that*?"

Celia's mouth twitched. Never again would she see the Queen in quite the same light. At the next Opening of Parliament, while her majesty sat regally on the throne in her crown and crimson-velvet-and-ermine ceremonial robes, making a speech that would be televised to the people of Great Britain, Celia would see, not a great monarch, not a sovereign of an ancient land with a thousand years' history of kings and queens who had ruled it, but "Gary," with a grandson in her arms and a scarf around her head.

They picnicked on a hill near Loch Muick, sitting on tartan rugs and enjoying the superb picnic prepared by the Queen's chef. There were ham and smoked salmon, hot sausages and Cornish pasties, freshly baked bread, and a variety of cheese and fruit. Wine was served, as well as soft drinks and coffee. The guns joined them, and as usual, the Duke of Edinburgh, Prince Charles, and Hugo talked of nothing but the size of the morning's bag. There were more than eleven thousand acres of grouse moors attached to Balmoral, as well as the river Dee, where they fished for salmon, so it was a paradise for these men who loved sport more than anything else.

That evening, as before, they dined at eight o'clock, and instead of watching a film, played word games. Julia and John Tetbury did not much like playing games, but they entered into the spirit of the thing rather than upset the Queen, and Celia watched in amusement as Julia, who was rather prim and proper, had to mime "Fatal Attraction."

Everyone went to bed early that night, as they would all have to be up early the next morning.

The Queen kissed Celia good night. "It's such fun having you both to stay," she remarked with her brilliant smile.

"Thank you, ma'am." Celia curtsied. "We love coming to stay too," she added sincerely. If she felt honored at being one of the ladies-in-waiting, she felt even more honored at being looked upon as a trusted friend. It had been an invigorating weekend, with lively conversation, much laughter, and the comfortable feeling that springs up among people of similar tastes. Tomorrow afternoon she and Hugo would be flying back to London and back to a normal life. It made her realize at that moment that if she was ever to lose her place in the affections of the royal family, her world would be a bleaker place. The excitement of being part of the court of Queen Elizabeth was both inspiring and thrilling and made her feel she was taking a part, although a tiny one, in the making of history.

Bidding the Queen a final good night, Celia reflected happily, as she and Hugo went up to their bedroom, that her next spell of Waiting began just after Christmas. Already the official royal diary was full of engagements and plans that included her.

Roland had spent the Friday night at Slingbacks, a gay club near Leicester Square, where the music was throbbing, the drinks expensive, and the clientele varied. Young black men in satin boxer shorts danced with bearded blonds, while insipid hairdressers glanced lingeringly at muscle-bound gymnasts as they strutted their stuff. Older men, fraying sadly at the edges, gazed with longing at virile young men, knowing their appeal had long since vanished, and chain-and-leather-clad youths stomped around in a macho display like peacocks showing off.

Roland had realized, while still in his early twenties, that he appealed to a certain type of middle-aged man who was successful in business, had money to squander, and frequently a wife as well. They felt they could trust him to be discreet, sometimes to such an extent that he even got invited to their dinner parties, passed off as a business colleague. They were easily able to persuade their wives that an extra man was very useful to balance the numbers.

Last night Roland had struck lucky again. He'd been at Slingbacks for only a few minutes and was standing by the crowded bar ordering himself a margarita to get himself going, when a good-looking man in his forties sidled up and offered to pay for the drink.

"Thanks," Roland replied readily, flashing his most engaging smile and removing his glasses. The man's face was familiar. After some artful questioning, Roland realized it was Melvyn Hart, a Member of Parliament who had recently won his seat in a by-election. Thankful that he had a memory for faces and names, Roland engaged in easy banter, being careful not to let on he knew who the man was. His first thought was to get the MP into bed and then blackmail him; the House of Commons was full of homosexuals, but who they were was a closely guarded secret and they would pay anything to keep out of the press. Then he had second thoughts. Having an MP as a "friend" could be useful. There was the social side to consider; an MP could affect all sorts of interesting introductions; there was also the possibility of having useful information to leak to the press. No, he would definitely befriend Melvyn Hart.

They went back to Roland's flat, off Sloane Street, and Melvyn did not leave until after midnight, saying he had to get back to his Westminster apartment, otherwise his wife would think his "constituency dinner" was going on very late.

"Let's meet again soon," Roland remarked, kissing him good-bye. "I've got some rather interesting friends you might like to meet. In fact, I'm giving a party in honor of Princess Ada of Bulgaria, and there are several fascinating people who've accepted to come."

"Sounds like fun. Where are you holding it?" Melvyn asked.

"Some great friends of mine, Lord and Lady Witley, are lending me their house in the Boltons. I'll send you an invitation."

"Good. That would be great. Could you do me a favor and put my wife's name on the invitation as well? You know how it is." His smile was weak and self-indulgent.

Roland didn't bat an eye. Sex with Melvyn had been

of the wham-bang-thank-you-ma'am variety and he knew he'd never feel emotional about someone so unimaginative. It was without the faintest pang that he was able to reply serenly: "Of course I know how it is. Your wife will be most welcome."

"Wonderful. Then I'll see you again . . . before that?" Melvyn licked his full bottom lip and searched Roland's face for a trace of responding lust.

When Melvyn had gone, Roland climbed back into bed. He hated spending the whole night with anyone, and as soon as he'd had sex, the one thing he wanted was to be on his own again. Now, relaxed and satisfied, he turned out the light and was asleep almost instantly.

The next morning, as he sat in his little kitchen with a mug of tea, he wrote the latest entry in his diary before turning to the back pages of the book. Here he kept a list of all the people he knew; that is, those who were of "interest"; those who had become part of the network of contacts who interrelated, whom he could play off one against the other; whom he could use, blackmail, threaten to blackmail, or who could in some way further his desire to be rich and powerful. He wanted to be accepted as "one of them," of course, but he was fast coming to the conclusion that maybe he could belong only by first incurring fear in others. That was the only way he could get a positive response, it seemed. When people were scared of losing their reputations, they would do anything. For some, of course, it was too late to redeem themselves in his eyes. Jackie Daventry had gone too far, and could never be forgiven. As for Celia Atherton . . . Christ, how he hated that woman! She'd stopped him moving into royal circles—where he'd been sure he could have found a niche for himself—and she'd humiliated him and made him feel small. One day he'd get even with her, he swore to himself. One day he'd be so rich and powerful he'd get even with all the people who had slighted him.

Thinking about money made him turn to another part of his diary where he kept meticulous accounts of all his dealings, accounts that no tax office would ever know about. These were his "earnings" from various secret sources, mainly blackmail or payment for selling drugs, and all of it in cash. There was the five hundred pounds he'd accepted to sit a student's A-level exams for him, something he did from time to time with great success; there was the "fee" he'd charged for introducing someone to a member of the Stock Exchange for a job interview, and how could he help it if the man, who didn't exist, failed to keep the appointment? There were several payments for promising not to inform the gossip columns about some indiscretion he'd witnessed, and a few payments from young men in return for his promise not to tell their parents they were gay. Added to that were the checks he'd received from various newspapers for the stories he'd sold them about people in high places, plus the money he'd got for the articles he wrote for the French scandal sheets *France Dimanche* and *Ici Paris*. Of course he wrote these under a *Nom de plume*, calling himself either Count Victor Leroy, because in Old French Leroy meant "the king," or else Jacques Duarte. They were easy to write, because they required no basis in fact, and one could say what one liked in a foreign newspaper, as it was beyond the boundaries of British libel. Recently he'd written a few delightfully spicy pieces: about the Queen seeking a divorce from the Duke of Edinburgh; Prince Charles having a girlfriend; Prince Edward having a boyfriend; and Princess Anne wishing to remarry.

Roland was sure his articles were causing fury in the press office at Buckingham Palace, but he knew there was nothing they could do. With a stab of self-pity he reflected that none of this need have happened. He had once worshiped the royal family, longed to meet them all, yearned to be in that rarefied, glamorous court circle inhabited by the nobility and admired by the world. He was sure he'd have been a great success too. How his gossipy wit would have enhanced Princess Margaret's little soirees! How his knowledge of art and heritage would have led to fascinating conversations with the Queen and Prince Charles! What a contribution he could have made to the entourage that surrounded Princess Diana and Princess Michael of Kent! How . . . But he wasn't quite sure where he'd have fitted into Princess Anne's world. He didn't like horses and he was scared of her abrasive tongue. He also had a feeling she probably didn't have much use for gay men either.

When his daydreams were disturbed by the phone ringing, he felt annoyed for a moment. Who could be calling him on a Saturday morning? But when a voice said: "Jim Osborne here, from the *Sunday Globe*," Roland's heart gave a great throbbing leap. Jim Osborne was no less than the editor of the sleazy tabloid which regularly ruined people's reputations each weekend, and who also paid large amounts of money for information of a salacious nature.

"Hello," Roland replied, trying to keep the excitement out of his voice.

"We're running the Atherton story tomorrow," he heard the editor say. "Our research has produced some incredible facts; we're making it the front-page lead, and we're also devoting the center spread to it."

"That's great," Roland gasped. "I was right, then?"

"You certainly were. Congratulations. It's a terrific story."

"Thanks."

"You'll be getting a check . . . a nice fat one this time, by the end of the month, as usual."

"Thanks," Roland said again, a great feeling of jubilation welling up inside him.

When he hung up, he gave a little dance of delight. What perfect timing! With the Athertons staying at Balmoral, it would maximize the effect of the *Sunday Globe*. Celia would be ruined. Wiped out. Persona non grata and definitely in purdah! No one would want to know her. She'd be finished. He could hardly wait.

9

*T*he skirl of the bagpipes under Celia's bedroom window at Balmoral Castle sounded particularly melancholy as they awakened her to the strains of the "Skye Boat Song," a lament that tugged at her emotions and filled her with a feeling of apprehension.

Speed, bonny boat, like a bird on the wing . . . over the sea to Skye. The words ran through her head as a sudden premonition clouded her mind and held her in the grip of some unknown fear. It was Sunday morning and Celia felt overwhelmed by the feeling that an impending disaster was hanging over her.

Sliding quietly out of bed so as not to disturb Hugo, she crept to the window and peered out. The mountains were draped in a thick mist, the glorious weather gone. A chilly landscape met her gaze and the echo of the sad music still lingered on the terrace below, although the piper had marched around to the other side of the castle to play under the Queen's bedroom window. Celia couldn't be sure whether she'd had a bad dream that accounted for her feelings of anxiety or whether, as happened with so many Irish and Scottish people, a flash of "second sight" had told her to beware of something. She'd had these strange feelings before, and it was as if some intense sadness, remote and unknown, was affecting her; as if she were suddenly bearing the burden of unknown tragedies, so that the air she breathed was impregnated with disaster, the walls around her saturated with despair, and the floor beneath her feet a mire of desolation into which she was rapidly sinking. The English called it being "fanciful," the Scots "fey." Whatever it was, Celia tried to shake off the unpleasant feelings that were swamping her as she dressed in a simple pale gray outfit that would be suitable, with her black velvet tam-o'-shanter, when she accompanied the royal family to morning service at Ballater.

Silent and withdrawn, although Hugo tried to engage her in lighthearted conversation as they got ready to go down to breakfast, Celia nevertheless felt unaccountably miserable.

"What's wrong, sweetheart?" Hugo asked at last. "Don't you feel well?"

"I don't feel ill, just sort of . . . I don't know . . . nervous, for no reason."

"What are you nervous about? The flight home today? You don't usually mind flying." He adjusted his tie in the mirror.

Celia shook her head. "No. It's not that." She shrugged. "I've no idea what it is, I just have a feeling something's wrong." She shot him a worried look. "You don't suppose the boys are ill, do you?"

"We'd have heard, darling. I told their housemaster where we'd be this weekend in case of emergencies. If anything was wrong, he'd have got onto us."

Celia looked only slightly relieved. "Of course you're right. I'm sorry to be such an old misery."

Hugo came over to her and kissed her on the cheek. "You're not an old misery. What you need is a good breakfast."

She looked up at him, wishing it was as simple as that.

"I probably do," she replied lightly. "Let's go down."

As they descended the stairs into the hall, she noticed Prince Charles deep in conversation with the Duke of Edinburgh and the master of the household just inside the main doors of the castle. They stopped talking as soon as Celia and Hugo appeared, and she paused, knowing by their expressions something was wrong. Dreadfully wrong. Prince Charles's brow was puckered, and the Duke looked strained. Quickening her pace, she hurried forward, curtsying first to one and then to the other.

"Ah, Celia," said the Duke before she had time to say anything. He had a newspaper in his hand. "For our sins we get copies of every newspaper that comes out," he said, as if it was an explanation for what was to come. "Have you heard of a rag called the *Sunday Globe*?"

"Yes, sir," she replied, puzzled.

"Why don't we go into the morning room," Prince Charles intervened. "We won't be disturbed in there."

"Good idea," replied the Duke.

The master of the household hurried ahead to open the morning-room door for them. As soon as they entered, he withdrew, leaving the four of them alone.

Celia looked around, bewildered. "What's happened, sir?" She addressed herself to Prince Charles.

As if Hugo suddenly sensed her earlier feelings of foreboding, he gripped her elbow in a supportive gesture. Celia looked from one to the other, waiting for someone to speak.

When Prince Charles quietly laid the newspaper on the round table that stood in the center of the room, Celia stared at the thick black headlines, feeling as if she were in the middle of some hideous nightmare, feeling none of this was happening to her, sure that she'd wake up in a minute and find everything was normal.

But it wasn't a dream, and the headlines that screamed at her were real, because there was her name, Celia Countess of Atherton, in black and white for all to see, together with a photograph of her standing just behind the Queen at a recent charity concert at the Barbican. Then, as the words sank in, as her stupefied eyes tried to read the text, bewilderment turned to anger.

"What *is* this?" she demanded. "Why have they printed these lies. Why have they written about my father like this?" In anguish she turned to Prince Charles. He looked back at her with sympathetic concern, his blue eyes reminding her of the Queen's in their honest directness.

"Have you any idea who could have done this?" he asked.

She shook her head. "It's unbelievable. My father a war criminal? A member of Hitler's SS? It doesn't make sense. Why have they written all this filth?"

The newsprint danced before her eyes, so that to read and make sense of all that had been written was impossible, but words . . . short phrases . . . her name and the fact that she was a royal lady-in-waiting, leapt out of the pages at her, making scorchingly compulsive reading.

"The Countess of Atherton's father" . . . "known as Ernest Smythe-Mallin" . . . "real name Ernst von Schmidt" . . . "escaped the Nuremberg trials" . . . "known to be a perpetrator of Nazi crimes" . . . "one of those responsible for 'clearing' the Cologne area of Jews . . . an organizer of the first pogram, the Kristallnacht in November 1938, which became known as the Night of Broken Glass, when a carefully planned program of violence against the Jews and their property broke out in various cities throughout Germany . . . demolishing their shops and homes."

On and on the article went, coolly documenting facts and ending with: "Ernst von Schmidt has been on a wanted list for the past forty-six years, while hiding in Southern Ireland under an assumed name. His collection of works of art may well form the bulk of Nazi loot that disappeared from occupied countries during World War II, and it is thought to be valued at about eight million pounds."

Celia sank heavily into a chair, her hands shaking.

"I don't understand . . ." she said brokenly as she looked at a photograph of a young Ernst von Schmidt in Nazi uniform, the swastika emblazoned on his breast pocket.

The Duke of Edinburgh and Prince Charles remained silent while she and Hugo skimmed the lurid pages, and it seemed as if a thousand years had passed since she'd awakened that morning.

"What does it mean, Hugo?" She looked at him, and there was something in his expression she didn't understand.

"Hugo? What is it?"

It seemed to Hugo, standing beside her, as if so many things hovered just below the surface of his consciousness. He began to speak, and then stopped, as if loath to put into words what was on his mind. Prince Charles and the Duke of Edinburgh were looking at him too, questioningly, wondering what he was going to say.

Intercepting their exchange of looks, Celia was filled with sudden resolution.

"You don't believe all this, do you?" she demanded. "You can't believe my father was a Nazi! This is some terrible mistake . . . but how did it happen? This is not my father they're talking about . . . it can't be." She looked from one to the other, seeking their support, but both the Duke's and the Prince's expressions were carefully composed, so there was no way she could tell what they were thinking. Only Hugo stood with his head bent and his hands hanging loosely by his sides. When he spoke, his voice was filled with regret.

"I think we have to accept the fact that while this story may be exaggerated, there is a basis of truth to it."

"*What?*" Celia's voice rose. "*Truth?* What kind of truth is this? This is a cruelly trumped-up story. Surely you can see that?"

Hugo put his arm around Celia's shoulders, then turned to Prince Charles and the Duke of Edinburgh. "Would you excuse us, please, sir?" he asked.

Both the Prince and his father looked relieved. The Duke spoke first.

"Of course. We'll leave you on your own to discuss this. We'll see you later."

"If there's anything I can do, please let me know," Prince Charles added. He indicated the phone with a wave of his hand. "If you want to use the telephone, please do. You might like to call your family in Ireland, Celia. I'm sure you want to get this sorted out as soon as possible." He smiled sympathetically at her.

"Yes. Thank you, sir."

When they had left the room, Celia realized that neither of them had protested her father's innocence. In fact, rather like Hugo, they'd seemed to presume him guilty.

She turned to Hugo. "You don't believe Daddy was a Nazi, do you? . . . And that he's wanted for war crimes? Oh, Hugo, it's ludicrous. It *can't* be true. And what about this bit . . . ?" She snatched up the newspaper again. "They say his art collection is a part of the Nazi loot! Daddy inherited all that stuff from his family. He told me so himself. The Smythes used to be rich landowners . . ." Her voice trailed off.

"But is he really a Smythe . . . or a von Schmidt?" Hugo pointed out. He hated, more than anything, having to inflict pain on Celia, but now he knew the truth had to be faced. "He is Austrian by birth, isn't he?"

She looked at him strangely. "He was born in Mittenwald, in the Bavarian Alps, but he came to England as a child, nearly eighty years ago, with his family."

"Did he? Do we know that for certain?"

Celia's pupils were sharp pinpricks of suspicion. "What are you getting at?"

"Have you ever asked yourself, darling, how he came to possess such fine pictures and furniture? And why he lives in seclusion so that nobody knows about the great art treasures at Kilfrush House?"

"He inherited them, Hugo, from his family. You know that! He lives quietly because he and my mother like it that way. As to the art treasures, he could never afford to pay the insurance premium, so that is why he doesn't want people to know what he's got. I don't understand what you're trying to say!" She sounded resentful, fear adding a sharp edge to her voice.

There was a long pause before Hugo spoke again. It was as if he were weighing up his thoughts once more, wondering how to put them into words. At last, with a sigh, he said gently:

"Although I'm chairman of Hamilton's Fine Art Auctioneers, I know I'm not a great expert on antiques. I know I was given the job because of my title and that it's a sinecure post, but I have learned a lot in the past few years—enough for me to realize that your father's hoard of treasures consists of works of art that have been missing from central Europe since the end of World War II."

Celia looked at him blankly. "What do you mean?"

"I read a report some time ago written by someone trying to trace what has happened to certain artifacts. They listed what is known to have disappeared. Some things were obviously destroyed during the war, others have now turned up in Russia, where they were taken by Soviet troops. These include paintings by El Greco, Goya, Cézanne, Monet, and Renoir. The report also went on to mention other paintings." He paused again, letting the words sink in, while Celia clutched her hands together in her lap and felt little bits of her heart crumble away. She knew what Hugo was getting at, but a wild hope that she might have misunderstood prevented her interrupting him.

Hugo continued: "There was particular mention of the Ernst Stuven *Still Life with Flowers,* the *Portrait of a Girl in a Hat,* by Renoir, the Corot of the harbor at La Rochelle, and the Utrillo. It was suggested that these works, along with antique furniture and *objets d'art,* were smuggled out of Europe by Nazi officers when the war ended; probably through Spain, which was the most commonly used exit point."

"Through Spain . . ." Celia echoed, and those words seemed like the final nails in the coffin of her ignorance. The next place that sprang to mind, automatically and indubitably, was the small island of Valentia, just fifteen miles along the coastal road from Kilfrush and linked to the mainland by a bridge. For centuries the Spanish fishing fleet had put in to Valentia harbor, and until a few years ago there had even been a pub that accepted payment in pesetas. That

well-known old sea route from Spain to Ireland would
have been the obvious way to smuggle in Nazi loot.

"Oh, my God," Celia said. "And of course Southern Ireland remained neutral during the war, didn't
it? It was a safe haven for anyone escaping from
Germany."

Hugo nodded. "There was even a German subma-
rine base in Southern Ireland during the war; they say
there are a lot of Germans living there these days. It
seems to me, darling, that this could be the answer to
a lot of questions I have been asking myself over the
years."

Celia looked up, her skin a sickly white now, her
shoulders hunched as if her life's blood was ebbing
away. "Daddy must have been frightened when you
joined Hamilton's and began to learn about the art
world. At any time you could have said something,
couldn't you?"

Hugo rested his hand gently on her shoulder. "I'm
sure nothing has ever frightened your father in his
life, Celia. He'd also know that even if I did suspect
anything, I'd never bring it up because of you."

She bowed her head, covering her face with her
hands, feeling sick. "It *can't* be true. It's my father
we're talking about." Yet even as she spoke, she knew
it was true. The photograph in the newspapers of the
young Ernst von Schmidt; the slight Austrian accent;
her mother's nervousness over the years; the fact she'd
been packed off to boarding school at an early age
and then sent to live in England. And finally, her
parents' reluctance to have strangers at Kilfrush. Even
so . . . Her mind reeled in a revulsion of thought as
she picked up the newspapers again. She could just
recognize the young man in the photograph. There
were the hooded blue eyes, the aquiline nose, the high
cheekbones and sculptured mouth of her father; but
the ornate uniform was repugnant to her, a symbol of
all that was demoniacally cruel and barbaric. What
she didn't understand was why all this had come out
now. Why, after over forty-five years, had the veil of

secrecy been torn away? What had occurred to finally reveal what had remained hidden for so long?

"It was all such a long time ago," she whispered. "Oh, Hugo, I don't think I can bear it. Who could have found out all these things about my father?"

"I don't know, sweetheart, but in the meantime you'd better phone your parents. They don't get the English newspapers, do they? We should warn them of what's happened. The media are now going to descend on them in droves, you know."

"Oh, I hadn't thought of that," she exclaimed, startled. "They'd better go to a hotel or something. They'll have to go into hiding."

Hugo looked grim. "I doubt if your father will agree to that. He'll want to guard his treasures."

"What's going to happen to him, Hugo?"

"Nothing for the time being, as far as the law is concerned, but I know the government is trying to get a bill passed which will enable them to round up those suspected of committing war crimes and putting them on trial. It still has to go to the House of Lords before the legislation can be carried out, but in the meanwhile they can't do anything to your father."

Celia looked aghast. "You mean if the Lords vote in favor of the bill, Daddy will be arrested . . . and put on trial? And if found guilty, he'll be sent to prison?"

Hugo's expression was solemn. "I'm afraid so, sweetheart. Your father and the many other war criminals who sought sanctuary in Ireland and Scotland after the war will have to stand trial. For the moment, though, your father is safe, but this story has a dreadful topicality about it. The Lords will be voting quite soon. I know, because I'll be there, having to vote myself. Whoever has written this story for the *Globe* must have realized your father's future is on the line."

Celia stared unblinkingly out the window at the mountainous gray landscape. This revelation, so astounding and shocking, was going to have far-reaching effects on them all that could only be vaguely guessed at; Colin and Ian, at Eton, would have a grueling time at the hands of bully-boys; Hugo, as chairman of Hamilton's, would find his position embarrassing as the son-in-law of a man who possessed a hoard of stolen works of art; and as for herself, one of the Queen's ladies-in-waiting, she'd already decided on the only possible and honorable course of action.

Jackie rolled over in her king-size bed, awakening with a pleasurable start when her hand came into contact with Gerald's arm. Then her eyes flew open as memories of the previous night came flooding back and a wave of happiness washed over her. As if he sensed her awareness, he opened his eyes too, and smiled lazily. His voice was husky.

"Good morning, my love."

Jackie snuggled closer. "Good morning. Did you sleep well?"

"Ummmm." He stretched out, placing his arm around her shoulders. "Did you?"

"Yes, I always sleep well, but you were in a strange bed." She slid long slim white arms around his neck and her face was close to his.

"Yes, but not with a stranger," he replied, kissing her tenderly, his mouth lingering on hers until he felt her blossoming in his arms and her lips seeking his with growing longing. Then he drew her closer still, feeling her pale breasts pressed against him and the perfume of her skin, like crushed flower petals, rising to his nostrils in its sweetness, sending darts of desire racing through him.

"I'm so glad you were able to stay all night," Jackie whispered.

"I'll be staying every night, as soon as I get my divorce," he promised, "and then I'll be staying forever and ever."

Jackie ran her fingers through the darkness of his hair, loving its silky texture. "I love you," she said simply.

For answer he kissed her again, deeply and with growing passion. "I love you too," he said at last, "more than you'll ever know. More than you could ever imagine. More than life itself, my darling."

"Gerald . . ." She clung to him, molding her body to his, breathing the air he breathed, wanting to become a part of this man who now filled her thoughts night and day.

"Yes, sweetheart, yes," he responded understandingly. Already, although he had not known her for long, he felt as closely attuned to the needs of her body as he did to his own, and as he slid his mouth down to her breast, he felt a surge of joy that this beautiful woman was his and that she gave herself to him without stint or reservation.

Their lovemaking was always swift and joyful, a celebration that lifted them to dizzy heights and transported them to a shining world, and this Sunday morning was no exception. The day stretched before them, long uninterrupted hours within the warm luxury of Jackie's flat, where they could spend their time exploring each other's minds and bodies. But theirs was a passion as fierce and fast as a hurricane, and so they could not wait, had no need to wait, wanting each other with an immediacy that demanded to be fulfilled; and so Gerald took her with a surge of longing, holding her tightly to him as she rocked her hips from side to side and then in a circular movement while he whispered hotly in her ear, cresting the wave with her, surging forward with her, peaking with such intensity of feeling that he cried out wildly. And all the time, as if carried along by a current, Jackie felt herself being swept helplessly away, her mind fragmenting with flashes of exquisite pleasure, her body playing the tune he played upon it, until, spent and gasping, she lay in his arms glowing and sated.

When they woke again it was nearly noon, a balmy, sleepy September Sunday, when Londoners sit in the park or stroll with their dogs, while children fly kites and pedal their bikes.

"I'll get us some brunch," Jackie announced, slipping into her toweling robe. She ran a brush through her black hair. "Hungry?"

Gerald surveyed her from the canopied pink bed. His smile was appreciative. "Starving."

"How about . . . ?" She came and stood at the foot of the bed, her hands on her hips, her head cocked to one side. "How about fruit juice, scrambled eggs with bacon and tomatoes, gallons of coffee, and toast and marmalade?"

"Oh," he groaned with pleasure. "That would be marvelous. Will you marry me?"

Jackie grinned. "Lucky you already asked me, before you knew I was a good cook."

"Ah, but I instinctively knew you were a good cook from the moment I set eyes on you," he teased.

"Liar!" she flashed back good-humoredly. "I was wearing my best ball gown, and I didn't look as if I was capable of making a cup of tea!" She turned to leave the room.

"Don't be long," he called after her, "or I shall get lonely."

"I'll be as quick as I can," she called back from the hall. "Meanwhile, you can be reading . . . Oh, Jesus!" She let out a cry.

"What is it?" he shouted. "Are you all right?"

Jackie came slowly back into the bedroom holding several Sunday newspapers under her arm. In her hands was one of the tabloids, and she was reading it with a shocked expression on her face.

"I don't believe it," she said slowly.

"What is it?" With a bound, Gerald leapt out of the bed and was looking over her shoulder at the headlines.

There was silence in the room as they both read about Celia Atherton's father. Gerald was the first to speak.

"What a nasty business! They can't do anything to him, though, unless the law changes. Anyway, he's an old man. I can't see the point in raking all this up now."

"Poor Celia. I wonder if she knew?"

"She must have known, darling. He's her father."

Jackie looked doubtful. "I suppose so."

"Christ, I hate the media," he said vehemently. "They're only interested in this story because Celia is a lady-in-waiting; if she'd been plain Mrs. Smith, with no social standing, no one would have cared a damn. Instead of which she and her whole family are going to be hounded now, and for what?"

"There are those who think we shouldn't ever forget what the Nazis did, and I think they're right."

"Oh, so do I, Jackie. Being a Jew, I don't think the world should ever be allowed to forget the holocaust, but on the other hand, it's too late now to go chasing one old man. Most of the evidence has probably been lost, and who on earth is going to remember that far back? No trial could possibly be fair. The odds would be stacked against a war criminal from the very beginning."

Jackie looked serious, sitting on the edge of the bed, the newspaper spread out before her. "I agree, but on the other hand, if this Ernest Smythe-Mallin, alias Ernst von Schmidt, really was responsible for murdering thousands of Jews, then he shouldn't be allowed to get away with it. There's no justice left in the world if that's the case. I mean, I'm terribly sorry for Celia, and, the sins of the fathers shouldn't be allowed to affect the children, but think of all those people in Cologne and in Belsen and Auschwitz."

"Yes, but making Celia's father stand trial won't bring them back, will it? Nor will it make any of us remember them any better. The death of six million Jews will go down as the grossest act of inhumanity the world has ever known, but what we have to do now is make sure nothing like that ever happens again."

"Yes, you're right," Jackie conceded. "Perhaps I'm one of those people who have a vengeful streak in them—an eye for an eye and a tooth for a tooth."

Gerald reached out and caught her hand. It felt cool and slim in his. "You're right to be angry, my love, but it won't do any good. Ernst von Schmidt is better left to live out the last days of his miserable life, because it's forty years too late to do anything about it.

The Nuremberg trials were the right time and the right place to punish people like him, but he got away. That's it. End of story."

"I wonder what Celia will do? I feel terribly sorry for her. I know how she hates publicity, and how she likes to keep a low profile in view of her position."

"Let's give her a ring, shall we? See if there's anything we can do."

Jackie started, as if remembering something. "Oh, my God!" she exclaimed.

"What is it?"

"We can't ring her. I remember her telling me that she and Hugo are spending this weekend at Balmoral."

"That *is* going to be embarrassing for her," Gerald agreed.

"Mother, why did you never tell me?" Celia exclaimed, her voice filled with anguish. From the morning-room window of Balmoral she could see the herd of red deer, so favored by Queen Victoria when she first saw them in 1848, grazing in the distance. She'd just finished telling her mother what was reported in the *Sunday Globe* and now she was waiting for her to say something. Anything. Say it wasn't true. Say it was a case of mistaken identity. Say . . .

But Aileen, far away on the most southern point of Ireland, did not know what to say to her daughter. She, too, stood by the phone looking out the window on this bleak Sunday morning, screwing up her eyes as she tried to make out the shape of the Great Skellig. With a great effort she tried to gather her thoughts together and find the words that would express her sorrow and her fear, but all she could say was: "Oh, Celia . . ."

"Why didn't you tell me about Daddy before?" she heard her daughter demand. "You could have trusted me, you know that, don't you?"

Yes, thought Aileen, she could have trusted her daughter, but she had not ever wanted her to be burdened with the knowledge in the first place; had never wanted her to know what a terrible shadow hung over them all.

"I had to try to keep it from you," Aileen said at last. "I never thought anyone would find out now. We live so quietly here, minding our own business. Your father doesn't even realize I know."

"What?" Celia was stunned. She'd always thought her parents were close. "You've been married to him all these years . . . and he's no idea you knew?" It seemed inconceivable.

"When I found out, by accident, I . . . well, I decided to keep it to myself. Your father would have been so angry at my going through his things, although I didn't know there was anything private among his books and papers at that time. I had no idea he'd kept things hidden from me." There was a raw edge to her voice now, and a bitterness that Celia had never heard before.

"What did you find, Mother?"

"Letters mostly. Your father is a vain man, Celia, and he'd kept several letters he'd received from Hitler, praising him and congratulating him on his achievements in the war. In one of them Hitler called him *'mein Sohn.'* My son. I found them, and also some memos from Göring, in a drawer of his desk, stuffed between the pages of a book of German poetry."

"Oh, Mother . . . how terrible for you. Was I born then? Had you been married long?"

The tears were coursing silently down Aileen's cheeks as she answered. "You were a small child, Celia. Of course I should have left him there and then, but I was so shocked, and the longer I left it, the more difficult . . ." Her voice cracked and Celia finished the sentence for her.

". . . And you loved him?"

There was a pause, and then Aileen whispered, "I suppose so. I suppose I did then. It was such a long time ago, you know, I can hardly remember now. You were just a little girl; you loved your father . . ." Her voice drifted off again. "I no longer love him, but it's too late to do anything about it now."

"Where is he?" Celia asked with sudden urgency.

"He's in the garden.

"Mother, why don't you come and stay with us? All hell's going to break loose, you know. The newspapers have mentioned where you live; you'll be besieged. Come to London and we'll look after you," Celia begged.

"Your father wouldn't leave here. You know that. He's refused to go anywhere for the past forty-five years."

"Yes, but surely—"

"No, my darling Celia. It's sweet of you, but I must stay with him now."

"But if you're not happy, Mother . . ."

"It's too late to change anything. I'm tired, and all I want is to be left in peace. Anyway, what would your father do without me after all this time?"

"Well," Celia said reluctantly, "if you change your mind, I'll come and fetch you. I've got to go and see Colin and Ian as soon as Hugo and I get back this afternoon; they may be having a bad time of it, but after that I'll fly over and collect you if you'd like me to." She knew she should have said "you and Daddy," but somehow, at this moment, she didn't think she could face her father . . . not yet, not until she'd got used to the fact that the man she'd loved all her life didn't really exist, and in his place was a terrible stranger.

"I shall stay here," Aileen was saying. "The tragedy is that it's unlikely any of this would have come out if you hadn't brought that tutor with you in the summer. I knew there was something wrong with him, and your father didn't trust him either."

"Roland Shaw?" Celia gasped. "What's he got to do with it?"

"He was always snooping around, as if he was looking for something. He was a very nasty young man, Celia. I can't think why you employed him." For the first time there was a note of reproach in Aileen's voice.

"And you think . . . ? Oh, my God, I never thought!" She remembered what John Tetbury had said the previous night about Roland Shaw, and her face flushed scarlet with a mixture of guilt and horror. "This is dreadful. Oh, Mother, what shall I do? I think you're right. I was warned about him only last night, and to think . . ."

"What is done is done," Aileen said resignedly. "My life is nearly over and I've known about your father for so long I've had time to grow used to the idea, but it's you and the boys I'm worried about now. It is I who should be sorry for what's happening to you . . ." Her tears had started to flow again and she was unable to continue.

When Celia put the phone down a few minutes later she knew that whatever her eventual feelings toward her father would be, her love for her mother would be tempered with deep respect for a woman who had kept a terrible secret to herself for nearly fifty years while she stood by the man she'd married for better or for worse.

The Queen's blue eyes were filled with concern as her reddened countrywoman's hand absently stroked one of the corgis. Breakfast was over, and in an hour she would be setting off with the rest of the house party to attend morning service at Ballater. Crowds of people would be waiting to catch a glimpse of the royal party, and there would be the inevitable press photographers and television crew, but meanwhile she sat at her desk in her study, regarding Celia with a look of sympathy.

"I'm so very sorry," she said, "but don't do anything rash, Celia. This will blow over in time, as everything does eventually, and it will be forgotten. People have very short memories, you know."

"I know, ma'am, but I don't want to cause you any further embarrassment," Celia replied. "If this was merely a libelous bit of journalism I'd fight to clear my father's name; I'd do anything to prove his innocence; but I can't, because it's all true."

"Are you quite sure, Celia? You know you can't believe a quarter of what you read in the newspapers."

"I'm sure, ma'am, I've just spoken with my mother and she's confirmed everything." Celia shook her head. "It's all true, I'm afraid." She paused; then her words came in a rush. "The incredible thing is that when she met my father she believed him to be Austrian, not German, and she thought he'd lived in the United Kingdom since 1910. It wasn't until after they were married and I was a small child that she discovered the truth. He'd told her, you see, that all his furniture and paintings were inherited from his grandfather, and she'd no reason to disbelieve him. She was also led to believe he'd been in British intelligence during World War II, when in reality he was . . . he was . . ." Her voice cracked, and for a moment she fought for control.

"How has all this come to light so suddenly, after all this time?" the Queen asked.

Celia told her briefly about Roland Shaw.

"I think you should get legal advice," the Queen suggested earnestly.

"I will, ma'am, but meanwhile, in view of the seriousness of the situation, I feel it is only right that I should stand down and resign from being one of your ladies-in-waiting."

The Queen frowned, distressed. "The Firm"—she always described the royal family thus—"have ridden out much worse storms than this, Celia. People have an enormous habit of forgetting, especially when another scandal breaks. Why don't you think about it for a while?"

"I can't think of anything that will reverse my decision, ma'am," Celia replied regretfully. "This nightmare is not going to go away, and as long as I'm at court I will be attracting more media attention than I would otherwise do. In fact, this is only a front-page story *because* I'm a lady-in-waiting. If I stay, I will be bringing discredit to you, and I can't let that happen."

"I'm sure you would never do that, Celia," she replied, but she didn't pursue the matter. They both knew Celia's position would be untenable by the following day, when the story had been picked up by the rest of the media.

"If you'll excuse me, ma'am, I think Hugo and I should return to London immediately. The press will have a field day if I accompany you to church."

The Queen nodded understandingly. "It's probably better to keep a low profile for the moment," she agreed with forced cheerfulness, "but let me know if there is anything I can do. Meanwhile, we'll get a car to drive you to the airport."

"Thank you, ma'am."

As Celia climbed the stairs at Balmoral Castle for what might be the last time, she knew with bitter certainty that it was the media, and the media only, who could prevent her enjoying the special privileges that went with being a lady-in-waiting. The Queen was deeply loyal to her friends, but even she would not be able to protect Celia from the onslaught that was about to happen.

The Athertons' departure was swiftly and efficiently carried out. Within a few minutes a maid and a valet appeared to do their packing, bringing with them Hugo's freshly laundered shirts and pajamas and Celia's lingerie. Then with professional expertise they started folding all the clothes in crisp white tissue paper; the shoulders and sleeves of Celia's lace evening blouse were padded out to prevent crushing, her skirts were layered with tissue, and more paper stuffed the toes of her shoes. Garments were placed in the suitcases, interwoven with each other to prevent creasing, and smaller items were tucked around the edges. Celia knew that when she unpacked again, everything would be in pristine condition.

Down in the stone-flagged hall the royal family were gathering to leave for morning service. As Celia and Hugo descended the stairs, she knew the hardest part was going to be saying good-bye, and suddenly she wanted to run away and hide her misery and shame in some private place where no one would see her. But years of discipline had taught her that controlled behavior was *de rigueur* in the presence of royalty, and so she managed to curtsy to the Queen and the Duke of Edinburgh, and Prince Charles and Princess Diana and Princess Margaret, with a composure that amazed even her. They all kissed her affectionately and with sympathy, but as she hurried to the Land Rover that would take them to Dyce Airport, she felt as if she was being cast out of heaven, the daughter of Lucifer bearing the sins of the father. It was a fanciful thought, but as she held her head high, willing the tears not to flow down her cheeks, she felt branded for life as surely as if she had been the one who had committed all those crimes against humanity.

For Roland Shaw it was a moment of triumph. He'd succeeded beyond all his expectations in bringing Celia down, and the proof now lay before him. It was Monday morning and every British newspaper was carrying the story in various degrees of maliciousness, and there were numerous pictures of Celia standing a few paces away from the Queen. Roland gazed with a satisfaction which was almost sexual in its intensity at the sensational headlines, and knew that Celia was finished. When he'd set out to seek revenge on her, he'd had no idea his plan would mushroom and explode so effectively, and he had to admit to himself he'd been lucky in discovering the secret of Kilfrush House.

Poor old Aileen! Roland couldn't help giving a little snigger as he sat on his bed and read article after article. It was one thing being suspicious about Ernest Smythe-Mallin's art treasures and wondering how he'd acquired them, but it was a chance in a million that he'd come upon Aileen talking to herself in loud and angry tones. The stupid cow, he thought gleefully, so unaware of her dangerous habit; so wrapped up in her own sad world, where she thought she was expressing herself only in the silent vault of her mind. For all these years she must have kept the secret of her husband's past to herself, spoken only in her mind, until loneliness and nerves broke those mute boundaries and she'd scorned Ernest resoundingly and loudly, as if he'd been in the room, for the criminal offenses he'd perpetrated in the name of the Nazi movement.

By the time she'd finished her diatribe, including expressing her disgust at the loot he'd stolen as Germany plundered the rest of Europe, Roland had all he needed to know.

As soon as he'd done a deal with the *Sunday Globe,* promising them the story exclusively because he'd be paid more that way, they'd done all the necessary research and he had to admit it was a superb piece of investigative journalism. No wonder the editor was delighted and had taken the trouble to call Roland himself.

But there was something else that thrilled Roland even more than the sensation his story had created, even more than the very large check he was about to receive. What pleased him most of all was that socially Celia Atherton was now one of yesterday's people.

The drawing room of the Witleys' house in the Boltons was crammed with people Elfreida hardly knew and Selwyn didn't know at all.

"What charity is this in aid of?" Selwyn kept asking the guests, who, in turn, looked at him most curiously and muttered something about "in honor of Princess Ada."

"What's that?" he demanded. "A nursing home?"

"You're thinking of the Princess Christian Hospital," cooed a lady in a quasi-Indian costume, which looked incongruous with her blond hair and blue eyes. "Princess Ada of Bavaria is royal! She's arrived in London, and she doesn't know anyone."

"Humph!" Selwyn surveyed the scene, looking for Elfreida and wondering where on earth she'd picked up this motley collection of people—mostly over fifty, mostly painted and primped women and effeminate men, and all rich-looking. The word that sprang to mind as he watched them cackling and rasping, as they pushed their way around the room in an effort to see and be seen, was "decadent." That's what his Welsh mother would have called this lot: decadent. He noticed a clutter of empty lipstick-smeared glasses on the white marble mantelpiece and signaled for a waiter to remove them. Some of the guests were even smoking, he realized, fouling the air. He hoped they weren't dropping ash on his priceless silk carpets.

At that moment a young man with glasses, wearing a neat pale gray suit, pushed past him, nearly knocking the drink out of his hand. Selwyn opened his mouth to say something, when the young man spun round angrily.

"Oh, for goodness' sake!" he exclaimed irritably, glaring at Selwyn.

"I beg your pardon?" Selwyn held his head imperiously. "And who are you?"

"I'm the host!" snapped the young man. Then he saw a new arrival hovering in the doorway. "My dear Violet, how wonderful of you to come." He shot away, hand outstretched, leaving Selwyn standing there looking after him.

"We'll see about this," Selwyn muttered under his breath, making his way between a large man in a loud suit, who was waving a cigar around, and an emaciated woman in black, to where Elfreida stood looking as bewildered as he felt. He grabbed her arm.

"I want to talk to you," he said fiercely. She allowed him to lead her into the adjoining study, where she looked at him with anxious eyes.

"Who the hell are all these people?" he demanded before she had time to say anything. "What the fuck's going on? I thought we were just having a few people for drinks, to help launch a charity function . . . not a bunch of faggots and fag hags taking over the entire house."

"They're not—"

"And who the fuck's that smart-ass who's calling himself the host?"

"He isn't the host—"

"I will not allow you to open the doors to all and sundry in this way, and at my expense! We've just given an enormous party that cost nearly fifty thousand pounds. What d'you want to give another party for, for Christ's sake? Get this lot out of here, Elfreida."

"It's to honor Princess Ada of Bavaria . . . she very important!" Elfreida's face was flushed scarlet now, and her ample breasts, encased in pink taffeta, were rising and falling alarmingly, heralding an emotional outburst.

"I don't give a damn if it's in honor of the pope!"

"But, Selwyn . . . baby . . ." Her voice took on its accustomed whine. "Roland asked me to invite a few friends to meet Princess Ada . . . she's related to our royal family, you know—"

"A few guests! A *few* guests! For God's sake, woman, there must be a hundred and fifty people here! . . . And who the hell is Roland?" Selwyn asked agitatedly.

"Oh, you know, my sweetness, you remember Roland? He came to our dance . . . he knows *everyone*. His name is Roland Shaw."

"Never heard of him. I'm going to tell the waiters to stop serving *my* champagne to a bunch of people I don't know and don't want to know," Selwyn headed for the door.

"Oh, please . . . please, darling . . ." Elfreida caught his sleeve and tugged at it. "Please . . . I will *die* of embarrassment. They will be going in a few minutes anyway. Please leave things alone or I shall never be able to face anyone again." She looked ready to weep.

Selwyn didn't reply, but strode back into the drawing room, cutting a swath through the melee as he headed for the bar. Elfreida followed him fearfully, ready to countermand his orders to stop serving drinks, but at that moment she was waylaid by a group of guests.

"*So* good of you to lend Roland your house for his party," said one.

"Isn't he a wonderful host?" cried another. "I always say his parties are the best."

"And how kind of him to arrange it so that you and Princess Ada could meet people and make new friends. You're both foreigners, aren't you?" gushed a third.

In truth, Elfreida was both dumbfounded and angry. She had invited only thirty people to drinks tonight, acquaintances she knew would be thrilled to meet the princess, but then, at the last moment, Roland had said he'd asked "a few more" . . . and well over a hundred had turned up. She no more knew who they were than Selwyn, and they were all far too old to help further her social advancement. Her first worry had been that they would run out of champagne and that there weren't enough canapés to go around; the waiters she'd hired were already looking disgruntled and resentful. But now this! How dare these people say Roland was giving the party so she could meet people! In her own house! The cheek of it inflamed her sense of self-importance; who did Roland think she was? An *au pair* still? The thought reminded her of the Athertons. Celia had been blazoned all over the newspapers for the past three days: pictures of her arriving at Heathrow on her return from Balmoral, her role as a lady-in-waiting speculated upon, her father's infamous past dissected in detail, the humiliation of the Athertons complete and utter, and it struck a fearful chord Elfreida. The fact that someone in such a seemingly unassailable position as Celia Atherton could be disgraced was a fearsome thought. It brought home to Elfreida how fragile public goodwill is, and how easily the bubble of popularity can burst.

She looked around for Roland, determined to have it out with him. Nobody used her in this way! How dare he say it was his party! Her eyes scanned the room; Selwyn was talking to the headwaiter, and from his gestures she could tell he was blowing the whistle on the whole thing. Large groups were standing with empty glasses now, and Roland was nowhere to be seen.

Furiously Elfreida went into the hall, which was also full of people she'd never before seen in her life. Roland stood in their midst, saying good-bye to departing guests and greeting late arrivals with all the largess of an ebullient host.

"Come in, come in," he exclaimed. "You'll find drinks through there. How good to see you, I'm so glad you could come."

Elfreida went and stood in front of him, her expression belligerent. Roland ignored her. She tugged at his sleeve.

"Who are all these people?" she hissed.

"What? Oh, for goodness' sake, Elfreida, I'll introduce you to everyone in a moment."

"I don't want to meet them, I want to know who they are. I didn't invite them, and this is my party. You said you would bring along a few people, but this is altogether too much." Her eyes flashed dangerously. "I hear them say this is *your* party and you give it so that I can meet people."

He regarded her with cold eyes through his highly polished glasses, so they reminded her of gray pebbles at the bottom of a pond. "But you *do* want to meet people. I thought that was our arrangement."

She dropped back, confused. "Yes . . . but they made it sound so awful . . . like I knew no one, like this wasn't even my house or my party."

Roland shrugged. "You employed me as your PR and I was under the impression it was because you wished to further your social standing and get to know more people. This party will help; Princess Ada isn't just anyone, you know!"

"But who are all these other people? They're too old for me . . . some are in their seventies," Elfreida protested.

With an expression of angry impatience he ticked off the names on his square-tipped fingers. "There's the Marchioness of Fitzhammond, Viscountess Sutcliffe, Lady Gascoign, Lady Murray, Lady Ingham, Sir Greville, Lady Hunt . . ."

As he spoke, Elfreida knew what he was saying was true because she'd heard those names before; they were mainly widows who kept their social life going by attending every charity function they could afford to buy tickets for. They did not, however, entertain themselves, nor were they in the mainstream; they were a bunch of rich old women who were clinging with all their might to the social scene, and it was obvious that Roland provided opportunities for them to have a little fun, as long as they paid for it.

As he got to the end of his list, which he thought would impress Elfreida, a young man came prancing up to him. Dandyish, in a brocade waistcoat, he spoke in an effete manner.

"They've stopped serving champagne, Roland! What sort of party is this? You said you were laying on gallons of the stuff, and now the waiters are refusing to give us any more."

Roland shot Elfreida a venomous look. "What's happening?"

"Selwyn is angry that there are so many people," she replied bluntly, for once sharing Selwyn's feelings because these were not her guests and she wasn't getting the credit for all this hospitality either.

"Who's Selwyn?" demanded the effete young man.

"He's my husband."

"And who are *you*?"

Roland intervened. "Elfreida, you can't let Selwyn do this. Some of the guests have only just arrived, and they haven't even had a drink yet."

"If it's your party, sort it out yourself," Elfreida snapped, walking away.

As soon as she'd gone upstairs and into her bedroom, her heart started hammering. What had she done? Roland had taken great advantage of her tonight, but on the other hand, she'd probably made an enemy of him now, and how would that affect her social standing in future? Would he go around saying dreadful things about her to everyone? Sitting on the edge of her turquoise-and-gilt king-size bed, with her head in her hands, she felt torn between keeping on the right side of Selwyn and not falling out with Roland.

Tonight had been a disaster. There were still over a hundred people downstairs, standing around with no drinks or food, a foreign princess who must be wondering what on earth was going on, and an irate husband. Elfreida made a sudden decision. Grabbing her handbag, she ran out of the bedroom without bothering to powder her nose or touch up her lipstick, and down to the drawing room again. People were still jostling around, talking loudly, and waving empty glasses; but in the window stood Princess Ada, talking to an elderly woman. She was looking bored and miserable. Elfreida rushed over, forcing a broad smile to her face.

"Ah, there you are, Princess. My husband and I would be so delighted if you would join us for dinner; we thought of going to the Connaught. I hope you can come?"

Princess Ada, seeing an escape route, looked relieved. "I'd be delighted to dine with you."

"Good. Shall we go?" Elfreida took her by the elbow and started steering her through the crowd. Selwyn stood by the doorway, a large whiskey and soda in his hand. He raised his straggly white eyebrows when he saw the two women approaching, and his eyes were steely.

"Selwyn, sweetness . . . you've met Princess Ada, haven't you?" Elfreida had to exert all her charm now to get round her obviously rattled husband. "You were quite right to stop drinks being served," she said immediately. "I never invited these people and I don't want them here either. You're so wise, Selwyn, and so clever." She turned to Princess Ada. "Isn't he clever? . . . and such a wise man. I'm so lucky to be married to him."

Selwyn stood looking at her, openmouthed with astonishment, and she pressed her advantage.

"Selwyn, sweetness . . . the Princess and I want to

get away from all these dreadful people. How about us all going to the Connaught for a little supper? Please, Selwyn baby?" She laid a hand on his chest in a gesture that was both proprietary and feminine. She gazed up into his eyes. "Let's slip away now," she added coaxingly.

"What about the house? I'm not going to leave all these people in my house," Selwyn protested.

"Tell the staff to keep an eye on everything, and lock the dining-room door, then the silver will be safe."

Selwyn still looked dubious.

"It will be all right, darling, I promise you. These are not bad people here tonight, just . . . just boring people."

"Well, I suppose it will be all right." With reluctance Selwyn went over to the headwaiter. They stood deep in conversation while Elfreida watched anxiously. If she could make a graceful exit now, carrying the guest of honor off to dinner, it would be a wonderful snub to Roland. Selwyn returned, nodding lugubriously.

"All right. Let's go. They'll look after everything."

"Thank God," said Elfreida under her breath.

With that, the three of them strolled nonchalantly down the front steps of the house and out into the street, leaving Roland to face a hundred and fifty thirsty guests on his own.

As Hugo stepped out of his car, blazing lights were switched on, a television camera pointed in his direction and a microphone thrust in his face. This was the fourth night that he'd been waylaid outside his house as he'd returned home from the office, and the questions were always the same.

"How is your wife feeling, Lord Atherton?"

"Is she going to be sacked as the Queen's lady-in-waiting?"

"Has she been in touch with her father in Ireland yet?"

Ever since they had returned from Balmoral, the media had been hounding them, first at Heathrow and now outside the house and on the phone. If he'd thought they'd been embarrassed by the debacle of their *au pair* running off with one of their dinner guests, it was nothing to what they were going through now. Celia had been unable to leave the house, and he'd had to go down to Eton and bring the boys home because they were being pursued by the media, which was disruptive for the whole college.

Hugo pushed past the reporters, disgusted by their persistence and insensitivity. "I've nothing to say," he snapped, letting himself in through the front door.

Celia was waiting for him in the drawing room, surrounded by some of the dozens of bouquets she'd been sent by friends and well-wishers. Beside her on the sofa sat Jackie.

Hugo bent forward to kiss Celia first, distressed to see her looking so pale, although her eyes were as clear and unwavering as ever. Then he greeted Jackie.

"It's pretty hellish out there, isn't it?" he remarked, nodding in the direction of the street. "You'd think they'd have something better to do. Have you both got drinks?"

"Yes, thank you, darling," Celia replied. "I invited Jackie to supper tonight because, with all her experience of the press, I thought she could advise us on how to handle this situation."

"Good idea," Hugo agreed. He went to the side table on which stood a silver tray of bottles. He poured himself a whiskey and soda. "More flowers, I see," he remarked, looking around.

"Yes, and some wonderful letters too, including one from a really nice Dutchwoman whose father collaborated with the Nazis; she was most sympathetic and said she understood how I felt," Celia replied.

"How very kind." He patted her shoulder, but knew that he couldn't reach the inner turmoil that was eating away at her. Never a man to be demonstrative, he felt helpless now in the face of such calm despair.

"So, Jackie, what do you advise us to do?" he asked, taking a seat facing the two women.

"If I were you, I'd give one press conference to say

what you have to say, and get it over. There's a good chance you'll be left alone after that, but if you keep trying to avoid the press, they will dig their toes in."

Celia looked horrified. "You mean make a statement in front of all those journalists and photographers?"

Jackie thought for a moment. "Have you been approached by any of the television channels?"

"Yes, all of them have asked if they can interview me."

Jackie nodded knowledgeably. "Then that's what you should do. Choose the BBC and invite them here. Say you will give them a five-minute interview, and add that that's all you intend to do. The newspapers will pick it up when it appears on TV, and hopefully that will be that."

"And you think I'll be left in peace then?"

"It will take the heat off, in the main, but why don't you also get the telephone operator to intercept all calls? You might even get your phone number changed to ex-directory."

"Jackie, you're wonderful," Celia exclaimed. She looked at Hugo. "That sounds like the best idea, doesn't it, darling? This thing's not going to go away by ignoring it, is it?"

"Tell me, Celia," Jackie asked. "How did this all start? Who told the *Sunday Globe* about your father?"

As Celia began to explain about the tutor they'd engaged to teach Colin and Ian during the summer holidays, Jackie's expression became first stunned and then incredulous. Suddenly she leaned forward and gripped Celia's wrist.

"You're not talking about Roland Shaw, are you?" she demanded.

Celia and Hugo both looked startled. "What do you know about him?" Hugo asked.

Briefly Jackie told them.

"My God!" Celia exclaimed. "How can we put a stop to this man ruining people's lives like this?"

"He must be off his head," Hugo commented.

"He's not mad," Jackie affirmed. "In fact, in a twisted way, he's probably cleverer than the rest of us put together. He's crafty and cunning, and he's obsessed by revenge. I'd say he was hooked on it. I wouldn't put it past him to set up situations that result in his feeling a *need* for retaliation. A psychiatric report would be fascinating, actually: what type of person puts himself forward, knowing in advance, as he must do, that he is going to be rejected, in order to have the pleasure of seeking revenge and hurting people?"

"Humph." Hugo looked skeptical. "I don't think one can wrap the whole thing up in a psychobabble. The man is obviously evil, and I shudder to think we let him near the boys."

Celia looked down at her hands, twisting her sapphire-and-diamond engagement ring around and around. Jackie intuitively knew what she was thinking.

"You're not the only one who has been conned by Roland Shaw, you know. I saw Bill Glass again yesterday, and he told me about a whole string of people who are being either blackmailed or set up in some way or other. People are petrified of him."

Hugo looked nonplussed. "Why?"

"Because he's so dangerous, and also, you know how the English like to pretend nothing's wrong while the whole world is blowing up in their faces." Jackie laughed. "Stiff upper lip and all that."

Celia and Hugo caught each other's eye and smiled, nodding in recognition of a national trait.

"It is a perfect breeding ground for Roland's machinations," Jackie continued, "especially as no one wants to appear stupid enough to have been taken in by him when they discover what he's really like. I mean, he pulls some of the oldest con tricks in the business . . . and people still fall for it! They are also afraid of being publicly humiliated by him, so they say yes to his demands rather than stand up to him. I've heard of several young men who have been invited to lunch by Roland at smart places like Claridge's or the Savoy Grill so that he can 'introduce' them to someone who can further their careers, and of course you can guess what happens. Roland turns up on his own, making an excuse for his 'friend,' who's suddenly indisposed, and then when it comes to the coffee stage, he thanks the young man for lunch and says he must dash, as he has another appointment, and the young man is left to pay the bill. I mean, these are corny con tricks, but people are frightened to cross him and so he gets away with it time and again."

"I had no idea," Celia said in amazement, "that people like him really existed."

Jackie looked serious. "That's the lighter side of his activities. There is also drug-pushing. Bill told me of a young man who was hooked on cocaine by Roland, and ended up stealing the family silver to pay for his habit—something the parents are too ashamed to admit happened, and so Roland gets away with it once again. This man is dangerous. He preys on the very young, and the old, the vulnerable and the gullible, the weak and the lonely, but all his victims are linked by one common denominator."

"Which is?" Celia asked.

Jackie said the word quietly. "Money."

"But we haven't any money."

"But you have the right connections, and that's where he *really* wants to be—part of the aristocratic scene. All the other things he does are merely to finance himself so he can join in on equal terms. He knows that it costs money to get into society, especially if you are an outsider. If you're a born aristocrat, it doesn't matter if you haven't got two farthings to rub together. People will still accept you."

"You're quite an expert on the English class system, aren't you?" Hugo observed, amused. "I hadn't really given much thought to this sort of thing, but you're right, of course."

"If he wasn't so evil, I'd feel quite sorry for the wretched man," said Celia, "but right now I could kill him." She shook her head from side to side, her eyes clouded. "He's done the most appalling damage to my family; no one will ever know how my mother is suffering at the moment. Colin and Ian are very bewildered and upset too, and none of this need have happened if Roland Shaw hadn't been so vindictive."

"Try not to upset yourself, darling," Hugo said. "It won't do any good."

"I can't help it, Hugo. How would you feel if you were to find out that your father had been a Nazi war criminal?" There was a dangerous edge to Celia's voice.

At that moment Mrs. Pinner knocked on the drawing-room door and announced dinner was ready.

"Thank you, we'll be right down," said Hugo. "Could you make sure the boys have washed their hands and brushed their hair, please?"

"Yes, m'lord."

"Such a treasure, I don't know what I'd do without her at the moment," murmured Celia when Mrs. Pinner had gone. "She offered to stay all day and do the dinner at night now the boys are home, and I couldn't be more grateful."

Down in the dining room, the candles had been lit, and the room was heavy with the perfume of more bouquets. Mrs. Pinner, in her element, was whizzing around with silver entrée dishes, and a bottle of wine, which was plonked on the table in front of Hugo. Colin and Ian were standing politely behind their chairs, waiting for the grown-ups to sit down.

"What are we having? I'm starving," Ian announced as soon as they were all seated.

"We do not tuck our table napkins into our collars," Hugo said quietly to his younger son.

"Oh, sorry, Dad. What are we having?"

"We're having," said Celia, forcing herself to sound cheerful, "smoked salmon to start with, and then roast lamb with lots of vegetables—"

"Yummy! My favorite!" Colin yelled.

"My favorite too!" echoed Ian.

"Hush!" said both parents simultaneously. Then Celia continued:

"We're having summer pudding—"

"Made with raspberries and red currants and blackberries?"

"And cream? Is there cream to go with it?"

Celia put her head in her hands in mock despair. "You will see, Jackie, that nothing, absolutely *nothing*, affects my sons' appetites."

Jackie grinned. "When I heard that menu, I nearly emitted the odd 'yummy' myself!"

Colin and Ian regarded her with growing respect, their unwavering gray eyes so like their mother's.

"Well, food is important, isn't it?" Colin declared.

"Oh, absolutely," Jackie agreed.

"Have you been talking about Grandpa?" Ian inquired suddenly, looking at everybody.

Hugo frowned, as if pained, but Celia looked unflinchingly at Ian.

"Yes, darling. Mrs. Daventry knows the wicked man who sold Grandpa's story to the newspapers."

Ian looked at Jackie with undisguised horror. "Is he a friend of yours?"

"No," Jackie replied firmly. "He most certainly is not."

"That's good. Will he make a lot of money by selling the story to the newspaper?"

"Yes, I expect he will." Jackie paused, struck by another thought. She turned to Celia with a wry smile. "I don't suppose you've heard the gossip about Elfreida Witley that is doing the rounds?"

Celia raised her eyebrows inquiringly.

"Roland wormed his way into Elfreida's life, and ended up getting her to give a party in her house for all his friends. She and Selwyn were so annoyed they walked out in the middle and left him to it."

"No!" Celia's mouth opened in amazement. "What happened?"

"I hear Roland's after her blood, swearing to get even with her for the way she's humiliated him."

Celia drew in a long deep breath. "My God, I wonder what he'll do."

Jackie shrugged. "Your guess is as good as mine. One thing is for sure: he'll want to see her ruined. He won't rest until he's wiped her out and she's unable to show her face in public."

*   *   *

Professor Arthur Rouse listened with a sinking heart, as Hartly Woodcroft recounted MI5's findings on Roland Shaw.

"The authorities are sure he's our man," he said succinctly. "He has a track record of drug-pushing and blackmail. He is a skillful confidence trickster, a stringer for down-market newspapers, and he has a reputation at two well-known gay clubs for picking up men in high positions so that he can later threaten to disclose discreditable information about them."

The professor looked startled. "Roland Shaw?" he queried incredulously. "Are you sure?"

"The authorities are sure, and that's good enough for me," Hartly Woodcroft replied crisply.

"But . . . but . . ." Arthur Rouse floundered, perplexed. "It's as if you're describing someone quite different. I never thought Roland Shaw was a homosexual, for a start. I certainly wouldn't have employed him to look after Tom if I'd known that. And he pushes drugs? And blackmails? It doesn't seem possible." He shook his head. "What happens now?"

Woodcroft shrugged. "That's up to MI5. They're keeping up a close surveillance for the time being, I gather, but his other activities are of no real interest to them. What they are looking for is some sort of evidence that he took the blueprints, I expect."

Arthur Rouse returned to his own office with a feeling of deep foreboding. Something was wrong, but he couldn't put his finger on it, but gut instinct told him that although Roland Shaw might be guilty of many misdemeanors, he just wasn't the type to steal secret nuclear-warhead designs.

Winter 1990

10

Selwyn's chauffeur always dropped him off at Witley House, the headquarters of Witley Construction, at nine-fifteen every morning. Although of retirement age, Selwyn was very much a working chairman, keeping a firm grip on the business and still making all the major decisions. Apart from his own company, his other commitments included being chairman of Burnett London Properties Management, vice-president of the Central City Museum of Art, and deputy chairman of the Greater London Construction Association.

On this particular morning the traffic was heavy as his limousine swung out of the mainstream and entered the courtyard of the building in High Holborn. It was nine-sixteen, and as he alighted, briefcase in hand, he turned to Jeffreys, his driver.

"Come back at noon, will you, Jeffreys? I'm lunching at the Savoy."

The chauffeur, who had been with him for the past ten years, touched his gray hat with his gloved hand. "Certainly, sir."

Selwyn glanced up at the sky. It was a typical overcast November day, and at that precise moment he remembered it was the twenty-second. Like almost everyone else, he, too, could remember exactly what he'd been doing on the same date twenty-seven years before when John F. Kennedy had been assassinated. He and Helen had been on their way out to dinner. He'd booked a table for two at the Dorchester Grill to celebrate a large contract he'd signed that morning. Then, just as they were leaving the house, the news had been flashed on television screens and broadcast on radios around a shocked world, and Selwyn remembered feeling as bereaved as if a friend had died. Twenty-seven years ago, he reflected; the time had gone so quickly, it didn't seem like twenty-seven years.

Turning into the building, he walked slowly to the elevator, his mind still clouded by the memory of that sad night so long ago. The hands of the clock above the elevator pointed to twenty minutes past nine.

By nine-forty-five a blow would have fallen that was to affect him almost as much as Kennedy's assassination.

Anne, his private secretary for the past twenty-two years, greeted him with her usual motherly smile, as ready as ever to protect him from the irritating trivia of the day.

"And how are we today, Lord Witley?" she asked cozily. "Would you like a nice cup of coffee?"

Selwyn, who enjoyed her cosseting, beamed at her as she stood with her hands clasped in front of her ample bosom. Sometimes he thought she was wasted as a secretary; in his opinion she'd have made the most marvelous nurse, with her comforting manner.

"I'd love some coffee," he replied. Then he settled himself at his vast desk, taking papers from his briefcase and squaring them up in front of him as he prepared for two and a half hours' solid work before entertaining a business contact for luncheon.

Anne took longer than usual to come back with the coffee, and when she did, her face was pale and she looked deeply distressed.

"I'm afraid there's some bad news, Lord Witley," she said in hushed tones. She almost tiptoed toward him, as if afraid of waking someone.

Selwyn looked up sharply. "What is it, Anne?"

"The Prime Minister, Mrs. Thatcher, has just resigned."

It was a body blow to Selwyn. He felt as shattered

as if Anne had announced the leader's demise. Margaret Thatcher gone! The woman to whom he owed so much, removed from the center stage of Great Britain! He couldn't have been more upset if the Queen had abdicated. Tears sprang to his eyes, hot and immediate. She had been betrayed! For a week or so now there had been trouble brewing in the government, brought about by failed and bitter men on one side and overweening ambitious men on the other.

"But she was fighting on, after the first ballot, when she was only four votes short of winning!" he gasped.

Anne nodded wretchedly. "I know, but it seems her Cabinet have advised her to stand down and not go for a second ballot. Apparently they told her she wouldn't win, and so, for the sake of the party and to avoid a split among the rank and file, she's stepped down."

Selwyn dropped his head into his hands. He knew her position was being challenged by another Member of Parliament, Michael Heseltine, but he had never for a moment imagined it would come to this.

"Oh, my God, this is dreadful. Absolutely dreadful," he muttered brokenly. He'd supported Mrs. Thatcher from the beginning. He admired her and agreed with her policies. Like all employers, he'd had trouble with the unions until she tamed them and made them more democratic; he'd backed her privately and publicly, and she, in return, had repaid him with a life peerage.

All the glittering prizes that had come his way in the past ten years were the direct result of the climate she had created for the entrepreneurial businessman like himself. His company had flourished, and then gone public. The share prices had rocketed; he'd made more money and generated more success as he'd diversified into buying and selling property; the world had become his oyster as the Spirit of Enterprise had flooded the eighties, making fortunes for those who seized the opportunity, and so many did. Millionaires had been created every week; young men were able to retire at thirty-five, having made themselves exceedingly rich; and new companies had started up all over the country as the competition to succeed had grown stronger.

But everything went in cycles; Selwyn knew that too much expansion had overheated the economy; businesses were in trouble now, and the stock market had slumped. He had been fully aware of an impending recession but he'd had enough confidence in Mrs. Thatcher to know that things would be restored in due course, and that as soon as the cost of living dropped and interest rates were lowered, the boom would return in full measure, and they could all enjoy the benefits of a rich economy once more.

"Oh, my God," he repeated as the implications sank in. "I can't stay here, Anne. I must go home. Get Jeffreys to come back with the car, will you?"

"Yes, certainly, Lord Witley. Are you all right?" she asked in concern. Selwyn looked gray and drawn, and his hands were shaking.

He gulped. "If you want to know, I'm gutted, absolutely gutted. She's been forced into resigning, you know that, don't you? This is all the result of a treacherous cabal. They've stabbed her in the back—those who owe their very positions to her!" Angrily he snapped his briefcase shut. "They were happy enough to give her their support when the going was good, but now that we're going through a sticky patch, although not as sticky a financial patch as in America, they want her out of the way! It's bloody disgraceful!"

"I'll get your car right away," she said soothingly.

"Oh, and, Anne . . ."

"Yes, Lord Witley?"

"I want to send Mrs. Thatcher some flowers. Arrange for one hundred and thirty-eight red roses to be sent to 10 Downing Street."

"A hundred and thirty-eight?"

"One for each month she has been Prime Minister."

As Jeffreys drove him home again, Selwyn realized how deeply disconsolate he felt. Nothing would ever be the same again. A golden era had come to an end, and the greatest peacetime Prime Minister had been

ousted from the Conservative party, although she had
done nothing wrong. It was unthinkable. And unbelievable too. A PM who had won three general elec-
tions in a row was being forced to step down in a coup
of appalling magnitude. Many of his old friends, who
had formed part of her entourage, all self-made men
like himself, would disperse too, while a shining new
brigade took over the running of the country.

Elfreida greeted him, still in her satin-and-lace neg-
ligee, although it was now after ten o'clock. Pop music
was blaring from the transitor radio she lugged around
the house with her, as if she couldn't bear the silence
of the empty rooms.

"Why you home?" she demanded in surprise.

"Turn off that bloody thing!" he shouted above the
din. "Haven't you heard what's happened?"

"No!" She turned the volume down, but the strains
of Tina Turner still filled the study.

"Turn that thing *off*!" Selwyn commanded, striding
over to the television set in the corner. "Mrs.
Thatcher has resigned and I want to see what's
happening."

As the screen flickered and blossomed into life, a
newscaster standing outside the leader's house in
Downing Street was giving an update on the dramatic
happenings of the morning.

". . . Mrs. Thatcher is expected to leave here at
eleven-fifteen to drive to Buckingham Palace, where
she will have an audience with the Queen."

Selwyn went over to the drinks cabinet and poured
himself a glass of whiskey, neat. Then he returned to
sit slumped in an armchair before the television set.

"This is a tragedy for the country," he muttered,
half to himself.

Elfreida perched on the arm of a nearby chair and
looked at the screen with disinterested eyes.

"She's been Prime Minister for a long time. A
change will be good."

"You don't know what you're talking about."

"Yes, I do," Elfreida replied stoutly. "Mrs. Thatcher
did a lot of bad things."

"She was a great Prime Minister, the greatest since Churchill," Selwyn insisted.

She shrugged, already bored by the conversation. "I hear people say she divided the rich from the poor, that she was a fascist, and that she encouraged greed."

"She can't be blamed for creating conditions that some people took advantage of," Selwyn reasoned, losing his temper. "Greatness is not the same thing as perfection, anyway. Nobody's perfect. Churchill wasn't perfect. He made mistakes and he made enemies, but he was still a great man. A society that provides opportunities will always produce opportunists; it's human nature. You can't blame Mrs. Thatcher for that."

"Well . . ." Elfreida gave the screen a final drifting glance. "I'm going to have a bath. How long will you stay here?"

"All day, I expect," he replied gruffly. "This is history in the making and it would do you good to watch. Mrs. Thatcher will be making a speech in the House of Commons this afternoon. I have to stay and watch that."

"I am going out." She was, in fact, seeing Roland, who had suggested, in spite of the debacle of her party, that they meet for lunch.

"Humph."

"Will you be all right? I thought you were having lunch at the Savoy."

"I've canceled. I might go to the club later on." It was obvious he didn't want to be bothered by her presence, so, shrugging, she left the room, taking her radio with her.

And so began Selwyn's vigil in front of the television as he watched the events of the day unfold, as little by little his world crumbled before his eyes.

Elfreida arrived early at San Lorenzo and was thrilled, as she sat at the table waiting for Roland, to see the place was packed with celebrities. Nearby, Princess Diana was lunching with her brother, Viscount Althorp; Joan Collins was with a group of friends at another table, and in the corner Robert Wagner and Jill St. John were lunching tête-à-tête. Elfreida glanced around the plant-filled, glass-roofed restaurant with ill-disguised fascination, glad that she was wearing her new Chanel suit. Roland certainly knew the best places to go, that was for sure. Perhaps he'd even be able to introduce her to some of these famous faces. Her mind raced ahead, imagining herself curtsying to Princess Diana, shaking hands with Joan Collins, and smiling—perhaps a little flirtatiously?—at Robert Wagner.

At that moment Elfreida was ready to forgive Roland Shaw for inviting all those people to her house and saying it was his party organized for her benefit. It was cheeky of him, of course, and Selwyn had been right to be furious, but one mustn't be too hasty. It would never do to fall out with Roland, Elfreida reflected.

Deciding to act sweetly and forget about how badly he'd behaved, she ordered a glass of champagne while she waited. Ever since the night of their ball she'd acquired a taste for champagne and the delightfully bubbly feeling it gave her. By the time Roland arrived, twenty minutes later, Elfreida was all smiles. She greeted him with outstretched arms.

"Hello! How lovely to see you," she exclaimed so loudly that several people turned to stare.

Roland avoided her embrace and sat down stiffly on the seat facing her.

"Are you well?" she cooed in the voice she always used when trying to coax Selwyn. "I must say you're looking very well . . . very handsome!"

With cold gray eyes he stared at her in a strange manner, and in the daylight that filtered through the lush plants above their heads, his skin had an unhealthy greenish tinge.

"What will you have to drink?" Elfreida continued, growing desperate as he sat in silence, just looking at her. "Waiter! . . . We'd like some drinks."

But when the waiter scurried over, Roland ignored

Elfreida and spoke directly to the young Italian who hovered unctuously.

"I'll have a Bloody Mary," he snapped.

For a moment Elfreida looked miffed, and then she said: "And I'll have another glass of champagne."

"Certainly, madam." The waiter bowed and then sped off, leaving them in silence once again, while Elfreida racked her brains, trying to think of something to say.

"Have you been to any nice parties lately?" she suddenly asked. As soon as the words were out of her mouth, she knew it was the worst thing she could have said. Blushing, trying to recover herself and change the conversation, she added hurriedly: "Have you seen . . . Princess Diana over there?"

But Roland's eyes were gazing fixedly at her again, making her feel deeply uncomfortable. Elfreida began to panic. What was she supposed to do? Apologize for abandoning the party and taking Princess Ada out to dinner? Say she was sorry? But it was Selwyn who had ordered the servants to stop serving drinks! She'd already decided to foot the bill for lunch today, although it was Roland who had invited her, but what more could she do? He was obviously deeply offended, and somehow she had to put it right or he'd stop helping her to get on in society.

"Roland," she began in her little-girl voice.

His mouth tightened.

"Roland . . . what would you like me to do?" She might have been a child begging for parental forgiveness.

"I'll tell you exactly what I'd like you to do." His voice was abrupt now, a sharp *rat-a-tat*.

She started in surprise. "Yes?"

"You've ruined my standing on the social scene, made me a laughingstock among my friends, humiliated me, wrecked my chances with the royal family, destroyed my credibility." *Rat-a-tat. Rat-a-tat.*

"No! No, I haven't!" Elfreida, scarlet and shaking, looked at him with real fear. If he thought she was responsible for all that . . . for unwittingly destroying the one person who had offered to help her . . . Her hands flew to her face, appalled.

"How can I have done that?" she quavered.

Through his clear polished glasses Roland's eyes pierced hers. "You know perfectly well. You don't deserve to be accepted into high society if you don't know how to behave. What you did was unforgivable, and you put Princess Ada in a very embarrassing position."

"But I . . ."

"You also insulted all the other guests, many of whom were friends of *yours*, I would remind you, by walking out like that."

"Yes, but I—"

"It was unforgivable behavior. I don't know who the hell you think you are." Roland's color had changed too, the sallowness replaced by a dark flush, and his voice was thick with intensity. "But nobody— I repeat, nobody—treats me like that."

"Roland!" Elfreida looked ready to cry, and several people had turned again at the shrillness of her voice. "I'll make it up to you, I promise. I'll give another party, a lovely party, and we'll invite all the press so that everyone will know—"

"No!"

"But, Roland—"

"*No!*"

"But we can make it a lovely evening. You can invite who you like. Oh, please, Roland . . ." She ran her fingers through her hair in agitation, ruining a very expensive wash and blow-dry. "I'll put it right. I'll—"

His voice was cutting. "Once I have been betrayed, that is that."

"What you mean? Betrayed? I no betray you, dear Roland. I—"

"You have betrayed me publicly and ruined me in the eyes of society."

"No, Roland, no!" The enormity of the whole situation was too much for her. If she'd ruined Roland, then she'd most certainly ruined herself. Tears ran down her cheeks, leaving little white streaks in her makeup. "What do I do, then?" she asked piteously. "Tell me what I do."

With the exception of Princess Diana, nearly everyone at San Lorenzo was looking at them now. Animated discussion on the resignation of the Prime Minister had dwindled to breathless silence as people strained to hear what was going on.

For the first time Roland smiled, but it was a bitter twisted smile and it did not reach his eyes.

"Oh, I'll tell you exactly what to do," he said confidently.

"Yes?"

"But I think you would prefer it if I didn't tell you here and now."

"Oh?" Relief mingled with a sense of intrigue filled Elfreida. Was he going to offer her a reprieve? A chance to make amends so that he would help promote her as they'd originally planned? "Anything, Roland. Anything," she vowed.

"Fine. In the meantime, we might as well eat." As he had no intention of paying for lunch, he picked up the menu, and peering at it through his polished glasses, studied it closely to see which were the most expensive dishes.

Two hours later, Elfreida was scrabbling frantically in her jewel box, dry sobs tearing at her throat, panic making her hands shake. Which piece should she sell in order to raise money to silence Roland? The aquamarine-and-diamond brooch? No, that probably wouldn't raise as much as ten thousand pounds from a quick sale. The ruby ring? She gazed through blurred eyes at the perfect bloodred ruby Selwyn had given her last Christmas, its platinum setting sparkling with diamonds, its value a great deal more than ten thousand. No, Selwyn would notice it was missing, because she often wore it. What else was there? The diamond earrings? The diamond-and-aquamarine bracelet?

"Oh, God, I wish I'd never met him . . . ," Elfreida

moaned, wringing her hands. "How can he do this to me?"

Roland had issued her an ultimatum as they left San Lorenzo.

"I want ten thousand pounds, within two days, or else I sell your story to the *Sunday Globe*," he said with odious clarity as they walked slowly along Beauchamp Place.

Elfreida had regarded him defiantly. "My story? But everyone knows my story! When Selwyn left his wife for me, it was in all the newspapers."

"Oh, I know."

"So?"

"They didn't print much about your past, did they? Before you went to work as *au pair*, to the Falk-Stanleys and then the Athertons?"

A dark flush started at the base of Elfreida's throat and then spread up to her cheeks. "I don't know what you're talking about," she retorted defiantly.

"I think you do." Roland's smile was smug, as if he were hugging a delightful secret to himself.

"No, I don't know." She tossed her head and pretended to look at the jewelry in Ken Lane's shop window.

"How you earned money when you first arrived in this country? You can't have forgotten that?" Roland said in a low voice, joining her to look at the dazzling array of sparkling earrings and bracelets, gold necklaces and ropes of pearls. Elfreida looked up and caught Roland's reflection in the glass, close to hers. Their eyes met and she gave a little gasp

"Remember?" he asked.

"I was an *au pair*, always an *au pair*."

"What about that club in Brewer Street? The Green Parrot?"

Elfreida turned and hurried along the pavement, elbowing him to one side, so that he had to step onto the road. A taxi hooted in warning.

"Leave me alone!" she cried.

Roland quickened his pace to keep up with her. "You were a stripper at the Green Parrot, weren't you? And you weren't particularly fussy who you went home with after the show, were you? . . . as long as they paid well."

"No! No!"

Along Beauchamp Place the shop windows glittered and glowed with expensive merchandise: silk-and-lace lingerie by Janet Reger; cocktail dresses by Princess Diana's favorite designer, Caroline Charles; ball gowns by Bruce Oldfield; beaded shoes and bags and bangles, extravagant hats and belts and scarves. Each little boutique in this exclusive shopping area was a cornucopia of exotic goods, but Elfreida saw none of it. With eyes fixed before her in a panic-stricken stare, she scurried unheedingly, her high heels wobbling on the flagstones of the pavement, while passersby jostled her, and Roland's words echoed hideously like a nightmare in her ears.

"You know it and I know it," Roland was persisting. "There's no point your denying it. I have a list of your . . . er . . . shall we say 'clients'? And the owner of the Green Parrot would be quite thrilled to have it known that one of his girls was now a titled lady!"

"*No!*" Elfreida repeated. She stopped suddenly and swung around to face Roland. "You can't do this to me! Not now, not when I've made a new life for myself. Please, Roland . . . I'll do anything . . ."

He raised his eyebrows in a fastidious fashion. "I'm only asking for a little money," he said in a voice that made his demands sound reasonable. "None of this *need* come out, if you'll cooperate. Unless, of course," he added artfully, "Selwyn would be prepared to give me what I ask?"

The single word exploded from her now. "No! *No!* Oh, God, he must never know. I'll get it somehow . . . but it may take a few days, it won't be easy. I have no money of my own, only my jewelry," she added piteously.

"The day after tomorrow. I'll call at your house at five o'clock."

Elfreida stared down at her feet. "Very well," she whispered.

With a polite inclination of his head, Roland smiled charmingly, so that anyone passing would think two old friends were taking their leave of each other.

"Oh, and thank you for a delicious lunch," he added as an afterthought as he strode away toward Brompton Road.

Now, as she held up a pair of diamond earrings to the light, she knew that they were the ones that must go to buy his silence. She would take them to a friend who owned a jewelry shop just off Bond Street. What she was going to tell him, she had no idea. It would have to be something good, though, otherwise why should a woman, married to an exceedingly rich man, want to sell a beautiful pair of earrings he'd given her only the year before?

"This situation is getting out of hand," Jackie observed, putting down the phone. She looked across the cluttered office at Rosie, who was studying some color transparencies of nubile models in beachwear.

"What is?"

"Roland Shaw and his machinations. You've no idea, Rosie. He seems to have woven a web of the most incredible complexity among the upper echelons of society. Wherever I go, and whoever I speak to, someone has a tale to tell about Roland Shaw. He's everywhere, creating havoc."

"Then why does no one stop him?" Rosie demanded. "It's simple enough, surely?"

Jackie shook her head. "That's just what it isn't. Look at poor old Bill Glass—being sued for slander! It doesn't matter that it may be a trumped-up case, the damage has already been done. Bill's lost several photographic jobs because people are scared of appearing to take his side. Roland Shaw is evil. I've just been talking to someone on the phone who has also received a writ, this time for libel. She wrote to her sister, saying don't have this disreputable man to the house because he sells drugs to young people, and the sister warned several of her friends, and of course it got back to Roland."

"Is there nothing that can be done?"

"You know what the British are like, Rosie. They seem to thrive on a conspiracy of silence, keeping secrets and pushing everything under the carpet rather than admitting they've been made fools of."

Rosie laughed. "I know what you mean. It's a basic fear of making a scene, I suppose, and from what you've told me about Roland Shaw, he seems to attack vulnerable people, doesn't he?"

"Yes." Jackie looked thoughtfully out the window. "The old and the lonely, people in high places, and people with a lot to lose, like Celia Atherton. His victims are either rich, and he's out for all he can get, or they've crossed him in some way, as I did, and he's out for blood. Something very deep-rooted must be motivating him to advance himself on one hand and destroy everyone who gets in his way on the other."

"Are there really a lot of people in his clutches?"

"I believe there are dozens and dozens, both here and abroad. He's been making inroads into foreign royalty, you know, by saying he can introduce them into English society. In one case, he even hinted to some deposed king from central Europe that he might be able to get the British royal family to give them a house in Gloucestershire to live in!"

"Then he's preying on the wishful thinking of various unfortunate people, who, I suppose, are prepared to grab at straws in the wind in the hopes of bettering their lives."

"Exactly," Jackie agreed. "It is mass manipulation on a grand scale. He's conning everyone, but in the end they are also conning each other as well."

Rosie grinned. "It's quite clever, I must say, if it wasn't all so pointless. I mean, who the hell cares if the Duchess of So-and-so did something dreadful in 1928, or whatever? Who cares about the social scene these days? Quite frankly, although you write a brilliant column, I can't imagine why anyone is interested in the activities of a lot of social butterflies."

Jackie laughed ruefully. "My sentiments exactly," she admitted. "But I don't know about anything else well enough to write about it. The point, though, is that society people care very much about their image, and who has been asked to which party, and who is new on the scene. It's a whole way of life, and right now Roland Shaw is snarling up the network, so that all these people are tiptoeing around, frightened of seeing him at parties because he's probably got something on them, and frightened of exposing him because they'd be exposing their own private lives as well if they did. At the same time, they don't want to stay away from the social scene in case they get forgotten. I tell you, he's got the very core of the social scene in his hands, and a lot of people are running scared."

Rosie looked at her in amazement. "You wouldn't have thought one young man could have such power. It's ridiculous."

"I know. I'm longing to write a feature exposing him and all he does, but when I mentioned it to Bertram, he nearly had a fit. Asked if I wanted the magazine to be shut down."

"So what's going to happen?"

Jackie shrugged. "Search me. Something will have to give eventually, I suppose, but who will crack first? Roland or the establishment?"

Rosie rose and went over to the coffee machine in the corner. "Christ, and I thought the world of fashion was cutthroat and ruthless! All this makes it seem like the Teddy Bears' Picnic by comparison."

Mrs. Pinner had polished and vacuumed the drawing room as if her life depended on it, in readiness for the BBC.

"I'm being interviewed at eleven o'clock tomorrow morning," Celia had told her. "I expect there will just be someone with a camera and the interviewer, so could you bring up coffee when they arrive, please?"

"Certainly, m'lady." If it had been exciting having an employer who was a lady-in-waiting to the Queen, then it was more exciting to have one who had become front-page news for the past week, even if the story was nasty.

"I feel sorry for her myself," Mrs. Pinner told Sidney. "It's not her fault, is it, if her father was on Hitler's side in the war? She wasn't even born then."

Sidney had grunted, more interested in the snooker match he was watching on the telly than in the activities of his wife's employer.

"She's had to give up her job, you know," Mrs. Pinner continued, "although I expects as the Queen will 'ave 'er back in time."

"Bloody lot, the Germans," Sidney observed, ". . . though the Japs were worse."

"It all 'appened fifty years ago, Sidney."

"Makes no difference."

"I don't see why 'er ladyship should be made to suffer now."

"I daresay she'll survive. Now, be quiet, I want to watch Joe O'Boye take this shot." Sidney turned up the sound, although the only thing to hear was the click of the snooker balls.

As soon as the front doorbell rang at eleven o'clock the next morning, Mrs. Pinner hurried to answer it.

" 'Morning!" said the burly chap in jeans and a crumpled sweatshirt who was standing there. "Is this Lady Atherton's house?"

Mrs. Pinner drew herself up, looking at the motley collection of people crowded on the doorstep. Some were bearded, all were scruffy-looking, and a girl with a clipboard clasped to her flat chest seemed to have her hair pinned up with large paper clips.

" 'Ere, 'oo are you?" Mrs. Pinner demanded, blocking the way.

"BBC, luv. Come to interview Lady Atherton." The first man spoke breezily, and then with a charming smile pushed past her into the hall. As if a floodgate had been opened, the other seven surged through after him. One carried some spotlights, another some coils of electric cable, a third had a camera, and a fourth a strong-looking tripod. Others followed with aluminum suitcases filled with assorted equipment, and then came the girl with her clipboard. Bringing up the rear was the only one Mrs. Pinner considered "respectable," because he was clean-shaven, well-spoken, and wore a nice dark suit.

"Good morning," he said courteously. And, "Thank you so much," when she shut the front door again after he entered the hall.

Celia appeared at the top of the stairs, looking startled.

"My goodness! So many of you!" she gasped.

The burly man, who seemed to be the spokesman, and was in fact the producer, ignored the remark, and mounting the stairs with outstretched hand, greeted Celia warmly.

"It's good of you to let us come into your home like this," he said.

"Er . . . not at all," Celia responded faintly, turning to lead him into the drawing room. "I thought perhaps . . . er . . . in here?"

He glanced around rapidly. Everyone followed him, crowding in with equipment and dumping it on the floor, so that the drawing room suddenly seemed to have shrunk in size. Mrs. Pinner, anxious to watch the proceedings, could barely squeeze in through the door at all.

The producer smiled at Celia. "I think we'll have you sitting on the sofa. You don't mind if we move a couple of things?"

"No, of course not," she replied politely, presuming he must mean the vase of flowers on the magazine table behind the sofa, or perhaps the gilded standing lamp that stood beside it.

"Right." He turned to the two men who had been carrying the suitcases. "I want that desk moved over there, and the chair also. Let's get rid of this table and that stack of books, they clutter up the background . . . and I think we're going to have to move that bookcase about a foot to the right. Jim, bring that stand of red glass ornaments forward a bit . . . and let's have that picture off the wall."

Celia watched, appalled. "Oh, do be careful of the

cranberry glass, it's very valuable," she cried out as the two beefy scene shifters started crashing about.

Meanwhile, another man was setting up the lights, some on stands, others clipped to the mantelshelf, one even hung from the drapery valance. Another man was crawling around on his hands and knees plugging cables into special sockets and disconnecting all Celia's table lamps.

"Do you have to . . . ?" she began, distressed, but at that moment the girl with the clipboard came up to her and began firing questions at her in an aggressive manner.

"Had you no idea, when you were a child, that your father had been a Nazi?"

Celia's gray eyes stared back at her stonily. "Are you doing the interview?" she asked pointedly.

"No, I'm the producer's assistant," the girl snapped back. "I want to get an angle on the line of questioning. What was your reaction when you found out about your father? Have you asked him about his part in the war?"

Before Celia could reply, the clean-shaven man in the dark suit stepped forward. "Allow me to introduce myself. I'm Ian Campbell. I'll be doing the interview, Lady Atherton, and I assure you there's nothing to worry about." He looked at her earnestly, making her feel he was a man she could trust.

"I'm not used to this sort of thing, you see," Celia replied diffidently. "I'm only doing it in the hopes of stopping the media interest once and for all."

Ian Campbell nodded understandingly. "I think it's a wise move. If we can cover the most important points in this interview, that should satisfy public interest. We just need a few statements from you, giving your side of the story."

"That's what I'm trying to do," said the producer's assistant acidly. Her name turned out to be Hilary and her ambition burned like a beacon for all to see. She gave Ian a withering look. "You've got to know *what* questions to ask."

At that moment the room was bathed in brilliant

light, making the cranberry glass glow and the Louis XIV mirror dazzle.

"Too bright," shouted the producer over what had now become a hubbub of babble. Adjustments were made, and one of the lights was fitted with an opaque filter to soften and dim the illumination. The camera, a large black affair with a big lens, was being screwed to the squat-looking tripod, so low on the ground that Celia knew all they'd get was a view of her chin and nostrils.

"Shouldn't it go higher?" she asked nervously. The producer shot her a surprised look.

"Why don't we get into position on the sofa and just have a little chat while they get on with it," said Ian Campbell soothingly. He was obviously used to the chaos of setting up, and hanging around while people fiddled with lights and microphones.

Celia looked around the room. "I'd no idea it would be such an upheaval."

"I promise you, everything will be put back exactly as it was," Ian assured her. "When it's all over, you won't even know we've been here."

A spotlight suspended from the end of a boom swung around to cast highlights on Celia's hair, nearly hitting Mrs. Pinner on the head in the process.

"Bloody 'ell!" she exploded angrily. "Can't you watch what yer doin'?"

"Perhaps you could make everyone some coffee, Mrs. Pinner?" Celia suggested desperately. The room had become so hot under the lights that she was already perspiring uncomfortably.

Mrs. Pinner looked around resentfully. " 'Ow many's that for, then?"

"Seven," replied the producer instantly. "Thanks, luv. And some biscuits too, if you can manage it.

With regal dignity Mrs. Pinner replied, "I'll see as wot I can do." Then she turned and left the room, her head held high. What a tale she'd have to tell them back in Fulham tonight.

Hilary crouched on the floor in front of Celia and Ian, making notes on her clipboard as they talked.

"So the first you knew was when you read the newspapers while you were staying with the Queen at Balmoral?" she interrupted at one point.

"I don't want to answer that sort of question," Celia replied, frowning. "I'm very anxious to keep the Queen and the royal family out of this. After all, the story of my father is a personal matter, and I wish to make a personal statement, not answer a lot of embarrassing questions."

Hilary looked resentful, pushing her large wire-framed glasses higher up her nose. "We have to operate within a framework," she retorted. "Ian has to be told how to angle his questions."

Celia turned to Ian in appeal. "Can't you just say something like . . . 'Will you tell us your side of the story?'—and then I can give my answer."

Hilary gave a deep sigh of impatience. "This has to be an *interesting* interview, you know. If you didn't want to answer questions, you shouldn't have said you'd do it in the first place."

"I'm prepared to answer fair questions, but not ones involving the Queen," Celia protested.

"Don't worry, I won't put you on the spot," Ian promised, stretching out to squeeze her arm. "But why not let Hilary ask you a few things, and then we can get a better idea of what to ask you . . . as well as what *not* to ask you?" he added diplomatically.

The producer himself leaned over them at that moment. "Can you move more into the corner of the sofa, Lady Atherton? We want to get a long shot as well as close-ups. Grand! Thanks, that's much better."

For another twenty minutes the film crew fussed and fiddled, altering position of lights and, to Celia's relief, raising the camera. They moved more furniture around, the Aubusson rug became hidden under a snakelike tangle of black cables, the room grew warmer and warmer, while the cameraman's body odor became more obnoxious by the minute. Meanwhile, Hilary continued to ask awkward questions, occasionally turning to Ian with an instruction, while she made copious notes.

At last Celia heard, through all the confusion, the producer saying: "Right. Are we ready?" A tiny microphone was clipped to the neckline of her dress, and the sound man was inquiring what she'd had for breakfast so he could get a voice level.

"Okay, let's go," said the producer, and Hilary withdrew to the back of the room and for a moment everything was quiet.

"Right, Lady Atherton. Look at Ian when you're answering his questions, and not at the camera. Forget we're here. Okay, everyone? Quiet, now. Okay. Camera rolling."

"Lady Atherton," Ian began, switching on a professional smile, "the last few days must have been very trying for you. Can you give us an idea of how you felt when—"

Tring-tring. Tring-tring. The phone rang loudly on the desk in the window.

"Shit! Cut!" the producer groaned. "We'll have to start again. Do you mind if we take the phone off the hook?" It was more a demand than a request.

Celia nodded, wishing she'd never agreed to the interview. The drawing room was a mess, there was tangled equipment everywhere, and so many people behind the camera they could hardly move. It was also stiflingly airless, as they'd insisted on shutting the windows to keep out the sound of traffic.

"Right! Okay, everyone. Let's go again."

Ian conjured up another smile and began again. Celia's throat felt dry and constricted.

"No, I had no idea about my father," she began in answer to his questions. "It did come as a big shock, but I think we should get things into perspective." Celia paused, gathering strength, the camera picking up her steady gray eyes and gentle mouth and the quiet way in which she spoke. "My father is now a very old man; all this happened a long time ago and he was of course acting under orders. War is a terrible thing and it does terrible things to people; it makes them act in a way they would not normally dream of doing."

"Do you think your father feels any remorse at the atrocities he is accused of committing?" Ian probed.

"Quite honestly, I haven't discussed it with him."

"How does your mother feel?"

Celia took a deep breath, wishing the interview was over. "Distressed, of course, as anyone would be," she replied diplomatically. "This is a very difficult time for all my family, but I would like to point out that it all happened before I was born, and certainly before my children were born, and so I do not think it is fair that they, in particular, should be made to suffer for something that happened nearly fifty years ago. We have had to fetch them home from school, you know, because of all the media attention, and that really seems very unfair to me."

Ian asked a few more questions and then closed in for the crunch.

"And what of your future, Lady Atherton? What has the Queen's reaction been to all this? You are, of course, one of her ladies-in-waiting, and so this must be very embarrassing for you."

A glint of steely anger showed in Celia's eyes and she stiffened visibly. "I have, of course, resigned as a lady-in-waiting," she said with dignity. The finality of her tone was obvious. She was not going to say any more.

Ian Campbell pressed on ruthlessly. "The War Crimes Bill, which received overwhelming support in the House of Commons recently, is about to be debated in the House of Lords, and if they pass the necessary legislation, your father could be arrested and tried as a war criminal. How do you feel about that?"

"I'm sure the Lords will come to a wise decision, whichever way they vote," Celia replied as calmly as she could, although she was inwardly seething.

"But doesn't this put your husband, the Earl of Atherton, in a difficult position? Will he vote in favor of the bill, which could lead to the arrest of up to seventy-five war criminals currently living in the British Isles, including his own father-in-law?"

This was a line of questioning Celia had not been prepared for. Of course, it had been paramount in her thoughts from the beginning. Her father's future might even lie in Hugo's hands if the voting was close, but it was something she couldn't bear to discuss, not even with Hugo. As she sat under the glaring lights, she felt sick and faint for a moment, exhausted by this grilling, exposed and nervous as the camera zoomed into a close-up. Taking a deep breath, she replied with dignity:

"That is entirely up to my husband."

But Ian still persisted with his line of questioning.

"There is still strong feeling in the country that a Nazi crackdown is desirable, that it is wrong for people like your father to have sought refuge in a neutral country like Southern Ireland for all these years and go unpunished. What do you feel about that?"

"My feelings about the past are of no importance," Celia retorted. "What we have to do is look to the future. I have sons of thirteen and fifteen, and naturally I do not want their young lives blighted by the past, by things that are a part of history as far as they are concerned. I also think," she added carefully, "that bringing these elderly men to trial as war criminals through such draconian legislation would be not justice but revenge, and there is a great difference."

Ian Campbell looked visibly impressed. "Yes, yes, I see, Lady Atherton, and you have no idea which way your husband will be voting in the Lords?"

"None whatsoever," she replied evenly.

"How did all this come to light?" Ian's tone had changed from interrogator to close chum. It put Celia more on her guard than ever. She knew this was the moment when she could so easily relax and then find herself up to her neck in damning questions and answers.

"I'm not sure," she replied evasively.

"But someone must have found out about your father and then told the newspapers?"

"I suppose so, but I've no idea how it happened."

"And you've no idea *who* made the discovery? Isn't that rather strange?" The charm had been abandoned again, and he was once more the inquisitor.

"I am not my father's keeper, Mr. Campbell," Celia replied frostily.

"I'm not suggesting you are, Lady Atherton, but doesn't it strike you as strange that your father's past, as a member of the SS, goes undetected for forty-five years, unknown, so you say, to yourself and your mother, and then suddenly all is revealed? And you say you've no idea who made the discovery?"

"I have no comment to make on this."

"Will the Queen in due course reinstate you as a lady-in-waiting?"

"I'm afraid I really couldn't say."

"But she has shown you sympathy and understanding during this difficult time?"

Celia glared, her mouth clamped shut. This is intolerable, she thought. There was long pause, during which time seemed to drag like a terrible blank void.

"I have nothing more to say," she murmured at last, shaking her head.

"Cut! Okay, everyone. Relax. That was great! Thanks, Lady Atherton. You were great."

"But I . . ." Her words became lost in the ensuing babble and sudden activity of the crew. Lights were switched off, the camera taken off its tripod, cables were gathered up, and a feeble attempt was made to restore her drawing-room to its former neatness.

"Just leave it . . . we'll do it," Celia said weakly as they shoved the table up against the back of the sofa again, making the ornaments on it rock and shudder. All she wanted was for them to go, so she could blot out the whole horrible experience; go, so she could collect her scattered wits, for the questions had disturbed her deeply, bringing to the surface aspects that she had tried to bury at the back of her mind ever since the story had broken. And the fact that the House of Lords would soon be voting on whether to pass legislation to put war criminals on trial only added to her present anguish. In view of Hugo's position as a member of the Lords, the situation was escalating into a nightmare from which she might never awaken.

*   *   *

Roland polished his glasses excitedly, then put them back on his nose to study the list. It was perfect. This was going to be the most wonderful dinner party he had ever organized, and in a mood of self-congratulation he studied the names once more. The greatest coup had been getting Queen Maria of Hapsburg to accept his invitation. He'd had to lie, of course, telling her in the carefully written note he'd sent round to Claridge's, where she was staying, that Crown Prince Gustaf of Luxembourg was also expected; but that didn't matter. On the night, he'd tell her that the prince was ill and unable to attend, and she'd be none the wiser. Meanwhile, having received her gracious acceptance, he was able to pull in a lot of other people who would not otherwise have accepted. People who could be useful to him in one way or another; people who would invite him to their stately homes for the weekend, or ask him back to dinner, or supply him unwittingly with some piece of gossip he could sell to a newspaper. Including himself, he now had twelve guests. All he had to do was telephone Jayne Summerville, the public-relations girl at the Brunswick Hotel in Mayfair, to confirm his table in the restaurant for next Thursday evening at eight-thirty. He'd organized that brilliantly too. When he'd telephoned her a couple of weeks before, reminding her they'd met at a charity ball, he put a proposition to her that he knew she'd jump at, especially as she was new to the job, and the hotel was keen to get a more prosperous clientele.

"I've got to give a dinner party for some royals," he'd begun in a rather bored and blasé voice. "You know what it's like: they arrive in London wanting to take part in the Season and longing to meet amusing people, and because they know that I know everyone, they call me."

"Oh, yes?" Jayne had sounded interested and alert.

"One of them is Queen Maria . . . of Hapsburg, you know. A sweet person. Old friend of my mother's. She arrives at Claridge's in a couple of days'

time, and I just know she wants me to give a party
for her. Then I've got to ask Crown Prince Gustaf of
Luxembourg to something, because he was so kind to
me last year, inviting me on his yacht; I also thought
I'd ask the American duchess who is so pretty . . .
Morgan, Duchess of Lomond, plus Lord and Lady
Ravensbrook, and Princess Ada . . . such a delightful
girl. In all, I'm planning to have a dozen people, and
I was wondering if the Brunswick would be prepared
to give the dinner and wines in return for my bringing
all these people to the hotel?" Roland paused, letting
the carrot hover, dangle tantalizingly, before he
added: "Of course, I'd be quite happy if you wanted
to invite Richard Young from the *Daily Express* to
come along and take pictures during the evening."

Jayne Summerville didn't so much bite as dive head-
long into the trap. "We'd be delighted," she purred.
"That's a real list of VIPs you have there, and I know
Mr. Colchester, the general manager, will be delighted
to arrange dinner for you. May I suggest you start
with aperitifs in the bar? Champagne and some nice
canapés? Then we can ask the chef to do his famous
turban de saumon with caviar sauce for the first
course—that's cured salmon and haddock mousse in a
caviar cream sauce, and it's deliciously light. And then
how about a main course of roast veal with chives and
wild mustard? The chef could then do *vacherin aux
fruits* for the pudding, which is meringue filled with
passion-fruit sorbet and served with oranges and
strawberries—it's wonderfully tangy and refreshing.
And then of course coffee and *petits fours* to end with.
I'll get the sommelier to suggest which wines will be
best, and you might like to offer your guests liqueurs
with their coffee."

Rather grandly Roland conceded that the suggested
menu sounded fine. "Very nice," he remarked casually as he did a quick calculation of how much it would
have cost if he'd been paying.

"Would it be all right," Jayne continued tentatively,
"if our own photographer took some pictures as
well?"

"Yes, that will be okay," Roland replied. "These people are used to being photographed all the time."

Now, as he contemplated his guest list, his pleasure became marred by enraged disappointment once more when he thought how he had been denied being able to say he worked for *Society* magazine. It had been his open-sesame to the drawing rooms of London, his passport to the Good Time. Every hostess had welcomed him, rolling out the metaphorical red carpet when he appeared, plying him with hospitality, and showering him with compliments. All that was changed now, thanks to that bitch Jackie Daventry and that old sod of a photographer Bill Glass. Grinding his teeth with fury, he thought how differently things could have worked out if he hadn't been thwarted in his attempts at being a leading social light.

Taking off his glasses to give them another polish, Roland thought about the funerals he'd ordered for Jackie. The trouble was, she hadn't been sufficiently scared. In fact, she was going to more parties than ever, and she'd gained a heroic aura as a result. Christ, how he loathed her! How he hated her smug face and air of self-assurance, as if nothing could ever hurt her. Maybe he could teach her a lesson that would change her mind about that.

11

Jackie looked at Gerald in consternation. "But we've been so careful," she exclaimed.

"I know, darling. How Candy found out about us, I don't know, but now that she has, she's really going for broke," Gerald replied ruefully. He'd come straight from the head office of the Goray Group to Jackie's apartment, and he looked tired and harassed. "She says she'll give me a divorce, but only on condition she gets a large settlement as well. Didn't I tell you she'd do this to me if she found out about us?"

"It's so unfair," Jackie broke in. "After the way she's treated you and tricked you into marrying her. I'm so sorry, darling."

Gerald pulled her down onto the sofa beside him, and putting his arms around her, held her close. "It's not your fault, my love. There was always a chance someone would see us together and it would get back to Candy."

Jackie snuggled against his side, pressing her face into the warmth of his neck. "But I feel so guilty, Gerald."

He pulled away from her, his face filled with astonishment. "Guilty? Why, for God's sake? You didn't take me away from Candy. Our marriage was over before it had even begun. She's had her boyfriend with her for the past four years, and he's with her now. Why should you feel guilty?"

"I'm not feeling guilty about Candy, I'm feeling bad

because I've a strong feeling that it was my *bête noire*, Roland Shaw, who told her about us."

Gerald sat still for a moment, his arms still around her, then spoke slowly and thoughtfully. "You're probably right. Judging by what he's already done, he's capable of anything."

"What shall we do? What *can* we do?" Exasperated, Jackie pulled away, sitting upright so she could look squarely at Gerald. "I'm sick of this, you know. He's making mischief all over the place and doing untold harm. I heard yesterday that Celia is on the brink of a nervous breakdown, and there are others too whose lives he is wrecking. We've got to do something to put a stop to his activities."

Gerald shook his head. "Yes, but what? We've taken legal advice, but we're dealing with a very slippery customer. He's tying people up in knots of their own making, that's the main trouble."

"Then what are you going to do about Candy?"

"I'm not going to give her a penny. She married me under false pretenses and she's not getting any of my money." Gerald's jaw tightened aggressively. Candy had made a fool of him and he didn't like it. All he wanted now was to get her out of his life.

"Don't look so angry," he heard Jackie whisper in his ear as she pressed herself against him. "We've got each other and that's all that matters."

His face softened immediately as he caught her close and held her fast. "I know we have, my love, and thank God for it," he murmured.

Gently Jackie nibbled his neck, just under his ear, and he groaned softly. His voice was husky when he spoke.

"Let's get into bed, shall we?"

"Why not?" Lingeringly she kissed his jawline and cheek, with light feathery kisses, while her hand slid caressingly inside his jacket. Then, still with their arms around each other, they went to the bedroom, where the dusk of evening muted the shadows and the large bed stood invitingly under its deep pink canopy.

They undressed quickly, knowing each other so

well, although they'd been together only a short time.
They could now sense each other's feelings and needs,
so that words were unnecessary. Once in bed, they
came together swiftly, on a rising tide of passion, the
firmness of his body sending tingling sensations of delight through Jackie as she stroked his back and felt
his tongue, hot and ardent, exploring her mouth. Usually it was Gerald who strove to stimulate her with
tender hands and honeyed words, but this evening she
felt a deep need to be the one to seduce him and lead
him down the path to fulfillment; and so she slid on
top of him, squeezing and stroking his buttocks before
bending over him to bite gently on the firm flesh.

"Oh, baby . . ." His voice caught.

Jackie sank her teeth into his tight bottom again,
leaving little marks, yet never hurting him, and then
with a swift movement she rolled him onto his back.
While he cupped her head in his hands, his fingers
lost in her cascading black hair, she licked his stomach
in a circular movement, then up to his ribs, around
his belly, and down his groin, her tongue leaving a
blazing trail.

"Oh, Jesus, yes . . . eat me, sweetheart . . . eat me
alive."

As her lips continued to gently tantalize him, she
brushed her nails lightly up and down the insides of
his thighs, so that he shivered and dug his fingers into
her scalp. Then, with her soft wet mouth and hot
breath, she slowly sucked the center of his universe,
making him gasp and writhe beneath her.

"Oh, baby, baby, baby . . ." He moved his head
from side to side on the pillow and his eyes were
closed. "Oh, yes, yes . . . don't stop . . . don't ever
stop . . ."

Curling herself around him, Jackie took him deeply
into her mouth, while her hands continued to stroke
and tease. This was a man she loved more than she
could ever have imagined possible. With him she
could forget Richard had ever existed; with him the
worries of the world slipped away and were as nothing. Gerald was her life now, as she knew herself to

be his, and nothing would ever come between them. From the moment she'd met him, she'd known they were destined to be together, and an overwhelming surge of love filled her now as she remembered the magic of that first meeting. He was everything she most admired in a man—strong, kind, powerful, and with a wonderful sense of humor. And he was all hers.

At that moment, as if he was aware of the great lassitude that was enveloping her as wave after wave of desire threatened to engulf her, he gently raised her head, lifted her so that he could kiss her, and then with a swift movement rolled over, pinning her under him. They moved in unison now, their breathing labored, their cries mingling until they became one cry, with one aim, one goal. Together they climaxed, gasping, sobbing, clinging to each other as if the world were about to come crashing around them, and Jackie heard him exclaim over and over, "I love you . . ."

It was dark when they awoke an hour later, and still in each other's arms they lay talking quietly for a while until Gerald said:

"I could do with a drink."

"So could I. There is a bottle of champagne in the refrigerator, if you'd like to fetch it?"

He slipped out of bed. "Stay there and I'll get it."

When he'd gone to the kitchen, Jackie also got out of bed, drew the pink curtains, and turned on the bedside lights. When Gerald returned a minute later, a rosy glow filled the room and she was sitting up in bed, a white satin robe draped around her shoulders.

"You look sweet," he remarked, eyeing her with unconcealed admiration.

Jackie watched him, tanned and naked, as he opened the bottle of Bollinger. A powerful-looking man, she reflected, and yet he possessed the gentleness of a lamb. Their eyes met. He handed her a glass of champagne.

"I think it's time we drank a special toast," he said, getting into bed beside her again.

She raised her eyebrows inquiringly. "To us?"

"Yes, to us," he admitted. Then he put his arm

around her and looked into her eyes. "But more than that."

"What more is there?" she teased.

"To us . . . getting married. We *are* going to get married, aren't we, sweetheart?"

"Oh, Gerald!" She'd hardly dare think that far ahead, and yet she knew it was exactly what she wanted.

"Well?" He paused, the glass half-raised to his mouth. His eyes twinkled. "Say something, for God's sake! Put me out of my misery. Are we going to get married or not?"

Jackie snuggled closer to him and there was a delighted smile on her face. "Of course we are!"

He sank back contentedly against the pillows. "That's what I thought. For a moment there I thought you were going to reject me."

She giggled. "As if I'd ever do anything so silly."

"And if Candy gets all my money, will you still have me?"

Jackie pretended to look serious. "You might have to apply again, in triplicate."

He groaned. "Triplicate? I'm not sure I've got the strength to do it *twice*." He reached over to kiss her lightly on the mouth. "On second thought, I could do it four or five times . . . with you."

"Really? Are we going to put this to the test?" Jackie's dark eyes looked wickedly into his.

"Let's have this drink first." He raised his glass to her, and his face was serious now. "To our getting married."

Jackie suddenly felt misty-eyed and her throat constricted emotionally. "To our getting married," she echoed in a whisper.

Because Candy had found out about their affair, there was no more need for secrecy. The next morning Gerald went back to his flat to change before going to the office, promising Jackie he'd move in with her on the weekend.

"I'm going to get rid of my gloomy flat," he said

when they awoke to the sound of the dawn chorus as the birds sang merrily in the trees below Jackie's windows. During the night, between sleeping and waking and making love, he'd whispered that all he wanted was to spend the rest of his life with her, and suddenly she'd known that it was what she'd wanted too. And if Roland Shaw had thought he could destroy her happiness by telling Candy Wyldman about them, his scheme had backfired. It's had the opposite effect, Jackie thought happily as she opened the bedroom curtains after Gerald had gone. The summer had long gone, but the weather was still beautifully dry, and the sun was shining in a clear blue sky. Down below, on Rotten Row, a group of neatly turned-out riders trotted sedately past. Stretching her arms above her head, she breathed in the gloriously fresh air and watched a sudden breeze cause a circling flurry of dust on a pathway, where an old man was feeding crusts to the pigeons and sparrows.

It was going to be a glorious day. She could feel it in her bones, and now that she'd found the perfect love, neither Roland Shaw nor anyone else was going to spoil it for her.

A few miles away in her suite at the Savoy Hotel, Candy Wyldman was getting ready to give a press conference. Her plan was to make a dramatic statement about how heartbroken she was at discovering her husband was having an affair with an American journalist. Tearfully she would explain that she and Gerald had been married only a short while before he'd betrayed her. She would add that she now had no option but to seek a divorce and ask for a settlement to compensate her for the humiliation and loss she'd suffered.

Putting the finishing touches to her thick panstick makeup, which this morning included false eyelashes, as there would be a lot of photographers, and a pale pink lipstick, Candy slipped into a white voile dress with matching tights and shoes, and then she fastened the clasp of a single row of pearls around her neck.

The demure dress made her look fragile and vulnerable, which was the image she'd decided to go for this morning. In fact it almost resembled a short wedding dress with its full skirt and puffed sleeves. She twirled in front of the long bedroom mirror, admiring her long slim legs and the blond hair which cascaded in loose curls and waves to her shoulders. Should she add to the demure look by wearing short white gloves? she wondered. They would be a very useful prop; she could fiddle nervously with the fingers and tug unhappily on the little pearl buttons at the wrists as she made her statement about her life being in tatters after the way Gerald had behaved. In the end, she settled on carrying the gloves with her white purse—a purse that would contain a lace-edged handkerchief with which to dab her eyes, being careful of course not to mess up her makeup.

With her acting skills she was sure she could convince every journalist of how much she was suffering and what great strain she was under, and then she'd get some great publicity.

A touch of Estée Lauder's Beautiful at her throat and wrists, a dab more lip gloss, and she was ready, a perfect picture of a decorously modest young bride who had been wronged. Her smile for the press would be sad but gentle, her voice a Jackie Kennedy Onassis little-girl whisper. Meanwhile she had to check the final details of the press conference with her personal assistant.

"Carol?" she yelled in her usual sharply pitched voice. "Where the fuck are you? Those cunts will be waiting in the River Room if we don't get down there soon. Have you done everything I asked you?"

Carol, a plain young woman of few words, came hurrying into the bedroom.

"I'm here, Miss Wyldman. I've been checking that everyone's arrived."

"Is Don there?" Don Lloyd was her personal publicity agent.

"Yes, he's offering them all coffee at the moment."

Candy's voice was harsh and piercing. "He'd better

offer them something stronger than frigging coffee if he wants me to get good coverage out of this. For Christ's sake, call down and tell the fucking bastard to offer them champagne."

"Yes, Miss Wyldman."

"And have you cleared an area for me to sit while I answer their questions?"

"Yes. I've arranged for a sofa to be placed near the window, with a pedestal of flowers beside it."

"But what's the lighting like there?" Candy eyed her assistant with suspicion. "I'm not going to sit in a place where the lighting's all wrong and it's going to make me look seventy!"

"The lighting's fine, Miss Wyldman. Anyway, they'll be taking flash pictures, so it doesn't matter," Carol said placatingly.

"What do you mean . . . it doesn't matter?" Candy stormed. "Fuck you . . . it *does* matter! Call Don and get him to check the lighting. We'll have to find another room to hold the conference in, if the lighting's wrong."

"Very well," Carol replied with barely concealed exasperation. "While I'm doing that, there is someone here waiting to see you."

"Who? You know people are not allowed to come up to my suite."

"It's a Mr. Roland Shaw. He said you were expecting him," Carol said in a low voice, indicating Roland was in the adjoining room of the suite.

"Oh!" Candy paused to think for a moment. Roland was her newfound friend and ally. If it hadn't been for him coming to the stage door the other night after the show and leaving a note saying he needed to contact her urgently, she'd never have known about Gerald's affair.

"I'll see him," she said decisively. "And tell Don to get his fucking act together and give those reporters a decent drink."

When she strode into the sitting room of her suite, her demure act forgotten for the moment, she found Roland hovering as if he was hoping to find something. At that moment she realized to her annoyance that her boyfriend, Tim, had left his sweater flung over the back of a chair. It was such a typically male-looking sweater too, there was no way Roland would think it belonged to her. Why couldn't Tim be more fucking careful? He was supposed to keep a low profile until she got her divorce, and there he was leaving his goddamn clothes all over the goddamn place.

For a moment a fleeting bad-tempered scowl marred her perfect features, but remembering she wasn't alone, she quickly recovered herself and switched on an appealing smile.

"Good morning, Roland. How are you?"

"Very well, thank you. And you look magnificent," he exclaimed, "quite breathtakingly beautiful."

"Oh, how sweet of you. Thank you so much," she simpered, her voice registering just the right amount of gratitude.

She let her pretty brow pucker. "Oh, it's all so up-setting. I haven't slept since you told me about Gerald. I mean, we had separated, but I'd really hoped it was only a temporary thing. I'd hoped that we'd get together again, because I really loved him, but now . . ." Her voice trailed off pathetically.

Roland nodded with sage understanding. "But you can still get several million pounds out of him under the circumstances, can't you?"

"Oh, sure, and this is going to be very bad for his image in the business world. I'm sure he'll see the need to compensate me for all this misery."

"Oh, quite." He spoke so softly his voice barely registered. Then he smiled, and for a second she thought she detected a trace of malice in his expression, but then she caught sight of her own dreamy reflection in a mirror and became distracted. Running her fingers through her long hair so that it swung like a curtain shielding one side of her face, she posed for a moment, before turning to leave the room.

"I'm afraid I must go now, Roland. The press is waiting for me downstairs."

Roland came nearer, pushing his face close to hers,

blocking her way. "As it was I who made you aware of your husband's infidelity, I'm sure you won't think it unreasonable of me to expect a percentage of whatever you get."

Suddenly Candy forgot all about her dainty performance. Stamping one neatly shod foot, she put her hands on her hips, washerwoman style, and let out a raucous yell.

"Give *you* a percentage, you motha-fucking little cunt!" she shrieked. "Get outta here! I owe you fuck all! Carol?" Her voice shrilled through the opulent rooms of her suite. "Call Security! I want this man removed immediately!"

As Carol came rushing into the room, Candy stomped off in the direction of the elevator, unable to believe that anyone thought he could pull a trick like that on her. Who the fuck did Roland Shaw think he was, anyway?

It took all Candy Wyldman's acting skills, between her suite on the second floor and the River Room on the ground floor, to switch on her sweet smile again and slip into the role of a frail girl. She thanked God she was such a wonderful actress, otherwise she'd never have suceeded.

There was deep consternation in the press office of Buckingham Palace that morning as James Ireland took stock of the latest collection of clippings about the royal family. For some time now, strange and inaccurate stories had been appearing in the daily newspapers, and although this was nothing new, for once the stories had not even the faintest bearing on fact.

"I don't understand this," observed James, passing a particular clipping to Jean Hopkins, the deputy press officer. "How did this particular rumor start? 'Prince Charles is planning to sell his country home, Highgrove, and move to another house in Gloucestershire.' There is no foundation in this story at all. Both he and the Princess of Wales love Highgrove; nothing would induce them to leave now they've landscaped the garden and got everything the way they want it."

"How about this one?" Jean held up another clipping. "It says here that Princess Diana is planning to breed Shetland ponies for Prince William and Prince Harry to have as pets."

James Ireland snorted. "Oh, it's all such rubbish. I wish they'd write something remotely true and sensible for a change." He'd started out as a journalist himself, before joining a television company as a foreign correspondent. When the Queen had appointed him chief press officer he'd been amazed. He was a large burly man from an ordinary background, and in his opinion possessed none of the courtly graces he would have thought necessary for the job. He'd soon discovered, however, that work in the press office of Buckingham Palace suited his strong blunt style of dealing with people, and he'd come to the conclusion that his appointment had something to do with "setting a thief to catch a thief."

"Look at this!" Jean exclaimed. "There's an article here saying the Queen is going to give up racing because it's too expensive to keep her thirty-six racehorses in training."

James laughed. "A likely story, I must say. The Queen may go around the palace at night turning off lights and telling everyone to economize, but she'd never cut out racing, it's one of her chief interests in life."

For the next half-hour they went through the large stack of clippings, sometimes laughing, as when they read Princess Anne had told a nosy photographer to "naff off," sometimes snorting in disgust at some particularly lurid report on the extravagance of the Duchess of York, other times nodding with approval, such as at the coverage of Princess Diana visiting patients in an AIDS clinic.

"That went very well," James remarked. "She looks good in the pictures too."

"Doesn't she always?" Jean sighed enviously. "She must be the most photogenic woman in the world. She doesn't even seem to *have* a bad angle."

All around them, phones were ringing, and fax and

telex machines were bleeping and pinging as secretaries dealt with queries and requests for information, and typists worked on press releases and schedules for forthcoming public engagements carried out by members of the royal family. The Court Circular of the *Times* and *Telegraph* had to be supplied with a daily list of engagements as well, and there were always radio, television, newspaper, and magazine journalists begging for details of interest. Worst of all, though, were the calls from the more lurid tabloids, who were interested only in salacious stories and were capable of inventing them if they couldn't get hold of a good factual story.

James Ireland and his team were very adroit at handling these "queries," and usually managed to get rid of hacks with diplomatic remarks that sometimes included the words: "No comment."

Suddenly there was a yelp from Phoebe Walse, one of the assistant press secretaries. She had been working at the palace for only six months, and so she was still learning the ropes. The others looked up expectantly.

"What is it now?" James asked.

"Who *is* this Count Victor Leroy, for heaven's sake?"

"Let me see."

Phoebe handed him a copy of the French magazine *Ici Paris*.

"Oh, this is always full of scandal, because they can say what they like and we have no control over them." He studied the article briefly, and his face whitened with anger. "This is preposterous! The Queen will be absolutely enraged!" he fumed. "To say these things about Prince Andrew is disgraceful."

"Do you think Count Victor Leroy is a pen name?" Phoebe asked.

"God knows, but I'd like to wring his bloody neck. At least the British press are not allowed to print this type of muck, but I wish we had the same control over the rest of Europe."

"Have they always been as bad as this?" She reread

the article, which would have been libelous if it had
been printed in the United Kingdom.

"Oh, yes." James nodded knowledgeably. "Before
my time, in the sixties, there were continual stories in
Ici Paris and *France Dimanche* about the Queen getting a divorce from Prince Philip, or abdicating, or
being pregnant again; nothing new, but this is a very
vicious attack on the Queen's son."

"Shall I ask around and see if I can find out who
this Count Victor Leroy is?"

James made a wry grimace. "You can try, but I
doubt if you'll succeed."

"What is the matter with you, Elfie?" Selwyn demanded as they got ready to go out to dinner. "That's
the third dress you've changed into in the past fifteen
minutes! Why on earth can't you decide what to
wear?"

Elfreida looked ready to burst into tears. The real
problem was that she no longer had the jewelry that
went with the particular evening gowns she wanted to
wear, and what she did have left looked all wrong for
a formal occasion, such as tonight, when they were
dining with the Lord Mayor of London at the Mansion
House.

"I can't make up my mind," she retorted, flushing.
Her pearls made her look old when worn with the
black chiffon, and her gold necklace looked flashy
with the turquoise silk. That left a few pairs of inconsequential earrings that were more suited to day wear,
a diamond bracelet, and her rings. Wishing she'd gone
to Butler & Wilson to buy some costume jewelry, she
tried on the salmon-pink dress with the ruched skirt
and puffed sleeves. Then she fastened the pearls
around her neck and stared at herself in her long bedroom mirror. She looked like an overblown, blowsy
debutante with high blood pressure. That was when
she had struggled out of the dress and Selwyn's temper
snapped.

"I don't know what to wear," she wailed, much too
frightened to tell him the truth.

He glared at her stonily. "How can you not know what to wear when you spend a hundred thousand pounds a year on clothes?"

She wrung her hands, which were sweating now. "Nothing goes with anything . . . don't rush me, Selwyn."

"For God's sake, woman, I'm not rushing you, but you've spent half an hour fiddling about, and we should be leaving. We can't be late for the Lord Mayor's banquet, for Christ's sake! If you're not ready in five minutes, I'm going!"

"Oh!" A sob burst from her lips. "I don't know what to do!"

Selwyn looked amazed. Even for Elfreida, this was over-the-top behavior. Perhaps she's unwell, he thought. Perhaps . . . Oh, dear God, she couldn't be pregnant, could she? Little cold darts of horror flickered through Selwyn's veins as he contemplated the idea. A screaming baby at his age? Prams in the hall and nannies in the nursery?

"Look, Elfie," he began, not unkindly, "put on that blue thing you were wearing, you know the one with the low-cut neck, and then the necklace and earrings I gave you, and let's go. You'll look fine in that." Turning to the long cheval mirror, he checked on his white bow tie, stiffened shirt front, and mother-of-pearl-and-gold shirt studs. For a man of his age he thought he looked quite distinguished tonight. Lord Witley of Vauxhall. Self-made millionaire. How amazed his mother would have been.

Then he heard a strangulated gurgle coming from his wife. She had flung herself down on the bed, her face contorted as if in pain.

"I . . . I c-can't," she said chokingly.

Fear held him for a moment. Perhaps she was really pregnant!

"What's the matter?" he asked, his voice sharp with anxiety.

"I can't w-wear my jewelry," she sobbed. Weeks of being constantly hounded by Roland, demanding more and more money, had taken their toll. She felt physically and emotionally wrecked, and at this moment she wished she was dead. When she'd sold the first lot of jewelry to meet his demands, he had come right back the next day wanting more, threatening to tell Selwyn as well as the gossip columns about her past. When she'd sold the second lot of jewelry, at way below its true value, she'd insisted that this was the last time he could get anything out of her. He'd smiled that cunning smile and his gray eyes had glinted through his glasses, and she knew, with the most sickening feeling of dread, that it wasn't the end. He'd demand the last bits of her jewelry next, before he started on the contents of the silver cupboard.

Elfreida's sobs grew louder as she thought of her aquamarines and diamonds, and her sapphires and rubies. All her life she'd longed to possess beautiful jewelry, and now most of it was gone.

"What *is* it?" Selwyn was asking, coming over to the bed. "What do you mean you can't wear your jewelry? Of course you can wear your jewelry! Everyone will be wearing jewelry tonight."

"Y-you don't u-understand." She looked up at him, her hair falling around her face, sticking to the tears that coursed down her pudgy cheeks. "I haven't g-got . . . g-got any jewelry anymore."

Selwyn frowned, not understanding. "What are you talking about? You've got lots of jewelry. Christ, I should know. It cost me a packet."

Elfreida shook her head. "But I haven't got it anymore. It's all gone."

"*Gone?*"

"G-gone . . ." She started sobbing again.

"What? Stolen?"

"No." There was a long pause, and then she said, "I had to sell it."

Selwyn sat down suddenly on the edge of the bed, his face gray.

"Sell it?" he repeated in a flat voice. "Sell your jewelry?"

"Yes. You see . . . Oh, I didn't want you to know, but Roland said he'd tell you . . . and the newspapers

. . . and I'd be ruined, and all because he said I humiliated him at that party here." Her voice rose hysteri-
cally. "I don't know how he found out . . . Oh, it's
the end of everything! You'll leave me now! It's all
o-o-over." She was rocking back and forth on the bed,
wearing only a lace see-through bra and panties, and
in spite of everything, Selwyn suddenly found her desirable at that moment. If only she'd calm down, he
thought, and stop crying, he might even be able to get
an erection!

"I don't understand, Elfie. Tell me what you're
saying."

"You really want to know?" The valley between
her breasts was a dark and exciting ravine. She looked
up at him with a tearstained face. "Roland is a bad
man, you know."

Selwyn reached out and ran his hand down the
length of her arm, from her shoulder to her wrist.
"What, exactly, has he done?" he asked, trying to
keep his voice steady.

As calmly as she could, Elfreida told him everything. She kept nothing back. She described the Green
Parrot, where she'd done two shows nightly, stripping
off in front of a bunch of lechers who leered and sla-
vered as their hands jiggled in their trouser pockets
and their eyes devoured her flesh. Then there were
the ones who loitered in the street outside afterward,
waiting for her to leave so they could stop her and
ask her how much she charged for sex. Desperate for
money so she could get herself a better room to live
in and better clothes to wear, she charged whatever
she thought she could get. For a year she worked at
the club, until a bout of pneumonia forced her to stay
in bed for two weeks and left her so weakened she
couldn't face returning. It was then she got friendly
with an Irish girl in the same rooming house, who
persuaded her that she could at least enjoy a better
standard of living if she got a job looking after
children.

"Get a copy of the *Lady* magazine," Maureen had
advised in her soft Irish brogue. "That's where all the

rich people advertise for nannies and chauffeurs and cooks and maids. You'll surely get a job through the *Lady*."

Elfreida wiped her eyes with the handkerchief Selwyn handed her. "That's when I got a job with the Falk-Stanleys, before I went to work for the Athertons."

"And Roland Shaw found all this out," Selwyn asked, "and blackmailed you about it?"

"Yes. Now everything's over, no? You finish with me?" The tears welled up in her eyes again.

Selwyn rose slowly, his ardor dampened, the muscles of his face slack with tiredness. He walked slowly, almost painfully to the bedroom door before turning to look at her. Watching him anxiously, Elfreida could not read his expression, had no idea what he was thinking. Then he spoke.

"I've got to go to this dinner tonight, for business reasons. You go to bed and rest. I'll say you're ill and we'll talk when I get back."

Their eyes met and she couldn't fathom what his feelings were. Humbly, acquiescently she nodded. "I'll wait up for you."

Selwyn left the room without another word, and she heard him going down the stairs. A moment later the front door slammed. She had three hours in which to compose herself and become resigned to the fact that by tomorrow he might well have kicked her out of the house—unless she could persuade him that the past was of no importance and it was him she really loved.

Clambering off the bed, she went to the mirror, groaning when she saw her reflection. Her face was red and blotchy and she looked a wreck. Wisps of hair clung to her forehead, dropping in limp tendrils to her shoulders. She knew she had never looked more unattractive in her life. It was going to take all of three hours to repair the damage, so that she could set about the task of seducing him. And then maybe, just maybe, he'd let her stay.

"Selwyn, how are you?" he heard a voice exclaim as he climbed the crimson-carpeted staircase of the

Mansion House, where three hundred distinguished guests had been invited to a banquet given by the Lord Mayor of London. Turning, he saw it was Celia Atherton, pale and very thin-looking, but still an elegant figure in a dark red silk evening dress with an exquisite sapphire-and-diamond tiara, which made her look very regal. It was the first time they'd spoken since his marriage to Elfreida, and he suspected it was because he was on his own tonight that she'd greeted him in such a friendly fashion.

"Celia, my dear." He kissed her on the cheek. Hugo appeared at that moment and the two men shook hands. "It's good to see you again."

Celia's smile was grave. "It's good to see you too, Selwyn."

"I'm sorry about all the trouble you've been having," he sympathized in a low voice. "It must have been a wretched time for you."

"It has," she replied candidly. "It's been the worst time in my life, and it's not over yet."

Selwyn nodded intuitively. "The House of Lords are voting tomorrow, aren't they?" He looked to Hugo for confirmation. "I don't think they'll pass the bill. Your father will be all right, Celia, I'm sure of it."

Hugo smiled tightly, looking past Selwyn into space. Around them jostled sheriffs in black velvet livery with lace ruffles at the neck and wrists, and women in rich gowns and jewelry, so that in the magnificent setting of the Mansion House the occasion resembled a ball at Buckingham Palace. Chandeliers blazed overhead, casting a dazzling light on the gilt-and-marble walls and the display of gold plate. Banks of exotic flowers stood on pedestals, and all around the opulence bore witness of the wealth of the City of London and the businessmen who had made it so over the past few hundred years. Tradition and heritage mingled in this unique setting, where the Lord Mayor himself, elected every year, held one of the most prestigious positions in the land.

Dinner was announced, and as everyone made his way into the splendid chamber where guests were seated at dozens of long tables joined at one end to the top table, Selwyn turned to Celia again and spoke in a low, confidential voice.

"I don't see how they can bring in the legislation to put war criminals on trial. I mean, most of the evidence will have been destroyed and people's memories are short. Who on earth can remember in detail what happened forty-five or more years ago? Where would the courts get their witnesses from?"

"Not everyone sees it that way." Celia's tone was even, but he noticed she was pointedly looking away from Hugo. He sensed the tension between them, and guessed at the strain on their marriage at this moment.

"I don't know how these things get into the newspapers in the first place," Selwyn snorted, more to change the direction of the conversation than anything else.

"Oh, we know how this one started," Hugo cut in suddenly, his voice harsh. "It all happened because we crossed swords with that bugger of a—"

"Hugo!" Celia said sharply. "We were warned by the lawyers not to say who was responsible—"

Hugo seemed to snap, as if all the previous weeks of trying to remain calm and objective had finally proved too much. He turned on Celia, his face livid.

"I don't care if he *does* sue us for slander or anything else he can think up! And if he sues us, he'll have to sue half of London, from what I hear, because he's causing mischief wherever he goes. The man's evil, and I don't care who knows it."

Selwyn looked confused. "What man?"

Hugo spoke clearly and deliberately, while Celia stood by his side, an expression of acute anxiety on her face.

"We hired a tutor for the boys, a young man called Roland Shaw. That is who I am talking about. That is the person who is selling scandalous stories to the newspapers, blackmailing people, pushing drugs on schoolboys—you name it, he's doing it! But the clever little bugger is so slippery no one can actually put a stop to his activities without harming themselves even more in the process."

Selwyn's mouth dropped open; then he closed it again and a look of incredulity crossed his face. Then his tired old eyes gleamed with something akin to amusement. So Elfreida wasn't alone in being victimized.

"You don't say," he remarked slowly. "Well, that's really most interesting. Humph!" He looked around the room at the men in evening dress, medals and decorations blazing on their chests, and at the women in all their fine silks and satins and glittering tiaras and necklaces. "I wonder how many people who are here tonight are being blackmailed by him."

Celia leaned forward nervously. "Oh, I don't think it's so much blackmail as his attempt to seek revenge if he thinks he's been slighted. That's what happened in our case. I refused to introduce him to the royal family and get him invited to Buckingham Palace and so he set out to find the best way of hurting me."

Selwyn regarded her with compassion. In spite of everything, Celia had lived a very protected life, unlike himself. He'd been born and brought up to be a street fighter, and little runts like Roland Shaw didn't frighten him. But then, he wasn't really a gentleman, he reflected. He wasn't scared of cutting up rough if he had to. Most of all, when it came to the crunch, he didn't give a damn what other people thought. That was where he differed from the real gentry; they were scared of making a scene, of losing their dignity. They'd been bred to act in a dignified way at all times and to close ranks and protect their own whenever there was a crisis. Most of all, the aristocracy liked to keep their skeletons hidden away and would go to any lengths to keep the closet door locked. For himself, he didn't care. He'd come up the hard way and it had made him impervious to public opinion.

"Humph," Selwyn growled. "I think we'll have to think of a way of dealing with this Mr. Roland Shaw."

Celia looked surprised. "He hasn't been giving you trouble too, has he, Selwyn?"

"It depends what you mean by trouble, but I believe

he's cost me something in the region of a million pounds so far," Selwyn replied dryly, "coupled to which Elfreida seems to be having a nervous breakdown, and I am about to get very angry."

"Elfreida?" Hugo queried. He said her name with a tinge of distaste.

Selwyn looked defiant. "Yes, Elfreida," he replied stoutly. Then with a brief wave of his hand he slid away to find his place at one of the long tables, which were set with magnificent City of London gold plate, cut crystal, and crested crockery. For the next two and a half hours he would have to make polite conversation to the people around him while they partook of a traditional menu that included turtle soup, roast lamb, and a confection of raspberries and meringue. There would also be fine wines served throughout the evening, followed by the loving cup, a large silver goblet passed around the tables for everyone to take a sip from. Speeches would follow and toasts would be drunk and an air of bonhomie would pervade, and all the time he would be thinking about Elfreida and what she had told him. He would also be trying to make up his mind what to do.

Celia and Hugo, seated at another of the long tables, went through the motions of accepted social behavior, although both were deeply unhappy and avoided looking at each other. This was the first time their marriage had faced a crisis, and for Celia it was an agony, all the more so because she felt Hugo was putting his principles before her. Night after night, although both of them tried to avoid the subject, Hugo's decision on how to vote in the House of Lords seemed to come up in the conversation, which always ended in a painful argument.

"Even if it wasn't my father we're talking about," Celia frequently told him, "I still think it's pointless bringing these old men to trial for something that happened so long ago. How can there be a fair trial? All the details must be lost or forgotten by now." It was the argument everyone who was against the War

Crimes Bill used, but she fervently believed it to be true.

"How can this country afford to get involved in trials that they say will last several years and cost twenty-five million pounds?" she continued heatedly.

"But it is fundamentally wrong that men who committed heinous acts of genocide should get off scot-free. Can't you see that, Celia? People must bear responsibility for their actions. We owe it not only to the families of those who perished in the holocaust but also to the victims themselves, all those who were gassed, or suffered in prison camps, or were shot in cold blood. Why should their murderers get away with it?"

Emotional distress, coupled with intellectual ability, fought for control in Celia's mind, although she still felt retribution to be as great a sin after such a long lapse of time as the crimes themselves. "If my father," she said, "and the others who are on the wanted list had actually stood trial at Nuremberg, that would have been fair; but some of them escaped, including my father, and I think it's too late to do anything about it. To drag these old men, in their seventies and eighties, into a court of law now would be quite wrong. How do we know they haven't made amends or suffered terrible guilt that must have been a punishment in itself?"

Hugo, who privately felt sure that Ernest had never suffered a single pang of remorse about anything in his life, replied as mildly as he could.

"So that means there's a time limit on being guilty or not being guilty? If you commit a crime last week, you are as guilty as hell? But if you're discovered to have committed a crime ten, twenty, thirty years ago, you're innocent . . . because no one can be bothered digging that far into the past? Come on, Celia, that's an absurd argument."

Heatedly she turned on him, her normally calm gray eyes flashing with anger. "No, it isn't! If you put someone on trial for a crime he committed last week, you have the opportunity to punish him in the hopes he will learn a lesson. What lesson are these old men going to learn, for God's sake? Some of them will be dead before a verdict is reached. Others, if found guilty, will languish in prison hospitals until they die."

"So they are to be allowed to get away with the most vile acts ever committed by one human being against another?" Hugo retorted. "Do you realize there are nearly seventy war criminals hiding in the United Kingdom?"

"They should have been tried at the end of the war. It's too late now."

"It's never too late! By sweeping the past under the carpet, you're denying rightful retribution to the innocent victims." Hugo felt so angry he could hardly contain himself.

"And the likes of you are just out for revenge," Celia shot back. "You're not interested in justice, you just want to rake up the past because you think it will make you feel better."

They glared at each other with cold hostility, divided on an issue for the first time since they had married. This was the most serious disagreement they'd ever had, and Celia couldn't believe that Hugo could have taken a stance against her and her family on such a sensitive and personal issue.

Now, as they went through the elaborate ceremony of passing the loving cup, they avoided eye contact, although both smiled and talked to the people around them as if nothing was wrong.

A marriage that had been extremely happy was slowly disintegrating, its very fabric tarnished by deep fundamental discord. Celia knew the House of Lords was basically against passing the bill, although the government had voted overwhelmingly in favor. It would take only one or two votes, either way, to swing the balance. Hugo's vote alone might be enough for the bill to be passed. And if it were . . . ? She tried not to think about it, horrified at the repercussions there would be if her father was arrested and sent for trial. The ordeal would kill him, and as for her mother, hadn't she suffered enough already?

*   *   *

Selwyn purposely didn't drink too much at the banquet, nor did he stay long. As soon as the speeches were over, he excused himself, and slipping away, hurried down the scarlet-carpeted staircase of the Mansion House once again, and out into the street, where he knew the faithful Jeffreys would be waiting. There was so much he had to say to Elfreida, and he wanted to be clearheaded in order to deal with what he knew might be her hysterics.

Throughout the banquet, at odd moments when they'd drunk a toast to the Queen, or passed the loving cup, or applauded the speeches, he'd experienced strange fleeting pictures flashing through his mind with such force he couldn't banish them. He saw Elfreida slowly stripping off to reveal full breasts and her melon-shaped bottom. Did she use fans? Would she have worn elbow-length gloves? Had there been twinkling circles of sequins covering her nipples? A silver-lamé G-string perhaps? Flash after flash, each more titillating than the last, inflamed his imagination with vivid pictures, so that he became aroused. *And this was his wife!*

Swiftly and smoothly the chauffeur drove him through the darkened heart of the city, past the Bank of England and down Threadneedle Street, where during the day all was activity and bustle, but at night became curiously still and quiet, as deserted as a graveyard, as silent as a tomb. Usually Selwyn regarded this as the most romantic part of London, built on the ruins of the Great Fire that had demolished the city in 1655, but tonight his thoughts were elsewhere. He knew now exactly what he wanted from life and he would tolerate no compromise either. He'd worked hard to reach the pinnacle of his career and he'd been rewarded for his efforts. Now it was his turn to do exactly what he wanted.

The lights shone brightly through the windows of his house in the Boltons when his car drew up outside twenty minutes later. By the glow of the street lamps, the ornate white stucco work looked more than ever like icing sugar applied in intricate patterns by some giant chef, and the windows beckoned tantalizingly, like open caskets of jewels. This had all been a status symbol when he'd bought it, a public demonstration that at sixty-five he had achieved what many men never achieve—a house that cost over six million pounds and a sexy young wife.

Bidding Jeffreys good night, Selwyn climbed up the front doorsteps with a surprisingly light step and let himself in through the glistening black front door.

Elfreida was waiting for him in the drawing room, curled up on a sofa, in a simple white cotton robe, her face scrubbed clean, her hair brushed so it hung straight and gleaming to her shoulders. The first thing that struck Selwyn was that she looked much younger without all the muck she usually put on her face, and there was a certain innocence about her that was strangely appealing.

"Hello, Selwyn," she greeted him in a small voice. She looked nervous and her eyes could not hide the anxiety she felt. "I wait up for you."

"I left the dinner as soon as I could," he replied, deciding that he needed a drink after all. Going to the cabinet in the corner, he poured himself some whiskey before sitting down on the opposite side of the fireplace, facing Elfreida.

Neither of them spoke. He sipped from his glass and she tugged at the silk fringe on a cushion, every line of her body slumped in hopeless despair.

At last she could bear it no longer. "All right, I'll go!" she yelled, jumping to her feet, her face crumpling. "I can see you don't want me. I can see you think I'm—how you say?—trash!"

Selwyn spoke calmly. "Sit down, Elfie, there's a good girl. I want to talk to you."

"What you want to say? What will you do to me?" she asked wildly. "I know I kept my past a secret, but not you, not *anyone* would have married me if they'd known what I did."

"Now, just be quiet and let me speak."

She sank back into the armchair, a mixture of defiant resentment and fear on her face. Like an angry child waiting for punishment to be doled out, she set her mouth in stubborn lines.

"First of all," Selwyn began, "leave that little bugger Roland Shaw to me. Do not give him another penny and refuse to speak to him or deal with him in any way."

"But it's too late, he has the money from my best pieces of jewelry."

"I know, and you were a fool to let him blackmail you in that way. You should have come to me immediately—"

"But—"

"There are no buts about it," Selwyn said sternly. "One must never give way to the demands of a blackmailer. You must tell me where you sold the jewelry, and I bet you didn't get the right price for those pieces . . . and I will deal with Mr. Bloody-Shaw."

"And then?" she questioned.

"And then," Selwyn said, sipping his drink again, "we will forget about the past; we will forget what you told me tonight; we will forget—"

"Selwyn!" Elfreida flung herself forward, her eyes round with surprise, her mouth gaping open. "Selwyn, do you really mean . . . ?"

"What I mean is, we'll forget what has happened, on certain conditions."

"Yes, all right, yes; what are they?" For a moment he thought she was going to fling herself on her knees before him, but to his relief she hovered instead on the edge of the sofa, her eyes never leaving his face.

"The conditions are as follows. First, we will sell this house and get a flat." Selwyn paused, expecting a wailing explosion, but there was none. Elfreida was looking at him as if she were ready to agree to anything. Smoothly he continued: "We will get a medium-size flat that is easy to run, with the help of a daily cleaning woman. I say medium-size because we are not going to be entertaining on a grand scale; we are going to live quietly. We are not going to be gadding around night after night."

Still Elfreida said nothing.

"We are going to stop this crazy social-climbing and publicity-seeking, and we are going to live normal lives."

At last she spoke. "Yes, Selwyn."

"You are going to find something useful to do, real charity work, not just sitting on these ridiculous committees squabbling over where you'll be sitting at the next ball," he continued, nodding as if encouraging her to agree.

"Yes, Selwyn."

"And you'll stick to these conditions?"

She nodded avidly. "Oh, yes, I will."

"And you'll discuss with me whom we ask to the house? You won't go throwing parties I know nothing about? You won't accept every single invitation that comes through the post, regardless of who it's from?"

"No, I promise, Selwyn. I'll do anything you say."

"And there'll be no more hustling to try to get to meet the royal family? You won't try to gate-crash private receptions or bullshit your way into VIP circles?" he persisted, driving home every point while she was still in such a receptive mood.

"I promise."

"Right." Satisfied, he downed the remainder of his whiskey. "We'll say no more about the past. It is done and finished with. Tomorrow I'll put this place on the market, though God knows it's a bad time to sell, and we'll find a nice flat. We might look in the Chester Square area. I hear that Mrs. Thatcher—or I should say Lady Thatcher, now that Denis has been given a baronetage by the Queen—has just taken a house in Chester Square. It would be nice to be one of her neighbors," he added dreamily.

Elfreida managed to look suitably enraptured at the prospect. "Anything you say, Selwyn. But what are we going to do about Roland Shaw?" she added. "What will happen if he puts that I was . . . well, that I worked at the Green Parrot, in the newspapers? Neither of us will be able to face anyone again."

"Don't worry. Nothing will happen. I know all the

newspaper proprietors, and I'll make sure they put an embargo on anything about us. They're in a position to tell their editors not to mention certain people, you know. Most of them owe me some favor or other, so there'll be no problem."

Elfreida looked bewildered. Up to now she'd only been interested in getting onto the lists of people who *were* mentioned constantly, not some blacklist of people the editors were instructed not to mention.

"Is that true?" she asked.

"Oh, yes." Selwyn was always pleased to be able to air his knowledge. "If you know the press barons, you can get a lot of things suppressed. First thing tomorrow, I'll ring them all up; most of them are old friends of mine anyway, who wouldn't want to see us harmed—especially by the likes of Roland Shaw. It was he who told the newspapers about Celia Atherton's father, you know. By the time I've finished, I'll see that no paper ever prints a story of us again . . . ever," he added vehemently.

Elfreida still looked puzzled. "Why didn't you stop them writing about us when you left Helen to marry me?"

"They'd already printed the story before I knew anything about it. I tried to put a stop to it, but it was no good. The horse had already bolted and the stable door was wide open! It won't happen again, though."

At that moment it struck him that the fuss he'd made at the time might well be the reason why no journalist had ever mentioned Elfreida since. Wisely, he decided to say nothing now.

"So I am safe? Roland won't be able to put in that I used to work at the Green Parrot?"

"You're safe, Elfie."

"Thank you, Selwyn," she said simply. "I'm very grateful and I'll do all you say."

He looked up at her, all pink and scrubbed and clean-looking, just the way she'd been when she worked for the Athertons. The surge of desire he'd felt earlier in the evening came rushing back now, and suddenly he felt quite young again. The relief at the thought of getting rid of their big house and their exhausting social life was so great he felt quite light-headed. Now anything seemed possible—even making love to Elfreida without suffering from a poor erec-tion, or worse still, premature ejaculation.

Rising from his seat, he went over to the sofa and kissed her ripe lips.

"Oh, Selwyn," she breathed, her voice catching in a little sob as she kissed him back. His hands fondled her untrammeled breasts as the cotton robe slipped off her shoulders, while all the time she responded with a gentleness she had not shown before.

"Look!" he said at last, standing jubilantly before her, his trousers around his knees.

"Oh, my God." She gazed in awe. "Oh, it's beauti-ful! I never saw it so big, Selwyn! Oh, I love it!" Eagerly she leaned forward, her lips parted, but he pushed her back and then climbed on top of her. His expression was ecstatic.

"I haven't felt like this for years," he gasped. "I'm going to make love to you tonight until you're begging for mercy."

Elfreida gave a moan of pure pleasure. "Oh, it feels s-o-o good. Oh, yes, that's just the way I love it . . . yes . . . yes . . ." She matched her rhythm to his.

"Can you feel how hard it is?" he boasted.

"Yes, so hard . . . so strong . . . so big."

"Elfie . . . I'll satisfy you yet."

"Oh, baby, you do . . . you do. . . . Oh, don't stop."

"Stop? I can keep this up all night!" he cried as he pumped away, and wondered if he could ever per-suade her to do her strip act just for him.

Ici Paris and *France Dimanche* were publishing more and more defamatory stories about the royal family, and although he couldn't do anything about it, James Ireland was getting increasingly perturbed.

"Who *is* writing this stuff?" he asked one morning as he and Phoebe did a rough translation of the latest batch of French clippings. It had been a bad week and the last thing he felt like was having to read stories over which he had no control.

"They all have the same . . . I don't know . . . something, don't they?" Phoebe commented, wrinkling her nose. "I wonder if 'Count Victor Leroy' and 'Jacques Duarte' are one and the same person?"

James shrugged. "God knows. Whoever it is, I wish he'd stop. I can hardly look the Queen in the face these days."

"Why does she have to see everything that's written? I wouldn't want to know what people were saying about me and my family if it was nasty."

"The royal family have always gone through their own clippings," he replied, sighing. "I think the Queen feels 'forewarned is forearmed.' "

James felt tired today, and thankful that the week, which had seemed particularly long, was over. At moments like this, he was convinced his was the most difficult public-relations job in the country. On the one hand, he had to promote his "clients" in the best possible light, while at the same time protect them from inaccuracies, abuse, and overexposure. It was like treading through a minefield and he'd had a bad time lately with the announcement that Parliament had granted the Queen and other members of the royal family, who received money on the Civil List, an increase in keeping with inflation.

The announcement had caused a flurry of angry articles and comments, which was deeply embarrassing to the Queen.

"It's most unfortunate that the figures have to be published," James remarked confidentially to Phoebe.

"What's the Queen getting? Nearly eight million pounds a year from the government in order to keep the show on the road? That's a hell of a lot of money, seeing she's supposed to be worth six billion as it is," Phoebe retorted. Privately, although it was part of her job to be loyal to the royal family, there were moments when she wondered if the expense to the taxpayer was worth it, especially when she considered that every member of the family, except for Prince

Charles, who lived on the proceeds of rents from land in Cornwell that he owned, received a large allowance from the government.

"Look at this feature. It's so vulgar," James groaned, breaking into her thoughts. He handed Phoebe one of the daily tabloids. She glanced at the page, which had photographs of various castles and palaces, with captions that read: "THE QUEEN'S HOMES: BALMORAL CASTLE, worth forty million pounds, including 7,600 acres of grouse moor and fishing rights on the river Dee; SANDRINGHAM, worth sixty million pounds, including 20,000 acres of farmland, 2,000 acres of woodland, and 700 acres of coastline, in which this mansion with 274 rooms, is set."

"You must admit it's a bit hard for people living in one room, on social security, to read this sort of thing," Phoebe protested.

"At least the Queen is only a custodian of Buckingham Palace and Windsor Castle; think what a fuss there'd be if she owned them too!"

"Yes, I know, but it still looks bad, and listen to this." She read aloud: " 'The running of royal establishments, which is paid for by government funding'— that's you and me, the taxpayer—'includes £100,000 on flowers each year, £63,000 on laundry, £200,000 on food, and a further £71,000 on wines and spirits, furnishings'—whatever they may be—'£180,000, and cars, horses, and carriages, etc., £176,000.' And those are only the *domestic* expenses, James. They go on to list 'office expenses,' which total around £460,000; household salaries, near three million, and finally household expenses, £1,336,017. My God, do you think these figures are right?"

"Those are only rough estimates," James explained, "but they're probably near the mark, and don't forget there are other government expenses too, like the royal yacht *Britannia*. That costs the Ministry of Defense nearly ten million a year; they have also just bought three new BAe 146 aircraft for the Queen's Flight, at a cost of forty million pounds, with running costs of seven million a year on top of that."

Phoebe looked deeply shocked. "My God, it does mount up, doesn't it? It says in this newspaper that the royal palaces are going to cost nearly twenty-six million pounds this year. What does that mean?"

"That refers to maintenance of Buckingham Palace and Windsor Castle, which, as I said, belong to the state and not to the Queen. She is merely allowed to live in them." He looked thoughtful for a moment. "Half that amount is to go toward paying for the refurbishment of Windsor Castle. The plumbing is antiquated, to say the least, and the wiring quite dangerous. There's been a real worry a fire could start, but it's such a massive job that the whole thing is going to take about seven years. That's why the Queen can have only a few people at a time to stay these days. It will be years before she can entertain the whole family at Christmas, like she used to, with up to fifty people staying at the castle."

Phoebe looked anxious. "What do I say if a newspaper reporter telephones and asks me about these figures? Do I admit they're true? How do I justify them when we're entering a recession? It looks so bad," she added, dropping her voice confidingly. "I feel quite embarrassed."

"Put them onto Jean or me," James advised. "As you get more experienced, you'll feel quite confident in answering questions of this type. After all, people seem to forget that the royal family are our greatest tourist attraction. Millions of foreigners come to this country every year in order to get a glimpse of one of them or to watch the Changing of the Guard at Buckingham Palace."

"Yes, that's true. I suppose I'm a socialist at heart, and it goes against the grain when I see here: 'Department of the Master of the Household, £1,667,462,' and that's just for salaries, while nurses working eighty- or ninety-hour weeks are only being paid something like eight thousand pounds a year. It seems so unfair."

James frowned, worried that her attitude might show in her dealings with journalists. It was important that those working in the palace press office showed a united front and not even harbor disloyal thoughts.

"If you feel so strongly about this, Phoebe, why did you come to work here?" he asked. "You're not being entirely fair, either. If you look at the salaries the Queen pays the palace servants, butlers, footmen, and maids, you will see they get way below the going rate. The Queen is very cost-conscious, you know."

"Then why do the servants work here? For prestige?"

"Yes, of course, and also the fact that once they've been employed by the Queen, it is sufficient recommendation to get a good job anywhere else," James explained.

"Or to sell their memoirs!"

James looked pained. "Yes, unfortunately, that's true too, in spite of their having to sign a declaration to the effect they will never reveal anything they may have heard or seen."

"But it's not binding in law, is it?" Phoebe pointed out.

"I'm afraid that's right."

"Not much point in having it, then, is there?"

"It is done in the hope," James said pompously, "of morally binding employees to a promise."

"And how many people break that promise?" she asked.

"Very few, considering how many employees work for the royal family. There was the case of Prince Charles's valet, who wrote an autobiography when he left, but his book didn't do as well as he expected, because when it came to the point, there was no dirt to dish. There are no dark secrets in Prince Charles's life, and there never were."

Phoebe looked impressed. At that moment James's secretary broke into the conversation.

"It's the *Morning News* on the phone, James."

"What do they want?"

"They want you to confirm rumors that the Queen, accompanied by her dogs, swims in the Buckingham

Palace pool every day, in the nude, compelling security to switch off the TV monitors that are linked to the police."

James burst out laughing. "This," he said succinctly, "is getting ridiculous by any standards."

12

*T*he Candy Wyldman interview was in all the newspapers, accompanied by pictures of her perched wistfully on a chair looking like a parody of a third-rate actress in a revival of *Oklahoma!*

"I loved Gerald so much," she was quoted as saying. "This betrayal has nearly killed me. I hope Jackie Daventry knows what she has done, breaking us up like this."

"Damned bitch!" Gerald stormed when he saw the papers.

They were having breakfast in Jackie's kitchen, as they always did in the early morning before he went to the office, but this morning the normally convivial atmopshere was disrupted by the latest turn of events.

"And damn Roland Shaw," Jackie said, thumping down the coffeepot with a bang on the table.

"It's time he was taught a lesson," Gerald admitted.

"He doesn't seem to scare easily."

"There must be a way. I wonder if we threatened him, or I mean pretended to . . . perhaps that would put an end to his activities."

"He'd go squealing to the police and that wouldn't help anyone. If only I could write an article exposing him for what he is, but in such a clever way he'd have no grounds for suing."

"Meanwhile, I've got to sort out Candy and her demands."

Jackie looked at him sympathetically. "Do you think she'll be reasonable about money, now that she's got all this publicity? This could make *Manhattan Starlight* the hottest ticket in town, and you can be sure she'll milk the situation to the hilt."

"Yes, encore after encore," he remarked dryly. "God, what a fool I've been! How I could have married her, I don't know. I see there's no mention of her boyfriend. I wonder how she managed to keep him secret?"

Jackie glanced at the newspapers again. "She's very pretty. I can quite understand a man falling for her."

"That's just the icing on the top, sweetheart. It camouflages what's underneath, and what's underneath is, I'm sorry to say, pretty rotten."

She looked across the white marble-topped kitchen table at Gerald, and as their eyes met, her heart caught in a little lurching spasm. He always had that effect on her when he looked at her with those dark penetrating eyes, and she couldn't help recalling how they'd made love the previous night. He was the most marvelous and unselfish lover she'd ever known, and coming into her life at this time, when she'd given up all hope of ever finding the right person, seemed like a miracle. Stretching out, she curled her fingers around his and smiled.

"It's all going to be different in future, isn't it? We're going to have such a wonderful life together."

Gerald smiled back. "You bet we are. As soon as I get out of this mess, we'll get married. Maybe even start a family."

Jackie blushed like a young girl as he looked at her with a knowing intimacy that made her feel quite faint with desire. The idea of bearing his child had not occurred to her before, and at that moment it seemed like the most wonderful thing that could happen.

"I hope I'm not too old."

"Of course you're not."

"I'd really love to have a baby," she said positively. "I always wanted children, but Richard wasn't keen."

Gerald's grip on her hand tightened. Leaning forward, he kissed her tenderly on the lips. "I promise you we're going to be the happiest people in the land."

"I know we are." Their eyes locked again. "Right now I wish I didn't have to go to work." Her smile was deliciously wicked.

He kissed her again. "I wish I didn't either. Can we have an early night tonight?"

"Not a hope." Jackie cast her eyes to heaven in mock despair. "I've got to go to that gala concert at the Albert Hall, and then I promised I'd drop in to the Butterfly Ball at the Dorchester. There are also three cocktail parties I've been invited to, but God, I don't think I can bear it."

"You work too hard, my love. Whoever heard of going to five functions a night?"

"Actually, Gerald, I'm thinking of leaving *Society*."

He looked surprised. In spite of her grumbling about the parties and the people, he'd always thought she basically loved her job.

"Why? I thought you liked being on the magazine."

"I used to like it," she explained, "and of course the perks are fantastic. I would have to be a million-airess several times over to actually *pay* for my life-style. I go to the best restaurants, travel first-class everywhere, attend every premiere and first night, stay in five-star hotels, and generally have the red carpet rolled out for me whenever I appear; but honestly, the gilt has crumbled off the gingerbread for me in the last few months. This Roland Shaw business has soured everything for a start, but apart from that, it's the predictability of everything that is driving me crazy."

"What do you mean?" Gerald helped himself to another cup of coffee, refilling her cup at the same time.

"Every night I see the same people, at the same places, eating and drinking the same food, wearing the same type of clothes, and talking the same rubbish; it's like being in a goldfish bowl, going round and round and round." She clutched her head with her hands, as if she had a headache. "It's so monotonous! Honestly, some nights I walk into a party and I think: Oh, Christ, I know all these people! And then all I want is to get out. I know the back exit in almost every hotel, and sometimes, as soon as I've been received by my hostess, I do a quick circuit of the room and then disappear through the kitchen."

Gerald laughed. "As bad as that? Maybe it *is* time you handed in your resignation."

"I think things have changed too . . . unless it's me," she continued thoughtfully. For the past few months she'd been experiencing a subtle change of feeling toward the social scene, which had begun as a vague sense of boredom but now bordered on an aversion.

"Maybe I've become disillusioned, but it seems to me that society is phony, Gerald, filled with phony people whose only thought is which party they are going to next. It's all so superficial. I'm also aware that eighty percent of my popularity stems from the fact I write a social column in which everyone wants to be mentioned—that's the only reason people suck up to me."

His mouth twitched. "Oh, I wouldn't say eighty percent, sweetheart. More like seventy-five."

Jackie burst out laughing. "You're just like Kip! But seriously, if I were to give up the column tomorrow, the flood of invitations would stop as if Niagara Falls had suddenly run dry. The majority of people would drop me like a red-hot brick, which is okay by me," she added, "because I never looked upon them as friends in the first place, merely people I had to list in the column. But it doesn't make me think very highly of them when I realize all that gush has everything to do with making sure their names are mentioned at every party, and nothing to do with friendship."

"Yes, people do fawn over you at parties, don't they? Did you think I wanted my name in print the night we first met?" he asked, intrigued.

"No." She smiled at him. "I can smell publicity seekers across a crowded room. I knew you were after

something quite different that night, and thank God
you were!"

"What will you do if you leave *Society*?"

"I'd like to get on a decent newspaper, like the
Telegraph or *Times,* and do interviews and features,
but I don't know if I write well enough. I suppose I
could work free-lance, but I need to earn a regular
salary, and free-lance work can be rather precarious
unless one's at the top."

"I don't think you ought to worry about money,
darling, not now we're a team. Not to put too fine a
point on it, I'm loaded, and what is mine is yours,
you know."

"That's sweet of you," she said, "but I have to earn
my own money. That's a bit of independence I'll never
give up. When I was married to Richard, I was the
'kept' wife, but I realize, looking back, it was a very
bad idea."

"Yes, but remember one thing. I've moved into
your flat, so it's only right I should use my money to
help us along," he pointed out. "Anyway, I'd like to,
so why not tell your editor you're going to leave and
then see what else is about?"

Jackie looked eager. "You really think it's a good
idea?"

"I think it's the best idea yet. For one thing, we
might be able to get to bed by ten o'clock at night for
a change!"

"I'd like that."

Gerald looked at her knowingly. "So would I," he
said fervently.

Why did people always cross him? Why did they go
along with his plans enthusiastically at first, but as
soon as he asked for a little recompense for this efforts, turn on him, abusing him and insulting him?
Roland walked quickly and unheedingly down Sloane
Street, back to his little two-room bunk-hole, where
he could lick his wounds and work out a plan for
getting even with whoever had rejected him.

Candy Wyldman. The common, vulgar bitch! Who

the fuck did she think she was? He'd been thunder-struck when she'd told him he wasn't to get a percent-age of her settlement. If it hadn't been for him . . . The words kept repeating themselves in his fevered mind. *If it hadn't been for him* . . . she wouldn't be getting a penny from Gerald Gould in the first place. She'd be dependant on her earnings as a third-rate actress in a crummy musical; she was a talentless tart; a worthless whore; a conniving cunt. He wished she would drop dead . . . preferably onstage.

He'd spike her guns, though. He'd teach her a les-son she wouldn't forget in a hurry. He'd ruin her chances of a good divorce settlement now. He'd ruin her with Equity too, and let them all see what a two-timing bitch she was. Nobody treated him like this! Nobody swindled him out of thousands of pounds, which he richly deserved, and got away with it.

As soon as he got inside his flat, he reached for the phone, dialing the number of the *Morning News,* which he knew by heart.

"Put me through to David York," he snapped when he got through.

A moment later he was telling the editor of the gossip column that Candy Wyldman had married the rich tycoon Gerald Gould only to get around an Eq-uity ruling about American actors working in Great Britain, and that all along she'd continued to have an affair with her longtime lover.

"Thanks, but we're not interested in the story," came the reply.

Dumbfounded, Roland looked accusingly at the phone, as if it had lied to him.

"Not interested?" he squeaked indignantly.

"Not interested."

Roland banged down the receiver. "We'll see about that!" he shouted to no one in particular. Then he dialed the *Daily Gazette.* Once again he asked to be put through to the gossip column.

"I thought you'd be interested to hear—" he began.

"Who is that?"

"This is Roland Shaw speaking. I've got a very good story for you—"

"I'm sorry, but we're not interested."

"What *is* this?" Roland exploded. "I'm offering you an exclusive for a really hot story, and you're telling me—"

"That's right. We're not interested. Good-bye." The phone clicked and there was silence.

A nasty suspicion began to cloud Roland's mind as he dialed another newspaper. The same thing happened again. It was at that moment he realized that somehow someone had blocked all press channels to him. Someone must have approached the proprietors, those rich press barons who looked after their own, and said no one was to take any more stories from Roland Shaw. The person would have stressed the risk of libel as being the main reason, but Roland knew better. Someone was out to destroy him. Someone wanted to prevent him becoming rich and powerful. It was a diabolical conspiracy to stop him bettering himself. Roland literally saw red as the blood surged to his head and he became engulfed with rage. Not only had he lost a regular source of income, but also his most powerful weapon—the ability to expose secrets and thereby ruin certain people by selling their stories to the newspapers.

With throbbing temples and shaking hands he racked his brains to think who could have done this to him. Names and incidents whirled through his mind in a confused maelstrom; there were the parents of the young viscount who'd been arrested for possessing heroin, which Roland had supplied in the first place. That had been a page-one story. Then there was the debutante who got pregnant by the black window cleaner who had also put the sparkle into the panes of glass at her parents' ancestral home. Had they sought revenge by blocking him? Or was it the titled lady who had asked him to introduce her plain daughter to some eligible young men in return for a "finder's" fee? . . . But the husband-hunting story had been leaked to the press and spoiled the girl's chances of finding anyone. There were also the dozens of stories about the royal family he'd manufactured recently; had the press office at Buckingham Palace found out it was him? At least *Ici Paris* and *France Dimanche* hadn't so far closed their doors, and did he have some spicy stories about the royals coming out in those journals in the near future!

For a moment he felt quite cheered at the thought, but then the bitter chagrin came rushing back. Everyone was against him. Everyone was out to get him. For some reason, people only took delight in frustrating him and impending his progress. It wasn't fair! He had as much right to a place in society as any of the morons born into the peerage, God damn their fucking family trees!

At that moment a sudden shaft of clarity penetrated the convolution and confusion making his senses reel: *of course* he knew who had told the newspaper proprietors to refuse any more stories from him. Why hadn't he guessed it immediately? There was only one person who had that sort of clout with the press, and that was Jackie Daventry—forever in his way. Forever trying to prevent him from getting on. She was jealous of him, of course. That was the reason, he assured himself. Jealous and vindictive. The funerals had failed to scare her. Candy Wyldman finding out about her affair with Gerald had failed to hurt her. He would have to think of another way to eliminate her from the scene.

Celia crept down the darkened stairs quietly and softly, not pausing until she had reached the bottom. The silence of the house was broken only by the ticking of the grandfather clock in the hall and the creaks that are part of an old house when all is still. Upstairs Hugo and the boys lay asleep.

Once in the kitchen, she closed the door and switched on the light. Instantly the room was flooded with a cheerful glow, and going over to the stove, she put the kettle on to boil.

This was the fifth night running when sleep had not come to her, in spite of taking one of the sedatives the doctor had prescribed and in spite of the activities like a warm bath, a hot milky drink, and something undemanding to read. At any moment she felt as if something inside her head was going to snap and explode into a thousand pieces, carrying her away on a downward spiral of hysteria, and she did not know how to control it. The feeling frightened her too; usually she was calm, composed, completely responsible for her actions, but now she feared she would go mad. Every day it got worse, the unrelenting mortification, the hell on earth that would not go away and from which there was no relief.

Tomorrow the House of Lords would be voting on the War Crimes Bill and she would know her father's fate. The voting, she knew, would be by a narrow margin, either way, so divided were the Lords, and there hung in the balance the most terrible consequences for her family. Her mother had told her on the phone earlier that her worst fears were now coming true, indeed had already come true, because even if the Lords turned down the bill, Celia's father was a marked man.

"Either way," Aileen had said wretchedly, "this is the end of your father. The strain is killing him and he certainly wouldn't survive a trial."

"And you, Mother? How are you bearing up?" Celia had asked.

"I feel I've been having a nightmare for the past forty-five years and I've just woken up to find it wasn't a nightmare at all, but reality."

Celia had sympathized, her heart bleeding for the woman who had done everything in her power to try to protect Celia from the truth. As to her own feelings about her father . . . That was the hardest part of all, she thought. How could she turn against the man she had looked up to all her life and loved so deeply? And yet, how could she overcome her horror and revulsion at finding out he was a monster at heart? This was the man who had taught her to swim and sail when she was small; this was the man who had taught her to appreciate beautiful works of art, the wonders

of nature, the culture of her heritage! And all the
time, he'd been responsible for the brutal extermina-
tion of his fellow human beings.

Celia's head reeled when she thought about it, and
she tried to rationalize it, wishing she'd never found
out because the guilt was hers now too; the enormity
of what he'd been and done was casting a black
shadow over her entire life, through which no glimmer
of light could penetrate.

Sitting hunched at the kitchen table, sipping a cup
of chamomile tea, the feelings of remorse threatened
to overwhelm her, although she knew it was not she
who had perpetrated those crimes nearly half a century ago. But her father had committed them, and so
the sins of the father . . . Celia covered her face with
her hands, her pain too deep for tears, her inexplica-
ble self-reproach carving a path through her mind like
a red-hot spear. *Her father* . . . Dear God, how was
she going to live with this thing? This thing that grew
more dreadful every day as the shock wore off and
the horror sank in? How was she going to go on bringing up Colin and Ian when she felt so inadequate and
unworthy herself? How was she going to continue to
be a good wife to Hugo, dear solid honorable Hugo,
when she felt herself to be born of rottenness?

Celia opened her eyes and noticed a large black
spider on the floor a few feet away. It was quite still,
as if waiting and watching, and she looked at it with
sad eyes.

"You see," she said aloud, addressing the spider as
if it was a friend, "I don't think I can carry on much
longer. I'm not sure what I shall do if my father is
arrested and there is a trial. I mustn't blame Hugo;
that would be wrong. He has his own conscience to
follow, but it is such a near thing . . . his vote might
just tip the balance."

The spider remained motionless, and she was convinced it was listening to her.

"What would you do if you were me?" she asked,
her voice calm and reasonable now. "If the Lords vote
against the bill . . . well, that will be a reprieve for us

all, I suppose, but everyone will still know what he did. Everyone will know that my father and Colin and Ian's grandfather was a Nazi war criminal. It's been in all the newspapers, you see, and I was even on television, trying to defend Daddy . . . trying to put as good a light on it as I could. What I don't understand is how he could have done all those things and yet be such a gentle loving man." Her voice dropped, became confiding. "I don't know how I'm going to live with the sense of guilt. I feel I ought to punish myself in some way . . . I should make amends. I've had too good a life, I've been too blessed . . . I don't deserve it. I don't deserve Hugo or the boys. What I have to try to do . . . try to do . . ." She felt confused, her thoughts so jumbled that she couldn't find words to express herself properly, and then, through a mist, as if from a long way away, she heard Hugo speaking.

"Celia, my darling, come back to bed. Come with me, my love. You're not well . . ."

She felt strong arms around her, his warm breath on her cheek.

"I shall have to try to do . . ." She was struggling with the words again. Try to do what? Her poor tired aching head couldn't quite grasp the meaning of what she wanted to do. All she could see, as in a flickering old black-and-white movie, were people herded in line, entering the gas chamber; standing in rows to be shot; women and children being brutalized, starved, eliminated overnight by unseen hands, as if they'd never existed. And these were the things her father had done.

"I shall never be free . . ." she whispered as Hugo half-carried her up to their bedroom. "I shall never understand . . ."

Later she was lying in bed, warm blankets tucking her in, the family doctor's face hovering above hers, his smile doing nothing to reassure her. A needle pricked her arm. She tried to speak again . . . to explain . . . to say she was sorry, but with the swiftness of a falling ax, merciful oblivion enveloped her in its gentle cloak.

*　　*　　*

"I'm so sorry, Bill. Is there anything I can do?"
Jackie asked sympathetically. The sight of his normally cheerful face looking so disconsolate distressed
her. The effect of Roland Shaw's harassment to settle
out of court, which was his latest tactic instead of
bringing a case, had changed Bill so that he seemed a
different person, she reflected. Gone were the relaxed
bonhomie, the philosophical attitude to life, the calm
chuckling demeanor. Gone also, which accounted for
his gloom, was a large part of his income.

"That's the worst of being a free-lance photographer," he explained. "People are frightened to be
linked with me in case Roland Shaw turns on them out
of revenge. Like rats deserting a sinking ship, they're
canceling jobs I was going to do by the score. I've
lost about ten weddings, which would have been very
profitable, two christenings, half a dozen dances, and
several sittings involving family groups. It's a financial
disaster."

"God, that's serious, Bill. I'll do what I can to get
you more work, but Roland really has a vendetta
against you, hasn't he?"

Bill hung his head dejectedly, reminding Jackie of
an old teddy bear from which the stuffing was slowly
falling away. "That's right," he replied gruffly. "I'm
as good as ruined; he wants thousands of pounds, otherwise the case will go to court." He raised his eyes
to look at her. "I can't afford the lawyer's fees to fight
the case, and I don't qualify for legal aid either, so
I'm just going to have to pay up."

"There must be something we can do."

Bill shrugged. "I'll have to sell my house."

Jackie looked at him, appalled. "That's dreadful! I
think *Society* should help you."

"Why should they? I'm not an employee; as a free
lance I sell photographs to other magazines too, and
newspapers. The only trouble is, I've not got much to
sell these days!" He smiled wryly, a faint echo of his
usual jovial grin.

"What will you do?"

"My wife and I will have to go and live with her widowed sister in Eltham. I'll lose my darkroom, which will mean taking my films to a laboratory, but it can't be helped."

"When is all this going to happen?"

"I've got a meeting with my lawyer in a few days. They'll have to wait for the money until I've got everything sorted out, though." His tone was resigned, as if he'd already come to terms with the fact that Roland Shaw had ruined his career and was about to cripple him financially.

"He can't be allowed to get away with this," Jackie said vehemently. "It's grossly unfair. Oh, God . . ." She brought her small fist crashing down onto the desk in frustration. "Roland Shaw's *got* to be stopped, Bill. This is the craziest situation I've ever come across. What do we have? One little con man who has no particular appeal or attraction, holding most of London society to ransom one way or another; all because people are scared of making a scene or being publicly embarrassed. I'm sure nothing like this would happen in the States. It's the English aristocracy closing ranks that allows people like Roland Shaw to operate."

"Surely there are cover-ups and closed ranks in America among the very rich, if things go wrong? Remember, privileged people feel very vulnerable, because there are always those who are ready to snipe at them out of jealousy or for political reasons. I don't think you can blame the class system in this country," Bill protested mildly.

"I don't agree. I think it's the absurd stiff-upper-lip syndrome that's to blame, this attitude of let's-pretend-everything's-all-right-and-maybe-it-will-go-away." Jackie spoke angrily. "As you know, I've wanted to write an article exposing Roland Shaw for a long time now, showing the absurdity of the situation."

"Bertram wouldn't allow it, would he? He can't risk having a libel writ slammed on the magazine."

Jackie leaned across her desk in a confidential manner. "I'm handing in my notice, you know. I've had it up to here with all these parties, and the inane conversation, and the shallow people, and the whole silly merry-go-round. Do you realize, Bill, we are sinking into a recession that could swallow up half the businesses in this country as if they were built on quicksand! How can I be interested in going to parties every night, when there are such serious issues happening in the country?"

Bill, who had never really experienced a world beyond the social round, looked nonplussed. His whole life, since he'd been nineteen, when he'd first taken pictures for the *Tatler,* had been photographing generations of aristocrats' families. His calendar had been filled up year after year with the regular functions that made up the social scene: starting with the Private View at the Royal Academy and the Chelsea Flower Show in May, through the summer with Glyndebourne Opera, Royal Ascot, the Derby, Wimbledon for the tennis championships, Henley Regatta followed by Cowes Regatta, and all the dances and parties, weddings and celebrations, that went with high society. World affairs were beyond the boundaries of his knowledge and interests, and now that society was turning its back on him, he was adrift, without direction or motivation.

Jackie continued: "Why don't you get into commercial photography, Bill? Fashion or advertising? It pays better too."

Bill shook his head. "I'm not a good-enough technician. My strength lies in speed with a flash, a good memory for faces, and a knowledge of the social scene. There's nothing else I can do, Jackie, except take pictures at parties—that is, if I'm allowed to."

"Cheer up, Bill," Jackie said encouragingly. "I'm sure things will turn out all right in the end. You'll get something sorted out. Maybe your lawyer will find a way of placating Roland's lawyer so you won't have to settle out of court."

He smiled wearily, rising from the chair opposite her desk. "One can but hope," he replied. But as she watched him leave her office, looking like a dog that has been whipped, she feared he was on the edge of a breakdown.

David's Club, opened only three weeks previously, was attracting a large crowd of gays every evening as they deserted Slingbacks in droves to seek new thrills in a louche new setting. The music was good, the drinks less expensive, and the ambience darker still. Needless to say, Roland Shaw was practically a founder member, and he liked to go at least once a week, provided he had a free night away from a party or a dinner someone else was paying for.

Situated just off Regent Street, bright pink neon lettering marked the entrance from a distance of a hundred yards. Inside it was all black velvet walls and fake zebraskin banquettes, with a small dance floor watched over by a larger-than-life version of Michelangelo's *David*, made of fiberglass. Under the shadow of this perfect body, couples gyrated energetically while a dazzling light show pulsed in time to the strident music.

Roland went straight to the bar, where deceptively macho-looking gays with thick mustaches and black leather gear were serving drinks.

"Vodka-ton, please, Jim," Roland said above the din to his favorite barman.

"Coming right up!" Jim replied.

Roland had become something of a celebrity at the club, where his tales of people in high society had at times caused gales of laughter and hysterical sniggers among the other gays. They especially loved the one about the drunken duchess falling off her chair during a dinner at Buckingham Palace, and the tale of the vivacious viscountess who had been caught in a parked car, making love to her daughter's boyfriend.

Roland reveled in holding court at one of the tables, while in a voice that sometimes became squeaky with excitement, he regaled the assembled company with accounts of his social successes. His stories and descriptions were vivid and detailed, and he did not hesitate to drop names, dish the dirt, and generally slander the very people who, on previous evenings, had offered him lavish hospitality.

On this particular evening, he soon found himself at the center of an animated group asking him what was new. One in particular, a man in his forties whom he had not met before, seemed intent on getting to know him better. Within half an hour he was suggesting they go back to his place.

Roland, who'd had enough of older men recently, curtly told him to "piss off, dear."

Inflamed, the man, who seemed to be called Stephen, started getting belligerent. "Who do you think you are?" he stormed.

"Not a failed pansy, anyway," Roland quipped back.

Humiliated in front of the others, and flushed with anger, Stephen lunged forward, attempting to hit Roland. Swiftly, out of the darkness and the pulsing lights, a bouncer appeared and grabbed hold of Stephen.

"Let me go, you fucking bastard," he yelled, struggling to get free, but the bouncer was stronger, and after a bit of a scuffle Stephen was evicted into the street, where he continued to shout obscenities.

"Oh, dear, you do seem to have made an enemy for life," said a joking voice in Roland's ear.

Roland turned and came face-to-face with a young man of about his own age. Trendily dressed in baggy trousers, army boots, an open-necked shirt, and a tweed jacket with patched leather elbows, Roland was instantly aware of the "street cred" that emanated from this handsome young man.

"Oh, hello," Roland replied, smiling ingratiatingly. "I think he must have been drunk, don't you?"

The chap shrugged. "Can I get you another drink?"

"Thanks."

"My name's Hal Taylor, by the way."

"Mine's Roland Shaw."

"Good to meet you."

"Yes. You too."

When Hal came back with the drinks, they fell into

conversation, but it wasn't until Hal said something about "my producer" that Roland's ears pricked up.

"Are you on the stage, then?" he asked.

"Television. I work on *First Thing,* the breakfast program for Star Television."

Intrigued, Roland asked, "Are you an interviewer?"

"No," Hal replied, "I'm a researcher, and it's up to me to find interesting guests."

"To interview, you mean? Film stars and that sort of thing?"

"Anyone who has something interesting to say. This morning we had an artist, who only paints on slate, and also a woman who has had eleven children and has educated them herself, around the kitchen table." Hal shrugged. "It makes good viewing."

Roland's mind began racing ahead of itself. If he could make a television appearance . . . talk about the social scene . . . turn himself into an authority on social matters . . . report on what was happening . . . even, perhaps, get a weekly spot that was like a diary of events . . . Excited and stimulated by the vodka, the music, the lights, and the atmosphere of David's, he thought nothing seemed impossible at this moment. If he could become a leading television personality, everyone would want to know him. This could be his big chance.

"Let me buy *you* a drink this time," Roland suggested. It was the first time he'd offered to pay for a drink in over a year.

"Thanks," Hal replied.

As he made his way to the bar, passing several delightfully fresh-faced youths whom he would have normally pursued, Roland decided he had bigger fish to fry. After all, what was a quick tumble under the covers compared to an appearance on the box?

The voices seemed to come from far away, blurred and indistinct. Celia strained to hear what was being said, but tiredness swept over in great waves, so that almost thankfully she surrendered herself to the sweet oblivion of being heavily sedated. For once in her life she was allowing others to take charge of everything, including her mind and her body, and the relief at handing over all responsibility was strangely wonderful. It was as if, no matter what happened now, it wasn't her fault. By opting out and allowing herself to become submerged in this floating black limbo of nothingness, she was relinquishing her grip on reality so that nothing could touch her. At moments, there would be a searing shaft of memory at what had happened, and then pictures would float into her mind: of her father being tried in a court of law, standing old and bent in the witness box; of the judge passing sentence, committing him to confinement for the rest of his life, while the sound of her mother sobbing heartbrokenly could be heard in the background. Then she would become aware of comforting hands and gentle reassuring voices, and she would realize the sobbing came from her.

"Celia, darling . . ."

She pretended not to hear, wanting to remain embedded in her own private cocoon of darkness.

"Sweetheart . . . Celia . . ."

She recognized Hugo's voice, but still she didn't want to acknowledge she'd heard. If only he'd go away, leave her in peace, leave her here in this safe place, where nothing could touch her.

"Everything's all right, Celia." The voice was persistent. "Nothing's going to happen to your father, darling. Everything's going to be all right."

It was a trick, of course. They were trying to make here wake up by telling her the Lords had voted against the bill, but she wasn't fooled by that one. She wasn't going to listen to Hugo, no matter what he said. Her father was in Ireland and about to be arrested at any time, and all she wanted to do was to go back to sleep.

"It's true, Celia. Listen to me. Nothing's going to happen to your father, I promise you. It's all over." Hugo's voice was louder now, and clearer.

She half-opened her eyes, wondering if she was dreaming. As her vision cleared, she could make out his face, close beside her, and his hands were gripping hers.

"Hugo?" she whispered uncertainly.

"Yes, my love. It's me. Did you hear what I said?"

"Yes. Is it true?" Did she dare to hope? Had her father and others like him really been reprieved?

"It's quite true," Hugo was assuring her. "The bill got rejected by only four votes, so it was a near thing, but you can stop worrying. Your father is quite safe." Wisely, he didn't add the fatal words: "for the meantime anyway." It was a known fact that the government was in favor of getting the bill passed, and would no doubt present it to the Lords again at some time in the future. It was really a question now, Hugo thought, of whether Ernest died of old age before that happened or whether he outlived the possibility if the bill were further delayed.

For the moment Celia seemed content, though. She was smiling and holding on to his hand, and she looked more relaxed than she'd done for a long time. A few more days in the Cromwell Road Hospital, tended by the best doctor, was all that was needed, he was sure. Hugo also came to a decision: no matter how much Celia might want to know which way he had voted, that was something he would never reveal.

The television studios sent a car to Roland's flat to collect him. It arrived at five-thirty in the morning, as Hal had told him he must be at the studios by six in order to be interviewed live at seven-fifteen, and Roland was ready and waiting and in a high state of excitement. Getting onto *First Thing* had been easier than he could ever have imagined. All he'd had to do was regale Hal with his social know-how—and he'd been very careful to keep it light, amusing, and breezily harmless—and before you could say "another vodka-ton," Hal had been suggesting he take part in a discussion in two days' time on the subject: "Does the Class System Still Exist?"

"You could give your point of view as someone who goes to a lot of smart parties," Hal had suggested, almost as if Roland might need persuading to appear.

"You could tell us things like . . . are the *nouveaux riches* really accepted by the aristocracy? . . . and what does it mean to be a debutante in the 1990's? How does it differ from when there were presentation parties at Buckingham Palace in the old days?"

Roland was nodding in avid agreement.

"That would be fine," he said airily. "There are so many things I can talk about, I could do a weekly slot on the social scene, like a diary, you know."

Hal nodded thoughtfully. "That could be quite interesting. Let's see how this first show goes! Also appearing with you on the program will be someone called Professor Julian Winterton, the sociologist; Lady Elizabeth Grinstead, who was a debutante in 1918 and is an earl's daughter; and a chap called Danny Fox. He belongs to an organization called Class Warriors and of course he hates anything to do with the establishment. It should be a lively item."

"Yes, indeed." Roland thought rapidly. This could be his big chance to make a name for himself. After all, there were several people floating around London, with no more qualifications than he had, calling themselves experts on all types of social issues; why shouldn't he become one too?

The car was on time. With a mixture of sick nerves and excited anticipation he climbed into the back and said rather grandly to the driver: "I'm appearing on *First Thing.*"

"I know," came the surly reply.

Through the still-dark streets of London, the car sped to the studios of Star Television in Greenwich, and all the time Roland was answering imaginary questions in his head, practicing witty retorts, and relating titillating anecdotes. He would dazzle everyone with his fluency. They would proclaim him a "natural." Viewers would write in, demanding to see "more of this amusing young man," and he'd be invited back on a regular basis. His success might even be so great that he'd end up with his very own chat show on which he interviewed celebrated guests. To hell with all the people who had tried to stand in his way. He'd show them! He'd really become a power to be reckoned with!

A scruffy-looking girl in jeans and a large chunky sweater greeted him in the lobby of the studios. Clutching a sheaf of papers, she had the busy air of someone who had already been at work for several hours.

"Come this way," she said briskly. "I'll take you to makeup first, then I'll introduce you to the producer. Would you like some coffee?"

Roland, who was feeling more heart-thumpingly nervous by the minute, muttered something about preferring tea, and a moment later found himself sitting in a chair with a pink plastic cape pulled up to his chin, while a tall thin girl in a white overall peered at the open pores on his nose.

"Tea. Milk and sugar?" asked the first girl.

"Just milk, please."

The makeup girl was still surveying him under the bright electric bulbs that surrounded the dressing-table mirror. Roland's skin had a distinctly sallow tinge to it. With swift movements and deft hands she started sponging his face with dark tan panstick.

By seven o'clock he was ready, waiting in a reception area they euphemistically called the Green Room, with the other people who were appearing on *First Thing*. The producer had greeted them all, but he did not introduce them to each other. The brisk girl with the sheaf of papers seemed to have been assigned to look after Roland, because she kept darting back to him, asking if everything was all right. There was no sign of Hal anywhere.

At last he heard the words he had been both longing for and dreading:

"Would you like to come this way?"

He followed as they filed down a corridor, up two flights of stairs, along a passage past some scenery propped against the wall, until they came to a large open space so brightly lit that Roland blinked. A room setting filled one end of the studio, with a sofa on which sat a female interviewer in a summery pink dress, although it was a cold winter morning. On a chair set at right angles sat a well-known pop singer, plugging his new record. Coiled cables snaked across the floor as the television cameras moved around on wheeled dollies manned by efficient-looking young men, and Roland stood petrified, wondering what was going to happen next.

The interviewer was thanking the pop singer for "dropping in" before telling the viewing millions that after the commercial break they would be posing the question to a panel of guests: "Does the Class System Still Exist?"

"Don't go away!" She beamed coyly into Camera One, and then the theme music for *First Thing* could be heard as the advertisements started.

"Okay," Roland heard an urgent whisper in his ear, and the brisk girl propelled him across the cluttered floor, pushing him into a chair, while Hal, who had suddenly appeared, guided the professor, the titled lady, and a chap with "Class Warrior" printed on the front of his T-shirt into other seats. Someone else was clipping microphones onto their lapels, the interviewer was smiling and nodding in a friendly fashion, and then Roland heard a voice boom across the echoey studio, which sent an icy shiver down his back.

"Ten seconds."

Oh, shit, what was it he'd planned to say? The others looked calm and assured, as if they'd done it hundreds of times, and he wondered who would be asked to speak first. Did they know his name?

"Five seconds."

Jesus, the tension was becoming unbearable. He could hear his heart pounding in his ears, and his hands were clammy. The interviewer was composing her face into lines of smiling welcome as the commercials came to an end, and then a red light lit up on Camera One, telling her she was back on the air.

Roland did not even hear what she said as she outlined the subject of the next item and gushingly introduced the guests to the viewers.

"Do *you* think the class system still exists?" she

asked the professor, a red-faced rotund man who looked more like the manager of a football team than a professor of sociology.

Roland sat tight, planning what he would say when he was asked the same question. Danny Fox, however, thrusting out his chest so that the words "Class Warrior" looked bigger than ever, cut in belligerently before Roland had a chance to say anything.

"It's the fault of them royals!" he stormed. "As long as we 'ave a royal family, we'll 'ave yer upper classes, yer middle classes, and yer lower classes."

Not to be outdone, the elderly Lady Elizabeth Grinstead entered the fray without being asked, and in a thin quavering voice spoke.

"When I was a gel, my good man, people knew their place!"

"And you'd like to keep it that way, because it suited the likes of you, didn't it?" Danny Fox jeered.

"There is actually more equality in this country than in—" began the professor in a pained voice.

"But how can people *expect* to be equal?" trilled Lady Elizabeth.

"The present system is unfair, that's wot it is!" Danny turned on her furiously.

She put her hand up to her throat as if to protect her ropes of pearls from his glare. "My dear young man, it's not my fault if I'm an aristocrat and you're not."

"I wouldn't want to be like you," he retorted nastily. "I don't envy you nothin'!"

As the rapidly escalating argument flowed around Roland's head, he realized he wasn't getting a word in edgewise. He'd been told the whole discussion was scheduled to last only seven minutes, followed by the weather forecast and then the seven-thirty edition of the news. If he didn't say something soon, he'd miss his big chance and be totally upstaged by this ill-assorted bunch of extremists.

"The landed gentry have always provided work for the proletariat . . ." Lady Elizabeth was warbling to no one in particular.

". . . and the insecurity of the upper classes manifests itself in the way they stick together," the professor was droning on.

Danny Fox returned to the attack. "If we got rid of the royal family, all that taxpayers' money could go to the National 'Ealth instead. That would cut the waiting list for operations!"

It was now or never. If he hung back a second longer, it would all be over. To hell with the subject of class; he had something far more riveting to tell the millions of viewers who tuned in to *First Thing*.

"The royal family," he piped up, "is riddled with insanity. It started with King George III, and has continued up to the present day. Most of the women in the royal family have given birth to at least one imbecile child, at some time or another, but of course these births are never acknowledged, never registered, never listed in *Debrett's Peerage*. The babies have been institutionalized since birth and never heard of again. This is the curse of all George III's descendants: there is a fatal flaw in the British royal family's genes."

That evening at six o'clock, Roland received a telephone call.

"May I speak to Mr. Roland Shaw, please?" The man's voice was cultured and he spoke with great courtesy.

"This is Roland Shaw speaking."

"Ah." There was a pause, as if the caller was appreciative of getting directly onto Roland. "My name is John Ashton," he continued, "and I wondered if it would be at all possible to come and see you on a highly confidential matter? I wouldn't take up more than a few minutes of your time, as I know how busy you are, but I would be most grateful if you could spare me a few minutes."

Roland was intrigued. The man spoke with the same aristocratic air as Hugo Atherton. At any minute Roland expected him to call him "old chap" or "my dear fellow," the way Hugo always addressed his friends.

And yet he'd never heard of anyone called John Ashton.

"Yes, of course," Roland replied automatically. "What's it about?"

"I can't really talk on the phone, but may I pop along and see you now? It is rather important, actually." The Oxford accent was marked, the politeness extreme.

"That would be fine. Come for a drink. Do you have my address?"

"Yes, I've been given your address," John Ashton replied. "This is really most kind of you," he added. "It might also be a good idea if you don't mention I'm coming to see you; you'll be on your own, I gather? I wouldn't want anyone else to overhear our conversation."

By now Roland was agog with curiosity. From John Ashton's tone it was obvious he was someone of importance. The way he spoke, too, was confiding, as if he were about to entrust Roland with some highly secret information. Perhaps he was the head of Star Television and he'd been so impressed by Roland's performance this morning, he wanted him to do a series on the royal family. Could it be that John Ashton was from the palace itself?

Hands shaking with excitement, and wishing his cleaning woman had come today, he plumped up a few cushions, got out some whiskey and gin, and changed into his best suit.

If he was to be paid the honor of a visit from royal circles, it was important he look his best.

13

"*I* don't believe it!" Stunned, Jackie gripped the phone when Bill Glass told her what had happened. "Roland Shaw dead? Are you sure? . . . I mean, he was young; how did he die?"

"I don't know," Bill replied. He sounded cheerful, almost like his old self again. "Apparently his cleaning woman went to his flat on Saturday morning, as she always does, and found his body."

"How did you hear about it?" It seemed unbelievable to Jackie that the man who had caused so much trouble to so many people was actually dead. Unbelievable and almost too convenient.

"Lady Atherton phoned me a few minutes ago to ask if I'd heard; she thought I'd like to know because she was aware how worried I've been about money, because Roland Shaw's lawyer was threatening me. Do you know what her first words were?"

"I've no idea!"

" 'Bill,' she said, 'I think your problems are over.' Wasn't that nice of her?"

"Yes," Jackie agreed dryly, "but how did she know he was dead?"

Bill was bursting with the news, longing to tell Jackie all the details. "Lady Atherton has a cleaning woman called Mrs. Pinner, who lives in the same block of flats, in Fulham, as the cleaner who did Roland's flat; a Mrs. Martin. Apparently they're old friends. I gather this Mrs. Martin was in such a state of shock after she found the body that she was taken home in a police car, and that's when Mrs. Pinner saw her and found out what had happened."

"How extraordinary. What else did Celia Atherton say?"

"That was all, really," Bill replied. "Just 'thank God he can't cause any more trouble.' She's been in hospital, you know. With nervous exhaustion or something. Anyway, I'm off the hook. I rang my lawyer a few minutes ago and he confirmed there's no need for me to worry anymore. Isn't that wonderful?" He sounded jubilant.

"I'm very glad for you, Bill," Jackie replied, but all her journalistic instincts clamored to know why and how he had died. She repeated the question.

"I've no idea," Bill said disinterestedly.

"Didn't Celia say anything more? Did his cleaning woman find him in bed? Collapsed on the floor? . . . or what?"

"She didn't say. All she said was, Roland Shaw had died and his body had been found on Saturday morning."

Jackie realized if she was going to find out the truth about the events of two days ago, she'd have to look elsewhere.

"Thank you for letting me know anyway," she told Bill. "It's so hard to believe that I can't quite take it in yet, but no doubt there'll be a huge collective sigh of relief when the news gets out."

The news, however, did not so much get out as leak slowly, passed by word of mouth in furtive tones among the incredulous victims Roland had left behind. People gathered in whispering clusters at parties, expressing relieved surprise, but there was no official announcement, no mention in any of the newspapers, no speculation in the gossip columns. Only those who did not wish to be connected with Roland in death any more than they had wished to be in life, passed the word around surreptitiously, and privately thanked God they were at last free of his machinations. The network of intrigue and secrecy he had created was continuing after his death, though now it took a different form. The hushed voices no longer spoke in fear but in suppressed delight, while still pretending they had never had any real interest in him in the first place. Over lunches at Claridge's and dinners at the Connaught, in the bar of the Ritz and the clubs of St. James's, while having supper at Annabel's or breakfast at the Savoy, the word went around: Roland Shaw is dead. No one cared how or why, only that their secrets were now safe.

Some, those few whom he had not directly harmed, could afford to sigh "Poor young man." Others went so far as to describe his demise as "sad." In death, it seemed, Roland Shaw was more popular than he'd ever been in life, among both his enemies and his acquaintenances, and Jackie thought with irony of how he'd have enjoyed being the center of so much interest and speculation. She also remained intrigued about his actual death, until one evening, while she and Gerald were dining at Harry's Bar, he pointed out that she seemed unable to talk about anything else.

"It's as if you're certain there's something sinister about this business," he remarked.

"I do think it's odd," she replied. "What makes me suspicious is the obvious cover-up that's been going on since he died. It's as if everyone has been sworn to secrecy and the press gagged."

"But Roland wasn't anyone of importance," Gerald reasoned. "Why should his death make the news?"

"I'm surprised it hasn't at least made the gossip columns. Everyone who reads them knew Roland Shaw. I think it's very strange. We don't even know how he died. *No one* seems to know."

Gerald looked at her quizzically. "Can we talk about something else, just for a change?"

Jackie looked contrite. "I'm sorry, Gerald. I'm getting obsessed by this business."

"That's all right. I've got some news for you, though."

"Something nice?" She reached across the table,

palm up, and he took her hand, winding his fingers through hers.

"I had a call from Candy today."

Jackie stiffened apprehensively. "What did she want?"

"She's agreed to a quick divorce—no settlement, no alimony, nothing."

"What?" Jackie looked astounded. "What's brought that on?"

Gerald grinned knowingly. "Certainly not an attack of guilt, that's for sure."

"What, then?"

"Apparently the _Daily Express_ rang her up and said they'd heard she'd only married me so she could work in England, and in reality had never stopped having an affair with her original boyfriend, therefore our marriage was one of convenience."

Jackie's eyes widened. "How did they find out?"

He shrugged. "From what she told me, I suspect it's one of the last stories Roland Shaw ever sold. They'd had a falling-out, I gather, and she admits he could have been after her blood."

"So what's going to happen? Are they going to print the story?"

"No, she denied it absolutely, and then rang me to say that if I deny it too, she'll let the divorce go through without any aggro; and she agreed not to ask for any money."

Jackie smiled in delight. "That's wonderful, darling. Oh, God, what a relief."

Gerald's grip on her hand tightened. "Isn't it good news?"

"Do you know something, Mr. Gould?" she teased. "I love you very much and I can't wait to be Mrs. Gerald Gould."

For a second he hesitated, as if about to say something, but then seemed to change his mind and the moment passed.

"What's the matter?" Jackie asked.

His smile was bland and his eyes gave nothing away. "Not a thing, my love," he replied smoothly.

*   *   *

In the red brick municipal atmosphere of a North London crematorium, an unending procession of funerals take place from early morning until late afternoon, every day of the week. With unrelenting regularity the conveyor belt of death grinds inexorably forward, hour after hour, in a constant turn-around of hearses bearing coffins, followed by large black cars carrying mourners. So swiftly does funeral follow upon funeral that the black-clothed bereaved are given only ten minutes after the service in which to look at the wreaths spread on the ground in a colorful carpet of blooms. They barely have time to read all the cards inscribed "In Loving Memory . . ." before an official whisks them away to make room for the next lot of floral offerings.

On this particular morning, jammed in between a funeral for a much-loved grandfather, who was departing this world surrounded by a large close-knit family, and a well-known businessman whose colleagues thought it only fitting to pay their last respects, came an unaccompanied hearse, within which was placed a cheap coffin, the cheapest coffin available. No flowers rested on its plain lid, and mourners there were none. The driver of the hearse, accompanied by the pallbearers who would carry the coffin into the chapel, waited quietly, the engine running, until the last of the weeping grandchildren from the previous funeral had come out of the chapel and made their way back to their own cars. Then he eased in the clutch and the hearse rolled forward to the entrance.

An official from the crematorium, whom the driver knew well, came forward to verify the name of the deceased.

"A Mr. Roland Shaw?" he confirmed, consulting his list.

"Absolutely right." The driver had an eccentric sense of humor. "He's on his own, too."

"On his own?" The official looked startled.

"Yup. No family, no friends. Here's one bake-and-shake that's not being seen off."

Unnoticed, though, a man had already slipped ahead of the coffin into the chapel, where he took a seat at the back. Dressed in gray flannel trousers and a dark blue quilted bomber jacket, which accentuated his bulky shape, he sat impassively, watching intently as the coffin was carried up the narrow aisle and placed on a platform in front of some dark red velvet curtains. Then an elderly clergyman appeared, and having glanced disinterestedly around the empty chapel, started to speak.

"We are gathered together . . ."

The man let his mind drift. He'd met Roland Shaw only the once, but he knew all about him, and he would have expected there to be quite a crowd today, even if only out of curiosity. Where were all the people Roland had surrounded himself with as he'd cut his swath through the drawing rooms of London? Most of those people, of course, the titled dowagers and deposed foreign monarchs, the social climbers and the misfits, had only hung around out of fear in the end, trying to avoid the ripples he had stirred up on the normally glassy surface of society, desperate to protect themselves from the revealing forces he had unleashed. But Roland was dead and he'd taken their secrets to the grave with him; so where was everyone now? Cynically the man stuck out his lower lip, knowing from experience the frailty of human relationships. If Roland Shaw had thought he could count upon one single person to be his friend at the end, he'd been mistaken.

". . . earth to earth, ashes to ashes . . ." The clergyman droned on in a flat voice. He might have been condemning a side of beef to the barbecue for all the emotion his voice expressed.

With a faint whirring sound that would have been drowned by music, if there'd been any music, the red velvet curtains parted, and the unadorned coffin lurched forward a couple of inches, shuddering to a halt like a train shunting into a siding, before moving forward again. Then it glided slowly on its tracks and the red curtains closed with a finality that was absolute.

Back in his car, which he'd parked a couple of hundred yards away from the chapel, the man picked up his mobile phone and dialed a number he knew by heart. When he got through, the conversation was terse.

"I've just seen him off."

"Everything go okay?" he was asked.

"No problems. Do you want the ashes?"

"There's no point. All the ashes get mixed up together at the end of the day . . . and who'd want them anyway?"

The man nodded, lower lip stuck out again. "No one," he agreed succinctly.

It was early December and Selwyn was not looking forward to Christmas and the New Year, with all their false gaiety and forced cheerfulness. Even the demise of Roland Shaw had done little to cheer him up, although Elfreida had been relieved beyond words.

"No one will ever know about my past now, thanks be to God," she exclaimed, crossing herself. "I am so happy and I will make you the most wonderful wife," she added, and she meant it. When he'd bought back her jewelry, she'd wept for joy and clung to him and promised to keep her side of the bargain; all of which Selwyn was relieved to hear, because he'd come to realize, with an ever-growing feeling of horror, that he was going broke. He'd been so swept along by Elfreida since he'd met her that he'd been ignoring all the signs of a deepening recession; not seeing what he didn't want to see, not cutting back because he'd somehow got himself into having a life-style that was a case of all or nothing. Elfreida had been so thrilled at having money to spend, but now reality had to be faced. Something had to be done. He owed several million pounds to the bank, at a fourteen-percent interest rate, his shares had plummeted in value, and his company had lost several major contracts which made the difference between a profit and a loss. As if that wasn't bad enough, he was also sitting in a vast white-iced wedding cake of a house that had cost him six million to buy and which he now couldn't give away.

His world, as he knew it, the world he'd built up and enjoyed, was disintegrating and his hard-earned fortune hemorrhaging away. Cursing himself for not having heeded the first signs of a recession sooner, and for allowing Elfreida to imagine his fortune was a bottomless well from which she could draw as lavishly as she wished, he decided to set up a meeting with his accountants and the bank. Drastic action was required if he was going to salvage any of his dwindling wealth.

Celia raised her eyes from the letter she'd been reading, to gaze thoughtfully out the window, down to the street below, where traffic wardens were wandering up and down South Eaton Place, looking for illegally parked cars. She did not register what she saw, though, so distracted was she by what she'd read.

The letter was from her father, written in his old-fashioned italic style that she had admired all her life, the lines so straight and even, so decorative and pleasing to look at. It had arrived by the morning mail and now, two hours later, she still sat in the drawing room reading and reflecting on the contents as the minutes slipped by.

" . . . I couldn't help becoming brutalized," he wrote, after he'd explained how things had been when he'd been a young man in Hitler's Germany. "I got sucked into the SS because all my friends had joined . . . and once in the Nazi regime, I had no alternative but to carry out the orders I was given. In time my emotions became so blunted I no longer felt pain or sorrow or compassion . . . I was like a machine, detached from any sort of normalcy, unable to register ordinary humane feelings."

The words echoed in her head as she wondered if his feelings of "pain and sorrow and compassion" had ever returned. Had he ever been able to love Aileen?

Had he experienced the normal feelings of a father for his child? Celia could only guess now, and surmise, she'd never know for certain, and that was one of the hardest things she was having to face. Perhaps, all along, Ernest Smythe-Mallin had been as false as his name, and his carefully calculated performance as a loving husband and father as untrue as everything else about him. Like his Austrian background? . . . the inherited art treasures? . . . his work for British intelligence during World War II? Or did Ernst von Schmidt really lurk behind the facade, a greedy criminal who had lived without guilt or remorse for over forty-five years, seeking protection behind the skirts of a kindly Southern Irishwoman whose country offered international neutrality?

Celia glanced down at the letter again: ". . . It was as if by preserving something beautiful, be it a painting, a bronze statue, or an antique piece of furniture, I was in some way redressing the ugliness that had taken over," continued the neat handwriting. "All I longed for was that the bloodshed cease, the war end, so that I could blot out all that had gone before and find a place where, in peace, I could appreciate and enjoy what I had collected."

Or stolen from your victims, Celia thought as she fought back the tears and clenched her fists until her nails cut painfully into the palms of her hands. What was she to believe? She sighed, knowing things could not continue as they were, knowing she would have to talk to Hugo when he got home tonight.

Ever since she'd returned from the Cromwell Road Hospital, discharged because there was nothing more they could do for her, she'd realized that finding out about her father had altered everything; not just her position at court as a lady-in-waiting, nor her social standing because all their friends, including the Queen herself, had shown great sympathy and understanding, but something so fundamentally deep within herself that her entire outlook seemed colored and changed. It was as if she too were now soiled by association with the atrocities her father had perpetrated, and so she must share his guilt. And what did her father expect of her? She picked up his letter again and reread the first few lines:

"Celia, I want you to try to understand . . ."

Understand? How could she ever understand the labor camps, the gas chambers, the torture and starvation and persecution? How was she expected to *understand* how the greatest massacre in the history of mankind could have been justified by the Nazis? More than that, how was she ever to understand that the father she had worshiped as a child had committed these appalling crimes? And yet . . . and yet . . . and this was the worst part of all . . . she wasn't able to understand either how it was she could still love him, did love him, deeply, while torturing herself about what he'd done.

When Hugo breezed into the drawing room that evening, she was sitting quietly by the fire doing her needlework. With Colin and Ian back at Eton, and Mrs. Pinner working only in the mornings again, the house should have been a peaceful haven in which they could rebuild their shattered lives and plan for the future. Instead, the atmosphere almost crackled with tension, exacerbated by Roland Shaw's recent death, rather than repaired, and it took all Hugo's willpower to maintain a cheerful countenance.

"Hello, darling," he greeted Celia, bending to kiss her.

"Hello, Hugo," she replied, looking up briefly from the petit-point cushion cover she was stitching.

"Let's have a drink," he suggested. "What would you like?"

"Whatever you're having."

"Gin and tonic?"

"That would be fine."

As Hugo poured the drinks, he found it hard to believe that they were reduced to the limited conversation of a couple who have nothing to say to each other. In the past, their coming together at the end of the day had always been like a little celebration, as they pleasurably recounted what had happened to each of them during the day, exchanging news and gossip and showing obvious delight in each other's company. Now, like strangers, they spoke in stilted tones, no longer sharing any interests.

"Have you been busy today?" Hugo asked in desperation, sitting down and picking up a copy of the *Times*.

Celia didn't answer at first, as if she were considering something. Then she put down her needlework and her voice was strong and positive.

"I want a separation, Hugo. We can't go on like this."

"A sep . . ." Suddenly gray and old-looking, he stared at her as if he couldn't believe what he'd heard. "What do you mean, a separation?" he asked, shocked.

The unwavering gray eyes looked into his, and he knew she meant what she was saying. "I can't go on, Hugo. Everything inside me has died. It isn't fair on you and it isn't fair on me either, to have to pretend things are all right."

"But, sweetheart . . ." There was anguish in his face now.

"It's no good, Hugo. I've given this a lot of thought. In fact I've thought of nothing else since . . ." She paused painfully, her brow puckering. "Don't you understand? How can I love you when I hate myself? How can I let you love me, when all I want to do is go away and hide with my pain? I've nothing more to give, Hugo. It's gone. If I stayed with you, we'd end up like strangers living under the same roof. Sometimes I think that's happened already," she added.

"Oh, Celia," he said huskily, coming to sit down beside her on the sofa. He tried to put his arms around her, but she pushed him away, her face averted.

"Don't, Hugo, please don't."

"But, darling . . ."

Wretchedly she rose and stood looking down at him. "I can't bear to be touched," she said quietly. "I don't think I'll ever want anybody to touch me again. You must understand, Hugo. I can't stay married to you. I simply can't.''

Hugo seemed to crumble and shrink, sitting on the sofa, growing smaller before her eyes. And older too.

"I'm sorry, Hugo." Celia's voice broke. "I wouldn't have had this happen for the world. The last thing I want to do is hurt you, but finding out about my father has changed me so deeply, I don't think I even know who I am anymore."

"We mustn't make it final, darling. I couldn't bear that," he pleaded.

For a dreadful moment she thought he was going to cry; Hugo, whom she'd seen cry only once, when Colin was born, but those had been tears of joy. Now he looked broken and desolate, so that, unable to bear seeing his pain, Celia looked away and wished she could feel the rush of deep affection that had always surged through her when she looked at him. But all she could feel now was a wrenching sense of pity for the man she had once loved, and in that moment she understood something her father had said in his letter: ". . . my emotions became so blunted I no longer felt pain or sorrow." Or love? she asked herself. Had her father also felt so dead inside he'd been unable to feel love?

With an effort, Celia strove to sound calm and businesslike. "I think it would be better if we separated for the time being; we can think about getting a divorce in due course, when the boys get used to the idea. Obviously we don't want to upset them more than is necessary."

"How can you do this, Celia? The boys are going to be devastated." Hugo turned glazed eyes on her. "Why don't you go away for a while . . . have a break on your own? Maybe you'll feel differently then. I think, right now, that you're under a lot of stress and it's all been too much for you, sweetheart. I'm sure if you got away for a while, you'd realize we can't possibly split up, not after all these years."

"It's not as simple as that," she replied, shaking her head. "My *heart* is no longer in our marriage, Hugo.

Going away isn't going to change that. Whatever we had is dead, as far as I'm concerned, and nobody is sadder than I am, believe me. I hate what I'm having to do, but I can't . . . well, I can't carry on." Her voice was so low he could barely hear her now.

A heavy silence fell between them, and in the distance the wailing of a police siren broke the stillness. It seemed to awaken Celia from the reverie she'd slipped into.

"I'm so sorry, Hugo," she said at last. "I'll get myself a flat somewhere. You must stay on here to provide a base for Colin and Ian."

"It wouldn't help to exorcise the pain if you went to stay with your parents in Ireland for a while?" Hugo suggested. "Sometimes facing the very thing that has hurt one helps one get over it and come to terms with it."

"I don't think I can ever go to Ireland again. I don't think I can even bear to see my father again, and I've decided on something else too."

"What's that?"

"I'm going to give my inheritance away when my father finally dies."

"The art treasures, you mean?"

"Yes. How could I possibly keep them, knowing how he acquired them? They are as soiled as if they'd been splattered with the blood of his victims; they were *stolen* from his victims. They represent the spoils of the holocaust. I wouldn't want Colin and Ian to sully themselves by inheriting anything from the collection either." Celia spoke vehemently and passionately now, her gray eyes sparking.

"What will you do with it all? Give it to a museum or something?

Celia considered the question. "No, I'll probably sell the lot and give the money to a charity."

"That collection's worth several million pounds."

"I know, and I shall never feel clean while it is in the possession of my family. It isn't much, but it's the only way I know of making atonement on behalf of my father for all the terrible things he did."

Hugo looked at her tenderly, never having loved her so much as at that moment. He knew she was serious about their separating, but something told him not to oppose her now. She was so filled with hurt and guilt and remorse, although none of it had been her fault, that she needed time to recover, time to make reparation for the wrongs that had been committed, before she could come to terms with the situation. Most of all, she needed time to learn to like herself again and to realize that the responsibility for what had happened all those years ago wasn't hers. He longed to take her in his arms and hold her close and show her how much he loved her, and would always love her, but he knew that this wasn't the time, and it wasn't what she wanted or needed at this moment either.

"Celia! Darling, you must do what you think is right, but you must stay on here in this house," he said instead. "I'll get a flat nearby so that I can see the boys during the school holidays and so that . . ." He found himself struggling for control, his throat seized in a painful stricture. "So that," he continued, swallowing hard, "we can perhaps . . . stay friends."

Suddenly Celia's eyes brimmed with tears. "Of course, Hugo."

Jackie arrived early at the Caprice restaurant for her lunch appointment.

"Mr. York hasn't arrived yet, madam," the maître d' smilingly told her. "Would you like to wait at the table? Perhaps we can get you a drink?" He led Jackie across the cold and clattering black-and-white restaurant, which was, as usual, packed with trendy showbiz celebrities, media personalities, and the smart crowd. As she took her seat, the babble of voices around her was proof that the Caprice was the "in" place these days.

Jackie had been invited by David York, editor of the *Morning News*, who had suggested they meet to discuss the idea of her contributing on a free-lance basis to the newspaper. She'd met him on the social round over the years, and as soon as he'd heard she was leaving *Society,* he phoned her with the suggestion she prepare a list of ideas for feature interviews. Now, as she waited for him, Jackie felt the tension of mounting excitement. It would be wonderful to work for the *Morning News,* she reflected, a real challenge after the monotony of writing up endless parties. In her handbag was a sheet of paper outlining the interviews she had in mind; she wanted to ask Albert Finney all about his string of racehorses, as opposed to his acting career, which was what most journalists questioned him on. Another of her ideas was to ask the Duke of Westminster what being a family man meant to him, instead of the usual angle, which was how does it feel to own the land of a third of London? Jackie wanted to do offbeat original articles, with unusual angles on famous people, and she felt her list was impressive. She hoped David York would feel the same. And, thank God, she reflected, her eyes darting about the restaurant to see who was lunching today, Roland Shaw was no longer around to get under all their feet. Ever since his death, the spate of stories about royalty had been reduced to the normal level; there was less dishing the dirt about those who appeared on the pages of *Debrett,* and people seemed to be going around as if they were breathing fresh air again for the first time in years. There were casualties strewn in his wake, of course, but on the whole, as she had predicted, a collective sigh of relief had spread around the social scene and already Roland's reputation had become yesterday's problems. Soon he would be a forgotten man and in time nobody would even admit to have known him.

"I'm sorry I'm late . . ." she heard a voice say, and there was David York, florid and energetic, always seemingly wearing a suit two sizes too small for him, but with a ready smile and large expressive hands. "Something suddenly came up, you know how it is . . ."

Jackie smiled, longing to be a part of the excitement that went with the newspaper world when a story suddenly broke and pandemonium ensued to get all the facts and write them up in time to put the paper to bed.

"Anything exciting, or can't you talk about it yet?"

"It's not an exclusive, so I'll certainly tell you all about it, but let's order drinks first. Is that mineral water you're drinking?"

Jackie nodded.

David made a grimace. "Ugh! Designer water. What next!" He turned to the waiter. "I'm going to have a whiskey and soda, please. What will you have, Jackie?"

"I'll stick to water," she replied, grinning. "Alcohol at lunchtime sends me smartly off to sleep by four o'clock in the afternoon."

"So?" he teased. "What has a beautiful girl like you got to do in the afternoon except have a siesta? Sure you won't change your mind?"

"Quite sure. Now, tell me about this scoop!"

David unfolded the white damask napkin and spread it on his lap. Then he offered her a bread roll, took one himself, and with his giant fingers started to break it into small pieces with fastidious delicacy.

"Ever heard of a man called Roland Shaw?"

Jackie sat upright, looking startled. "I most certainly have. Why?"

"Well, he died a couple of weeks ago."

"I know that. I also know his death is something of a mystery. No one seems to know how he died, although it's bound to come out at the inquest."

"Hmm." David looked thoughtful. "He was cremated last week."

"Really? Was there a postmortem? I suppose there must have been. Have you found out what caused his death? I heard a rumor it was suicide, although I myself think that's very unlikely."

"I don't know how he died"—David didn't sound interested either—"but I'm very interested in how he lived!"

"Why? What's happened?" Jackie leaned forward curiously.

"There's a good old panic going on. It seems to

have started late last night; by this evening most of London will be humming with hysteria."

"Why?"

"Roland Shaw's 'diary,' for want of a better word, containing all the details of his victims, has gone missing."

Jackie's face was a study as the implications of what he said sank in. "Gone missing?" she repeated. "How do you know? I didn't even realize he kept a diary."

"I don't think many people did, but they soon will. It all depends who's got hold of it now."

"How did this story break?"

David took a sip of his drink, then replaced the glass with care on the table. Like all large men, his movements were almost dainty in their carefulness.

"Apparently Roland Shaw was selling drugs to quite a few people, including a young man named Walter Grahame," he explained. "Two nights ago, not knowing Roland was dead, he went round to Roland's flat, desperate for more supplies of cocaine, or whatever he was on. Getting no reply, he went berserk and smashed the lock and got in. He knew where Roland kept the dope hidden, you see, and where, incidentally, he also hid his diary. Walter looked in the usual place, which was behind a loose section of the fireplace, and it had all been cleared out. There was no dope—and no diary either."

Jackie raised her eyebrows. "What happened then?"

"He flipped! Started smashing up the place; that's when the neighbors called the police. They arrested him and he admitted what he'd been after, although by doing so he also incriminated himself as a drug addict."

"My God! What about this diary, though?"

"Under questioning, he said he'd been quite close to Roland at one time and knew he kept a diary listing everyone he was blackmailing. Apparently he kept detailed accounts, itemizing how much money he'd received, who from, and when. Walter even admitted he'd had a quick look at the diary one day and seen for himself how Roland had written down the details of everyone he knew, and what he knew about them. The lot."

"Had someone else already broken into the flat before this Walter Grahame got there, and stolen the diary?" Jackie asked.

"Apparently not. I gather there was no sign of a previous entry. I think whoever bumped Roland off took the drugs and the diary at the same time."

"You think he was murdered?"

David looked at her speculatively. "Don't you? Surely all your journalist instincts tell you there's something very fishy about this whole business?"

"Yes, but why has there been a cover-up? Why, for instance, hasn't your newspaper printed the story of his cleaning woman finding his body?"

"We had a directive from the proprietor, forbidding us to mention anything about Roland Shaw's death," he said shortly.

Jackie's eyes widened in astonishment. "Are you serious? You mean your great white chief, Ralph McPherson, asked you not to report Roland's death? Isn't that strange?"

David shrugged. "It's so unusual that I'm highly suspicious."

"But what does it mean? Do they know who killed Roland Shaw, but it's someone of such importance he has to be protected?"

"Something like that."

"How incredible." Jackie thought of all the people she knew who'd got involved with Roland. "Have you any idea who it might be?"

"Your guess is as good as mine," David retorted. "There were plenty of people who wanted him out of the way."

Jackie protested, "But surely the law is the law? No one's above the law?"

He looked at her quizzically. "Oh, no?"

"No, of course not! Or are we talking about the Mafia?" Then she smiled at the absurdity of her question. Roland Shaw had been a small-time crook, swin-

dler, and blackmailer, whose pray had been young
boys and old women, stupid socialites and rich fools,
and then of course those who had stood in his way,
whom he'd set out to savage. "Are you going to be
able to do a piece about this missing diary of his?"
she asked eagerly.

"I'm waiting to hear from the great white chief. I
very much hope so, because it's a great story, but even
if I can't, the news of its disappearance will still spread
like wildfire. There will be a lot of people quaking in
their shoes," he said with relish.

Jackie looked askance. "You can say that again."

"If I get the go-ahead to print, will you write an
article about Roland Shaw for us? Eighteen hundred
words on the sort of man he was? How he arrived on
the social scene, what his background was like, that
sort of thing? Write about the tricks he got up to,
without naming names, of course. Explain to the
reader how this type of con man is able to operate in a
close-knit society where people care desperately about
appearances and will go to any lengths to protect their
social standing. Can you do that?"

Jackie's eyes sparkled. This was the first time she'd
been given a serious journalistic brief, and she was
thrilled. "I'd love to," she replied enthusiastically.
"When will you need it?"

"Tomorrow afternoon. By four o'clock. That is, if
we're allowed to go ahead and print the whole story.
I'll know later on today."

"No problem," she replied, hoping she sounded
professional. This was far removed from writing about
yesterday's society wedding, where "the bride looked
radiant" and "among those present on this happy occasion were . . ." followed by a long list of names.

Jackie decided to start on the piece as soon as she
got home that afternoon, whether she got the go-
ahead or not. It would be excellent practice, and a
good example of her ability to show David York,
whether or not he could use it.

"Can you tell me one thing, without breaking a confidence?" she asked as they finished their coffee at the end of lunch.

"If I can."

"Whom would your proprietor have been approached by, asking him to put a stop on any mention of Roland's death? I mean, what sort of person has that power?"

"In this particular case I honestly don't know, but a request of this type can come from the government, the Foreign Office, maybe MI5 or MI6—"

"You've got to be joking!" Jackie cut in, amazed. "As high a level as that?"

"Yes, certainly."

"My God, I'd no idea. I'd heard about D-notices being issued, referring to defense and the country's security, but do you think that someone in such high authority has really stopped the press mentioning Roland Shaw?"

"Yes, I do. You see, I'm not the only newspaper who's had an embargo on Roland Shaw's death; we've all been told to lay off the subject. I think something very sinister happened and that was why he was cremated so quickly."

"Has there been an inquest?" Jackie asked.

"Not that I know of." David beamed with the satisfaction of a newspaperman who knows he's onto a good story.

"I hope you can print the story."

"So do I," David agreed, "and while I think about it, I'd like you to be a regular contributor to the *Morning News*. You're still interested in working on a paper, are you?"

"You bet I am," Jackie replied with alacrity. "With assignments like this, who wouldn't be?"

14

*J*ackie realized, as she started writing the article on Roland Shaw, that London was trembling on the brink of a series of scandals that threatened social catastrophe for those who had been listed in his diary. The more her research continued, and the more she talked to people, the worse the situation looked, because the scandals were so widespread. She remembered a case, years before, when the madam of a brothel had threatened to publish her list of "clients" unless they paid her a fortune to keep quiet, and how this had caused ripples of hysteria among half the well-to-do men in the city. Husbands had quaked in their shoes as they saw their sordid secrets about to be made public, and money exchanged hands at a rate of knots until the police got wind of what was happening and arrested the madam for keeping a house of ill repute. The implications of exposing the contents of those records had been bad enough; marriages would have broken up and divorces would have ensued. But it was nothing compared to the mayhem that would follow if anyone made public Roland's diary now.

As Jackie phoned as many people as possible who might be able to give her more of an insight into his character, a picture emerged that was chilling. There were even more corruption and acts of pure revenge than she'd imagined.

At six o'clock that evening David York called her to say he'd had the go-ahead to print her article.

"Great," she replied, delighted. "I've got enough

information to make this a compelling feature. I'll let you have it tomorrow afternoon."

That night, as she lay in bed with Gerald, going over the draft of what she'd written, she remarked, "This doesn't make pretty reading. The people he was involved with were almost as sleazy as he was; in some cases I'm not sure they didn't deserve each other."

Gerald looked up from the *Financial Times*. "He must have been very sick."

"So were some of the people he tangled with. I wish I knew who'd stolen his diary."

"What do you think they'll do with it?"

Jackie leaned back against the pink pillow of her bed, and her expression was reflective. "They'll either sell it to a tabloid for a fortune, or they'll take over where Roland left off, and start blackmailing the relevant people themselves."

"No wonder some people are nervous."

"Have you heard from Candy?"

He looked startled. "No, why should I?"

"I just wondered." Jackie tried to sound non-committal.

"You mean, you're wondering if whoever has got the diary has been onto her, threatening to expose our sham of a marriage?"

"Ummm."

"As we've agreed to a quickie divorce, with no financial strings attached, I don't expect to hear from her," Gerald said firmly. "What's wrong, my love? Is something troubling you?"

"Of course not," she lied, smiling quickly. In fact she wasn't worried about Candy in connection with Roland's diary at all; her disquiet went back to the night she'd joked that she was looking forward to being "Mrs. Gerald Gould" and Gerald had suddenly acted evasively. Could he still be hankering after Candy, regretting their marriage hadn't been a real love match? Pretending to study her article again, she knew that she certainly had no reason to doubt his love. Never had he been so ardent and passionate; never had he seemed to want her so much. If he'd changed his mind about their getting married and only wanted them to live together, then she was prepared to go along with it. Anything would be better than losing him altogether. That was something she could not even contemplate.

"Have you heard?" Elfreida looked at Selwyn with stricken eyes. It was the early evening and she'd just got back from having tea at the Ritz with Princess Ada, with whom she'd become good friends.

"I've heard most things," Selwyn replied rather sourly as he poured himself a drink. "I've heard I can't sell this house because the bottom's dropped out of the property market; I've heard the recession is going to get worse before it gets better; and I've heard that we've lost another construction job. Can you improve on that for interesting news?"

"Oh, Selwyn, what shall we do?" she said, her voice catching on a dry sob. "All my secrets will come out now!"

He turned to look at her with sunken eyes. "What do you mean?"

"Roland Shaw . . . he keep a diary, listing everyone he knew and all their secrets, and it's missing."

"Missing!"

"Yes, oh, the Princess is frightened too! She has secrets, she told me all about it! She had a baby some years ago, as a result of being raped when she was fifteen. You can imagine how dreadful it would be for her and her family if it got out. And there are others, she told me, many people Roland was blackmailing, people who did things to be ashamed of. How did he know so much? How did he find out all these things? Oh, God, he was a dangerous man. And now I'm so afraid, Selwyn, afraid people find out that I was . . ." She looked at him piteously.

"Well, you'll certainly be in good company," Selwyn quipped with unaccustomed humor.

"It no joke."

"It *is* no joke," he corrected her. "Well, there's nothing you can do about it. Who the fuck cares anyway? What if it does get out? It will only shock a bunch of hypocritical socialites whose one thought will be: Thank God it isn't me that's been found out. Everyone has skeletons in the cupboard, Elfie. If our friends don't stand by us, they aren't worth having. There's too much smugness around for my liking," he added vehemently. "If we become unpopular because of your past and my dwindling fortune, then to hell with the lot of them. I'll take you back to Wales, where I was born, and we'll get out of the whole sodding social scene."

"Out of . . . ?" She looked stricken. "I don't think I'd like living in Wales, would I, Selwyn?"

She looked like such a sad plump child that Selwyn went over and took her in his arms. "You'll like it," he promised her. "You'll bloody love it."

The call came through to Jackie late the following afternoon. It was David York from the *Morning News,* and he sounded enthusiastic.

"I loved your piece on Roland Shaw," he said immediately. "We're still not allowed to print an investigative article on his death, but we can go ahead with this."

"You can't report on how he died?" Jackie asked, stunned.

"Nope. We're only allowed to print your piece because it's more of a fascinating insight into the way a social climber can infiltrate the homes of the aristocracy and find out all their secrets, and then cause havoc, rather than a hard report on how, or why, he died. You've done a very good job, Jackie, striking just the right note, and I like the way, without naming names, you've managed to convey what goes on beneath the glossy surface. You've painted a very vivid picture of the hypocrisy and double standards that exist. I just wish we could back it with some evidence of what we suspect really happened. That would make one hell of a story."

"I'm glad you like it," Jackie replied.

"Yup," said David York. "So much so, in fact, that

I wondered if you'd like a job in our features department, rather than writing for us on a free-lance
basis?"

"Oh, I'd love it," Jackie exclaimed. To work on a
leading national newspaper had been her ambition for
a long time.

". . . Could you possibly start next Monday?" she
heard David say. "We're planning a series of articles
on Wives Who Are the Power Behind the Throne—
you know, interviews with women who have helped
their husbands succeed, but at what cost to themselves? We want to get interviews, obviously, from
the wives of famous men: sportsmen, businessmen,
politicians, artists, and actors. The conclusion, of
course, is why aren't there more men who are supportive of their wives? Could you think about it between
now and Monday?"

"Sure, it's a great idea," Jackie agreed. "Perhaps
we could actually do two series of articles—one on
wives who support their husbands, and one on husbands who support their wives."

"If you can find any, that would be great. Only
Denis Thatcher springs to mind at the moment, but if
you can find any others, let's have them."

"I'll do my best," Jackie promised. "By the way,"
she added, "has Roland Shaw's diary turned up anywhere yet?"

"No. As far as I can tell, it's completely vanished.
I'd have heard if one of the other newspapers had
been offered it, and there's been nothing. Whoever's
got it is sitting on it."

"The question is," Jackie remarked, "for how
long?"

"The little bugger!" Candy said with soft venom.
"If those diaries are published, it could ruin my career. Equity will stop me working in England. I might
have to leave *Manhattan Starlight*!"

Tim, her lover, made a grimace. "How could this
guy have known about us? Christ, even your fucking
husband didn't know about us."

"I've no idea."

They glared at each other, seeing their plans wrecked if the trick they'd played on Gerald became exposed, each ready to blame the other for what was happening.

"Why did you have anything to do with this Roland Shaw in the first place?" Tim snapped irritably.

"How was I to know he was a con artist?" Candy replied angrily. "It's me that's going to suffer if this gets out, not you. It may affect my divorce too. You know how tricky lawyers get about show-biz people having arranged marriages in order to get around work permits. I might not even be *granted* a divorce! Oh, God, imagine having to remain married to Gerald! I don't think I could bear it."

The brief coded report was headed "TOP SECRET." No name was mentioned. It referred merely to T/5486 J and ended with the words: "obliterated as instructed." The document was undated and it would have been impossible for the layman to make out to whom or to what it referred.

But the man who had attended Roland Shaw's cremation knew what it was all about. It was he who had carried out the instructions under the alias of John Ashton. It was he who had "obliterated" T/5486 J, and it was he who had made sure that T/5486 J had been "dispatched." All that was required now was to pass the report and the diary to the highest quarters, those who had given him the instructions in the first place, and then his part of the operation would be over.

Placing the document and the thick volume into a specially reinforced envelope, he sealed it securely, ready to be delivered to a secret address. He would take it himself, of course. There must be no risks of a leak under any circumstances.

The man smiled wryly. It had been a piece of cake, actually. Roland Shaw, or T/5486 J as he had become, had been so impressed when he'd called and asked if he might come to see him, that an invitation to drinks had been issued on the spot. Of course the fatal ingredient he'd slipped into T/5486 J's gin and tonic had worked within moments, and left no trace in the body. Not that there'd been a postmortem in this instance. A complete cover-up had been ordered, and the media silenced by a few judicious phone calls to the newspaper proprietors themselves, from someone they couldn't refuse.

The man held the package in his left hand, feeling the weight and thickness of the diary. A lot of secrets were contained in those thin, closely written pages. How the hell all that had been gathered, he had no idea, except that T/5486 J must have been a nosy little bastard, who would have probably made a first-class investigator if he hadn't been so screwed-up. In the end, of course, he'd known too many secrets for his own good. The list of victims was impressive, to say the least, but this job of "obliterating" hadn't been done to protect the secrets of those who swanned around the social scene. They, with their petty indiscretions, were of little consequence. The country would not be rocked to its foundations because someone had given birth to an illegitimate baby, or been a hooker, or a drug addict, or a swindler. No, the secret information that had finally been T/5486 J's fatal undoing had made him too much of a security risk.

"John Ashton" rose from his desk, put the package in his briefcase, and left his office. As far as he was concerned, the file on T/5486 J was just about to be closed.

It was almost like the old days, Celia thought as she drove out of London, threading her way through the heavy traffic going west, as she headed for Windsor Castle. Just like the good old days, except this time she was alone.

"Come in time for tea," the Queen had said on the phone, "so we can be on our own before the others arrive."

"The others" she was referring to were six couples whom she had not met before but who had been invited for their outstanding contributions and achievements in the country, for the traditional "Dine and Sleep" visit to the castle. To help make the atmosphere more relaxed, there were usually several other members of the royal family present on these occasions, as well as a few personal friends and members of the household, which might include the lord chamberlain, the mistress of the robes, the ladies of the bedchamber, and several lords- and ladies-in-waiting.

"Thank you, ma'am, that would be lovely," Celia replied.

In spite of everything, the Queen still looked upon her as a friend. Maybe someday in the distant future she would be able to resume her duties at court, but not for a long time yet. Not while her father was still alive, and not while there was a divorce pending between her and Hugo. There had already been several sensationalized stories in the newspapers when their separation had become known, and it would happen all over again when they got divorced.

"When," not "if," Celia thought with conviction, although she knew Hugo hoped it was "if." Haunted by the specter of her father's victims, feeling tainted by the fact she was his daughter, born of his flesh and with his blood flowing through her veins, Celia was still racked by guilt day and night, her emotions blocked so that she felt as if her feelings had become fossilized in stone a thousand years ago. Would she ever love again? Feel affection? Intense desire? Ardent passion? She doubted it very much. The cold, still feeling inside her encompassed everything and everybody now. Hugo, she regarded with distant impartiality; Colin and Ian aroused a sense of duty only, whereas in the past her maternal instincts had been strong. All she could think about was what had happened in Germany between 1939 and 1945. All she could feel was guilt. And every day she wondered how she was going to atone for what had happened, so that she could finally awaken from this nightmare and get on with her life. Yet she had to admit there was a curious sense of peace in the nothingness that filled the vacuum created in the eye of the storm; it was a respite from all that had gone before, a welcome lull, like dreamless sleep.

Now, as she drove along the M4 motorway, she could see ahead of her the dramatic outline of Windsor Castle silhouetted against the sky, its crenellated battlements of gray stone a fortification against past enemies, and today a perfect protection from terrorists or intruders. From the famous Round Tower, built on William the Conqueror's Mound in 1066, the royal standard fluttered in the breeze, its vivid blue and gold silk telling the people of Windsor that the sovereign was in residence.

Normally Celia experienced a rush of excitement as she entered through the archway of King Henry VIII's Gate, feeling she was stepping into the pages of history; but today she felt nothing. It was of course a great honor to be ranked among the Queen's coterie of close friends, especially after what had happened, but her anticipation was no greater than if she'd been entering a supermarket. The policeman waved her on as soon as she told him her name, and driving carefully through the Tudor arch, she turned right, changing gear to drive up the steep incline to the heart of the castle, past St. George's Chapel and the Dean of Windsor's private residence, past the rows of small Tudor houses occupied by some of the gentlemen-at-arms and their families, up to the second archway, which led to the foot of the Round Tower, and the Quadrangle, from where one entered the royal home. As soon as she drew up at the east entrance, she noticed an equerry coming out of the ancient doorway, through which kings and queens had entered for hundreds of years. It was the Earl of Slaidburn, whom she'd seen only once since the Buckingham Palace garden party in the summer.

"Hello, my dear Celia," he greeted her warmly, kissing her on the cheek. "The Queen will be delighted you are here," he added.

As Celia followed him into the castle, servants ap-

peared to unload her luggage and take her car off to
be washed.

"How is everything?" Robin Slaidburn asked. For
a military man his tone was almost tender.

"I'm all right, Robin," she replied briefly.

"You've had a bad time, m'dear," he said gruffly.
He paused and then asked, "How's Hugo bearing up?
I was very sorry to hear you'd split up."

"Yes. Thank you. It has been a rather sad time
for us all." *But I don't feel sad because I don't feel
anything.*

Leading the way, Robin climbed up the wide oak
staircase to the Grand Corridor, with its richly molded
ceilings, paintings, and antique furniture and clocks
that lined the walls on either side. On this floor were
innumerable state rooms, including the Grand Reception Room, hung with priceless Gobelin tapestries, the
Van Dyck Room, the Waterloo Chamber, which the
Queen used for banquets and which seated forty
guests at one long mahogany table, the smaller King
Charles II Dining Room with its exuberant Grindling
Gibbons carvings, and the Rubens Room, famous for
its magnificent paintings of King Philip II of Spain.
Today, though, Robin led Celia past the small royal
chapel, the Green and the Crimson Drawing Rooms,
to the Queen's own private drawing room.

"Do sit down until the Queen arrives, my dear," he
urged. "You must be tired after your drive."

"It takes only thirty minutes from London," Celia
replied mildly. "It's not exactly the Monte Carlo
rally!"

He smiled remotely and she could see he didn't
think her remark was amusing, but then, she thought,
Robin had never had much of a sense of humor. She
remembered Hugo saying that even at Eton Robin
had been a very earnest and serious boy.

As she looked at him now, she regretted the lack
of even a faint twinkle in his eyes. "Well-meaning"
was how Hugo always described him, and that just
about summed him up.

Rather than sit down, Celia went to look out the

window at the formal garden and its central fountain on the east side of the castle. Beyond, encircling the large smooth lawns, were the battlements, complete with cannon. This part of the castle had been built in 1194, and she loved it because there was something immensely reassuring in the thickness of the stone walls, weathered to a soft silvery shade. On one side the Orangery stood protected from the elements by a high wall, and in this sheltered spot flowers still bloomed, although it was winter, in neat rectangular beds. Celia turned back to the room, realizing that nothing here had changed in this ever-changing world. On either side of the elegant fireplace, two sofas covered in white brocade stood as they'd always stood; exquisite paintings hung on the walls, and in the window a large oak table supported a three-foot-high arrangement of tiny pale green orchids, a present no doubt from an ambassador or visiting head of state. Underneath the table, on the floor, was a very large television set.

This was the drawing room of a rich county woman whose taste was perfect, she thought. The chintz cushions and plain silk lampshades were understated good style, as were the ornaments on the mantelpiece, and the books and magazines conveniently placed on low tables. It might have been a room belonging to a thousand aristocratic women; this just happened to be the private sitting room of the Queen of England, set in the most magnificent castle in the western world.

At that moment, and with the usual flurry of dogs, the Queen came bustling into the room, kissing Celia on both cheeks and smiling a bright acknowledgment to Robin.

Celia, dropping a deep curtsy, returned the Queen's greeting. Robin, with a bow, then excused himself, his job of escorting Celia to the private quarters done. Quietly he left the room.

"Now, come and sit down and we'll have some tea," the Queen said briskly, seating herself at a small table covered with a lace cloth on which fine bone china cups and saucers had been arranged on a silver tray.

There were also plates of scones, some biscuits, and a homemade Dundee cake. A moment later a maid appeared with a silver teapot and a large jug containing boiling water.

The Queen sat back contentedly, the dogs asleep around her feet. "I do think teatime is the best part of the day," she remarked. "One's got all one's work done, you know—those dreaded red boxes—and it is a good moment for relaxing before one gets swept up in the evening's activities."

"I know," Celia agreed, smiling. It was a well-known fact among members of the royal family that everything stopped for tea, unless they had a public engagement.

For a few minutes they exchanged pleasantries of an inconsequential nature, and then the Queen turned and looked directly at Celia.

"I'm very sorry to hear you and Hugo have parted. Is there any hope of a reconciliation?"

"I don't think so, ma'am," Celia replied truthfully. "What has happened has changed everything; the trouble is, I no longer feel the same."

There was understanding in the Queen's expression. Her sister had been divorced, and her daughter had separated from her husband, so she knew the heartache they had suffered.

"That is sad," she observed. "Roland Shaw had a lot to answer for, hadn't he?" She began pouring the tea into the delicate cups.

Celia was startled. It never failed to surprise her how *au fait* the Queen was with everything that was going on. Far from being cocooned in an ivory tower, she seemed to be aware of everything that was happening in the country, and no fragment of gossip ever escaped her.

"I think he ruined several people's lives, and I don't think any tears were shed when he died," Celia said. "I shall never know how I came to take him on as a tutor for the boys. That was the biggest mistake of my life."

"You weren't to know what he was like," the

Queen replied reasonably. "You should have seen the things he wrote about us in the French papers! I thought the press office were going to have a seizure. No, you're right; I don't think anyone was sad when he died."

When they'd finished tea, Celia was shown to her room, where a maid had already done her unpacking and laid out her dark blue velvet evening dress ready for her to change into for dinner. In the closet, her other clothes had already been hung on coat hangers marked with the E II R cipher. It was a charming room, comfortable in a chintzy way, rather than glamorous, with a good supply of writing paper and pens on the desk, magazines and books which the Queen had chosen personally, on the sofa table by the fire, and a pretty arrangement of flowers on a table in the window.

This was not the first time Celia had been invited to a dine-and-sleep occasion and she knew the form. At seven o'clock, and still wearing her day clothes, which consisted of a cherry-red tweed suit and silk shirt, she would go down to the Green Drawing Room, where everyone would be gathered to greet the special guests who had been invited. The Queen, who had already been briefed on who was coming, had told Celia they were expecting a well-known film producer, a professor of science, a publisher, an archbishop, and a leading sports commentator. Unlike her luncheons, when they were invited on their own, spouses were included on this occasion, though never lovers. It was up to the royal household and equerries to put guests at their ease while they waited for the Queen, and although no longer a lady-in-waiting, Celia easily and automatically started talking to people and introducing them to each other as soon as they were ushered into the long spacious room, where everything, from walls to gilded furniture, was covered with emerald-green silk brocade. This was, in fact, her least favorite state room in the castle, casting as it did a bilious tinge to the guests' skin under the glittering chandeliers, making them look even more strained and nervous than they already were. Much more welcoming was the adjoining crimson drawing room, where every available surface was covered with red silk brocade and gilt.

By the time the Queen made her entrance, surrounded by her bevy of prancing dogs, everyone had got acquainted and the party was going with a swing. For another ten minutes the footmen circulated with silver trays bearing small glasses of sherry, and then, at a given signal, the guests dispersed to go and change for dinner. They had been instructed to be back in the Green Drawing Room by eight-thirty, and were warned not to be late. To Celia's amusement, she saw several of the guests scurrying along the corridor to their bedrooms, some of which were more than five minutes' walk away. One couple were actually sprinting, the wife's Chanel handbag dangling from her shoulder, the husband with his hands in his pockets to stop his keys and small change jingling, while he whispered: "Hurry, for goodness' sake. We mustn't be late."

Back in her own room, Celia quickly showered and changed before applying a minimum of makeup. Then she brushed her neatly cut hair, put on her drop pearl earrings and the long rope of pearls Hugo had given her as a tenth-wedding-anniversary present, and was just about to return to the drawing room when there was a tap on her door.

"Come in," she said, thinking it must be one of the maids. The door opened a few inches, and she heard a man's voice speaking softly. "Celia? Can I come in?"

Puzzled, she strode over to the door and flung it open.

"Robin!" she exclaimed.

"Celia, can I talk to you for a moment?" He was looking at her strangely.

"What do you want?" she asked. Beyond him, down the long wide corridor of the castle, she could see some of the other guests coming out of their rooms, looking curiously in her direction.

Celia frowned, her stomach suddenly tightening with apprehension. Looking at Robin again, she realized there was concern in his eyes, and it seemed as if he was at a loss for words.

"What is it?" she asked urgently.

"There's been an accident, my dear . . ."

Her hands flew to her face. "The boys . . . ?" This had always been her worst fear, that something should happen to her beloved sons.

Robin nodded gently. "Colin has been knocked down by a cyclist in Eton High Street."

"Oh, my God." She felt herself grow cold, while every part of her mind screamed out in silent agony. No, oh, no . . . oh, please, God, no. She hardly dared ask the question that sprang to mind. "Is it bad? How is he?"

Now that he'd broken the news to her, Robin seemed stronger, more in charge of the situation. "He's pretty badly bashed up, my dear, and they've taken him to Windsor Hospital. I've arranged for a car to take you there immediately."

Unthinkingly Celia went to the closet to get her tweed coat. There was no time to change out of evening dress. Her only thought was to get to Colin.

"Oh . . . the dinner!" she exclaimed, aghast.

"Don't worry," Robin assured her. "The Queen knows what has happened. She's not expecting you for dinner now."

Hurrying down the corridor, Robin's hand lightly cupping her elbow, Celia started to pray as she'd never prayed before. If God spared her Colin, she would do anything, *anything*, she vowed; but please let him be all right. Please don't let it be too bad. Please, God . . . punish me any way you like for being my father's daughter . . . but please don't let it be this way. . . .

Out of a doorway stepped a motherly figure in a lilac silk evening dress, a blaze of amethysts and diamonds around her neck and in her ears, her hands outstretched.

"Celia, I'm so very sorry."

Startled, because Celia had forgotten for a moment where she was in her desperation to get to the hospital, she stopped in her tracks, realizing it was the Queen.

"Thank you, ma'am," she replied automatically.

"If there's anything I can do, please let me know." The Queen turned to Robin. "Hugo's been informed, hasn't he?"

"Yes, ma'am. He's on his way from London now."

"Good." She turned back to Celia, kissing her on both cheeks. "It may not be so bad, you know," she said comfortingly. "Windsor Hospital is first-class; he'll get the best attention, and luckily it's only a few minutes away. You must stay here at the castle and use it as your base until he's better."

"That's very kind, ma'am." Automatically she dropped a deep curtsy.

"I'll see you into the car," Robin was saying as they hurried on along the hundreds of yards of red-carpeted corridor and then down the wide staircase to the courtyard. "I wish I could come to the hospital with you, but with all these guests for dinner, I've been detailed to look after several of them."

"Don't worry, Robin. I know what it's like. I quite understand."

A car with a driver was waiting, the engine already running.

"The Queen meant what she said, you know, Celia," he assured her as he saw her into the car. "You must use the castle as your headquarters; just come and go as you like. Tell Hugo the same. It will be so much easier for you if you're near the hospital. Good luck, my dear. Things may not be as bad as you fear."

Celia nodded, unable to speak. Then the car was speeding across the silent Quadrangle, leaving the warmth of the castle and the glittering company behind. Ahead, she knew not what she would find, or what horrors the night might hold, but as the Rolls-Royce swooped down the hill from the main part of the castle and then out through King Henry VIII's

Gate and into Windsor High Street, she realized with a painful start that her feelings had returned. She was actually hurting, agonizingly, brutally, as if a dressing had been wrenched from a wound. Tears were streaming down her face, and for a moment she wished she could recapture that blessed deadness of spirit that had been like a cocoon shielding her from the sharp edges of the world for the past few weeks. Instead, sobs were tearing at her chest as fear and anxiety sent waves of panic through her. Colin mustn't die! He mustn't!

Sitting in one of the Queen's most luxuriously appointed cars, she reached for her handkerchief, trying to pull herself together before she arrived at the hospital.

In a medieval building near Whitehall, the stonework blackened with age, the entrance a heavy oak door, two men sat facing each other in a small office on the second floor. Between them on the cluttered desk lay a folder and a thick black bound diary filled with neat, even handwriting. One of the men was "John Ashton." As he glanced out the deep mullioned window, seeing in the distance the Houses of Parliament veiled through the heavy rain that had been falling since dawn, he was unable to believe what he was hearing. He glanced at the other man, his chief, the head of this very special department whose activities were known to only a handful of the topmost people in the land, and he shook his head with incredulity.

"I'm afraid that's the position," his chief was saying calmly. "Most unfortunate, I grant you, but from time to time these things happen."

All those months of surveillance . . . all the inquiries they'd made . . . all that phone tapping and bugging and tailing . . . only to find they'd disposed of the wrong man. It was enough to shake your faith in the system, a system that had managed to eliminate more people who were high security risks than anyone would ever know. In this office, which did not even exist as far as Parliament was concerned, dark deeds had been planned before: "accidents" had been contrived; incidents of "heart failure," as in the case of T/5486 J, had been plotted; and many a break-in, organized to look like common burglary, had been masterminded. More scheming, in the name of national security, had been devised within the walls of this ancient building than the general public would ever have dreamed, and yet they'd got the *wrong* man.

"How did it happen?"

His chief shrugged. "We made an error, I'm afraid. Make no mistake, though, Roland Shaw was up to every trick in the book, but the one thing he wasn't guilty of was stealing nuclear secrets. He wasn't a security risk at all, just a damned nuisance in the highfalutin world of high society." He sounded scornful.

"All this started because he was a tutor to Professor Rouse's son?"

"Exactly. When the professor reported his designs for a nuclear warhead were missing, he rushed off like a scalded cat to his boss. Top brass were called in. The professor swore he'd put the designs in his safe over Easter, when Roland Shaw was staying in his house, but he only discovered they were missing three months later."

"So that's when the finger of suspicion fell on Roland Shaw?"

The chief sighed. "You know the saying 'give a dog a bad name'? That's what happened in this case. It turned out to have been a bad mistake on our part, but when we sent you to do the job, we really thought we had our man. Especially when we found he made a living by selling information, even if it was only of a scandalous rather than a security nature."

"So what happens now?"

"Nothing. He has no relatives and no one to make inquiries or cause a fuss."

"And the death certificate?"

"It won't divulge any useful information. It will read 'cause of death not ascertained,' and below, the word 'open,' meaning 'open verdict.' "

The man who had been responsible for Roland's

elimination shook his head. He was used to receiving orders and carrying them out without question, but for as long as he'd worked for this department, nothing like this had ever happened before, to his knowledge.

"What about the diary?" he asked at last. "It contains a lot of damaging information about a hell of a lot of people.

"So I've noticed." The chief made a wry expression. "I think we'd better shred it, along with the file referring to T/5486 J."

The man rose to leave the room, and then, pausing in the doorway, turned to look at his chief.

"What *had* happened to the blueprints? Who stole them?"

The chief's expression was inscrutable, but there lurked in his eyes a hint of black humor. "Ever heard the one about the absentminded professor? It turned out Professor Rouse had taken the designs up to his bedroom one night, and because he was too tired to go back to the study to return them to the safe, he'd stuffed them under his mattress. His housekeeper, in a fit of spring cleaning, found them two days ago."

Through the blurred vision of tears, Celia sat watching Colin, oblivious of her surroundings. She did not even seem to notice the comings and goings of doctors or nurses, or the bustle of a busy hospital. Locked away in a private world in which only she and Colin existed, she willed him to live. All she wanted was for him to open his eyes; to look at her and recognize her; to squeeze her hand in awareness. Most of all she wanted to hear his voice, those piping adolescent tones that had in the past so often prompted her to tell him to stop shouting. Now she would give everything she possessed to hear him speak again. Colin was in a coma as a result of hitting his head on the curbstone when he was knocked down, and it was too soon for the doctors to be able to say how bad it was.

On the other side of the bed, Hugo also kept vigil, as concerned for Celia's mental fragility as he was for his son's well-being. Once or twice he reached out to take her hand, and was rewarded by the briefest response, but then she turned back to Colin again and the moment was gone.

It was noon now, sixteen hours since she'd got the message that Colin had been in an accident; sixteen hours since she'd got herself dressed for the dinner party at Windsor Castle. Suddenly she looked down, realizing she was still wearing her blue velvet evening dress under her coat. For a moment she looked perplexed, as if trying to remember what had happened. Watching, Hugo intuitively knew what she was thinking.

"I'm going to make a phone call, Celia," he whispered.

"We mustn't whisper, we must talk loudly," she replied. "They always say you must keep talking to someone in a coma; and play music too."

"I know, darling. I'll be right back." Hugo hurried from the small private room that led off the main hospital ward and went in search of the nurse on duty.

"May I make a local phone call?" he asked when he found her in the dispensary room.

"Of course." Bowled over by his good looks and charming manner, she indicated a phone fixed to the wall. "Unless it's private, you can use this one."

"Thanks." Hugo dialed the number of Windsor Castle. "I'd like to speak to Lord Slaidburn," he said when the girl on the switchboard answered.

"Certainly, sir. Can I say who it is, please?"

"Atherton. Lord Atherton."

"Certainly, Lord Atherton. I'll put you through."

There was a click and then Hugo heard Robin's voice.

"Hugo! How are things? We've all been very anxious. The Queen has asked me to keep her posted. How is Colin?"

"He's still in a coma; they're doing a brain scan later on this afternoon," Hugo replied, managing to keep his voice steady. "All we can do is sit and wait. Nothing will induce Celia to leave his side, and already she's exhausted and suffering from strain."

"My dear chap, I'm so sorry." Robin Slaidburn's

voice was full of sympathy. "What a dreadful thing for you both. Is there anything I can do?"

"I was going to ask a small favor. Can you arrange for some of Celia's day clothes to be sent over to the hospital? She's still wearing last night's togs and I know she'd be more comfortable if she could change."

"Consider it done, old chap. I'll get one of the maids to pack a case and send it right over. What about you? Is there anything you need?"

"I'm fine, Robin, and I can send my driver back to London if I need anything."

"Well, you'll let me know, won't you? And what about Ian? Does he have an exeat from Eton this weekend? I'm sure the Queen would be delighted to have him stay at the castle. Princess Anne's children, Zara and Peter, are coming over, so he'd have company."

"That's very kind. Can I let you know? So much depends . . ." Hugo's voice, in spite of his rigid self-control, cracked.

"Of course, of course, old chap," Robin cut in hastily. "We'll keep in touch. Right?"

"Right."

An hour later, a driver from the castle arrived with a change of clothes for Celia, plus her makeup and toiletries. The maid who had done the packing had even included the bottle of perfume she'd left on her dressing table the previous evening.

"How thoughtful," Celia said as she looked at her things. "Thank you for arranging this, Hugo." Her steady gray eyes were red-rimmed as she looked at him, and he longed to take her in his arms, but it was as if she'd built a shield around herself and Colin's accident had only reinforced that protective barrier. Then she rose with such quiet dignity it broke his heart.

"I'll find somewhere to change," she said quietly as she left the room. "I shan't be long."

The driver had brought something else from the castle: a picnic hamper, which Hugo found contained cold pheasant, ham, freshly baked bread rolls, fruit, cheese, and a thermos of coffee. The attached note merely said:

"The Queen requested me to send along some provisions for you both so that you will not have to leave Colin's bedside." It was signed "Slaidburn."

Hugo showed the hamper to Celia when she returned, neatly attired now in the cherry-red suit she'd worn to travel down to Windsor the previous day.

"How very kind; that's typical of the Queen's thoughtfulness," Celia murmured, sitting by Colin's side again. "Has there been any change, Hugo?" She leaned forward, looking closely at her son. His skin was a transparent white except for the black and purple bruising which disfigured one side of his face, and his closed eyes had a hollow look that frightened her.

"Nothing so far," he replied, forcing himself to sound cheerful. "Now, would you like a ham roll? Or would you rather have pheasant or cheese?" In order to give himself something to do, he fussed with the contents of the hamper, insisting Celia have something to eat.

"I'll just have a cup of coffee," she said distractedly.

"No you won't. You'll eat something. You've got to keep your strength up, sweetheart, in order to be fit enough to nurse Colin when he goes home in a few days." Hugo spoke with such conviction Celia turned to stare at him wonderingly.

"Have you spoken to the doctor again . . . ?"

He shook his head. "No, but I have great faith in Colin's powers of recovery. He's a tough little chap and a great fighter. He'll come through this, I promise you." Hugo surprised himself by the conviction in his voice.

Celia's shoulders sagged, as if in disappointment. "I hope to God you're right," she replied. "But suppose there's permanent brain damage?"

"We'll cross that hurdle when we come to it," Hugo said firmly.

"It will soon be Christmas." She sounded forlorn as she reluctantly accepted a wedge of Stilton and a bread roll.

"I know."

"I don't think I'll be able to bear Christmas if Colin . . ." She faltered, stifling a sob.

"Don't think like that, Celia. We've got to be brave for Ian's sake."

"Yes, I know." She made a visible effort to regain control. "Have you spoken to him again today? Is he all right?"

"He's okay, and I've promised to go and see him later on. He's been invited over to the castle for the weekend, which will be better for him than staying at school or sitting here with us in this atmosphere."

"Yes."

They fell silent again as they continued to sit on either side of Colin's high narrow hospital bed. At one point a nurse came in to check on his drip and take his blood pressure, but she said little except that the doctor would be coming back later. Otherwise only the overwhelming horror of what had happened pervaded the oppressive atmosphere, draining them of energy and impetus, so that they sat helpless and devitalized.

At last Celia spoke. "It's been a terrible year, hasn't it?"

"Yes," Hugo replied hollowly.

"This time last year we were such a happy family, weren't we? Getting ready for Christmas."

"Yes."

"So much has happened; if only I'd never engaged Roland Shaw . . . if only we'd never gone to Ireland . . ." Her voice trailed off, an echo of a thousand regrets.

"It's no good looking back," Hugo reminded her. "Nothing has actually changed, you know, it's only that we've discovered the truth, and sometimes that can hurt. But I wish that knowledge hadn't affected us, you and me, Celia. That's the worst part of it all."

"We can't go back, Hugo. Nothing will ever be the same again; nothing." She was stroking Colin's hand as she spoke, such a smooth childish hand, the hand

of someone, she reflected, who hadn't even begun to
live a full life yet.

Hugo didn't reply, his pain too deep at the realiza-
tion that he'd already lost his wife, and might now
lose his son too. And so, in silence, they continued to
keep watch by Colin's side, waiting and hoping for a
miracle to happen.

The freezing blizzards that were to mark the end of
1990 and the beginning of 1991 had not yet set in to
bind both town and city in icy clutches. Selwyn, with
his accustomed gloominess, looked forward to the
coming year with about as much rejoicing as a man
with a terminal illness.

"You must cheer up," Elfreida informed him early
that morning. "Something good might happen."

"Humph!" He clambered creakily out of bed.

"You go to the office today?" she asked, propping
herself up against the mound of lace-and-lawn pillows.

"I've got to try to save what I can of my business,"
he replied. "Even some of the banks are going broke
these days. It worries me they'll call in the thirty-
million-pound loan I've got."

Her mouth dropped open. It was even worse than
she'd thought. Thirty million! She couldn't even imagine such a sum.

From the adjoining bathroom Selwyn was still grumbling loudly about the recession, the rising cost of living, interest rates, and unemployment, so that he
didn't hear the phone ringing until Elfreida yelled at
him to come and take the call.

"Who the hell is it, at this hour?" he asked crossly,
trying to smooth the spiky tufts of hair sprouting from
his head, as if by answering the phone he was also
going to be seen.

"I couldn't make out. Mackrell Jones, or Mackrell
something . . ."

Selwyn snatched the phone from her hand.

"Lord Witley here," he barked pompously.

"Good morning, Lord Witley, this is Roger Holland
of Mackrell, Sebastian, and Jones. I'm sorry to ring

you so early, but I thought you'd like to know that we've managed to rent your house for you, to a very wealthy Arab family, who have come to live in London because of the situation in Kuwait—"

"How much?"

"—and they are here for at least one year and—"

"How much?"

"I beg your pardon?"

"I asked how much rent they're proposing to pay," Selwyn demanded testily. "I told you at the beginning that if you couldn't sell my house, to try to get as high a rent as you could."

"Oh, yes. Two-and-a-half." The voice of Roger Holland sounded deeply self-satisfied.

"Two-and-a-half what?"

"Two-and-a-half thousand pounds," he replied in an aren't-I-clever voice.

"Per . . . ?" Selwyn queried.

"Per week, of course, Lord Witley, and they'd like to move in as soon as possible."

"Right." There was a pause while Selwyn rearranged his thoughts. "That's fine," he said at last. "They can move in as soon as you can find a flat for my wife and me to live in."

"Certainly, Lord Selwyn. What type of accommodation are you requiring? We have some lovely penthouse flats in Eaton Square, or a pied-à-terre with a conservatory and large garden in Knightsbridge—"

Selwyn cut in succinctly. "I'll tell you what I want. I want a small flat with one bedroom, one living room, and a kitchen and bathroom."

The silence on the other end of the phone was more dumbfounded than thoughtful. "I see," Roger Holland said, adding carefully: "Are you particular which area you'd like to live in?"

"Not at all."

"Right." There was another pause, and then Roger asked, rather tentatively this time: "And rent? What sort of rent did you wish to go to?"

"No more than a thousand."

"A thousand pounds."

"Yes, and that is a thousand pounds per *month*," Selwyn snapped. "There's a recession on, young man, and we've all got to tighten our belts and it's going to get worse before it gets better, mark my words!"

"Yes, of course, Lord Witley. I'll see to it right away, and in the meanwhile I'll get a contract drawn up for the letting of your house and—"

But Selwyn wasn't listening anymore; he was doing a few quick calculations in his head. Two and a half thousand pounds a week added up to one hundred and thirty thousand a year. Even allowing for tax, that meant he and Elfreida could live in comfort, if not a little luxury, without him having to draw a penny from his company. That way, and provided he kept his head, he might survive this financial crisis as he'd survived all the other crises in his life.

Africa knocked on the bedroom door at that moment with Elfreida's breakfast tray.

"Come in," Elfreida called out. "Have you got the newspapers?" She asked out of habit these days, more than in the hopes of seeing her name in print.

"Here, madam."

"Thank you." She surveyed the tray with pleasure. Warm blueberry muffins nestled in a basket with almond croissants; two fried eggs glistened alongside the tiny sausages she liked so much, and the pot of coffee steamed fragrantly. If they were economizing, it would not be on food, Elfreida determined.

From the wide pocket of her apron Africa withdrew a bundle of mail. "Here are your letters, madam," she crooned, smiling all the time.

"Thank you." Elfreida flipped through them avidly to see if any contained nice stiff engraved invitations, for in spite of her promise, she still hoped to go to a few parties. Meanwhile Selwyn pottered back to the bathroom, greatly cheered to be getting rid of what he'd come to think of as "Elfreida's Folly." The house had cost him a bomb and in recent months it had come to resemble, to his way of thinking, a great white elephant that nobody wanted. They'd be much happier in a little flat, he assured himself, and if Elfreida objected, he could always silence her by threatening to make her live in Wales.

Suddenly he heard a scream from the bedroom. "Selwyn, oh, Selwyn!" she was yelling at the top of her voice.

With a towel slung around his reedy body, he hurried back. Elfreida was out of bed, her great voluptuous body dancing around the room in all its pink nakedness amid the turquoise-silk-and-gilt hangings.

"What the hell's the matter?" Selwyn roared, badly shaken.

"Oh, Selwyn, you'll never guess! It's too amazing . . . too marvelous . . . it's . . . it's *wunderbar!*" She was waving a letter about, raising her arms so her full melon-shaped breasts stood out like jutting buttresses.

"Cover yourself up, woman!" Selwyn exclaimed, before he remembered they were alone in their bedroom. "What on earth has happened, for God's sake?"

"This letter! It's from a charity that looks after old and poor people . . ."

"I didn't think they knew about me already," Selwyn responded dryly, but Elfreida wasn't listening.

"They want to hold a series of fund-raising events, beginning with a concert, and they've asked me to be chairman of the whole project! All the functions! There is to be a ball in the summer and a sponsored polo match at Windsor, and . . ."

Selwyn was looking at her despairingly. Had nothing changed? Was she still on this frenzied social-climbing ladder? Being chairman of all these charity events would cost a lot of money, just when he was trying to economize. He turned to tell her she'd have to refuse, but she was still talking, like a wound-up speaking doll.

". . . they're planning a fashion show too, but the best bit of all, Selwyn, the very *best* bit of all is the president of the charity is Princess Diana! They say . . . let me see . . ." She read the letter again. "Yes, they say: 'Her Royal Highness the Princess of Wales has already agreed to attend at least two of the functions this year.' Isn't that wonderful? Can you believe it? As chairman, I'll be hostessing these events, receiving her when she arrives, looking after her all evening . . ." Elfreida clasped her pudgy little hands together and cast her eyes upward in a state of cerebral ecstasy.

Silence followed her enraptured outburst. She was smiling at Selwyn with an expression of the purest happiness he had ever seen.

He couldn't say it; couldn't destroy this overgrown child's moment of triumph and joy, when she'd achieved her life's ambition. It would be too cruel, too devastating. Everyone had to have something to aim for, and if Elfreida's aim was to be a leading social light, so be it. Somehow he would have to support her in this much-sought-after venture, and do it with a good grace.

"Well done, Elfie," he said warmly, going over and giving her a kiss. "Congratulations. You've done very well."

"It's wonderful, no?" she replied, clinging to him. "Oh, Selwyn, I have so much to thank you for."

Selwyn thought of her doing her stripper act. "Oh, I don't know," he replied modestly. "I think we give each other a good time, don't we?"

Across London, Jackie and Gerald were already up and dressed, having breakfast in the kitchen. Now that she was working on the *Morning News*, she did not have so much time to herself, and her day was much more structured. She did, however, finish work by the late afternoon, and so she and Gerald were now able to enjoy their evenings together, doing what they wanted to do.

Tonight was New Year's Eve, and for once they had decided to stay at home.

"I'll cook your favorite dinner," Jackie announced.

"I can't think of anything nicer; I loathe New Year's Eve parties," Gerald responded. "If we stand on your balcony and lean right over the side, we might even hear the chimes of Big Ben striking midnight while we drink champagne."

Jackie giggled. Life had become increasingly romantic since Gerald had come to live with her. With Richard it had all been about getting ahead, making money, hustling ambitiously for more work, seeking more recognition. She'd been made to feel that if she didn't use her father's diplomatic contacts to further Richard's business, she was somehow letting him down. Then there'd been all the dinner parties she'd had to give, the dreary clients she'd had to be nice to, the whole business of helping him to be successful; only to find he was having an affair with his boss's daughter.

With Gerald, who had no social aspirations and who had succeeded in business through sheer ability rather than pushiness, Jackie was able to enjoy his companionship as they relaxed together in the evenings, talking, reading, watching videos, or going to bed early to make love. Each new day seemed to reveal a facet of their personalities and interests that blended together so naturally she could barely remember a time before Gerald had come into her life. Even when their opinions differed, they rejoiced in a discussion, sparking each other off in the friendliest of arguments, scoring points as if in a verbal game of tennis; and always, always respecting each other's point of view, even if they disagreed.

The only fear that came to Jackie's mind at odd moments was the thought that it was all too good to last. Gerald's divorce wouldn't be through for some time yet, and it niggled her, the curious way he'd sidestepped the issue when she'd remarked she was looking forward to being Mrs. Gerald Gould.

As tonight was New Year's Eve, she decided she wanted to start 1991 with no shadows between them. The moment had come to ask him why he'd been evasive on that point.

"I wonder what the coming year holds for us?" she began. Pouring them both cups of steaming coffee, she tried to sound casual, as if speculating for the amusement of it. "Me with my new job on the *Morning News* and you with an ever-increasing empire and the Goray Group shares still going up in value on the stock exchange."

"Ummm." Gerald looked thoughtful. "It's going to be tough for everyone. The recession is going to get worse, too."

"So people say, but shops are still busy and so are restaurants," Jackie replied.

"Shops that sell essentials, and restaurants that are good," Gerald agreed. "But wait until mid-January. There will be a dramatic decrease in spending . . ."

"It's worrying, isn't it?" Jackie wondered how she could get around to talking about them. Right at this moment the state of the economy was not uppermost in her mind.

"There's one thing to look forward to, though," Gerald said, brightening suddenly.

"What's that?" she asked cautiously.

" 'What's that?' " He looked at her incredulously. "*What's that?* We're only getting married, sweetheart . . . unless you've forgotten?"

Jackie felt her insides melting with relief. "Really? You mean it?" she asked breathlessly.

Gerald looked startled. "Of course I mean it. What are you talking about? I thought we'd planned all along to get married as soon as my divorce came through. You haven't changed your mind, have you?"

"Of course not." She squeezed his hand. "It's just that you went, well . . . sort of funny the other day when I happened to say I was looking forward to being Mrs. Gerald Gould."

"Ah." Gerald smiled mysteriously.

"What does 'Ah' mean?"

"Just that you won't be Mrs. Gerald Gould this year, or any year for that matter."

Jackie frowned, something telling her that in spite of Gerald's reaffirmation they were going to get married, something odd was happening.

"I don't understand what you're saying, Gerald. Do you mean you want me to be all women's lib and go on calling myself Jackie Daventry?"

His smile was mysterious. "That's entirely up to you, sweetheart."

"Then what do you mean? I don't mind taking your name . . . unless you'd rather I didn't, of course."

Gerald didn't answer for a moment, and it seemed to her he was weighing something in his mind. When he spoke, it was with caution. "I had thought of surprising you."

"In what way?"

"Tomorrow is New Year's Day, when the Honors List is published, when all the people who deserve recognition for their various services to the country are given titles, or Orders of Chivalry . . ." He was trying very hard to control the grin spreading over his face.

Astounded, Jackie looked at him wide-eyed. "You mean . . . ?"

He nodded, and he was laughing delightedly now. "I'm being given a knighthood for my services to the clothing industry, because of Goray's remarkable success in exporting. I've known for some weeks but I was sworn to secrecy, as one always is, until it is formally announced; but the Prime Minister put my name forward and the Queen approved . . ."

As he spoke, it dawned on Jackie what he'd meant when he'd said she'd never be 'Mrs.' Gould. Jumping up, she rushed around the table, arms outstretched, her face radiant.

"Oh, Gerald, I'm so pleased for you. You deserve it, you've worked so hard. It's the most wonderful news. Will it be in the newspapers tomorrow with the list of new life peers and all the other people who have been given an honor?"

Gerald nodded roguishly, pulling her down onto his lap, nuzzling her neck as he held her close.

"So," he asked, "how are you going to enjoy being Lady Gould?"

Jackie giggled. "About as much as you're going to enjoy being Sir Gerald, I should think."

His kiss was tender. "We're going to make London

buzz, aren't we? Between us? American journalist and deprived inner-city boy making the big time?"

"My family will be tickled pink!" she chortled.

"While my family will probably completely disown me!" he rejoined, joining in her laughter.

"Ian, could you put another log on the fire?" Celia asked as she set up a small table in front of the sofa in the drawing room where she'd planned to have supper while they waited to see in the New Year.

"Sure, Mum," he replied. "Want any help with that tray? It looks heavy." Ever since Colin's accident he'd been much more thoughtful and considerate, helping Celia as much as he could, being very much the man around the house.

"Thank you, darling." Gratefully she handed him the large silver tray on which she'd brought up plates, glasses, and cutlery from the kitchen.

"What are we having?" asked a piping voice from the depths of the sofa where Colin lay, miraculously fully recovered, but still ordered to rest by the doctors.

"All your favorite things," Celia said, smiling. It was such a relief to have Colin home again, and with no lasting effects, that nothing seemed too much trouble these days. That morning she'd been to Harrods and come home laden with smoked salmon, violet cream chocolates, the most expensive tournedos steaks, and lemon sponge cake topped with whipped cream—all the things she knew Colin and Ian liked best for this special New Year's Eve supper they were having together.

"I'm starving," Colin announced.

"You're always hungry," Ian grumbled goodnaturedly.

"I've got to get my strength back," Colin reminded him stoutly.

"*Any* excuse to stuff your face!"

"Dinner won't be ready for a while yet; would you like some nuts and crisps to be going on with?" Celia asked them.

"Yes," the boys chorused. Ian, who had been putting more logs on the fire, straightened and looked at his mother.

"Can we have a Coke too, Mum? After all, you're having a gin and tonic."

"Help yourself."

"Thanks." As Ian bolted from the room, Celia sat down near Colin and picked up her needlework.

"You're not getting tired, are you, darling?" she asked.

"I'm fine, Mum," he replied contentedly.

Celia looked around the drawing room at the Christmas tree which she'd hurriedly decorated to welcome Colin home, although he'd not returned until the twenty-seventh, and at the hundreds of cards that had been sent by friends and well-wishers. She'd received more cards than in previous years, containing messages of thankfulness for her son's recovery, and they warmed her heart and made her thank God every time she looked at them. One, in particular, in pride of place on the mantelpiece, was a photograph of the Queen and the Duke of Edinburgh, bearing the handwritten inscription "Elizabeth and Philip, with love."

It seemed to Celia, as she stitched her cushion cover, that the trauma of Colin's accident had overshadowed the nightmare of finding out about her father, and that therefore it had put a perspective on events, removing the acute pain she'd felt. Her father and his life belonged to the past; Colin's lay in the future; and in the future lay hope and expectation and prospects. She would never look back again, only forward, she vowed to herself. She would show her gratefulness to God for sparing her Colin, by justifying her own existence every day for the rest of her life, and she would try to find a way of rebuilding her relationship with her father.

Colin spoke, breaking into her thoughts. "It's a pity Dad's not here with us, isn't it?" he observed. "It would make New Year's Eve . . . well, more complete, I suppose."

Celia looked into her elder son's face as he lay back

among the tapestry cushions, and she noticed how wan he still looked, with purple smudges beneath his eyes.

"Yes," she said evenly, "it would have been nice."

"Why don't we ask him?" Colin suddenly sat bolt upright. "Why don't we ask him to dinner, Mum? We've got enough steak, haven't we?" The underlying pleading in his voice made Celia's heart contract, as if a hand had squeezed it. "Couldn't we give him a ring, Mum? Please?"

Ian came back into the room at that moment with two cans of Coke. He handed one to Colin. "Who are you talking about? Dad? Yes, why don't we ask him to dinner?" He looked at Celia enthusiastically. "That's a terrific idea. New Year's Eve won't be the same without him."

Celia was silent, unable to summon up the courage to tell the boys that she was scared; too scared to ask Hugo to come. The last time she'd seen him had been four days ago when he'd helped her bring Colin back from Windsor Hospital. He'd suggested they get together again and put the past behind them, but she'd been unable to agree then. Some demon, some terrible resistance within her, had still seemed hell-bent on punishing herself as well as others, forcing her to say no. She knew it was a perversity, of course, a self-inflicted wound into which she could only seem to twist and twist the knife, hurting herself as she did so; much worse, hurting dear Hugo, who deserved so much better.

"I expect Daddy will be busy," Celia said, playing for time. "He's sure to have had lots of invitations for tonight."

"But there's no harm in ringing him, is there?" Ian pointed out. "He *might* be free."

"Yes, he might," Colin echoed.

Supposing Hugo refused! The thought struck her forcibly, increasing her nervousness. She'd treated him so shabbily, he might well refuse. She wouldn't beg; she was too proud for that, and too afraid that even with begging she might be refused. At that moment she thought of a possible way out, something that would lessen the hurt if he turned down her invitation.

"Why don't *you* give Daddy a ring, Ian?" she suggested in a falsely bright and coaxing voice. "Ask him to join us for supper in front of the fire, that is, if he isn't doing anything else."

"He won't be doing anything else if he can be with *us*," Colin said confidently, with the conviction of a child who has known only love and security. Celia smiled tremulously, suddenly hoping he was right. She and Hugo did belong together and she must have been mad to think otherwise. But suppose he'd already gone out? It was unthinkable he'd be alone in his small apartment, seeing in the New Year by himself, when they had so many friends who were fond of him, so many hostesses who would clamor for his presence at one of their parties.

Celia poured herself a second, rather stronger gin and tonic as Ian went over to the phone and started dialing Hugo's number, and she braced herself for the rejection that she was sure would come.

"Hello? Dad?" she heard Ian exclaim.

Sitting down rather heavily, she took a gulp of her drink, hardly able to bear listening to the one-sided conversation.

"Dad, we were wondering if you could come to dinner. That is, Mummy says it's supper by the fire, because Colin has to rest on the sofa." There was a long pause and Celia thought the suspense would kill her. Then Ian spoke again.

"Yes, just us. No, it's not a party. There'll just be the four of us, and Mum bought enough steak, which is lucky, and we're starting with smoked salmon . . . What?" There was another pause as Ian seemed to be listening intently to what his father was saying, and Celia was digging her nails into the palms of her hands until she left little scarlet half-moons on her pale skin.

"Okay. Right. Okay," Ian was saying. Did she detect disappointment in his voice? Was Hugo saying, regretfully of course, for Ian's sake, that he was already going out? Celia felt a terrible sinking sensation plummeting through her, leaving her cold, her heart hardly seeming to beat. Ian had hung up and was coming back to the fireplace. Colin twisted around on the sofa to look at his brother.

"Well?" he demanded. "Is Dad coming?"

"Of course! I told you he'd come if we asked him, didn't I? Oh, and he gave me a message for you, Mum."

"What is it?" Celia asked faintly.

"He said to tell you he'll bring a bottle of champagne with him."

"Oh! Oh, thanks." Her voice wobbled and her eyes suddenly brimmed with tears. Half-laughing and half-crying, she hurried from the room to powder her nose and brush her hair and apply a touch of the perfume Hugo always gave her for Christmas. Then she went down to the hall and waited by the front door. The rest of the evening and for the rest of her life, she would share him with Colin and Ian, but for these first few moments she wanted him just to herself.